**Praise for *The Darlings* by Cristina Alger**

"Alger, who has worked at Goldman Sachs as well as at a white-shoe law firm, knows her way around twenty-first-century wealth and power, and she tells a suspenseful, twisty story." —*The Wall Street Journal*

"What happens to the Darling family in the course of a weekend is what carries this tale along, but it's Alger's description of quintessential New Yorkers, and how they survive, that adds the extra layer. . . . Alger has what it takes, in the best sense of the phrase." —*USA Today*

"Forget *Gossip Girl*: If you really want a peek into the scandalous lives of New York City's elite upper class, Alger's debut novel—set during the financial downturn of 2008—gets you pretty close. The hedge funds, designer clothes, and lush Hamptons homes are all on display. But Alger also deftly juggles a complicated and myriad cast of characters who orbit around an It Family, the Darlings, who are at the center of a Madoff-like Ponzi scheme. *The Darlings* moves so fast that it feels more like a thriller than a social drama." —*Entertainment Weekly*

"Penned by a former banker, this is a dishy yet thoughtful portrait of greed gone too far. . . . A page-turner." —*Good Housekeeping*

"Two parts *Too Big to Fail*, one part *The Devil Wears Prada*, Alger's debut is taut and compelling." —*Publishers Weekly*

"Probably the most compulsively readable fiction to come out of the Wall Street financial scandal so far . . . Alger knows the ins and outs of both Wall Street and an upscale NYC lifestyle, nailing all the details, from the plush, hushed atmosphere of high-end law firms to the right tennis togs for a 'casual' weekend in the Hamptons. Delicious reading." —*Booklist*

"A financial thriller with a tone that fits somewhere between the novels of Dominick Dunne . . . and Tom Wolfe's *The Bonfire of the Vanities*." —*Library Journal*

"Cristina Alger is so good, you just know she's an inside trader—as intimately familiar with the inner workings of Wall Street investment banks as she is with haute Manhattan social life. She's also a gifted storyteller. *The Darlings* is an utterly compelling novel, as knowing about family as it is about money and social status, and may be the best literary product of the financial crisis to date."

—Jay McInerney, *New York Times* bestselling author of *The Good Life*

"For those who have only gazed up at the palatial residences of Manhattan, this is a glimpse from the penthouse down."

—Tom Rachman, *New York Times* bestselling author of *The Imperfectionists*

"Cristina Alger's debut novel offers a fresh and modern glimpse into New York's high society. I was hooked from page one."

—Lauren Weisberger, *New York Times* bestselling author of *Last Night at the Chateau Marmont*

"A rare, glittering glimpse into Manhattan's banks, bedrooms, and private clubs, a material and psychological world rendered with extraordinary detail. A smart, gripping tale . . . complex and mesmerizing."

—Sarah Houghteling, author of *Pictures at an Exhibition*

"Cristina Alger has written a racing, vivid, multivocal chronicle of the new gilded age, with equal shades of Jay McInerney and Bernie Madoff. Start reading it and in three hundred pages or so you'll feel like a consummate New York insider, too." —Charles Finch, author of *A Burial at Sea*

PENGUIN BOOKS

# THE DARLINGS

Cristina Alger graduated from Harvard College in 2002 and from New York University School of Law in 2007. She has worked as an analyst at Goldman, Sachs, & Co. and as an attorney at Wilmer, Cutler, Pickering, Hale, & Dorr. She lives in New York City, where she was born and raised. Alger is at work on her second novel, coming soon from Pamela Dorman Books/Viking.

Cristina Alger

PENGUIN BOOKS

PENGUIN BOOKS
Published by the Penguin Group
Penguin Group (USA) Inc., 375 Hudson Street, New York, New York 10014, U.S.A. • Penguin Group (Canada), 90 Eglinton Avenue East, Suite 700, Toronto, Ontario, Canada M4P 2Y3 (a division of Pearson Penguin Canada Inc.) • Penguin Books Ltd, 80 Strand, London WC2R 0RL, England • Penguin Ireland, 25 St. Stephen's Green, Dublin 2, Ireland (a division of Penguin Books Ltd) • Penguin Group (Australia), 707 Collins Street, Melbourne, Victoria 3008, Australia (a division of Pearson Australia Group Pty Ltd) • Penguin Books India Pvt Ltd, 11 Community Centre, Panchsheel Park, New Delhi – 110 017, India • Penguin Group (NZ), 67 Apollo Drive, Rosedale, Auckland 0632, New Zealand (a division of Pearson New Zealand Ltd) • Penguin Books, Rosebank Office Park, 181 Jan Smuts Avenue, Parktown North 2193, South Africa • Penguin China, B7 Jaiming Center, 27 East Third Ring Road North, Chaoyang District, Beijing 100020, China

Penguin Books Ltd, Registered Offices: 80 Strand, London WC2R 0RL, England

First published in the United States of America by Viking Penguin,
a member of Penguin Group (USA) Inc. 2012
Published in Penguin Books 2012

10 9 8 7 6 5 4 3 2 1



A Pamela Dorman/Penguin Book

Publisher's Note
This is a work of fiction. Names, characters, places, and incidents either are the product of the author's imagination or are used fictitiously, and any resemblance to actual persons, living or dead, business establishments, events, or locales is entirely coincidental.

THE LIBRARY OF CONGRESS HAS CATALOGED THE HARDCOVER EDITION AS FOLLOWS:

Alger, Cristina.
The Darlings : a novel / Cristina Alger.
p. cm.
ISBN 978-0-670-02327-1 (hc.)
ISBN 978-0-14-312275-3 (pbk.)
1. Investment bankers—Fiction. 2. Financial crises—Fiction. 3. Family secrets—Fiction. 4. Upper class—New York (State)—New York—Fiction. 5. New York (N.Y.)—Fiction. I. Title.
PS3601.L364D37 2012
813'.6—dc23 2011036292

Printed in the United States of America
Set in Warnock Pro with Amasis MT Std and Snell Roundhand Script
Designed by Daniel Lagin

*For Mom*

## ACKNOWLEDGMENTS

This book would not exist were it not for the tireless work, general brilliance, and high-risk tolerance of everyone at McCormick & Williams and Viking Books, most especially Pilar Queen, Pamela Dorman, and Julie Miesionczek. Working with you is a pleasure and privilege.

A number of wonderful folks offered their support, insight, love and encouragement throughout this process. Particular thanks to: Lucy Stille and everyone at Paradigm; David McCormick; Leslie Falk; Jamie Malanowski; Anne Walls; Joan Didion; Tom Wolfe; Ben Loehnen; Jennifer Joel; Sara Houghteling; Charlotte Houghteling; Edward Smallwood; Lauren Mason; Andrew Sorkin; Andrea Olshan; Michael Odell; Christina Lewis; Daniel Halpern; Joanna Hootnick; Sharon Weinberg; Cristopher Canizares; Carolina Dorson; Redmond Ingalls; Francesca Odell; and Jonathan Wang.

There are no words to appropriately thank my mother, Josephine Alger, for all she has done for me. This book's for you, Mom.

# THE DARLINGS

# INTRODUCTION

*This is it,* he thought, as he clicked on his left blinker. *The end of the road.*

The sign for the bridge had snuck up on him. He had done this drive before, but not at 2 a.m, and he had never been much of a night driver. There had been a little traffic leaving the city, but now there was almost none. Every time a car passed him on the left he wondered who the driver was and why they were on the road this late. He wondered if they were thinking the same about him.

More than one driver had turned to look at him as he passed by. *Checking out the car,* he thought. He probably shouldn't have brought the Aston Martin. Even in the dark it was a real showstopper. Of all his cars, it was his favorite. It was a near-perfect replica of the one driven by James Bond in *Goldfinger* and *Thunderball.* The original had sold at auction two years before for over $2 million; he would have bought it in a heartbeat if he had had the opportunity. But this was the next best thing: perfectly restored and refinished in classic silver; even to a professional's eye, it was almost indistinguishable from the genuine article.

As he merged toward the bridge turnoff, a white Kia pulled up alongside him. For a moment, he locked eyes with the driver. The guy gave him an approving smile, a thumbs-up. Usually he got a little rush from impressing guys like that: some accountant from Westchester who probably made less in a year than he could in a day. This time it sent his heart racing, and not in a good way. It was a miscalculation. This wasn't the time to be attracting attention.

He hated miscalculations. There had been a lot recently, which was, of course, how he had ended up parked at the base of the Tappan Zee Bridge at 2 a.m. on a Wednesday. Not exactly Plan A. His mind whirred as he parked the car and switched off the headlights. The engine fell silent and all he could hear was the white noise of cars crossing the bridge and the rush of his own blood roaring in his ears. He sat still for a minute, and stared blindly at the bridge. It looked different than it had last week. In the daylight, it looked like a steel cage suspended over the river, more like a carnival ride, a roller coaster with two peaks. The top beams were lit up and the reflection danced across the black water below. It was beautiful.

This was harder than he had thought it would be. Maybe impossibly hard. He knew he had to stop thinking and just move, but his heart was pumping so hard that he felt faint, almost as if he were having an epileptic seizure.

He reached for the bottle of Dilantin that he kept in the glove compartment. He had bottles stashed in every car, just in case. His hands shook as he twisted off the cap and the bottle slipped out of his hands. He scooped up the pills from the passenger seat—there were only two left—and put them in his pocket.

*You know this bridge,* he told himself.

*It's three miles long and seven lanes wide.*

*And there are four phones, two on each side.*

The storm was churning up the river. He couldn't see it in the dark, but he imagined it now, the cold, tufted rush of black water slipping endlessly beneath the belly of the bridge. Already there were sustained winds of up to 40 mph with gusts of up to 60 mph, so the current was moving faster than normal. If someone were to jump, his body would be pulled down and under into the river, swallowed whole. They might not even find the body; just a heart-deadening splash, and gone.

*In the past ten years, there have been more than twenty-five suicides from this bridge. They put in the phones to connect callers to a suicide prevention hotline.*

*The weather is optimal. This has to be done now.*

Running through statistics and scenarios, especially the outside or unlikely ones, the ones that others might discount to zero, usually calmed him. His breath slowed a little, enough so that he could get out of the car. His shoe hit a patch of loose dirt, causing him to slip slightly. He stopped and wiped a bead of sweat from his temple. He couldn't see the phone in the darkness, but he knew it was there. Just yards away. For the millionth time, he reminded himself that this wasn't just the best exit strategy; it was the only exit strategy. He had done the math, run the numbers, analyzed the risk. This was it: the only way out.

# TUESDAY, 9:30 P.M.

Paul slipped in through the side door just as the applause was ending. He stood at the edge of the ballroom until the clapping faded and the music started up again. His wife, Merrill, was up front near the stage. She looked on as a photographer snapped pictures of her mother, Ines, the gala's chairperson. Around him, partygoers wafted from table to table; a giant amoebic mass, shimmering in the incandescent light of a thousand cocktail glasses and candles. As Paul wended his way toward his wife, he caught a couple of cold stares tossed in his direction. His hand shot reflexively to the knot of his tie, straightening it. It was one of his favorite ties; part of what Merrill called the "first-string rotation" in his closet. He felt good in it, usually. Tonight, amid the sea of tuxedos, it felt woefully inadequate. He kept his eyes trained on his wife and tried, without luck, to recall the name of Ines's charity.

The live auction, it seemed, was over. This was a slight disappointment; he had been told it would be a spectacle. This was his mother-in-law's first year as chairperson, and she wasn't one to be outdone. For months, she had run around soliciting the most extraordinary auction items she could think of: a weekend at Richard Branson's house on Necker Island; private piano lessons with Billy Joel; a baseball signed by Babe Ruth. While Paul couldn't imagine someone throwing down six figures at a charity auction in the middle of a recession, Ines seemed unfailingly confident that she would raise more money this year than ever before. Bullheaded confidence was part of Ines's charm. She hired a Sotheby's auctioneer, ordered oblong bidding paddles with the name of the charity stenciled on the back in gold, and called in favors to get as much press buzz going as possible. She wheedled her way into the pages of some social magazine or other, posing with a handful of other women who also listed their occupation as "philanthropist."

From the looks of the stage, Ines had been right. Posters of the auction items had been set up on easels behind the podium. Each one now bore a bright red Sold sticker, the kind that got put on car windshields at the dealership. On the last easel, the auctioneer was using a thick marker to ink a staggering "Total Dollars Raised" figure on a large placard.

Ten yards short of Merrill, a hand reached out of the crowd and snagged him by the shoulder. "Bro!" Adrian appeared before him. "I was wondering if you were going to show." Adrian's cheeks were flushed and a mist of sweat had appeared at his hairline, from dancing or drinking, or both. His bow tie, a polka-dot number that matched his cummerbund, hung undone around his neck. Adrian was married to Merrill's sister, Lily. Even though he and Paul were the same age, it was hard for Paul to see Adrian as anything other than a younger brother.

Paul went to shake his hand, but Adrian held up two bottles of beer instead. "Want one?" he said, offering it up.

Paul suppressed an eye roll. "Thanks. I'm all right. Just came straight from work."

"Yeah, me, too," Adrian nodded thoughtfully and took a swig of beer. This seemed highly unlikely to Paul. Adrian was in a tuxedo, for one thing, with those velvet slippers he loved to wear to formal occasions. Also, he was suspiciously tan. Now that he thought about it, Paul hadn't seen Adrian in the office since last Thursday.

"I mean, not the actual office," Adrian added quickly. "I was down in Miami with clients for the weekend. Had to run here from the airport."

"Looks like you got some sun."

"Weather was killer down there. Got in nine holes of golf this morning." With a big grin, Adrian drained the beer. "Mother's milk," he said, with an approving nod. "You sure you don't want this one?"

Paul shook his head. "Glad you had fun," he said, turning away.

It was, he recognized, Adrian's job to entertain. But the market had been bouncing all over the place, and the call volume from clients was up nearly five times, and Paul's patience for anyone at the firm who wasn't working at least eighty hours a week was limited.

As he glanced over Adrian's shoulder, Paul saw Merrill slipping farther into the crowd. "Hey," he said, "I've gotta go find Merrill. I'm already late as it is."

"Yeah, yeah, go do that. She was asking where you were. You coming to the after-party?"

"I don't think I can swing that. I'm pretty shot. It's late."

Adrian shrugged. "East Hampton tomorrow? Lily and I are going to leave around lunchtime to beat the traffic."

"Doubtful. Work, and all that. We're planning to drive out Thursday morning."

"Cool. Gotta be there by 12:30 p.m., though, to see the kickoff. Darling family tradition."

"Who are they playing this year?"

"Tennessee. Looks tough. Okay, Bro. We'll look for you before we hit the after-party." Adrian threw Paul a "you-da-man" nod and dropped the empty bottle on a passing waiter's tray.

"Right. Later, then." Paul watched Adrian roll off like a tumbleweed, hands in his pockets with signature nonchalance. He joined his brothers at the bar. All four were tall and thin as matchsticks, with thick heads of charcoal-black hair. The oldest, Henry, was telling a story while Griff and Fitz, the twins, laughed riotously. From all sides, women instinctively slowed as they passed by them, like stars getting sucked into a black hole. The Pattersons were so handsome that each had his own magnetic pull;

together, they became the universe's gravitational center. When Adrian pulled up, Henry tossed his arm casually about his shoulder. Perfect white teeth flashed as they greeted each other.

Adrian wasn't as stuffy as Henry, and he wasn't as frivolous as Griff or Fitz. He was actually a reasonably nice guy, the kind of guy that Paul liked in spite of himself. As Adrian laughed with his brothers, Paul wondered briefly if there was any way he could find Adrian's total indifference to stress inspirational instead of infuriating. He was trying to be more understanding with Adrian now that they worked together, though market conditions were making that tough.

A light touch on his arm stirred him from this consideration.

"There you are!" Merrill said. She was flanked by Lily; both were dressed in blue. Or perhaps it was Merrill who flanked Lily: Lily bloomed at these sorts of social events, unfurling her petals like a flower in a hothouse. Her cornstalk blond hair had been spun into a complex series of braids, not unlike that of the dressage horses she still rode on summer weekends. From her ears dangled two teardrop diamonds, each stone larger than her engagement ring. Her father had given them to her, Paul knew, on the occasion of her wedding.

Merrill looked quietly beautiful—the simplicity of her dress brought out the blueness of her eyes, the tone of her shoulders—and though she was smiling, her face was taut with frustration. Paul sensed that he was about to be reprimanded. He leaned in, kissing both sisters on the cheek.

"I'm sorry I'm late," he said preemptively. "And I know I'm supposed to be in black tie. I came straight from the office. You both look great, as always."

"You're here now," Merrill conceded.

"You missed Mom's speech, though," Lily protested. She blinked her big eyes impetuously at him.

"I know. I'm sorry. How was the party?"

"Great," Lily said absently. He had already lost her attention. Her eyes scanned the room just beyond his shoulder. "Are you guys coming to the after-party? Looks like things are winding down."

"Of course," Merrill said.

"Doubtful," Paul said, in tandem.

They stared at each other, and Lily let out an awkward laugh. "I'll leave you guys to discuss," she said. "I think you should come, though. It'll be fun. Even Mom and Dad are stopping by."

Lily turned and flounced off, the bustle of her dress trailing behind her. The dress was cut low in the back, and Paul noticed how uncomfortably thin she was. He could see the articulation of all her vertebrae, and small hollows beneath the blades of her shoulders. Lily was forever dieting. She had an evolving list of foods to which she claimed to be allergic. Sometimes Paul wondered if she had cut out food entirely.

"We have to go to the after-party," Merrill said once Lily was out of earshot. Her voice was strained. "Tonight's important to my parents."

Paul pulled in a deep breath and let his eyes flicker shut for a half second. "I know," he said. "But I've got to weigh that against sheer exhaustion. I've been working around the clock. Which is important to your dad, too, by the way."

"There are things he values other than work."

Paul ignored the snappishness in her voice. "Look, I'm doing the best I can. I'm just exhausted. I'd love to go home and just fall asleep with you."

The crease in Merrill's forehead relaxed. "I'm sorry," she said, and shook her head. She reached up and wrapped her arms tenderly around the back of his neck. Paul pressed his nose against her golden brown hair; he could feel the slope of her skull beneath, and she smelled warm, like maple syrup. When she pulled back, she kept her hands resting on his shoulders. He slipped his grasp to the small of her back and held on to her, admiring her at an arm's length. "I really do understand," she said, and sighed. "Work's been crazy for me, too. I barely had time to change. I look terrible. I didn't even do my hair."

"You look stunning, actually. Great dress."

Her eyes lit up. "You're sweet." Her round cheeks flushed, the color of peonies. She smoothed her dress at the hip. "You should see my mother's. She's literally been talking about it for months. She had it made by some Latin designer."

They both looked over at Ines. She was basking in the attention of Duncan Sander, the editor of *Press* magazine. Duncan's hands fluttered like birds' wings as he spoke, and Ines was laughing grandly. It was the kind of image that would end up in the Styles section of the Sunday *Times*. *Press* had run a two-page spread on the Darlings' home in East Hampton the previous summer, called "The Darlings of New York." Ines loved to reference "the article" in casual conversation, and she spoke of Duncan Sander as though they were old friends. In truth, it wasn't really an article, but more of a blurb attached to a glossy photograph of Ines and Lily, inexplicably attired in white cocktail dresses, frolicking on the front lawn with Bacall, the family Weimaraner. To Paul's knowledge, Ines never saw Duncan except at events like this.

Tonight, Ines's dress was long and emerald green, festooned with a ruffle that looked as though a python were in the process of consuming her whole.

"I really do appreciate you being here," Merrill said, staring cynically at her mother.

"Of course. It's a great cause. Dogs? Cancer? Dogs with cancer? Remind me."

"Tonight's New Yorkers for Animals. Jesus, Paul. Pay attention."

"I'm for them, myself. The groups against animals just seem so heartless."

Merrill burst out laughing. "They auctioned off a rescue dog," she said. "For eight thousand dollars." She stared at him, allowing him to absorb that information.

"That's possibly the most absurd thing I've ever heard."

"I think it's nice!" she exclaimed, her eyes wide in mock seriousness.

"It's for *charity*. The poor thing was so sweet. It's a retriever or something, not a pit bull. They actually had him out on stage, wearing a little bowtie."

"Mmmm. One of those rescue retrievers."

Unable to help herself, she laughed again. "It's for charity," she sighed. "Anyway. The bowtie was from *Bacall*."

*Bacall* was Lily's year-old line of dog accessories and clothing. It was her sartorial nod to her family, a first and only attempt at gainful employment. Merrill was convinced that the enterprise was costing their father nearly twice what it was earning, though to Lily's credit, it appeared to be staying afloat, despite the market crash.

In the background, the band had started playing their last reprieve before the clock struck the witching hour. The band leader swayed around the mic, summoning his best Sinatra baritone. Paul couldn't think of a black-tie event in Manhattan that didn't end with "New York, New York." It had been the last song at their wedding. Now, they stood together on the edge of the dance floor, watching as the last few dancing couples slid by with varying degrees of grace.

"Want to dance?" Paul asked, though he was a bit too tired for it. What he really wanted was a drink.

"God, no. I think what we need is a drink," Merrill said. She slipped her hand into his, leading him in the direction of the nearest bar.

The bar was stacked three deep and the bartender was topping off last-call orders. As Paul and Merrill waited their turn, Merrill's father appeared behind them.

"What's going on over here?" Carter asked good naturedly, clapping them both on the back. He was tall enough that he easily captured them both in his wingspan. "Paul, who let you out of the office?"

"You're working him too hard, Dad," Merrill said.

"Yes, well. It's been an interesting two months, hasn't it, Paul? Opportune time to come over to the investment side." Carter laughed lightly.

Though he was, as always, perfectly groomed, behind his glasses his eyes were small and seemed rimmed with fatigue. His hair was thinner, too; a little more white than silver these days. He wore it well, but for those who knew him, the change was perceptible. The market collapse had come at a bad time for Carter. Word around the office was that he would've retired at the end of the year if the markets had stayed on course. Now he was working more of a junior analyst's schedule than a CEO's, seven days a week, sometimes sixteen hours at a stretch.

"Lily and Adrian look as though they're leaving," Merrill said, looking over Paul's shoulder. "I'm going to go tell them we may not make it to the after-party. Don't talk shop while I'm away." She flashed them a sweet smile and then was gone.

Father and son-in-law stood together in comfortable, familiar awkwardness.

"This is a nice event," Paul offered as they surveyed the landscape.

"Isn't it?" Carter nodded vigorously. He seemed grateful for the introduction of a topic. Paul found that casual conversation with Carter often felt like a high-wire act, and it was even more difficult now that they worked together. To discuss work felt overserious, anything outside of work, frivolous. He sensed that Carter felt similarly unsure of how to navigate their new dynamic.

"Ines put a lot of effort into this," Carter volunteered. "It was hard to get people to open their wallets this year. They lost all the corporate tables, too—Lehman always used to take one and AIG and, of course, Howary. It's amazing to think that all those firms are actually gone now."

Paul nodded. He remembered seeing his old boss, Mack Howary, at this same event the previous year. He had been holding court at the Howary LLP table, entertaining a few clients and their wives. Mack was grotesquely fat and very loud for a lawyer, and his ego was still soaring from a recent write-up in *Barron's* that had crowned him as one of "the Street's most influential power players." Mack had waved Paul over and introduced him ("One of our rising stars," he had said to the table), but only after he saw Paul standing with Carter Darling and Morty Reis, the founder of Reis Capital Management.

Paul wondered where Mack was tonight. He had heard rumors that he was under house arrest at his estate out in Rye, a piece of property so enormous that it didn't really seem like much of a restriction. Howary LLP had gone under only ten weeks before, fewer than two months after Mack had been indicted for six forms of tax and securities fraud. It had been a swift fall from grace. For more than a decade, Howary LLP had been the golden child of Wall Street law firms. Mack, the firm's founding partner, was one of the few attorneys who enjoyed almost mythical status among young associates and law students. Paul had seen him pack a lecture hall at NYU, students sitting on stairwells just to hear him speak about structured transactions. When Paul had interviewed as a second year law student, associate positions at Howary were by far the most coveted.

Howary had always been an unorthodox sort of place. With only 150 attorneys on staff, it was a small shop, but it punched way above its weight. The firm specialized in corporate tax and capital markets transactions, advising clients on derivatives and structured products offerings, cross-border equity deals, privatizations of public companies. It was a sophisticated, highly lucrative practice, and Howary was the best in the game.

Unfortunately, it turned out that Mack was really more of a corporate tax evasion specialist than anything else. The authorities had been watching him for years, waiting for him to make a mistake. When one of his largest clients admitted to laundering close to a billion dollars of Colombian cartel money through a bank in Montserrat, the end was swift and merciless. Within days, the IRS, the Department of Justice, and the New York State Attorney General's office were picking through everyone's desks like vultures, subpoenaing files, desktops, expense reports, e-mails, anything that wasn't nailed to the floor. Client work stopped entirely. Assisting the Feds became a twenty-four-hour seven-days-a-week job.

Paul slept nights on a couch in his office, going home only to shower and kiss his sleeping wife. Though the end terrified him, he was grateful when it finally arrived. It had been like manning the deck of a sinking ship.

When Howary LLP folded, it got less press than it might have in normal market conditions. But it was the fall of 2008. Next to Freddy, Fanny, Lehman, AIG, Merrill Lynch, the loss of a 150-person law firm was a paper cut on a carcass. Still, the shot of Mack in cuffs outside his Park Avenue pied-à-terre graced the cover of every newspaper on the newsstands. The other partners simply disappeared to houses in Connecticut or Florida or the Caribbean, where they hunkered down and waited for the storm to pass. Some took other jobs, but most didn't; no one wanted to hire a Howary partner. The Howary name reeked of illegitimacy. It was the stuff of cocktail party chatter, another Bear Stearns or Dreier. The associates were unceremoniously dismissed via e-mail. Not knowing what else to do, Paul had gotten drunk and gone to the movies. He still dreamed about it sometimes, waking up in a cold sweat.

The first night he was unemployed, Paul couldn't sleep. Merrill was cradled tightly in the crook of his arm, and as her breath rose and fell against his skin, he ran the numbers in his head, over and over, until light crept across the ceiling. He had been well paid at Howary. Extremely well paid in fact, but the problem was that they lived well, too. He could sustain their lifestyle for six months. That wasn't long; he could see the sand running through the hourglass. After that, he would have to cut back substantially, draw from Merrill's trust fund, or he would have to find a job. The former two options made him sick with worry. The latter would prove nearly impossible. The Street was crawling with the unemployed. None of the big law firms would touch a Howary associate with a ten-foot pole. Seven years of practice had positioned him decently well for an in-house job at a hedge fund, but the vast majority of those funds had either blown up or battened down the hatches. It was a bleak situation.

A few days after the pictures of a handcuffed and angry Mack became tabloid fodder, Paul got a call from Eduardo Galleti, an old classmate from

Harvard Law. Eduardo had been a JD/MBA at Harvard, and was one of the smartest people Paul had ever met. They studied for finance classes together and quickly became drinking buddies. When Eduardo found out that Paul was interested in Merrill, he offered to teach him Portuguese. "Latin women, they want to know they can bring you home to Mom," he said one night over beers. "To get in good with a Brazilian mom, you've got to speak her language." By the end of law school, Paul spoke Portuguese with reasonable facility, though he wasn't sure if this, or anything he did, would ever impress Ines.

Though Eduardo had been a groomsman in Paul and Merrill's wedding, they had lost touch during the intervening years, both bogged down by family obligations and grueling work schedules. They e-mailed from time to time. Paul had heard that Eduardo had recently taken a senior position at Trion Capital, a private equity firm in the city that invested heavily in Latin America. The firm was doing well, one of the few that was actually expanding. Though he wasn't feeling particularly sociable, Paul took the call.

"Hey, man," Eduardo said when Paul answered. "Glad you picked up. Figured your life is pretty crazy right now."

"That's one way to put it. Good to hear from you, sir."

"Listen, I heard about Howary. I don't know what you're thinking in terms of next steps, but I've got an out-of-the-box proposal for you. We're building up Trion's office down in São Paulo. I'm moving down there myself next month and taking a small team with me. We could use an attorney who understands international tax and has an accounting background, and it's gotta be someone who speaks Portuguese. Not perfect, but you know, passable. Merrill's fluent, isn't she? Anyway, if you're interested, come on down to the office."

Eduardo's voice always had an infectious clip to it; fast and enthusiastic, as if not a minute could be wasted. Paul's heart rate quickened as he considered the possibility of escaping New York altogether. He had always wanted the chance to live abroad, and this job sounded like a dream opportunity. *São Paulo!* The thought exhilarated him. It took him only a moment to dismiss the idea. Eduardo was right—Merril was fluent—but still, she would never go for it. He didn't even want to ask her. New York wasn't just a city to Merrill, it was a part of her being. Though he told Eduardo that he would sleep on it, Paul's mind was made up by the time he hung up the phone.

"I got a call from Eduardo today," he said to Merrill casually that evening, as they were getting ready for bed.

"How is he?" Merrill replied. She pulled back the duvet and crawled in. "Oh, my God. Bed feels great. I'm beat." She closed her eyes, her face peaceful.

"Seems like he's doing really well. He's at Trion Capital. Actually, he sort of offered me a job with them, but in the São Paulo office. He's moving there next month."

Merrill opened her eyes. "Oh?" she said. She sat up. "What did you say?"

"I said thank you, and I'd think about it. Didn't want to be rude. I was going to call him tomorrow and say that, you know, we love New York and have no intention of moving."

"Oh," she said, and nodded thoughtfully. After a minute she slid back down and closed her eyes again. "Listen, did you still want to talk to Dad?" She sounded sleepy. "He's serious about the general counsel position, you know. He's gonna hire someone soon anyway, and I know he thinks you'd be great."

She had floated this option by him a few days before. He had hedged, saying he wanted a few days to think about it. In another market, he wouldn't have considered it. Paul firmly believed, or he had up until then, that the only way to be a part of a family as powerful as the Darlings was never to take anything from them. Otherwise, they owned you. Of course Adrian had worked for Delphic for years. Paul imagined that Adrian didn't have a wealth of offers at other hedge funds in New York, but Carter graciously employed him as a salesman, putting him in front of clients at dinners or on the golf course where Adrian fit in best. It was a quiet yet obvious arrangement: Carter provided for Adrian, Adrian provided for Lily. It wasn't the kind of arrangement that sat well with Paul. But with

São Paulo and unemployment as his other two options, working for Carter seemed like the obvious solution.

"Really generous of him," Paul said. " I'd like to. Very much. You sure this is okay?"

Merrill reached for his hand and squeezed it. "Absolutely," she said. "I think it's a perfect fit."

---

There was no Howary table at the New Yorkers for Animals benefit that year; no Lehman table, no Merrill Lynch table, no AIG table. Still, it seemed as though most of Manhattan was present. Paul had to hand it to Ines: She knew how to get things done.

"There's practically no floral budget," Ines declared when she had been named committee chairwoman. "We'll have to get creative. Opulence is out, anyway." She wasn't lamenting; Ines simply stated unpleasant facts with a sort of stoic fortitude. She was right, of course; no one wanted to see orchids at a five-hundred-dollar-a-plate charity event, not with the Dow hovering around 8,400. Instead, the tables had been sprinkled with tiny silver stars, which were turning up everywhere, stuck to lapels and elbows. Yet it looked festive somehow, not cheap. The food, too, was spartan but passable: chicken Marsala and some kind of wilted root vegetable. But then, no one really ate the food.

As he looked around the ballroom of the Waldorf Astoria, Paul wondered how many of the guests had also been laid off. Everyone appeared confident and relaxed, seemingly unaffected by the financial maelstrom. They laughed as they always had, exchanging stories about their children, swapping plans for the upcoming Thanksgiving holiday. The mood was slightly more somber than it had been the previous year, but not by much. The women had turned out in couture. Maybe it was last season, but Paul couldn't tell the difference. Necks still dripped with jewelry, the kind that spent the rest of the year locked away in a safe. Town cars and chauffeured Escalades idled their engines out front. Of course, it was all an illusion. It had to be. This was a finance-heavy crowd in a finance-heavy town. There wasn't a single person in this room—not a one—who could claim they weren't worried. They all were, but they were dancing and drinking the night away as they always had. They had to know the end was coming; it was probably already here. It was like the final peaceful moments at the Alamo.

"There's Bloomberg," Carter said to Paul, tipping his glass in the mayor's direction. "Did you see him? Bill Robertson was here, too, but he left before the dinner started. Everyone's talking about how he'll run for governor in the fall."

"I'm sure there will be some folks here glad to see him gone as attorney general," Paul said drily. Over the past few years, Bill Robertson had become an increasingly controversial figure in New York politics. Though his own father and brother had made fortunes in finance, Robertson had garnered a reputation as the so-called Watchdog of Wall Street. He had tripled the resources of his white-collar crime division, and had successfully prosecuted several high-profile financiers for various securities-based scandals, everything from insider trading to market timing to tax fraud. He had made enemies along the way. Wall Streeters saw him as a turncoat. Attorneys and politicians christened him a power-hungry megalomaniac. He was routinely flogged in the press for his antics in court (his rodentlike features lent themselves particularly well to caricature), which some saw as nothing more than grandstanding and obvious campaigning. And still, his power grew. When Robertson was in the room, everyone, even men like Carter Darling, took notice.

Mayor Bloomberg was standing twenty feet away, slightly apart from a cluster of very serious-looking men. Leaning in on his left was a woman in a strapless black evening gown. Her eyebrows were furrowed and she was nodding at whatever he was saying, her arms crossed at her chest. She had a razor-sharp jawline and cheekbones, all angles assembled in the most striking way.

Unlike most of the women at the party, this woman wore no jewelry and almost no makeup except for a sweep of crimson lipstick. Still, she was drawing attention. To her left, a few young men in tuxedos chatted among themselves. They seemed to be on call; every few seconds, their heads would rise slightly as if to check on the mayor and the woman with the red lipstick. Paul wondered if they were her staff or his.

"Who's the woman he's talking to?" Paul asked. Though she was well out of earshot, she looked up like a deer, sensing that she was being watched. For a brief second she locked eyes with Carter. To Paul's surprise she nodded at him in acknowledgment before turning back to her conversation. "Oh, you know her?"

"That's Jane Hewitt." Carter said, sounding grim. "She runs the New York office of the SEC. We've met through Harvard College fund-raising."

"Ah. More adversary than friend?"

Carter let out a dry chuckle. "A little of both, I suppose. There was an article in today's paper saying she's on the short list to be the next commissioner. That's why everyone seems to be staring at her."

Carter himself was staring. Paul shifted uncomfortably at the mention of the SEC and turned to find a surface on which to place his empty glass.

"Speaking of the SEC," Paul said, clearing his throat, "That lawyer keeps calling around. David Levin. I've pushed back, but he's . . . well, he's persistent."

Carter grunted. He signaled a passing waiter with two fingers. "Probably some low-level staff attorney trying to impress his boss. What's he after now?"

"I'm not entirely sure. He's been asking questions about some of our outside managers. RCM, mostly. Just the stuff I mentioned to you last week."

"Well, call him back, but don't give him anything you don't need to." Carter handed the waiter his glass. "Another round," he said. The waiter seemed to know what he meant. Paul was certain it was his customary ginger ale out of a wineglass. Though he hardly ever drank alcohol, Carter liked to give the impression he was having fun.

"Tell him we're running a business here," Carter said gruffly. "If they want more stuff from us, they need a subpoena. Period. We don't have the time to pansy around sending them shit."

Paul began to say something, but thought better of it. "Sure," he said instead. "I'll take care of it."

Carter nodded, which meant the conversation was over.

From across the room, Merrill waved. She was listening to Lily, who was midstory. When Lily finished gesticulating animatedly, Merrill clapped her hands and beamed at her sister with a smile that was equal parts encouragement, indulgence, amusement. Paul had seen that scene countless times before. Though Lily was more classically assembled, Paul found Merrill's innate, unstudied gracefulness endlessly appealing. There were moments when it took the wind out of him, how unfathomably lucky he was to be her husband.

"She looks beautiful, doesn't she?" Carter said, his voice tender with pride. "All my girls do tonight."

"I'm a lucky man, sir."

"We both are. It's been a tough fall, but we have plenty to be thankful for in our family."

"Indeed. I know I do."

Carter patted Paul on the shoulder, acknowledging Paul's gratitude. He had told Paul to stop thanking him for the job, but Paul continued to do so, in quiet ways.

The band had stopped playing, and the crowd had begun to trickle out in groups of two and four. Carter pointed toward Ines and Merrill and said, "Should we get the girls to the after-party?"

Paul hesitated. "I think we may head home," he said finally. "It's my fault; I'm a little tired tonight. Will you be in tomorrow?"

"Ines wants me to go out to East Hampton with her and get the house ready. I'll be on my cell, if you need me, or call me at the house. Ines gets testy when I take too many work calls on what she considers to be 'family time.' I've been doing a lot of that lately, so I'm a bit in the doghouse."

"Understood. I'm sure nothing will come up that I can't handle."

"Good man. You're coming out Thursday morning?"

"Yes, sir."

The men shook hands. "All right, son. Be there in time for the game. The Lions need all the fans they can get this year. Tennessee's going to give us a run for our money. I'm counting on you."

Paul stood outside the Waldorf for a few minutes before Merrill emerged. He watched as she said good-bye to a couple he didn't know, and from the way she lingered at the hotel entrance, he could tell she was about to stand him up.

"Shall we walk home?" Paul said when she finally slid beside him. He extended the crook of his elbow to her.

"I think I'm going to stop in quickly at the after-party," Merrill said. She busied herself with her fur coat and stared at the ground, knowing she was disappointing him. "I'm sorry! Lily convinced me. I'll only stay for a drink."

"Okay," he said. He was disappointed, but not entirely surprised.

"Why don't we walk together, though?" she offered quickly. "The party is just up the street; it's on your way home. These shoes are actually pretty comfortable." She laughed as she lifted the hem of her evening gown, the cold night air pricking at her exposed toes. Her toenails were painted a deep vermilion red. Her fingernails were short and unpolished. Merrill never got manicures; she claimed she couldn't sit still for that long without using her hands.

"That can't be possible," Paul said, shaking his head, "but I can carry you the five blocks."

She laughed. "It'll feel warmer if we start walking." She burrowed into his side. Feeling her head against his shoulder bolstered his spirits a bit. They started up Park Avenue together, moving as briskly as her dress would allow. Paul noticed when a man passing in the opposite direction checked Merrill out; it gave him a small burst of pride and he hugged her closer to him.

Even at night, Paul loved this walk. After so many years in New York, midtown Manhattan still felt like the epicenter of the world. The steel buildings glowed with life. Outside, sleek black town cars lined the curbs while young bankers and lawyers stood in the lobbies, awaiting the delivery of their dinners. In their offices, the deals that would make tomorrow's papers were being negotiated; large sums of money were changing hands; wealth was being created. It was reassuring to see the lights still on.

They walked quietly together for a few blocks, their feet falling in rhythm on the sidewalk. "Your mom did a great job tonight, I thought," Paul said, after a time. "Good crowd."

"She really did. It was so hard this year, with everything that's going on. It was strange, didn't you think, to have so many people missing?" Merrill shivered involuntarily, pulling her fur tight to her body.

"I certainly noticed Mack not being there."

"You know who else wasn't there? Morty. I was surprised. He was supposed to be at Mom and Dad's table."

"He probably got stuck at work. It's been rocky lately. RCM's had a lot of redemption requests."

"He's spending Thanksgiving with us," Merrill said softly. She drew to a stop on the corner as the light began to flash Don't Walk. "I worry about him sometimes. Julianne is apparently off skiing with her friends in Aspen." She raised her eyebrows disapprovingly. "Can you imagine us not spending Thanksgiving together? I mean, for God's sake. It's a family holiday. She should at least pretend to enjoy her husband's company."

"Well, I suppose second marriages can be different." Paul said, as diplomatically as possible. An image of Julianne in a white bikini and mesh sarong popped into his mind, which he tried to dismiss. This happened anytime anyone mentioned Julianne; it was what she was wearing the first time Paul met her. Julianne had a tight body but she was still just a little too old for most of her wardrobe. Her hair was thick and slightly too orange and when she smiled, Paul got a distinct sense that someone was about to be conned out of something.

"We have such a good thing, you and me," he said. "I'm so lucky."

Merrill laughed. "I'm no trophy wife, that's for sure."

"You're my only wife," he said. "Only one I'll ever have."

She smiled. Before the light changed, she drew close to him, her lips lingering at his ear. "I'm the lucky one," she whispered.

As they passed the Delphic headquarters, Paul looked up at his office. The Seagram Building was a colossal steel structure that shimmered bronze, even at night. At the time it was built, it was the most expensive skyscraper in the world. The solidness of it gave Paul a strange sense of confidence, as though the weight of the building assured him that his job would be there in the morning. *I'm still here*, he thought to himself, pulling his wife closer.

"Here's where I leave you," Merrill said, when they reached the corner of Sixty-second Street.

Paul pulled her in for a quick kiss. Their lips lingered on each other's, soft and familiar. She tasted like chocolate cake, and he could smell the faint trace of champagne on her breath. "Please come home soon," he said. "I miss my wife."

Merrill smiled. "I will," she said, and kissed him again on the cheek. "Just one drink, I promise."

His eyes followed her. Just before she turned the corner, she looked back at him and gave him a little wave. The collar of her coat was up, obscuring her elegant, slender neck from view. He loved that neck. Then she reached into her purse and pulled out her BlackBerry and held it up to her ear as she disappeared into the night air.

As Paul made his way uptown, the offices gave way to residential buildings. The sidewalks grew quiet, populated only by couples walking their dogs or coming home from a late dinner. The temperature had dropped and the wind had picked up, ruffling the awnings overhead and the branches of the trees. By the time Paul reached home, his nose was raspberry red. He sprinted the last block, straight through the lobby, and pulled off his tie while he was still in the elevator. Too tired to do anything else, he stripped off his suit and crawled into bed without brushing his teeth. When Merrill crawled in beside him a few hours later, he was already in a deep and dreamless sleep.

# WEDNESDAY, 6:23 A.M.

For once, the morning news was focused on something other than the turmoil in the markets. Traffic reports streamed in, along with lighter fare about holiday weight gain and teaching kids the true meaning of Thanksgiving. The local channels were all focused on the winter storm that was approaching the Northeast. It had moved quickly up the Florida coastline and was threatening to clog roads and delay flights from Washington, D.C., to New Hampshire.

While the coffee was brewing, Paul flipped aimlessly through the channels. He paused on CNBC in the hopes of a market update. The *Squawk Box* anchors were discussing the debut of Papa Smurf, the newest balloon in the Thanksgiving Day Parade. They were dressed casually, in turtlenecks. After the footage of the balloons stopped, one commentator said with a bland smile, "Everyone needs a holiday right now, don't you think? I know Wall Street does." Paul raised his mug. *Cheers to that*, he thought. He was fighting a mild hangover from the night before, and his temples were pulsing. Even a scotch or two got him drunk these days, and he wasn't used to staying out late on a Tuesday. The other anchors nodded in concurrence and then went to black as Paul clicked off the screen.

"It's gotten chilly out there, Mr. Ross," said Raymond, as he opened the lobby door for Paul. He was wearing a navy overcoat atop his doorman's uniform, and black leather gloves. Raymond was a beefy Irishman, with light blue eyes and fingers like salamis. The kind of man who seemed to thrive in cold climates. If Raymond was wearing a coat, it was cold.

Raymond's ruddy cheeks glowed as he made this pronouncement. He always liked to comment on the weather. "That coat's not going to do it for ya this morning, I don't think." He said, nodding at Paul's Barbour jacket.

"Thanks, Raymond," Paul said. He paused just inside the lobby, zipping up. "Still early. Hoping it'll warm up a bit."

"You and Mrs. Ross taking off for the holiday?"

"We are. Driving out to East Hampton first thing in the morning. Are you working tomorrow?"

Raymond shook his head. "No sir. You couldn't pay me enough to work on Thanksgiving. They pay us double, you know, so some of the boys like to take the holiday shift. But nothing more important than family. Not for me, sir."

"Couldn't agree with you more, Raymond. Nothing more important than family."

Paul turned up his collar and walked out onto Park Avenue. The *Wall Street Journal* was tucked beneath his arm. He felt bleary-eyed, and the air hit him like a punch. It wasn't yet 7:30 a.m. and the sun was still lingering behind the buildings to the east. For a moment, he thought about returning upstairs for a scarf. He checked his watch and decided against it.

"Have a good holiday," he called over his shoulder to Raymond, his breath hanging heavy in the morning chill.

It had been two months since Paul had started at Delphic, almost to the day. He had only just begun to find a rhythm. It was hard to feel settled; the markets undulated so wildly that even seasoned professionals felt unhinged. Every day began with a quiet hush, like horses lined up at the gate, pawing nervously at the dust. Though everyone was polite and apologetically busy, no one at Delphic had the time to show Paul much more than the men's room. Paul had never filled a general counsel role and Delphic had never had a general counsel, so the job was largely a project of mutual invention.

Paul's only form of orientation had happened at the same time as his interview. When Carter had called Paul into his office, Howary's doors had been closed less than two weeks. From the window behind Carter's desk, Paul had watched the flow of dark suits on their pilgrimage down Park Avenue. For years, he had gone to work just two blocks north; a part of him couldn't entirely believe that it was over. The surreality of sitting in a leather armchair in his father-in-law's office, resumé in hand, implicitly begging for employment, made the situation almost bearable.

Carter started off the meeting graciously, almost apologetically, as if Paul were doing him a favor by showing up. He gestured for him to sit, then pressed an intercom button and asked for coffee. "I appreciate you coming down, Paul," he said. "Do you want anything to eat?"

"I'm fine, thank you."

"I was glad to get Merrill's call. It's been a crazy quarter, and we could really use another hand on deck."

"I appreciate you thinking of me, sir."

The door opened and a woman came in, wheeling a silver cart. After they had helped themselves to coffee, Carter thanked her and she disappeared wordlessly back into the hallway. Once the door was closed, he said, "So here's the thing. My job used to be eighty percent offense, twenty percent defense. Now, it's completely inverted. I barely have time to respond to all my preexisting clients, much less go out and get new ones. Everyone wants to redeem out. If they aren't pulling their money, they're thinking about it. They want to talk about it. Investor Relations has turned into a triage center."

Paul nodded soberly. "How many people do you have in the IR department?"

"A couple top guys. But it doesn't really matter." Carter shook his head. "I've had relationships with a lot of these folks for years. Some of my clients have been with me since JPMorgan. They don't want their hand held by some pretty Investor Relations girl wearing a nice suit. They want to talk to me, or to Alain, or at least someone who works directly for me or Alain."

"How far down are you?" Paul asked.

Carter began to clean his glasses. Paul wondered if he wasn't supposed to be asking questions.

Still cleaning, Carter said, "Good question. Some of the funds are doing better than others. We're divided into five main funds, each with a different tilt. An inside manager here at Delphic oversees each of the funds. Alain oversees all the inside managers. As you know, we're a fund of funds, so our inside managers aren't directly managing the assets under their control: They're hand selecting outside managers. Only one of our funds, the Frederick Fund, is a single-manager strat. That means a single outside manager holds primarily all of its assets; in this case, it's RCM, Morty Reis's fund. Our other funds are generally subdivided among multiple outside managers, between three and ten depending on the fund and the timing. Some of the outside managers are doing fine, a few are doing abysmally, and one I'm going to get rid of in"—Carter stopped to glance at his Patek Philippe watch—"about twenty-five minutes."

He placed the glasses back on the bridge of his nose. "We'll discuss details later," he said, nodding quickly. It was clear he felt almost as awkward about this interview as Paul did. "I don't keep a big staff here at Delphic. We've been resisting the idea of getting a general counsel for years. For a few years we had a CFO with a law degree so he wore both hats, so to speak. But we lost him a year ago, and we've been on autopilot since then, relying on outside counsel when we need it. But with the markets the way they are, it's just too risky for us not to have someone in-house. Candidly, it would be of particular use to me to have someone whom I can put in front of clients as my proxy. If they can't see me, they can see my son-in-law. See what I'm saying?"

"I'm not a pretty Investor Relations girl wearing a nice suit."

Carter chuckled. "Don't sell yourself short, Paul. You deserve this job. But you're also great with people, and right now there are a lot of folks who need seeing. When things calm down, we'll get you back into more of a traditional GC role if that's what you want. But for the moment, I'd like it if you could come help me out with the client side of the business. You don't ski, do you, son?"

"No, sir. Last winter in Vail was my first time."

"Was it?" Carter's left eyebrow rose in slight amusement. "Didn't show."

He couldn't tell if Carter was being serious. Paul had spent the entire vacation with his knees turned into an uncontrollable pizza wedge, hoping not to run into his wife. All of the Darlings were expert skiers. Every President's Day weekend, the family spent four days together out in Vail or Gstaad or Whistler. Paul had been able to plead his way out of the trip in years prior, claiming one work obligation or another, but the previous year, Merrill had insisted. When she found out that he had never set foot on a ski slope in his life, she surprised him by arranging for a private instructor—a peppy woman named Linda—to babysit him all weekend. It was one of those misguided presents, simultaneously thoughtful and completely thoughtless. Generous and hopelessly emasculating.

"I started alpine skiing at the age of six," Carter announced. He had told Paul this before but Paul smiled encouragingly anyway. Carter always seemed to relax when he talked about one of his sports. "I still enjoy it, but telemarking is my true love. Do you know what telemarking is, Paul?"

"No, sir."

"I like to think of it as a blend of cross-country and alpine skiing. The binding of the boot attaches only at the toe, so your heel can come up off the ski. You get the rush of downhill, but with the flexibility of cross-county. Best of both worlds, I think. The boots allow you to really feel the mountain, to work with it." Carter's eyes grew soft and the corners of his mouth turned up slightly. "I think good investors tend to be good skiers," he said. He leaned in, as though he were sharing a trade secret. "They stay on their toes. They react fast. Even if that means changing course on a hairpin."

Paul shifted in his chair, trying not to look bemused. "Given my performance in Vail, sir, I'm not sure that bodes well for me."

"Ahh, we'll make a skier of you yet, Paul," Carter said solemnly. "Point is: These markets require agility. If we're going to survive, we're going to have to stay flexible."

"Indeed." Paul concurred, wondering if he was in over his head. It was a done deal now. Maybe it had always been, and everyone but Paul had the prescience to understand that.

"It's going to be hectic around here for a while. You'll have to hit the ground running."

"I understand."

"Take a day or so to think it over, if you like. Come back to me when you're ready and we'll talk compensation. And Paul?"

"Yes, sir?" Paul said, jumping to his feet.

"Call me Carter, for chrissake. I was just going to say, think up a title for yourself while you're at it. General Counsel, SVP; don't care what it is, as long as you don't come off sounding like a member of the Windsor family."

---

In his first few weeks of work, Paul was surprised to discover how big an operation Delphic actually was. He felt as though he had opened the back of a giant clock: The bullpen computers buzzed, the conference rooms sparkled, secretaries slipped quietly up and down the halls like well-oiled gears. Even the day before Thanksgiving it hummed along like a machine. As Paul swiped in through the large glass doors, a rush of filtered air and kinetic energy hit him. The lights were on and a few associates sped past him down the hall. Paul was surprised to see so many people at work. He nodded to Ida, Carter's secretary, who was talking into her headset. She signaled him over with one hand, like an air traffic controller bringing him in for a landing, and he waited in front of her cube as she wrapped up her call. The firm's mascot, a gleaming bronze lion, stared at him with unmoving eyes from across the hallway. The statue stood perpetual guard over Carter's office, a gift from Carter's lawyer, Sol Penzell.

"Terry's out today," Ida said crisply, when she hung up. She gave Paul an efficient smile. "I'm filling in for her. Anything you need, you just give a shout."

"Thanks, Ida," he said. "I appreciate it." He turned toward his office. His was the next door down from Carter's. Paul still found the proximity vaguely unnerving.

"Oh, Paul," Ida called. "A woman from the SEC named Alexa Mason called for you. She said it was urgent."

"Alexa Mason?" Paul stopped and turned around, his hand still on the door handle. "This early? Did she say what about?"

"She left a voice mail. She said she's working with David Levin. She told me to say that."

Paul nodded. "Thanks, Ida. I'll get back to her."

"Do you need her number?" Ida asked, but Paul had already shut the door.

In the safety of his office, Paul closed his eyes and took a deep breath. His shoulder blades rose and fell gently against the wall. The message light on his phone flashed an insistent red. It elevated his heart rate just to look at it.

*I'm not ready to talk to anyone at the SEC,* he thought. *Even Alexa.*

He sat down at his desk and, after a minute, turned the phone to face the wall so that he couldn't see the light.

By noon, Paul had worked his way through a stack of agreements that needed his sign-off. Since most of the senior management was out of the office, he had kicked off his loafers and was sitting crossed-legged on his desk chair. He had forgotten Alexa's call, or, at least, pushed it to the recesses of his mind.

Outside his window, the November sky had turned to silver. The few pedestrians he could see on the sidewalk below were swaddled in hats and coats, their faces tucked up behind lengths of fabric. Paul regretted not having his scarf. They were predicting that the snow would hit earlier than expected; a shiver of excitement passed through his body as he checked the weather report online. One thing he loved about New York was the sharpness of the seasons. There was something electric about winter coming to the city. It was gritty and cold but also wondrously beautiful. The dark army of trees on Park Avenue came alive with lights at night; the store displays on Fifth Avenue were gaudy and gorgeous, as were the throngs of holiday shoppers that clogged the sidewalks. Snow in New York turned quickly into a blackened slush along the curbs, but for the first brief moment, it would dust the sidewalks like confectioners' sugar and transform the city's skyline into a perfect, tiered wedding cake.

Suddenly, Paul was itching to leave the office. He put on his headset and dialed Ida.

"Ida, it's Paul. Listen, please go home. No one else is here and I doubt anyone's going to call. You can roll Carter's line over to me if that makes you more comfortable."

"Are you sure that's okay?" Ida said gratefully. "It's only lunchtime. I'm happy to stay."

Paul was about to wish her a happy Thanksgiving when she said: "Actually, a call is coming in now. It's Merrill. Do you want to take it?"

"Sure, just forward it to me. Now get out of here."

He switched his phone to line two and put Merrill on speakerphone. "Hi there," he said affectionately, relaxing back into his chair. "Almost done with work?" Merrill had planned on taking a half day so that she could pack for the weekend. "Any chance you're stopping by the drugstore on your way home?"

There was a pause. When she spoke, her voice was hollow, as if the air had been sucked out of her. "Who is this?" she said.

"It's Paul, Mer," he said, snatching up the receiver. His body instinctually flushed with adrenaline; something was wrong. "Ida's rolling your dad's calls to me."

"I need to talk to him. I called his cell phone, but it's off. Where is he?"

"I think he's driving. What's going on? Talk to me."

Merrill was mute. He could hear the television on in the background. It buzzed like white noise, the sound reverberating on the line between them.

"Turn on the television," she said quietly. "It's on every channel."

"What is?"

"Morty's dead."

"I'll call you back from the conference room," Paul said, fumbling beneath his desk to put on his shoes.

"I have to go. I'm at the office. There's a deposition."

"You don't need to go to that," he said, trying not to raise his voice. "You don't need to do anything if you're upset."

"No, I can't—I just can't. I'm sorry; I'm a little overwhelmed right now. I'll call you later. I love you."

And then she was gone, before he could say, "I love you." Before he could say anything at all.

# WEDNESDAY, 11:20 A.M.

The day began badly for Lily, with all the hallmarks of a hangover. She awoke with a throbbing headache and the disheartening realization that she had slept in her makeup. Her eyes blinked open, and finding the bedroom saturated with light, immediately closed again. For a minute or two she went still, counting her drinks from the night before like sheep and wishing she weren't awake. The hangover felt disproportionate to the amount of fun she remembered having.

Lily always drank too much when she was with Daria. It was possible that Daria was her best friend; at least, Daria was the person with whom she spent the most time, next to Adrian and her mother. Ines didn't approve of Daria; she described her, arch eyed, as "having an agenda." Ines was wary of girls whom she perceived as not being from nice families; girls who insinuated themselves into New York society by tactically befriending the right sort of people at the right sort of parties. Women with Agendas: Lily had been cautioned not to befriend them. Women with Agendas were, in Ines's estimation, more dangerous than gold diggers because they were clever, and because they wanted things that girls like Lily could provide for them.

If Ines was to be listened to, the world was populated by people waiting to take advantage of Lily. Boys without means were interested in her money. Boys with means were still interested in her money because children of the wealthy lacked a work ethic and wanted a spouse who would make sure their club memberships would never go unpaid and their children would be admitted to the right schools and there would always be pleasant dinner parties and charity events in the evenings. And all women wanted something. Ines felt strongly that women were rarely friends with one another unless they could get something out of it. Female friendships were like strategic alliances: Each party had to bring something to the table in order to maintain equity. The simple fact was that Lily didn't need anything from anyone. She had money, she had connections, she had beauty and style and a house in the Hamptons. Therefore, she would inevitably be on the losing end of any friendship. Lily found it difficult to find people to spend time with as a result.

Lily didn't altogether disagree with Ines's assessment of Daria. Daria was a shrew. But she was lively and fun and Lily enjoyed her company. Unlike most of Lily's Spence friends, Daria actually had a job: She ran Investor Relations at a large private equity fund, a job that suited her looks and her Type-A personality and her unwavering commitment to surrounding herself with highly liquid men. Daria knew everyone in New York. It was her job to. And her boundless energy was infectious: It was nearly impossible to feel listless around her. *Bored on a Tuesday?* Daria had an extra ticket to an art opening and would pick you up in an hour. *Single?* Daria knew a gorgeous hedge fund manager who had just broken up with his girlfriend. *Marital trouble?* Daria would escort you to the New Yorkers for Animals benefit and buy you Bellinis beforehand.

Only, of course, if you were the kind of person who invited her to your house in East Hampton every August and could introduce her to a managing director at Goldman Sachs. Fortuitously, Lily had done both.

When Adrian had called to say he would meet her at the party, Lily's first thought was to call Daria. They met for a quick drink first at the Library of the Regency Hotel, a snug bar that was exactly equidistant between their apartments on Park Avenue. The clientele was mostly neighborhood types: older women with shellacked hair and suspended eyebrows, bankers who needed a scotch before going home to the kids. It was a place where two women in formal attire would not be incongruous.

"All right," Daria said when Lily arrived, "What's going on with Adrian?" She had staked out a corner nook with leather couches, ideally located for watching people and people watching her. Daria loved being watched. She cut a sharp figure in a strapless, plum column of a dress (plum was the color of the season, and it looked decadent against Daria's perpetually tan skin). A fox fur bolero was wrapped neatly around her shoulders. She had tucked a black feather in her chignon, something Lily felt looked sensational on Daria but that she herself could never pull off. Daria's arms draped languidly across the back of the couch, and she yawned lightly, as if she were so accustomed to wearing a ball gown that it might be just another Tuesday.

After kissing Daria hello, Lily perched gingerly on the edge of the opposing couch, trying not to wrinkle herself.

"Oh, it's nothing," she replied, looking away. As she said it, she realized this was true. "He's just stuck at work, that's all."

"Is he not coming?" Daria probed, trying to assess the problem. Though she looked stunning—Lily always looked stunning—she seemed not herself. She had sounded sensitive on the phone. This had been the case a lot lately, and Daria wasn't sure what could be done about it.

"Oh no, he'll be there. Just a little late. I didn't want to walk in alone."

With a pinched brow, Daria signaled for the waiter. Lily felt her eyes misting over with tears. She could sense that Daria was growing mildly irritated with her or, at least, tiring of her. And why not: Lily was tiring of herself. She couldn't explain why, but the inarticulable sensation that something was wrong had been following her everywhere, like a shadow. It lay heavy on her lids in the morning when she woke; it sat with her in the afternoons, gnawing away at her insides as she went about checking her e-mail, having lunch, running on the treadmill. She was becoming a bore.

"I'm being silly," she said.

"Of course you're not. He adores you. You know that, don't you?"

The waiter came with their drinks.

"Oh, I know. It's really nothing. It's not his fault. He's just a little—I don't know, distant?—lately. My father's the same. It's stressful at their office right now. And Adrian's off with clients a lot, too, and I'm alone. I hate being alone. It makes me feel needy, you know? I wasn't like this before."

Two middle-aged men, both in red power ties and pinstriped suits, sat down at the adjacent table. They stared predatorily at Daria. One leaned in and whispered something to the other; they both grinned. Daria recrossed her coltish legs and ignored them.

"Everyone's stressed right now," she said. "Jim's been a maniac, honestly. He takes calls from Asia in the middle of the night. He screams at waitresses who take too long with our food. Last week he bit my head off for ordering too much Pellegrino on Fresh Direct. Pellegrino, honestly. The guy gets driven around in a chauffeured Escalade and he's bitching at me about Pellegrino. I love your bracelet, by the way. Is that new?"

Lily managed a weak smile. She held out her wrist. The bracelet was new. Though she knew it was counterintuitive, there was something about the downturn that made Lily want to buy more, not less. She had been shopping a lot lately, with almost reckless abandon. She would "stop in to look" on her way to somewhere else, and somehow emerge with an espresso maker or a pair of espadrilles. She bought birthday presents for no one in particular, dresses without occasion. If the wares were small enough (a pair of earrings; lingerie) she would stuff them in her purse and dispose of the shopping bags and price tags and put the receipts into a wastebasket on the street. The closets were bursting with new things. It wasn't even that she was hiding them from Adrian; seeing new things, tags still on, made her uncomfortable.

The satisfaction of a new pair of earrings or shoes had an immediate satiating effect, but one which would be replaced later in the day with a tidal wave of guilt. *This is it for the month,* she would think furiously. But then a particularly dull Monday would confront her; Adrian would be out of town and her girlfriends were busy and her date book was glaringly empty, and Lily would find herself once again wandering though the aisles of Bergdorf Goodman or Williams-Sonoma or even Duane Reade, hungrily snapping up things she hadn't known she needed until she saw them.

"Maybe you're bored," Daria suggested, shrugging. "Have you been working lately?"

"A little. Barney's is taking our holiday leash line. So that's fun." In truth, *Bacall* was moving sideways, and Carter was unwilling to sink more money into it until the economy picked up. There was still an occasional online order, and there was the Barney's deal, but at the end of the day, it was still a net-negative cash-flow situation. More of a vanity project than a job. Lily found herself working on it less and less, her productive hours dwindling from nearly full-time to decidedly part-time, then finally to scant, now-and-then hours, the kind tucked away for hobbies or household chores.

Lily swirled the drink in front of her, watching as the ice melted and wet beads began to form on the outside of the glass. "Do you ever worry about Jim?" She asked casually.

Daria's eyes widened. "Worry?" She put down her drink. "What do you know?"

Lily looked up, and catching the worried look in her friend's eyes, felt instantly terrible. "Nothing!" she exclaimed. "I'm sorry. I didn't mean to imply anything. Really, Jim is smitten with you."

Daria nodded uneasily. She glanced away; one of the middle-aged men at the next table caught her eye. *They look like traders,* Lily thought. *Or hedge fund managers. A little too slick to be investment bankers.* Daria smiled back, adjusting her bolero.

"I was really talking more about me," Lily added, watching Daria watch the trader. "I know it's stupid, but sometimes I get nervous when Adrian's out with clients. Women in this city are shameless. Last week we were at a party and I watched two girls just go right up to him, as if I weren't even there. Gorgeous girls. Both younger than me. Definitely prettier. Do I sound paranoid?"

"Yes," Daria said. "Well, no. I don't know. I mean, look, Adrian's a handsome, successful guy. And New York's a shark tank. There're always going to be girls around. We're going to get older and they're going to stay the same age. You're going to have to get used to that." One of the traders answered his cell phone. He stood abruptly and strode out of the bar's door, into the hotel lobby. Daria's eyes followed him until he was out of sight, and then she turned back to Lily. "Look," she said sternly, her hand on Lily's shoulder for emphasis, "The only thing you can do is look your best and not get insecure. Guys are like dogs: They smell fear. You're *Lily Darling*, for God sake. Adrian's lucky to be married to you. If you don't forget that, he won't either."

Lily nodded quietly, her eyes downcast. The ice in her drink had melted. It was forming a ring on the table, the cocktail napkin wrapped around it like a giant Band-Aid. "Thanks," she said, her voice small. "I just don't feel like myself lately."

"Don't be crazy," Daria said curtly. She straightened up and signaled for the check. "Come on—what would Ines say? She would tell you to buck up and enjoy the party."

"I know. My mother's a master of appearances."

"She taught you well," Daria said, rising to her feet. She tapped her wrist. "Let's go," she said, and offered Lily her arm.

Ines had indeed taught her daughters a great many valuable things. Most could be filed under the topic heading of style and etiquette. (*Never leave the house without makeup; you never know who you will run into. Nice girls wear nice lingerie. Ignore the latest trend if it doesn't suit your shape. Always send a handwritten thank-you note.*) But she imparted grander axioms of wisdom, too, which Merrill largely disregarded and Lily accepted as gospel. With the exception of a long-running disagreement over whether or not navy could ever be appropriately worn with black, Lily had found that Ines was almost always right.

Lily had, therefore, accepted her mother's determination that Merrill was smart and Lily was pretty. The distinction was made so early on that Lily couldn't remember a time when anyone in the family thought otherwise. Of course, Ines had never come right out and said this. But she did say it, again and again, in those countless small ways that leave a distinct impression, like footsteps on a stone stair. Merrill found books in her Christmas stocking; Lily found Clarins makeup sets and self-tanner. Merrill had French lessons when Lily had ballet. Ines took Lily to Elizabeth Arden once a week, where they would have lunch and get their nails done. It was assumed that Merrill was too busy pursuing important intellectual things to join them, so they never invited her; but then, she had never asked to come along, either.

Lily understood her mother well enough not to take offense. That Merrill was smart and Lily was pretty wasn't a value judgment. It was, instead, an acknowledgment of the world's ordering. Merrill was one genus, and Lily another; separate but equal sub-branches of the same family tree. If anything, Lily secretly suspected that Ines placed a slightly higher premium on looks than on brains. Anyway, Lily was smart enough to keep her mother laughing and engaged when they were together. "Smart *enough* is what's important" was a favorite phrase of Ines's.

In any case, Ines was a firm believer that neither looks nor brains much mattered if you didn't know what to do with them. "The greatest strength you can have is to know your own strengths," she said when Lily was rejected by Tisch, her top choice for college. "You've got to figure out what you're good at and make the most of it."

That stuck with her. Lily made the most of her looks, her sense of style, her ability to entertain. Life was simple, really, when you knew what you were good at.

Lily had always thought that Merrill's Achilles' heel was being good at everything. She was an excellent athlete, facile at every sport she tried. In school, A's came easily to her. Friends did, too; all the girls wanted Merrill to be part of their group. While she was friendly with everyone, Merrill always kept a close circle: girls with names like Whitney and Lindsey and Kate, girls with snub noses dusted in freckles, and ponytails and the luminous skin of the very well cared for. They dressed the same: Patagonia zip-ups and pearl earrings and sherbet-shaded cable knits. They were the "nice girls": liked by everyone, not too fast for the parents but not too slow for the boys, either. They went off to New England colleges, mostly, Middlebury and Dartmouth and Trinity, to play lacrosse and date boys from Connecticut. They won awards for qualities like "general excellence" and "most well rounded." The Spence admissions catalog filled its pages with photos of them in the classrooms and in the library, faces beaming, arms looped around each other's shoulders in enthusiastic sorority. On the other hand, Spence treated girls like Lily with casual indifference, like a movie sequel that had gone straight to DVD.

From the time she was six, it was clear that Lily had no real business at a top-tier school. She would be kept on, of course, out of respect for her father, and because she was Merrill Darling's sister, expected to muddle through with C's, and discreetly shuffled out the door to some college or other at the end of it. There would be no fanfare at graduation, as there had been with Merrill. No awards, no crying teachers, and no celebratory family lunch at the '21' Club. Instead, there would be quiet relief on everyone's part that she had made it through.

Having been a failure as a student, Lily tried her best at adulthood. At twenty-four, she had been the first in her circle to get married. Adrian was exactly what Lily imagined her parents wanted for her: He had gone to Buckley and lived on Seventy-third and Lex; he worked in finance; he was a member of the Racquet Club. In a suit, he looked remarkably like Carter: vertical frame and the smile of a winner. Adrian was the most outgoing of the famously attractive Patterson boys. Ines disliked everyone that Lily dated, but she seemed to dislike Adrian least.

Every girl on the Upper East Side between the ages of twenty-two and thirty-five knew the Patterson boys. All four were tall and tanned with impossibly perfect teeth and jet-black hair. Their father, Tripp Patterson, was handsome in a terrifying, patrician sort of way. He carried himself with the assurance of a pedigreed show dog; he was, after all, the president of the Racquet Club, an ace tennis player, and damn good at backgammon. Tripp, who had never really worked, now managed the family's assets. This took up little of his time as, after several generations of idle Pattersons, there were few assets left to manage. An unfortunate detail that could only be surmised by the keenest of observers; Tripp's wife, CeCe, did a remarkable job of keeping that under wraps. She herself worked as a real estate broker, keeping the family afloat on her commissions. She made sure that the whole family was always perfectly turned out, and ever present on the New York, Palm Beach, and Southampton social circuits, even if only as guests of other families. Ines threw out the occasional wry comment about the Pattersons' lifestyle, which she felt was "financed on fumes." Still, Ines saw CeCe Patterson as a compelling social ally, and made a point to befriend her long before her daughter took an interest in CeCe's son.

The Pattersons' Christmas cards were legendary. Each year, the family wished their friends happy holidays from the ski slopes of Aspen or the beaches of Lyford Cay or the golf course at St. Andrews. Each year, the daughters of family friends would steal the card and tuck it away in backpacks and bedside drawers, so that they might stare lovingly at the face of Henry or Griffin or Fitz or Adrian well into the new year. Any girl who went out with a Patterson boy in middle school was immediately elevated to interschool royalty. Marrying one was like landing a Kennedy.

Theirs was a storybook courtship, the kind that begins on a tennis court at the Meadow Club in Southampton and culminates in a two-hundred-and-fifty person wedding at the Maidstone Club in East Hampton. Lily was fresh out of Parsons, living at home with Carter and Ines, when Adrian mistakenly hit an errant serve in her direction. Though Lily would later come to terms with the fact that Adrian would neither inherit nor make any real money, he pursued Lily grandly, with resources that most boys her age could never hope to offer. For a twenty-two-year-old, dating a thirty-year-old felt hopelessly sophisticated and titillating. Lily was hooked. After a year of preparing for dates with Adrian and going on dates with Adrian and discussing dates with Adrian with her friends, Lily said "Yes." And after a year of preparing for what *Quest* magazine called "the Society Wedding of the Summer" Lily said "I do." It wasn't until the honeymoon photos had been uploaded and the registry china had been delivered and the thank-you notes written, that Lily once again began the business of figuring out what came next.

---

Down the hall Lily heard the shower shut off, and it occurred to her that Adrian was still home. She rolled over and checked the time. Her heart sank; it was much later than she had thought. She groaned and flipped herself face down into the pillow. She was still lying like that when Adrian banged open the bedroom door, a bath towel wrapped around his waist like a kilt. Without looking at him, Lily could tell he was upset.

"You set the alarm for 7:30 p.m. instead of 7:30 a.m.," he said when she sat up. The muscles between his shoulders rippled as he moved. "I missed a call with Asia." He stood with his back to her, yanking through a rack of suit pants like pages of a boring magazine. The moist heat of the shower steamed off his body, and the back of his neck was taut, as though strung with electrical cords.

When he had settled on a suit, Adrian let his towel slide off him. It formed a puddle at his feet, blue and wet. Lily stared at it and tried not to be annoyed. Just a week before, Adrian had fired their maid, Marta, as part of an overzealous campaign to reduce household expenses. Marta had actually seemed grateful for the release, which embarrassed Lily terribly. They were, she knew, exhaustingly messy. Lily was always underfoot, padding around the house in a bathrobe while Marta vacuumed or urging Marta to hurry up and go before their friends came over for cocktails at six. Adrian managed to leave behind a trail of dirty running socks and pocket change and cereal bowls with a crust of oatmeal still clinging to the rim. Marta could always tell when Adrian and Lily were home. She would follow the mess: a briefcase in the foyer, shoes scattered on the living room floor, a suit jacket thrown over a dining room chair, a half-drunk soda on the kitchen counter, only to find Adrian, feet up on the coffee table, watching *SportsCenter* in the den or Lily, tossing dresses on the bed as she decided what to wear for the evening.

"I'm sorry," Lily said weakly, her head pounding. "I, *ehm*, drank a bit too much last night."

"Yeah, I saw."

"Ugh, was I terrible? I'm so embarrassed. Did I embarrass you?"

She flopped onto her back, her head sinking into the pillow. Her blond hair splayed out around her head like a halo. The duvet fell back from her shoulders, exposing her naked torso. Lily never wore anything to sleep. In the morning, she looked as fresh and clean as a newborn. Her skin was a soft, milky white, and the color of it matched the sheets almost exactly. She was the same size, the same smoothness, as she had been at sixteen. There had never been a moment, not one, where Adrian saw her and didn't want to sleep with her.

He sighed, carrying his shoes over to the edge of the bed and sat beside her. Lily braced herself for a lecture, but instead, he leaned in and kissed her gently on her temple.

"It's fine," he said. "You were fine. I just want you to take it easy, you know, if we're going to be trying and all that. Or not not trying."

"Will you lie down for just one minute?" she asked, her eyes still shut. "My head's killing me. Just a minute, I promise. I feel like I never see you anymore."

He swung his legs up onto the bed. Then his arm was around Lily, and she snuggled into it, her nose pressed into his damp ribs.

She looped her leg gently over his, but he didn't move. Then she pressed her lips to his. Maybe she was imagining it, but she felt him stiffening away from her, and her heart sank as she wondered what he was thinking. *Was he annoyed that she was delaying him? Was he just counting the seconds until he had held her for an acceptable amount of time?* It was wrong to try to sleep with him in the morning when he was already late to work, she knew that logically, but lately she just felt so hungry for him, and the further away he drifted the hungrier she became.

Lily had never before worried about their sex life. When she was being rational, she could acknowledge that there wasn't really a reason to start worrying now. She and Adrian had sex regularly (at least, regularly if the lives of her two married girlfriends with whom she was comfortable enough to share this sort of information could be taken as a guide); they were adventurous (as adventurous as Lily thought people from nice families ought to be); and, as discussed, they had stopped using birth control on their third anniversary. Nothing had changed, to date.

They weren't trying, but they weren't not trying, either. *Not not trying.* That was Adrian's expression, repeated like a party line to increasingly expectant friends and family. It was said with a big smile, and met with approving nods. Every time he said it, Lily rolled it around in her head like a marble, inspecting it for traces of unacceptable indifference or nonchalance. *Not not trying.* She couldn't find anything wrong with it, but then, she couldn't find anything not wrong with it, either.

According to Adrian, they discussed having a baby ad nauseam; according to Lily, not nearly enough. She didn't know why, but the conversation felt unresolved, like a project that hadn't been given a red light but didn't quite have the green light, either. It was all she could think about. It wasn't unlike *Bacall*: a live deal, but temporarily held up, waiting in limbo for approvals and funding.

"I hate when you say that," she said. Her head throbbed: *I will never drink like that again.*

"Say what?"

"Not not trying. It's just the way you say it. It sounds so . . . passive."

Adrian put his finger beneath her chin and lifted it gently until her big blue eyes flickered open. He examined her tenderly, his eyebrows knit with an almost paternal compassion. There were freckles on her nose, like little flecks of chocolate. She was so frustrating when she was like this: childish and defiant and hopelessly attractive. "Okay," he said, eyebrows raised. "We're trying. Better?"

"No," she said stubbornly and shut her eyes, though she knew he was saying everything right. For all of Adrian's childish foibles—his messiness and his perpetual lateness and his tendency to overserve himself at the bar—Lily knew Adrian was a good husband, devoted to her, and to the idea of children, if for no other reason than that it was the right thing to do.

Adrian's was a neatly ordered world. It was a world Lily knew well, and would be happy to live in for the rest of her life without much thought of any alternatives. Sure, Adrian broke a rule now and then—a brief suspension at boarding school for smoking weed and a DUI or two—but that was all part of the game anyway, nothing Tripp Patterson hadn't done, or Henry Patterson Jr. before him. For the most part, Adrian followed the handbook to the letter.

He dressed as he did—Nantucket reds and bow ties and hunting jackets—without irony. He played lacrosse and drank his way through college, never doubting that a spot in the Morgan Stanley Investment Banking program would be available to him upon graduation (it was), and after that, a job at his wife's father's hedge fund. That was just the way it was, the way it always had been. The examples of his brothers, all married, each employed by a hedge fund or large investment bank, one summering in Nantucket and the other two in the Hamptons, offered validation to Adrian's baseline assumptions. As long as Adrian was in charge, Lily was certain the world would always be as she had known it under Carter's management. This was deeply reassuring.

"I just need to know we're ready."

Lily could feel Adrian's presence beside her, the weight of his body pressing down the mattress and his head partially blocking the light from the bedside lamp. Skin touched skin at the shoulders and elbows and her knee draped softly over his. The musculature of his arm was tight beneath her head and it made her feel safe, if only for a moment. She wanted him to stay beside her all day, to snuggle back down beneath their piled-high duvet and put his forehead to hers and tell her that today was theirs and theirs alone. As long as her eyes were shut he wouldn't leave. The clock would stop its ticking and they would be suspended in the moment, together, like the second of silence after a performance is over and the applause has not yet begun.

"I'm thirty-four," Adrian said simply. "It's time. I don't know what else there is to say." He reached out and massaged her temples. He smelled like the cedar drawer linings they used in the closet, the smell of home.

The phone rang, breaking the moment. No one ever called their home phone, except for the doorman and telemarketers. They glanced at each other briefly, each wondering who it could be.

Adrian pulled his arm from beneath her head to answer the phone, forcing her to sit up. Lily's eyes popped open and the light rushed in.

"You've got to be kidding," Adrian said after a few seconds. Through the phone, Lily could hear the staccato sounds of a man talking rapidly on the other end, though it wasn't loud enough to hear what he was saying. Lily was awake now, charged by the current of nervous energy that seeped through the phone wire.

Adrian cupped the receiver and hissed, "Turn on the TV." Startled, Lily grabbed for the remote and flicked it on, smarting a little from her husband's directive. Adrian was rarely sharp with her. Her nipples grew hard as the sheet fell away from her body and she shivered, suddenly aware that she was naked.

As she flipped aimlessly through the channels, Lily felt her insides grip with a sickening self-conscious tightness, a familiar feeling. Her mind raced furiously through the events of the past few days. *Had she done anything wrong? Had she forgotten to pay the maintenance again? Overdrawn the household account?*

Her stomach churning, she whispered, "What's wrong?"

Adrian shook his head and waved her off. "When did you find out?" He asked the person on the other end of the phone, his brow furrowed tightly into a hard V. Then: "Does Carter know?"

Lily's eyes widened, "Know what?" she insisted, louder this time. When he didn't answer, she focused on the muted figures flickering across the television screen.

*Uncle Morty's house. Why was it on television?*

She turned on the sound.

"Jesus, Lily," Adrian whispered, and grabbed the remote. He muted it again, and covered the ear that wasn't pressed to the receiver. "All right," he said to the voice on the other end. "I mean, that's obviously terrible news. Yes, yeah, I understand. I'm going into the office now. I'm with Lily. . . . No, I haven't spoken to him. Have you tried his cell? All right, Sol. Yes, thanks for calling. Talk soon."

Adrian clicked off the phone and lay back against the headboard.

"Holy shit," he said.

Lily turned away from the television, still not quite sure what she was seeing, and her entire body prickled with goose bumps. Adrian's perfect tan face was a sickly green. He looked, she thought, exactly as he had the time she had found him lying on the floor in the fetal position, and had rushed him to Lenox Hill with what turned out to be appendicitis.

"That was Sol? What did he want?" Lily said, her voice small, almost inaudible. She wanted to reach out to him but she felt frozen, like a rabbit in the road. *This was it,* she thought. *I knew something was wrong.*

"Lil," he said, and took her hands in his. "He's trying to get in touch with your dad. He wanted to let him know—to let us know—that Morty Reis . . . Uncle Morty . . . he passed away." His eyes stared straight into hers, strong, alert, alight with adrenaline. "I'm so sorry, sweetness. I'm so sorry."

Her head shook back and forth in disbelief. Her hand gripped his tightly but she couldn't look up. Tears began to fill her eyes.

"How?" she breathed. "He's still . . . he was young."

Adrian held her tighter. Her skull was nestled in the crook of his neck, her forehead pressed tenderly against his Adam's apple.

"He killed himself, love. He jumped off a bridge." He swallowed. "It's horrible, I know."

She was crying hard now. "Oh, my God!" Her pretty face contorted with pain. "Does Mom know? We have to call her. I want to talk to Mom."

"Of course," said Adrian, fumbling for the phone. "Of course."

The conversation with Ines was short and loving. After a few reassuring words to Lily, Ines asked her to put Adrian back on the line.

"Hi," he said, nodding solemnly. He listened as Lily went to the bathroom, reemerging with a shining face, damp and pink from scrubbing. "Yes, I understand completely. No, we're fine. I haven't talked to him, no . . . I'll take care of her. Yes, call if you need me. No, no, of course I'll stay with her."

"Tell her to come over," Lily panted from the bathroom door, her voice ragged from crying. She hiccupped.

"Lily's asking for you, if you'd like to come over . . . No, I understand. Well, call us once you've reached him."

After Adrian hung up, he opened his arms and she joined him in bed. He held her quietly for a long time. She didn't ask what it meant for the business and he didn't tell her.

Eventually, their bodies were intertwined and they were kissing fiercely, salt-stained kisses. Lily's face was swollen and ugly from tears and their bodies became wet from sweat and as Adrian pushed himself hard inside her, they both exploded, with all the passion of two people painfully aware of being alive. It was the kind of sex they hadn't had since their honeymoon: raw and unadulterated.

"I love you so much," he said tenderly when they were done. He kissed her hard on the forehead and saw that she was crying again. "Hey," he said, pressing his forehead to her cheek. "Hey, now."

She shut her eyes and shook her head . . . *How could they have just made love? It seemed so selfish, so indulgent . . . and so irresponsible . . . not not trying . . . what a fucking time this would be for her to get pregnant . . .*

*but she had so desperately wanted to feel close to her husband . . . and lying here like this, it was the closest she had felt to him in a very long time . . .*

"Are we still ready?" she said, her voice tiny. "No matter what?"

"Of course, Lil," Adrian said, drawing her body to his. He stroked the soft skin of her back, running his fingers lightly down the curve of her waist in a way that made her shiver. "Of course we are. You'll see, it's going to be fine."

# WEDNESDAY, 12:56 P.M.

Toby, the neighbor's dog, had been causing problems for years. He was a typical urban mongrel, some sort of pit bull or Staffie, with a squat, spark-plug body and a square mug of a face. His ears had been clipped. They were pinned back to his head in a way that made him look as though he were already running headlong at you, about to lunge for the jugular. You knew Toby's story just by looking at him: Animal Care and Control had picked him up in the projects. A rescue group had saved him, probably when he was a puppy and still reasonably cute. Somehow, he had made it to the Dunns' backyard in Staten Island. Not heaven, exactly, but a quiet purgatory, where he could pass his final dog years pacing and barking and scaring the neighborhood children without the threat of imminent euthanization.

Chris was terrified of Toby, but then Chris was terrified of most things. The previous Thursday, Chris had come home from his after-school program shaking, his face blotchy from crying. At first, Yvonne couldn't get a peep out of him, but eventually she wore him down, plying him with Oreos and Coke. It was Toby, he said, when the snot-soaked tears subsided. Toby had scared him. He had thrown himself against the Dunns' fence when Chris had walked by; he could feel Toby's hot dog breath on his arm, that's how close he got. Yvonne suspected the tears had to do with something else—the kids at school, probably—but she didn't push. Chris didn't like to talk about it when he got bullied. Especially in front of his big brother, Pat Jr. It would only make Pat Jr. angry, which would make Chris even more upset, and no good would come of it.

"They should have that dog put down," Pat Jr. fumed, draping his arm protectively around his little brother. Pat Jr. was still wearing his football jersey, even though Yvonne had told him to change it before dinner. "Seriously, he's scary as shit."

"Language," Yvonne said.

"Sorry, Mom. But it's true. He really hates Chris."

"That dog hates everyone. He's just a very angry dog."

"Yeah, well. Joe Dunn's an asshole for letting him off the leash."

"*Language*," Yvonne said again, more sternly this time. It was hard reprimanding Pat Jr. when he was standing up for his brother. Her heart softened as she watched them settle into the couch together. The pale freckled skin of the one blended into the other's so that when they touched it was almost hard to see where one ended and the other began.

Pat Jr. wordlessly flipped on the television to the Discovery Channel, Chris's favorite. They had a quiet rhythm, like a couple who had been married for years, like a set of uneven bookends. Though Pat Jr. was nearly twice Chris's size, they were undeniably brothers. Both boys had their father's piercing blue eyes. A blue so brilliant it made you want to squint, like looking straight up into the sky on a sunny day. Irish eyes, Yvonne's mother used to say. Chris might've had an athletic build, too, but all the complications at birth left him warped and small, with a sunken rib cage and legs like spindles. To the rest of the world, Chris would always look sickly. To Yvonne, he was just the smaller of her boys. She tried to treat him the same way she did Pat Jr.—the worst thing in the world for him, she knew, would be for his mother to act as if he were a cripple—but sometimes her heart got the better of her. She would hug him just a little longer; ask him how he was doing more than once in the same conversation; let him sneak a cookie before dinner. She kept the house stocked with all his favorite foods: Oreos and Fruit Roll-Ups and mini microwaveable pizzas.

Yvonne went to muss Chris's hair but he flinched when her fingers grazed his scalp. He was getting older, she reminded herself. Boys his age didn't like to be coddled by their moms. His eyes stayed trained on the television set, focused as a race car driver. Yvonne felt a twinge of love.

She straightened up and headed back to the kitchen, where she had been chopping onions for the pasta. Her eyes stung from them, and she wiped away a tear with the elbow of her shirt.

"Go change your shirt, Pat Jr.," she said, over her shoulder. "And both of you wash your hands."

"I washed my hands already!"

"Your shirt then. No jerseys at the table."

The boys scampered up the stairs. Before they reached the second floor landing, she thought she heard Chris say, "Joe's an asshole." His stutter caused him to stop a half step on the *a*, like a record skipping. Chris never cursed.

Yvonne stopped midchop, her knife poised just above the cutting board. "Joe Dunn?" She called after them, but they were gone; the muffled thumps of their sneakered feet against the carpet had fallen silent behind their bedroom's door. Above her head, she heard the rush of water fill the pipes as one of the boys turned on the sink.

Yvonne turned slowly back to the onion, piercing its flesh with the tip of the knife. "Language," she said, shaking her head, though there was no one there to hear her.

Pat Jr. was right: Toby did seem to have it in for Chris. Yvonne had seen it herself. Toby could sense Chris's fear. He barked mercilessly at him whenever he passed by.

Kids were the same. Chris had always been picked on because of his size, because of his stutter. It had been worse this year, worse than ever. Yvonne couldn't figure out why. Chris had always been a little different, but what had been a gap between him and the other kids had widened to a chasm. His grades had dropped to C's and D's, though his test scores still showed above average capabilities across the board. He had no friends, except for his brother. In the past, Chris had carried on in his own quiet way, almost as if he was unaware of just how different he was. Then he turned twelve, and everything seemed to change. Yvonne kept trying to track it (had it been a year since things had gotten really bad? Maybe since the summer?), but it had been a gradual deterioration, a slow burn.

At first, she had thought it was the girls in his class. They had come back to school after the summer tall as beanstalks, and keenly aware of the boys. They wore their hair flipped over to one side now, with deliberate cool. Little stud earrings—hearts and peace signs and stars—peppered their earlobes. *Alli Shapiro*, Chris reported, awestruck, *had gotten a nose ring.* Yvonne saw them clustered on the sidewalks and in front of the school, giggles and whispers passing through them like wind in the reeds. The girls all dressed the same, which was the part that concerned her most. You could tell where each of them fell in the pecking order by how closely they adhered to whatever style dictum was setting the curve that semester. Twelve: the age of conformity. Anyone who was different didn't stand a chance. The girls' lack of interest in Chris caused him to drift farther and farther toward the margins, in a little life raft that Yvonne feared wouldn't hold up against the open waters of high school.

When he was seven, Yvonne found Pat Jr. on the curb outside the house, his hands cupped in front of him like a nest. In them was a baby sparrow. Pat Jr. had found it in the gutter; a car had almost parked on top of it. It had a broken wing and was so covered in dirt that it hardly looked like anything at all. He kept it in a cage that he found in the basement and fed it mashed bananas three times a day until it had grown to full size. He would take it out to the backyard in the afternoons until one day it flew away. Pat Jr. was a protector; he had to be, with a younger brother like Chris. She thought of this more often, especially now that he was getting into these fights.

The first time the school called about Pat Jr.'s fighting, his father had said, "This had better not have anything to do with your brother. You can't always fight the kid's fights."

The second time, Pat Jr. came home with a black eye and a day of suspension. Yvonne was called in to see Pat Jr.'s guidance counselor. Teresa Frankel was a middle-aged woman who looked as though she resided permanently at the intersection of boredom and disinterest. She didn't let Yvonne say much of anything, but told her that if it happened again, there would be "serious ramifications."

That was three weeks ago, and Pat Jr. had been sullen ever since. Yvonne had a bad feeling that whatever was going on with him wasn't over and, in fact, had probably just begun.

Her stomach had been tied in knots all week, and not just over the boys. She thought maybe it was the vacation: She hadn't taken one in four and half years. Sol kept referring to it as her "two weeks off" even though, with the holiday, she was only taking six actual vacation days. Still, Sol wasn't used to fending for himself, and the idea of it made them both nervous.

He had been driving her crazy all week with little tasks that "had to get done before she left" and questions that he already knew the answer to: *How do I print documents on the color printer?* And: *What is my voicemail password?* Part of her suspected he was doing it on purpose; overloading her so that it was almost not worth taking the vacation at all. Fortunately, he was out in Westchester with a client today and wouldn't be back in until Monday.

The office administrative staff had been told they could leave at noon, though most of the lawyers were still around. The lawyers were always around, so it was as quiet a day as Yvonne was going to get.

Sol had forwarded his work number to his cell phone, so the desk had been eerily calm all morning. When the phone rang, she practically jumped. She had her own line, but almost no one used it.

"Mrs. Reilly," Teresa Frankel's voice came in nasal and weary, "It's about your son Patrick." The bottom fell out of Yvonne's stomach, as though she were in a plane that had suddenly dropped in turbulence.

"But it's a half day," Yvonne started. She was holding her sandwich with one hand, the meat and bread pulled back like a bandage. "Is he even still at school?"

"He was just outside the school, still on the property. He got in a fight with Joseph Dunn. We're going to need someone to come down here to pick him up right away."

"Is he hurt?"

"Patrick's fine. Just a few scrapes on his knee but the nurse put some antiseptic on it. Joseph has a black eye."

"Isn't Joe in high school?" Yvonne said suspiciously. She put down the sandwich and buried her forehead in the palm of her hand.

Though no one was within earshot, she spoke at a near whisper. Yvonne's desk was open on three sides so anyone rounding the corner could hear what she was saying before she saw them. The hallways of Penzell & Rubicam were typically quiet. The lawyers kept mostly to themselves behind the doors of their private offices. Secretaries were trained to keep their voices low and their conversations short. For confidentiality reasons, there were no outside visitors on the floors where the lawyers had their offices. Penzell & Rubicam hired its own cleaning, security, and mailroom staff, which was more tightly vetted than those provided by the building. Clients went directly from the lobby to a conference room on one of the five "hospitality floors." Attorneys reached the hospitality floors via keycard-protected internal stairwells, but the clients had to use a separate bank of elevators, a different one for each floor. So discreet was the firm that the elevators' schedules were tightly controlled, so as to prevent even passing intraclient interaction.

"Joe Dunn is still in eighth grade," Teresa Frankel snapped. "The point is, your son hit him on school property. Frankly, Mrs. Reilly, from the sound of things, it wasn't provoked. So you or your husband better get down here as soon as possible. I can't release him without a parent present."

"Where's Chris?" Yvonne said. "My other son," she added testily.

"Christopher is waiting here in my office. He's very upset. He keeps saying something about a dog."

"Toby."

"What?"

"Nothing. The dog's name is Toby. That's the Dunns' dog—Joe Dunn's dog. They're our neighbors. Never mind. I'm leaving work now."

"The school closed twenty minutes ago, Mrs. Reilly," Teresa said, crisp as paper off the printer. "If I were you, I'd get down here as soon as I could."

Yvonne was slipping on her jacket when the phone rang again. She froze, one sleeve hanging from her shoulder. *What now,* she thought, when she saw the number.

"Hi," she said, as neutrally as possible.

"I need you to get a pen immediately and write this down. Got a pen?"

"I was on my way out. How important is this?"

Sol paused, stunned into silence. Yvonne's eyes instinctively blinked shut. She had rarely pushed back on him, never in an emergency, and so neither of them quite knew what to do now that she had.

"What?" he said, stupidly.

Yvonne weighed her options. *Better to stand her ground than back down and apologize,* she thought. *If I apologize, he'll feel justified in being pissed off, and then he'll be even more difficult than usual.*

"You said I could leave at noon," she said. Her voice came out loud, a little too aggressive. "Everyone else left. I have some business at my kids' school. So unless it's really important, I can't get to it right now." She winced, immediately regretting the last sentence.

"It *is* really important," Sol said, sounding vaguely triumphant. "It's an emergency. Get a pen."

*Damn it,* she thought. *Never argue with a lawyer.*

In the background, Yvonne could hear the distant ding of elevators opening and closing, and the murmur of voices around him, as though he was in a tank filled with water.

*He's in a lobby somewhere. He must be desperate.*

Sol never called from unsecured spaces, unless it was about daily logistics, confirming a dental appointment, or having her reserve a conference room, that sort of thing. He was paranoid—no, obsessed—with the fear that an outsider (a taxi driver, a teenage hacker, Yvonne's cousin visiting from Boston) would happen upon some shred of confidential information. He talked about these possibilities all the time.

Yvonne had taken off her headset, so the phone's receiver was scrunched up between her ear and her shoulder. A dull ache ran down her spine. She switched ears and sat back down. She wanted to put him on speaker phone, but he hated it when she did that.

Behind her back, the fabric of her coat bunched uncomfortably, causing her to sit up straight as if in a state of high alert. She took a pen from the top drawer and cocked it between her finger and thumb, its tip poised over the stenographer pad that she always carried with her. She was on the last page of it now; she hoped he wouldn't be talking long.

"All right," she said, when she was ready. "Shoot."

# WEDNESDAY, 1:25 P.M.

The networks were all broadcasting from the same street corner. It took him a moment to process the image, but it was unmistakably Seventy-seventh Street, just off Park Avenue.

Paul stood alone in a conference room, his eyes fixed on the flat screen mounted to the front wall. His arms were crossed tightly over his chest, and his fingers drummed against his biceps.

*This isn't happening to someone I know,* he thought. *This isn't happening to us.*

He settled on channel five, though most of the channels were airing the same feed. Pedestrians passed aimlessly across the screen; the street corner was being filmed in real time. The cameras focused on one town house, its bright red door punctuated by a door knocker shaped like a stag's head. Flanking the entryway were two round topiaries. They were meticulously clipped, like green poodles, and potted in stone urns.

He knew that town house. It belonged to Morty and Julianne Reis. On the television, it looked at once familiar and remote.

Morty Reis had been one of Delphic's outside managers since its inception. Until he'd joined Delphic, Paul hadn't realized how much of the fund was under Morty's control. The Frederick Fund, Delphic's only single-strategy fund, had 98 percent of its assets invested with Reis Capital

Management; other Delphic funds had varying smaller percentages. Paul wasn't sure of the numbers, but he would have estimated that about 30 percent of Delphic's total assets under management were held by RCM.

Morty was a brilliant investor. Year after year, RCM produced consistently strong returns. In large part, Delphic's success was directly attributable to RCM. Clients jostled for "admission" to RCM as though it were an exclusive golf club, and Carter's fund of funds provided them the access they were looking for. There had been quarters when Delphic actually turned away money, though those heydays felt far away now.

Over the years, Morty and Carter had become close friends. On Carter's desk sat a photograph of Morty toasting Ines on her birthday; another showed the two men in waders and baseball caps, fly-fishing in the brilliant sunlight of an autumn weekend in Jackson Hole. They dined together, they vacationed together, they celebrated milestones together. The Reises were frequent visitors to the Darlings' home in East Hampton. Paul had seen Morty only a few weeks ago, at a surprise birthday party for Julianne.

The party had been held at the Reises' town house, the image of which now was glaring at him from the conference room television. Paul remembered making a passing comment about the door knocker on the way into the party. Merrill, his co-conspirator, usually had a greater aversion to ostentation than he did, especially when it came to interior design. She smirked at first, but then whispered, "Julianne just redid the house," in the tone she used when he was being rude. "Just tell them you like it." Merrill and Lily had always been quietly respectful of Morty, perhaps because he was one of the only people to whom their father deferred.

Julianne was a self-proclaimed interior decorator, though this was a subject of some controversy among Morty's close friends. As far as Paul was aware, Julianne had never decorated any interior that didn't belong to Morty, though these alone provided her with ample canvas. The town house was her first top-to-bottom job. Previously, Morty had limited her to smaller projects with reasonable budgets, like a pool house or a guest room. Julianne's taste was ornate and obvious, heavy on gilding and marble, and in direct contrast to Morty's bland aesthetic. She had been begging him to do the town house for years. The project must have taken her months, and Paul couldn't imagine how much financing.

The Reises were like many couples in New York. Morty met Julianne at a charity event, shortly after his first wife left him. Julianne was pretty in an obvious way, the kind of beauty that read better from across a room. She had large, wide-set eyes and high cheekbones; her auburn hair was highlighted and coiffed into a veritable mane that she wore layered around her shoulders. Her body was phenomenal, tanned and cross-trained within an inch of its life. She was taller than Morty, and her thinness gave the impression of a B-list actress or model. Julianne was the kind of woman Paul's mom would call "a showstopper," the kind of woman who was a dime a dozen in Manhattan.

At first blush, Morty and Julianne seemed like a mismatch. Morty was a recluse and a schlubby dresser. He loved to make money but he didn't particularly care to spend it; he wasn't cheap, but he didn't seem to derive much pleasure from personal acquisition, either. Among his possessions, he seemed only to care for his extraordinary car collection. He wore off-the-rack suits from Bloomingdale's and shirts bought in bulk online. He had no hobbies except for collecting cars, and rarely traveled except on business or to one of his four houses. His houses were all built like fortresses, with state-of-the-art security. He opened them to guests infrequently, typically only when Julianne demanded it. Carter had seen him disarmed by only one person: Sophie, his first wife. He had loved Sophie deeply. When she left, he had sunk into a terrible depression, one that had lasted for months. He wasn't the type to take solace in a trophy wife, and Julianne seemed to bring him headaches more than anything else. Now that Sophie was gone, Carter sensed that Morty really enjoyed only two things: working and being left alone.

Paul tried to remember where Julianne was now. The Reises were so often apart that he thought of them as loosely affiliated but separate entities.

*Aspen?* Paul thought. *It was earlier there. She might be skiing.*

Paul wondered if she knew that Morty was dead.

*Someone should tell her; someone she was close to, preferably. But anyone really, before she saw it on the news.*

There was no movement in or out of the town house. At the bottom of the screen was the caption: 23 East Seventy-seventh Street, Home of Morton Reis. Paul half listened as a reporter described Morty's business: "Reis Capital Management opened its doors in 1967, trading mostly penny stocks in the over-the-counter market . . . Firms like RCM made their bread and butter by capturing what's known as the 'spread' or gap between the offer and selling prices on these stocks . . . It wasn't until a regulation change in the 1970s that RCM was able to capture market share on the New York Stock Exchange and began to trade in more expensive blue-chip stocks . . ."

The reporter's head bobbed up and down as she spoke, her hair tousled by the wind. She gripped her microphone tightly and frowned, indicating that she was reporting something of a serious nature. It sounded like a lecture in the history of securities regulation; no real information there.

Paul flipped to another channel. This time he heard: "His wife, Julianne, is said to be vacationing at the couple's home in Aspen today . . . It remains unclear how much time elapsed between when his car was found and when he allegedly took his own life . . ."

Paul felt a cold chill ripple through his body, like a wind off the water. He glanced through the glass door of the conference room into the semidarkness of the hallway and realized he was alone in the office.

*Morty Reis killed himself.*

*Morty Reis. Killed himself.*

*Holy shit.*

He wanted to be able to bounce that off someone, just to hear himself say it. In his head, it didn't sound plausible.

He changed the channel, but the news was the same.

"Morton Reis managed in excess of fourteen billion dollars . . . He produced consistently strong results for a number of high-profile institutions, families, and charities . . . Reis was born in Kew Gardens, the son of Jacob and Riva Reis . . . He graduated from Queens College in 1966 with a degree in accounting . . . His father was a well-known professor of mathematics at Queens College until his death in 1980 from lymphoma . . . Mr. Reis had no children of his own and was married to Julianne Reis of New York and Aspen . . . His car was found parked near the Tappan Zee Bridge early this morning, a bottle of pills was said to have been found on the floor of the car . . . No one from his firm, Reis Capital Management, was available for comment . . ."

Eventually, a new topic was introduced: drilling in Alaska. The screen filled with the tranquil purples and brilliant blues of the Arctic sky, and the slow, loping migration of a herd of caribou. Paul stood frozen for a few minutes, watching as the caribou traversed an ice-filled river. The littlest ones were kept to the center of the pack. When they were safely across, he switched off the television. He dialed Merrill's office line from the conference room phone but got no answer. As he listened to the sound of the phone ringing, he stared at his reflection in the conference room window. He looked tired, and thinner than he thought himself to be. He felt the life draining out of him as he stood, receiver to his ear, phone ringing over and over until her voice mail picked up.

He didn't leave a message. He couldn't think of anything to say.

Carter wasn't answering his cell phone, either. Paul was momentarily grateful. He didn't want to be the one to have to break the news to Carter. Morty's death would be devastating; Carter had many acquaintances but few friends, and Morty was probably the closest of those. There was also the unfortunate but undeniable fact that RCM was holding up Delphic's performance. While most of the other managers were losing money daily, RCM was only slightly down on the year. His heart fluttering, Paul wondered if Delphic could stay afloat without RCM.

As he walked back to his office, Paul tried to recall whatever details he could about RCM. *Was it possible that the business was failing?* He didn't think so. Two of Delphic's outside managers—Lanworth Capital Management and Parkview Partners—were considered the dogs of the Delphic portfolio. Both funds had frozen redemptions after severe net losses. There were rumors that Lanworth might fold altogether. E-mails about both funds circulated between senior management on a daily basis. Paul hadn't seen anything like that about RCM. In fact, he had heard very little about RCM at all.

From what Paul had seen, Alain handled the RCM relationship by himself. He had brought RCM to Delphic's platform years ago, and was quick to remind everyone that the relationship belonged to him. "RCM's his golden goose," one of the other managers had explained to Paul when he had started, his voice dry with irritation. "No one deals with RCM except him. I mean, look, RCM's knocking it out of the park, and Reis is supposed to be difficult as hell. So if Alain wants to deal with him, fine with me. Long as it keeps making us money."

Now that he thought about it, there *had* been some e-mail traffic about RCM in the last few weeks.

Andre Markus, a senior sales guy, had been concerned about increased investor inquiries into RCM's counterparty risk. Specifically, a few of Markus's clients had asked about the liquidity of the counterparties who bought and sold RCM's options trades. A valid concern given the stability of some of the financial institutions, but Alain wouldn't give Markus the names. Markus balked: How could his investors rest easy until they knew who was on the other side of the RCM trades? As he pushed harder on Alain to produce the names of the options counterparties, the e-mails had become increasingly heated.

Not getting the answer he wanted, Andre had cc'ed Paul and Sol, Delphic's outside counsel, midway through the dialogue. Paul couldn't tell whether Alain knew who the counterparties were and was just being stubborn, or if he didn't know them and was being irresponsible. Sol had been handling Delphic's risk management far longer than he had, so he figured if there was a problem, Sol would speak up. But then Andre asked Paul to weigh in, and he was general counsel after all, so he felt he ought to say something. He decided to raise it with Carter first, before he stepped in to mediate what appeared to be an ongoing office power struggle.

"Alain and Andre butt heads a lot," Carter explained kindly. "I wouldn't get too involved. Andre's kind of a lapdog with his clients."

"I understand. But the counterparty names . . . Alain should at least know who RCM is trading with, right? Even if he doesn't want to give the names out to clients, we should know just for our own peace of mind."

Carter hesitated. "Look," he said. He rubbed his temples, which he did at the onset of one of his tension headaches. "Alain's been working with Morty a long time, and Morty can be very private. He's had a tough life in a lot of ways and he gets paranoid about disclosing information, even to us. So you have to know how to play him. If I were you, I'd tell Andre to back off. Things are pretty stressful right now, for everyone. Alain will get the counterparty names eventually. In the interim, just have the client service teams tell investors that, while we don't give out the names of counterparties, they are all well-established financial institutions rated A or better. Or something like that. That's all they want to hear."

Paul wondered if that wasn't playing it a bit fast and loose, but he had let it go, too tired and unprepared to propose an alternative. His response to Andre and Alain was met with radio silence from both. Paul found this to be a quiet relief; he was learning quickly that the general counsel role meant a lot of mediation and political navigation, often in situations on which he wasn't fully briefed. Quickly, he forgot the counterparty issue altogether, tabling it beneath a long list of other items requiring immediate attention.

---

Now everything seemed relevant. What if one of RCM's counterparties was about to default? What if one already had? The fall of Lehman

Brothers had made it painfully clear that no counterparty was too big to fail. While some funds had seen the writing on the wall and reduced their exposure to Lehman before the collapse, others hadn't. The ones that hadn't faced a deluge of redemption requests from investors on assets that had vanished into the ether.

Who was to say that RCM wasn't one of these funds? If Morty played as close to the vest as everyone said he did, God knows what he had been hiding from his investors. They could already be dead without anyone knowing it, like a plane than had lost its engine midflight and was still cruising silently along on momentum alone.

Delphic had nearly a third of its assets invested with RCM. If RCM went up in smoke, in all likelihood, so would they. Paul shuddered, reliving the feeling of freefall he had experienced when the Feds showed up at the Howary offices for the first time. It had happened before. It was happening all over the Street. As he walked back to his office, a lightheadness came over him, and the halogen glare of the hallway felt dizzying.

When he opened the door, his phone was ringing. The sound buzzed in his ears like alarm bells.

"Merrill?" Paul said, snatching up the receiver.

There was a pause. "It's Alexa," the voice on the other end of the phone said stiffly. Paul could hear traffic in the background; she was calling from a cell phone on the street. "I guess I shouldn't even ask if it's a bad time."

"I'm sorry," he said, flustered. "I'm just in the middle of . . . a family situation. I know I owe you a call."

"That's okay. I know I'm bugging you. So you've heard about Morty Reis."

"Yes. Horrible. He was like an uncle to Merrill. Was. How did you—?"

"That's why I called you so early this morning. Look, I need to talk to you. In person. I know you're busy but it's important. I'm in midtown, near your office. Can we meet?"

Paul paused. "Alexa, what's this about?" he said, slightly exasperated. "If this is just a friendly phone call, it needs to wait." He took a deep breath. He was being rude, perhaps unduly so, but it bothered him to think that she'd use her job at the SEC as an excuse to see him. Ever since their last encounter, just the thought of Alexa Mason set him on edge. That was a year ago; they had spoken only twice since. He felt guilty about it, cutting her off as he had. But she had to understand that he was married now, and that being friends with her just simply wasn't going to be possible. Not in the same way.

"This isn't a friendly phone call," she said testily. "I've never asked for anything from you before, have I? Just trust me. It's important."

He pressed the receiver between his ear and his shoulder, and squeezed his eyes shut. She was right: She had never asked him for anything. Not even an explanation when he stopped returning her calls, something she had certainly deserved. He regretted the acidity in his voice, and the haughty assumption that she still had feelings for him as anything more than an old friend.

He had a short fuse lately. He had barked at a cabdriver over the weekend. He hadn't realized how gruff he sounded until Merrill had put a soothing hand on his forearm. Then Katie, his sister, had called asking for help with her mortgage. Though ordinarily he would have done anything for her, he had very nearly bitten her head off for interrupting him during work. He had called her back and apologized, but the smallness of her voice made him feel like an ogre. And now he was snapping at Alexa. Sweet Alexa, who had never been anything but devoted to him since the ninth grade. Sweet Alexa, who still sounded excited to talk to him, even after he had told her that he no longer had a place for her in his life.

He sank into his chair. Paul had thought it would get better after he had started at Delphic. Nothing could have been more stressful than Howary, particularly after the indictment. But he was sleeping worse now than ever before. Sleeping pills made him sluggish. Instead, he wrestled through the nights, his thoughts pulling him in and out of consciousness. The constant mental fight made him irritable. He had never had a temper before. Some days, he felt as if his entire body were a raw nerve, its membrane receptive even to the smallest passing slight.

"Listen, Alexa, I'm sorry," he said. "I'm just having a really bad day. I can meet. Not for long, but I can meet. How close are you?"

He heard the plaintive wail of an ambulance through the phone, and then realized that he could hear it just outside his window, too.

"I'm a couple of blocks from your building," she said. "Near MoMA. Can we meet there?"

"I'll be right down," he said. "I'll meet you just inside the doors."

# WEDNESDAY, 3:06 P.M.

Marina Tourneau stood in the doorway, watching her boss. Duncan was hunched over the light-box table in the corner of his office. It had been custom built to match his desk, and the glow from it illuminated his silver hair. Her eyes were instantly drawn south to his argyle socks. Duncan didn't like to wear shoes while he worked. He typically took them off before entering his office and left them in the hallway, beneath the coat rack. No one knew whether this was a matter of comfort, or if he was trying to preserve the pristine white carpets that he had also had custom installed, or if it was simply one of his cultivated eccentricities. Duncan's socks were like most men's ties: a flash of color, a punctuation. Argyle was his favorite.

The shoe issue had gotten his last assistant, Corinne, fired. Or at least, that was the water cooler version. After the carpets were put in, Duncan had suggested to Corinne that she should remove her shoes before entering his office. This was her last straw; a screaming row ensued. Corinne threatened to file a sexual harassment claim against him (the rest of the office found this very funny). Duncan promptly fired her, or threatened to and she quit, which was how Marina had gotten her job. Marina had been at *Press* for less than a week when someone told her this story. Overwhelmed, she had picked up a pint of frozen yogurt on the way home, eaten it for dinner in front of the television, and cried. All she could think was how embarrassing it would be if she were required to pad shoeless around her boss's office, like some sort of geisha. *She had gone to Princeton, for God's sake . . . Would she have to buy new socks?* She certainly couldn't afford to, given what *Press* was paying her.

After eighteen months as Duncan's assistant, this story had lost all shock value. Marina had grown accustomed to his peculiar brand of fastidiousness, and to his outrageous and sometimes morally questionable requests, and to the tantrums he threw when his world order was tampered with. She had become, she thought, a remarkably patient person.

Duncan's face was so close to the surface of the light box, and his arms were splayed out in such a way that for a split second Marina thought he might be dead. She stepped closer. He was looking at some photographs through a loupe. When he was working, Duncan had an uncanny ability to remain still for minutes at a time, far longer than the average person. It seemed to absorb him wholly. Sometimes, Marina found this inspiring. On the days she wanted to leave at a reasonable hour, it was profoundly frustrating. Holidays were the worst. It was almost as though he wasn't aware of them. Marina often wondered if this was because he had no one with whom he could celebrate. That was sad, but not sad enough for her to feel anything but irritated by him.

The sound of the cleaning lady's vacuum filled the hallway behind her. Marina sighed.

She had said good-bye to the last editor over an hour ago, and she was beginning to give up hope that she could leave the office in time to get her hair done. Her boyfriend's parents' annual "Thanksgiving Eve" party began promptly at 5 p.m., and she would feel much better with a blowout. The Morgensons' party was a very big deal. Their apartment was on Eighty-first Street and Central Park West, a prime perch from which to watch as the balloons for the Thanksgiving Day Parade were inflated on the street below. Since 1927, New Yorkers and tourists had gathered in the cold for this spectacle. They jostled behind police lines, their faces growing red in the frigid night air. Some had staked out small squares of the sidewalk for their kids, who invariably had to pee or had forgotten their hats in the car. It never felt worth it until the balloons came alive overhead, puffing up like giant, animated cumulus clouds. The Morgensons' guests enjoyed it from seventeen floors up, beside a crackling fire and a tower of cocktail shrimp. For one night a year, The Beresford was the best building in Manhattan, and Grace Morgenson made sure to capitalize on it. She invited everyone. Friends, cousins, business associates. Also, any New Yorker of particular note with whom she shared even a tenuous connection: a *Times* columnist; the mezzo-soprano from the Metropolitan Opera; a principal dancer from the New York City Ballet; a state senator; a talk-show host; the head of the teacher's union; a designer known particularly for her wedding dresses; a hotelier who had recently made the papers for leaving his wife for a minor British royal.

Tanner had asked Marina twice what she was planning to wear. Nervously, she had modeled three outfits for him; he seemed most content with the tweed skirt and cable-knit sweater combination from Ralph Lauren that was now hanging in the office coatroom. She'd brought it to work in a hanging bag so that it would not wrinkle, and planned to change into it in the women's bathroom. It was clear that the Morgensons and their friends would be evaluating her as potential wife material. She had been unfocused all day, unable to think of anything other than last-ditch measures that might improve her by the evening. Now, it was game time. Every minute mattered.

"Duncan," Marina said, trying not to sound anxious. "How're you doing?"

He looked up from the light-box table and frowned at her, as though he was trying to place her. "These photos are atrocious," he said, finally.

"Which photos?"

"The ingénue spread!" He exclaimed, waving her over to look. "These women *do not* look like The Ingénues of Fashion Week to me. They look like tarts. Tarts or hookers."

Marina sighed, audibly this time, and crossed the threshold into his office. *Tart* was Duncan's new favorite word. It would bore him in a few weeks, but for right now, everyone was a tart. Paris Hilton was a tart; the night receptionist was a tart. Duncan was certain that the Bush twins—and possibly their mother—were tarts. For all Marina knew, she was a tart when she wasn't around. He had that difficult tone of voice, the one that meant that nothing was going to be good enough. She took her place next to him at the light-box table but refused to look through the loupe. She had seen the photos countless times; everyone had. This was the first time she had heard him complain about them.

"Look at this one!" He plunged back toward the table, like a porpoise after a fish. "She's far too thin. She looks like a heroin addict! You can practically see the track marks on her arms."

"Do we have the time and the budget to reshoot?" Marina said, knowing the answer.

"Of course not. Of course not," Duncan snapped. "This is for *the January issue*. We're absolutely out of time. And we're so far over budget it is appalling. No. These are going in. Well, some of these are going in. That can't be helped. But it just upsets me, printing this sort of trash." He closed his eyes and turned his face to the heavens, as if to say, God help us all.

Every fiber of her being told Marina not to roll her eyes, not to open her mouth. If she rolled her eyes, he would fire her. If she opened her mouth, she was afraid a torrent of screaming would pour out, and every single frustration she had with Duncan and the magazine and her boyfriend and the snobby Morgensons and the fact that she got paid less than $30,000 to work eighty hours a week and was treated like a total peon even on Thanksgiving eve would be aired, and she would not be able to stop it.

Instead, Marina said timidly, "Maybe the piece stays in, but you could add the finance piece you were describing to me yesterday, to provide, you know, a little balance?"

Duncan looked at her for a few seconds, and then switched off the light box and went over to sit at his desk. He didn't answer. Marina realized that by speaking, she was at best prolonging her departure, and at worst, she was enraging Duncan with the implied presumption that he gave a shit what she thought about the magazine's content.

"Remind me what I said yesterday," he said, tapping his fingertips together.

She took a deep breath and tried to recall what he had said, word for word. Duncan liked to hear her repeat his own words back to him, but she had to be precise. "Yesterday, you were saying that we had to be careful not to seem like we're out of touch with the financial crisis. That if we published too many pieces on fashionistas and socialites, we would seem irrelevant and frivolous and too many magazines are falling apart precisely for that reason. Then you said that Rachel's suggestion for a piece on Lily Darling and her new line of dog accessories was exactly what you didn't want to hear." Marina paused, and then blurted, "I have to say, I agree with this; I can't imagine anyone would actually buy designer dog sweaters right now, and Lily's too young and ridiculous to actually run a business. But that's just my opinion." She fell quiet again; she shouldn't have editorialized. The wall clock ticked away. Though she desperately wanted to, she refused to look directly at it. If he caught her wanting to leave, it would end very badly.

"Go on."

"Anyway," she resumed quickly, "you said that instead, we should be running a piece on her father, Carter Darling, who was actually a person of interest and substance who ran a real business that people would want to read about. Then you said that dedicating four pages of the January issue to a photo spread on twenty-year-old models was mindless and unmemorable."

Marina looked up. She had a tendency to look at the floor when she spoke. She felt her face hot with embarrassment and wondered how long she had been talking. It was probably the longest she had ever spoken inside Duncan's office.

To her relief, he wasn't glaring. Instead, his eyes were closed behind the frames of his tortoiseshell glasses.

"I was right about the ingénue piece," he said. He opened his eyes and nodded thoughtfully, as though he were acknowledging someone other than himself. "That's exactly the issue. Relevancy. Right now, the only thing anyone in New York cares about is Wall Street. No one gives a shit about some twenty-two-year-old anorexic model at Fashion Week. We simply don't have time for frivolity right now. We can't afford it."

"I—"

"Agreed. It's too late to cut the ingénue piece. But if we ran it in the January issue next to some exposé about the board of Goldman Sachs, or some hedge fund manager who has done something naughty, I think we're in business. I love this idea. It's very high/low. That's what this magazine is all about. We just have to develop it, and quickly."

Marina nodded, still a little dazed from being addressed as though she was a working member of the team.

What came out of her mouth next surprised them both.

"What *about* a piece on the Darlings?" she said, with unprecedented boldness. "Remember last summer, when we did that spread on their house in East Hampton? You said there was tension between them. They fought in the kitchen when they thought no one could hear them? And then Ines Darling was such an utter bitch to everyone all afternoon, bossing everyone around, micromanaging the photo shoot."

Duncan sat forward. He nodded, prodding her to continue.

Marina paused. They stared at each other in silence for a minute, each waiting for the other to say something.

Finally she said, her voice a little small, "Well, that's all I've got. I just meant you could write an article on them as a power couple. I don't know. Maybe it's a stupid idea. It's just a thought. I think people love to read about the personal lives of billionaires. Especially if they're kind of screwed up."

Duncan smiled and sat back in his chair. "Yes, there's a certain schadenfreude about these finance people, isn't there?" He was feeling magnanimous suddenly; Marina was there, after all, to be journalistically nurtured by him. "I mean, look, we've all secretly hated them for years. I'm the managing editor of this magazine and I make less than Carter Darling probably spends on lawn care in East Hampton. But the game's up, it seems . . . All right, let me think about this. I'm not sure Carter Darling is the right person for this piece. He might be too squeaky clean, if you know what I mean. I just saw them the other night at the New Yorkers for Animals benefit. Ines had on a hideous dress. Lorenzo Sanchez, I think it was? You know, that new latin designer who puts ruffles on everything? She's a bitch, but he seems like a nice old-fashioned WASP and I don't think they are the type to throw parties in Sardinia on the corporate AMEX, you know? I need to noodle this over."

*Yes,* Marina thought, *please go home and think about this, or noodle this over, or whatever it is you do. That way I can finally get out of here.*

She turned to go. "Marina," Duncan said, in that voice that stopped her cold in her tracks, "You'll make yourself available over the weekend if I need you for anything." His words ended flatly, more of a statement than a question.

Marina closed her eyes and choked back frustration. She waited a second before turning around, so that he wouldn't see her falter. When she did, a brilliant smile was pasted on her pretty face. "Of course," she said. "Happy to."

Duncan gave her a single quick nod. "All right, then," he said, and swung back to his computer. "You're off. Have a good night."

"Same to you!" She called. "I hope your family has a wonderful Thanksgiving!" She moved so quickly toward the door that she did not see the spark of sadness that registered in Duncan's eyes. After she was gone, he sat a while longer at his desk, her words ringing in his ears against the silence of an empty office.

# WEDNESDAY, 3:45 P.M.

Paul spotted Alexa through a sea of Japanese businessmen, like a peacock in a flock of penguins. She was standing under a wire mobile, part of the Calder retrospective, wearing the same bright blue coat that she had worn the last time Paul had seen her. She didn't notice him at first. Instead, she was looking up at the mobile overhead, a constellation of red stars or birds on the wing. Her mass of thick black curls fell gently behind her ears. She looked smaller than he remembered, more like the Alexa from college than the Alexa he had seen most recently. He had a distinct memory of wandering through the galleries with her at UNC's Ackland Art Museum during a high school field trip. They were sixteen then, and though he was desperately in love with her, they were just friends. A year later, they would sleep together, complicating everything.

Theirs had been the kind of love that blooms in a small town but fades when exposed to the elements of the wide open world. As adolescents, they were united by a desire to get the hell out of North Carolina. Alexa, the stronger willed of the two, was the first to go. She had always remained at arm's length from her peers, carrying herself with the quiet complacency of someone who knew that she would be moving on soon enough to something better. Paul had thought she'd become an academic, maybe, or a curator. He wasn't surprised when she was offered a scholarship to Yale. "Not bad," she had said, "for a girl from Charlotte."

Paul stayed behind, taking a full ride at Chapel Hill. When Alexa left, their parting was tender and tearful and they vowed to stay together despite the distance. For a few months they were steadfast, each logging hours on trains and planes when they could. But as the weather turned cold and the calendars filled with parties, exams, and football games, their visits became less and less frequent, and the phone calls shorter and more perfunctory. By the time Alexa came home for the holidays, they both knew it was over. They stayed friends, but afforded each other a respectful distance, especially when it came to the subject of current flames.

Alexa wasn't pretty, exactly, but she was pleasant to look at. She had a brilliant smile, and a maternal way about her that set dogs' tails wagging. Her curvy figure was the kind that played better in the South than in Manhattan. She had come close to marriage once, to a guy with whom they had grown up; Paul knew him only in passing. But "the bar exam had gotten between them" was the way she put it, which Paul took to mean that she hadn't been willing to give up her career for a life as a suburban mother in Charlotte. He didn't blame her.

"She's intense," Merrill had said flatly after their first meeting. "I mean, what was she wearing? Is that some sort of statement?"

Paul couldn't recall what Alexa had been wearing, but she did tend to err on the side of casual. "That's just Alexa," he said. He had underestimated how it would feel for Merrill to meet Alexa. They had, he realized, spent the majority of the dinner talking about home, a topic to which Merrill was rarely subjected. Alexa had meant to bring a date but she hadn't, and so the two women sat awkwardly beside each other on the banquette like a panel of interviewers, staring at him and not quite at each other. "She's just not that into the way she looks."

*She's not from New York,* Paul thought. Then a stab of guilt: he shouldn't defend his ex-girlfriend to his wife, if only in his head.

After a pause, Merrill said softly, "I bet she thinks I'm a brat."

This was Merrill's tender spot. Her warm eyes grew earnest and worried; Merrill was not accustomed to people disliking her, and the thought that someone might always troubled her deeply.

"I promise she doesn't," Paul said, wondering if that was true. "All she cares about is her work. She doesn't think about much else."

"She cares about you."

"She does. But as a friend. That's all, I promise."

He kissed her on the head, and then the conversation was over, for that evening anyway. He knew it would come up again, if only in a raised eyebrow or slight shake of the head, anytime he mentioned Alexa's name. It became easier not to talk to Alexa at all. Being with her was like a detour off the main highway. Scenic, pretty but ultimately a distraction.

Paul had hoped that with time and a little distance, the complications of the past might slip away. The moment he saw her, he had the uncomfortable feeling that the exact opposite was about to happen.

"Hi, stranger," Alexa said, giving him a fierce hug. She was happy to see him, but strain radiated from her eyes and the tightness of her jaw. "Thank you for seeing me."

"Course." He gave her a quick squeeze and then snapped back, fast as a rubber band. He hated that it felt good to see her again. "Look, I don't have much time, so . . ."

"I know. I don't, either. Let's walk? There's a new Rothko exhibit upstairs."

"Sure."

She took a deep breath and stepped onto the escalator. As they ascended to the permanent collection on the fourth floor, she glanced behind them. No one was in earshot. She seemed jumpy, like a person being followed. "I'm just going to start talking," she said in a low voice, "and maybe you could just listen. And when I'm done, then you can ask questions. Okay?"

"You're the boss."

He extended his hand to her as they stepped off the escalator on the fourth floor. "Okay. Here's the situation," she said. "You've spoken to David Levin. He's technically my boss at the SEC; I report to him, he reports to Jane Hewitt. Also—" she shifted awkwardly now, fumbling to tuck a strand of hair behind her ear "—we've been seeing each other. For quite some time now. We live together."

Paul was quiet. He stared straight ahead at the painting in front of him: a dark brown canvas, punctuated by thick strips of black and blue. At the top was a wispy streak of white, hanging like a lone hopeful cloud in a brooding, storm-filled sky. He could tell Alexa was looking at him, gauging his reaction.

Then she said, with slight irritation, "It's not exactly a big secret."

"Hey," he raised his palms. "No judgments."

"Anyway, a couple of months ago, David started spending more and more time at the office. He wouldn't talk about it, but he seemed completely consumed with something. He couldn't sleep. Then one Saturday he didn't show up to dinner with some of our friends. No call, nothing. I started to wonder if he was seeing someone. This was, I don't know, early September? Pre-Lehman? I let it go, but he just kept getting more and more distant."

"Mmm," Paul said noncommittally. He would have said that Alexa was too pragmatic to drag him out of the office for relationship advice, but with women, you never did know.

Alexa stopped walking. In a low voice she said, "This is all confidential, okay? I know you know that, but I still think I have to say it. I'd get fired for sure if anyone knew we spoke about this."

"I got it," Paul said, not entirely sure that he did.

"Okay. Thanks." As they moved together to the next gallery, the sleeve of her coat brushed against his. "So this weekend, David finally sits me down and tells me that something's up at work. He was freaked out, talking about it with me. Frankly, I'm scared now, too. That's why I'm here. I need your help."

Paul's pulse had been steadily increasing since they arrived. Alexa was usually so calm, but today she was completely on edge, a little wild-eyed, almost paranoid. Not the girl he knew, and yet the girl he knew almost as well as anyone. He surged with the impulse to put his arm around her, but he stopped himself.

"Okay," he said slowly. "Can you talk about it?"

She nodded nervously. "It started because David got a call from this woman named Claire Schultz; she was a classmate of his at Georgetown. She's an attorney at Hogan & Hartson. Claire found out that her mom, Harriet, had given over a substantial portion of her retirement money to this no-name accounting firm out in Great Neck. Firm's called Fogel & Moritz. It's basically just two guys and a desk—trust me, you've never heard of them. Anyway, in addition to doing Harriet's taxes, Gary Fogel also offered to invest some of Harriet's savings in an investment vehicle. He said he could guarantee her twelve percent returns. Harriet's not a rich woman and she's not a particularly savvy investor. But she trusts Fogel because he's done her taxes for years. So she hands him eighty grand without asking a lot of questions, and wouldn't you know it, a year later she gets back just over twelve percent on her investment. When the same thing happens again the next year, she calls her daughter Claire and brags a little about how smart she's being with her money. Now Claire's a securities lawyer, and so alarm bells go off when she hears about the 'guaranteed' returns that Fogel & Moritz are promising her mom. She asks Harriet to send her the offering documents. In the meantime, Claire does a little digging of her own and discovers that Fogel & Moritz isn't a registered investment adviser. In fact, its nothing more than a three-man operation in a strip mall off the Sunrise Highway."

"Uh-oh."

"Right. Not good. So she ends up calling David, the only person she knows personally at the SEC. David goes out to visit Harriet in Great Neck, just on an informal basis. Harriet, of course, is embarrassed at the suggestion that she's been had. In her defense, she tells David that a number of her friends in the neighborhood have been investing money with Gary for years. That Gary has some 'in' with a big-shot hedge fund manager in New York, who happens to be his brother-in-law. Long story short, the brother-in-law is Morty Reis."

"No shit."

"Harriet shows David some statement that appears to be from RCM. So on its face, it looks as though the money's being invested in a real investment vehicle and not just some scam. But the returns just seem eerily consistent, so he starts talking to her mother's friends who are also Fogel's clients."

"At this point, no one's lost any money with Fogel, right?"

"No. They're all getting twelve percent, pretty much year after year. Some of them had been doing it for seven or eight years, in fact. But they all use the same words when they talk about Fogel, 'guaranteed' and 'bullet-proof'—stuff an investment adviser should never be saying to a client."

"Harriet and her friends must not have been too thrilled that David was out there suggesting they hop off the gravy train."

"No kidding. Most of them were just reinvesting their earnings in the firm or at least letting their initial investment ride. But a few redeemed out and were quite pleased with their net profit."

Paul was getting impatient. He had begun rattling his keys in his pocket, a habit that drove Merrill crazy. "So the point is, twelve percent year after year is too good to be true."

"That's what Claire thought. Oh, look at this . . . " Her words trickled off, and she was lost for a moment in a painting. Her eyes gleamed, transfixed, and her forehead relaxed as if her worries were momentarily washed away.

Paul looked at the painting, but to him it was just a swirling mass of color and light. "Insider trading." Paul prompted her. "Is that what you're thinking? Fogel's in on it, or at least, he's capitalizing on it."

"Something like that," she said, looking away from the painting.

"Fogel's too small a fish to run some kind of insider trading ring himself. Not effectively anyway. So David started focusing on RCM. That's when things got scary."

"Scary how? What did he find?"

"Nothing. That's the thing. There's no information on these people. The way David describes it, there is no RCM."

Paul frowned. "That doesn't—that doesn't make any sense. They're one of the world's largest hedge funds. They're in the news all the time."

"Maybe so," she said. "But there's no *real* information. They've been operating as one of the biggest hedge funds in the world for over fourteen years, but they aren't a registered investment adviser, either. We have no file on them. As far as the SEC is concerned, RCM doesn't exist."

Paul felt his heart drop into his feet. The key rattling stopped. "No. That must be some kind of mistake. Someone would have complained. RCM has a lot of very sophisticated investors. Us, for example."

"Someone did complain. His name's Sergei Sidorov; he's a money manager up in Waltham, Massachusetts. It took David a year to find him. He's a total recluse now. Sidorov himself was invested with RCM for a while. But he got suspicious about the lack of transparency, so he pulled all of his clients out of the fund. A lot of them weren't happy about it. But RCM wouldn't give Sidorov online access to their accounts, so he never felt as though he knew what they were doing. He says RCM's a black box."

Paul shook his head. "I don't know about that. Alain Duvalier is the head of our investment team. He's always dealt directly with RCM, so he's the one monitoring their trading activity. I just assumed he had online access to their accounts. I'm sure he does."

"Paul!" Alexa said, loud enough to turn the heads of two mothers with toddlers in tow. Her eyes fell, embarrassed. She lowered her voice to a whisper. "Look, you realize the implications of what we're talking about here, right? This is a multibillion-dollar fund. And it's a fund that Delphic's heavily invested in. You're their general counsel, for chrissake. If there's an issue here, you can't just tell your investors, 'Sorry, I didn't know.'"

They had stopped walking, and stood alone in an empty side gallery. Alexa went to sit on a bench in front of a large triptych. She patted the spot beside her. When he sat, she said, more gently this time, "I'm sorry. But I needed to tell you. With Morty dead, there's a spotlight now on RCM. You know that. The press, the authorities—everyone is going to want to know why a successful hedge fund manager with a beautiful wife and four houses would jump off the Tappan Zee Bridge the day before Thanksgiving. It won't take them long to figure it out."

Paul wasn't feeling right; his throat was tightening on him, and the air around him felt heavy, like water. He pulled at his collar. The chaotic sounds of a school group in the adjacent gallery reverberated off the ceiling. Paul felt as though he was in a giant fish tank, drowning in their noise. "Killing yourself isn't an admission of fraud," he said hoarsely. "There are other reasons he could have done it. Health. Tax issues."

"No, Reis knew that David was closing in on him. They spoke two days ago. He must have seen the writing on the wall and panicked." Her hand had found its way onto his knee. "Are you okay?" She said. "You don't look okay."

He moved away from her. "Why are you telling me this, Alexa? I mean, is this just a friendly heads-up? 'Hey, my boyfriend's about to indict you?' What do I do with that?"

"Honestly, I don't know. I know that Reis's death has accelerated the timetable on David's investigation. He's been talking to someone at the NYAG's office about a case against RCM and its three biggest feeder funds: Weiss Partners, Anthem Capital, and you guys. They'll look to indict senior management, the people who should have known, so to speak. But it's not my case, and I'm not sure of the particulars. Or the timing."

"'Should have known'? I *told* you I didn't know. I've been there for two months. I still don't know, beyond what you've just told me." His voice was reaching a hysterical clip.

"That's why I want you to talk to David. Now, before everything comes out in the open. If you work with him, well, maybe you guys can work something out."

"*Work with him?* What does that even mean?"

"Well, that's the thing. It's hard to isolate exactly what was going on over there, without someone from inside. They need e-mails, internal memos. My point is, you could help each other."

"You understand what you're asking, right?"

"Just talk to him, Paul. He'll show you the case. If he can't prove to you that there was fraud at RCM, and that people at Delphic knew about it, then by all means, walk away. But if he does have a case, save yourself. I'm not telling you what to do. I'm telling you that you're a sitting duck. Also," she paused. "He told me he talked to you. Just be honest. You lied to him about some things, right?"

"Why do you say that?" His eyes darted inadvertently to the ground. He knew he should be looking at her, but his body seemed to be responding viscerally to the conversation, all the ticing and key jangling and collar pulling of a nervous man.

"David said he asked you directly to give him the names of RCM's counterparties. Don't you remember? And you said you didn't typically disclose that information. But the truth was you didn't know whom RCM was trading with! You couldn't have, because RCM wasn't trading with anyone. Their trades were just illusions, made-up transactions that existed only on paper. If you had bothered to call Goldman Sachs or Lehman Brothers or whomever RCM pretended it was buying and selling from, you would have found out that these places weren't doing any business with RCM. RCM wasn't doing any business at all."

"I have to go."

Alexa sighed. "All right." She stood, gathered up her coat, and then held out a manila envelope for him. "Take this, okay?"

Paul gave Alexa a short nod and took the envelope. For a moment, he thought about opening it, but instead he folded it in half and tucked it into his pocket. There was too much information already—his mind was thick with it—he wasn't even sure he could read words on a page. He gave Alexa a quick kiss on the cheek.

"This isn't just about work for me."

"I know."

He gave her a quick nod. "I'll be in touch," he said. Then he turned away from her, leaving her alone in the gallery.

Outside, the sky had grown dark with clouds. He felt bad leaving her there. Alexa had no umbrella, he realized, and her coat was too thin for so late in the season. He wondered where she would go now. Perhaps she would wander MoMA for a while, as lost in thought as he was.

---

He had to find Alain. He didn't need Alexa to tell him that Morty's death would turn a thousand eyes in RCM's direction, and eventually in Delphic's, too. If there were problems with one of Delphic's outside managers, now was the time for Alain to raise them. Paul went straight from the elevators to Alain's office, his pulse racing as he walked himself through the best way to open the conversation.

Alain had the biggest office at Delphic, bigger than Carter's. He had insisted on that when they had moved into the Seagram Building. Stylistically, it was a major departure from the rest of the floor. For the most part, Carter ensured that the Delphic office was understated, and things only got replaced when necessary. The conference rooms were appointed in muted shades of olive and beige. A tasteful collection of landscape photographs hung above the gleaming tables. Nice enough that the firm appeared successful, but not so nice that a client would balk at how their fees were getting spent. Carter did insist that Alain have a frosted glass door for his office instead of a clear glass one. That way, the opulent interior was at least obscured from view.

Paul met Alain for the first time at a dinner party at the Darlings' home, and the impression that Alain left that night was how Paul would always think of him. Alain had arrived late, just as they were being seated for dinner, and immediately all eyes were on him. He introduced the young blonde on his arm as Beate (not his girlfriend, Beate, but simply Beate) and then promptly left her to fend for herself. An irked Ines was forced to cut short a conversation with an art dealer who seemed to be deeply engrossing her so that she could fuss about until an extra seat at the table had been carved out.

"I'm *so sorry* we didn't have a place set for you," Ines said to Beate, looking not sorry at all, "I had *no idea* he was bringing a guest." She cast a slit-eyed glance at Alain, who was busy showing Carter his new watch and either didn't notice Ines or didn't care. When he looked up, Alain flashed Ines his signature rakish smile. Then he shrugged his shoulders, adjusting the sleeves of his cashmere blazer just so, and with a flourish pulled out the chair for the woman beside him. She seemed thoroughly charmed. Despite best efforts, even Ines's frost thawed slightly.

"Thank you, I'm so glad to be here," Beate murmured, looking nothing of the sort.

Ines seated her at the far side of the table, next to Paul. She was beautiful in a placid, glacial way. Paul couldn't tell if she was bored or simply not entirely fluent in English, but she was nearly impossible to engage in conversation. From what he could gather, Alain had gone home to Geneva for the holidays and returned with Beate in tow. It wasn't clear how permanent he intended the move to be, but from the way Beate looked at Alain, Paul could tell that she was smitten. The only time she seemed to light up was when Alain was telling a story. When he spoke, he used his hands artfully, reeling in his audience like a fisherman. It was hard not to be taken in by him. Even men seemed captivated by Alain; he could talk about the equity markets, scotch, the World Cup, women, other people's children, health care policy, race-car driving, commodities pricing, inflation concerns in emerging markets. "He's like James Bond," Carter had once said about him. "James Bond meets Gordon Gekko." Carter always sounded like a stern older brother when talking about Alain. He tried to appear mildly disapproving of Alain's flamboyance, but anyone could tell he was secretly proud to be associated with him. After all, Alain was the real deal. He was one of the best investors on the Street. For all of his antics, his confidence was entirely founded.

Paul never saw Beate again. A few weeks later, he saw Alain at a restaurant downtown with another woman. She was voluptuous this time, raven-haired and beautiful in a different way than Beate. "Oh, I don't know," Merrill said when Paul asked her about it. Merrill flicked her hand in an easy-come-easy-go manner. "He's been engaged more than once, I think. Dad's says he'll never get married. He's the consummate bachelor." Paul wondered for a moment if Beate had stayed in New York, tried to make a go of it on her own. The thought was fleeting. How many Beates were there out in the world? How did Alain have the time to find them, court them, and then dispense of them while managing a multibillion-dollar portfolio? Though he stood for everything that disgusted Paul about New York, he had to hand it to the guy: he did it with incredible style.

---

The door to Alain's office was locked, and inside the lights were off. He was gone. The hazy outlines of paper stacks, like skyscrapers, were visible through the frosted glass.

Across from his desk, Alain had removed the standard-issue bookshelves so that he could hang three large photographs depicting industrial buildings in Milan. His files were stored in rows of black cabinets in the hallway outside the office. The filing cabinets took up a good amount of space. Alain was old-fashioned; he printed out everything, even e-mails, and kept them neatly organized as hard copy.

Paul stood in front of the filing cabinets assessing. Five large drawers were labeled "RCM." He tried the first one and realized that the cabinets were locked. He wasn't sure that Alain intended the files for public use, but the circumstances seemed extenuating.

*What now?* He surveyed the office. Most of the doors were closed. From the analysts' cubicles, sleeping computer screens glowed with the Delphic lion insignia. A few chairs were pushed back as though the analyst had departed quickly, rushing to make a flight. Paul felt like the last man in Pompeii.

"Hey, Paul."

He was startled by the voice. He turned to see Jean Dupont, the associate who worked under Alain, standing in the hallway. Beside Jean was a small rolling suitcase. He was wearing a stylish winter coat, collar up, and held a cashmere cap in his hand. "If you're looking for Alain, he left already. I thought I was the last one here."

Paul smiled tightly. "So did I," he said.

Paul had never liked Jean. He was the son of a Swiss businessman who was a social friend of Alain's and a longtime Delphic client. The other associates grumbled that Alain had hired him as a favor to the Dupont family. Unquestionably, he was less qualified than others at his level. He was a good-looking kid, in a slick *I-own-you* sort of way. His whole demeanor at work felt like an act, as though, deep down, he knew the rules would never really apply to him, but would play along for the time being. Maybe he couldn't touch his trust until he was thirty, Paul thought. Maybe his dad thought working for a year or two would be character building. Whatever it was, it wasn't a good enough reason for Paul.

It was late to see Jean in the office, Paul thought, especially with everyone else gone.

"So Alain left for Geneva?"

"Yeah, he took off this morning. He's probably midflight now. Can I help with something?"

Paul hesitated; he hated asking Jean for help. Then a sense of urgency overwhelmed him and he caved to it.

"Actually, yeah. Could you open up the files on RCM for me? I'd like to review some of them before I go."

Jean paused and inhaled sharply, as if he was about to say something but thought better of it. "Do you need something in particular?"

"I'll find what I need myself."

Jean looked at him reluctantly.

Paul sighed. "Listen, you will probably see this on the news later, but Morty Reis committed suicide." Jean turned ashen. "I just want to get some basic materials organized to bring out to Carter in East Hampton. There's going to be some fallout."

"Jesus." Jean let out a whistle. "Wow. That's crazy. How did he do it?"

"I think he jumped off the Tappan Zee Bridge. Early this morning. Or late last night."

"Holy shit. Right before Thanksgiving, too."

"Yup. Obviously very unfortunate."

"I'll say." They made eye contact. Jean put his cap down on his suitcase and began opening the locks on the filing cabinets.

"Okay, see here?" he said after a minute. "It's organized by date. All the trade confirmations are in the first two drawers. They go back six months; Alain has the old ones scanned to disk so they don't take up too much space."

"Trade confirmations? They send actual, hard-copy paper trade confirmations?" Paul had never heard of anyone who still relied on paper trade confirmations. They were a thing of the past. For years, it had been standard industry practice for funds like RCM to provide their investors with online access to their accounts. Investors demanded real-time information. Relying on the postal service was hopelessly archaic; millions, billions even, could be lost in a matter of minutes, not to mention the time it would take for a trade confirmation to be printed out at RCM, mailed, and finally reviewed by someone at Delphic. Paul couldn't imagine why Alain would ever agree to invest in a fund that didn't provide him with up-to-date trading information.

Paul felt a chill as he remembered what Alexa had said about the manager who pulled out of RCM because of a lack of access. *Sidorov? Sergerov? Fuck.*

"Yeah, RCM doesn't allow anyone access to their accounts. They send daily trade confirmations by mail. It's kind of weird because we get them on a five-day delay, but it's the best they're willing to do."

"*A five-day delay*? They can't fax them? I've never heard of not having online access. That's insane."

Jean shrugged. "Reis's famously paranoid. Or was, I should say. He said he didn't trust fax machines. Thought there could be a confidentiality breach, or something like that. I don't know. It's a little crazy. Working with RCM is like working with Blackwater or something. They're really protective of their information. Who knows, maybe they were in bed with the Russians or something." He gave a sour smile, aware that a joke about Reis felt awkward under the circumstances. Then he said, "That's why I'm not sure if Alain would be happy with my opening up his files. But there you go." He gestured at the cabinets as if to say, *you asked for it.*

Paul nodded. "Thanks. It's important. Don't worry if you need to take off; I'll close up here."

"Yeah, I gotta catch a flight. Have a good holiday. Will someone tell Alain about Reis?"

"I'll send Alain an e-mail. I imagine it'll be all over the news, but I'll make sure he knows. Check your e-mail this weekend. This is gonna shake things up around here."

"Yeah, I figured. The guy's running thirty percent of our money." Jean shook his head. "When you're done with the files, do me a favor and just close the locks for me." Paul nodded. He was already digging though the first drawer when he heard the *ding* of the elevator doors closing behind Jean.

Paul had no idea what he was looking for. Most of the files were unlabeled, except for dates. Feeling helpless, he decided to take what he could carry and try to make sense of them later, when his mind had slowed. The files were chronological, so Paul pulled the last six months. It was an aggregation of trade confirmations, e-mails, investor documents. He locked the cabinets before heading back to his office.

Paul dropped the RCM files on his desk. On top of the stack, he laid the envelope from Alexa. He stared at it for a minute before the stillness of his office got the better of him. He pulled open the tab and withdrew a thin sheath of papers, loosely joined at the top by a paperclip. The top page was a chart, colorful and computer generated, like something out of a textbook. It bore no label, but it only took Paul a moment to comprehend it. The chart's Y-axis was marked Q1—Q4 of years 1998 through 2008, and the X-axis showed Net Asset Value. Across the chart was a single red line, marked simply "RCM." The red line rose from right to left in an unnervingly steady progression, forming a forty-five degree ellipse on the chart.

In the upper right-hand corner of the page, Alexa's tiny handwriting caught Paul's eye.

It read: Perfect Performance. She had underlined it twice.

Below that:

(1) Unusually high and consistent returns (<5 down months in 7 yrs)
(2) S&P 500 performance has no bearing on RCM's performance. If RCM's whole strategy is split-strike conversion based on the S&P 500, this doesn't make sense. The two return curves would appear correlated. RCM could theoretically outperform the index, but it was still going down when the index went down, and up when the index went up. Here, RCM's curve appears untied to anything. It's essentially statistically perfect.

Paul's heart fell to the pit of his stomach.

He pushed his chair back from his desk, as if that would distance him from what he'd just read. Even from three feet, all he could see was the perfectly formed red line. He didn't read anything else; he didn't need to.

He knew what it said. It all said the same thing: RCM was a fraud.

That fact had been slowly sinking in all day. Or perhaps it had been longer than that. Paul felt as though he had been sitting in a rowboat in the middle of a lake, watching as the water level rose slowly up the boat's side. It wasn't until someone threw him a life preserver that it occurred to him that the water wasn't rising; rather, the boat was sinking. And if he didn't jump now, he would go down with it.

He flipped the chart over while he made the calls. The first was to Merrill; again, it went straight to voice mail.

"It's Paul," he said. "Call me when you get this." Then he hung up, and his hand lingered for a moment on the receiver.

It felt as though days had passed since they had spoken, instead of mere hours. Paul imagined that she was sitting across a sterile conference room from her client, a trader maybe, or a hedge fund manager, quietly jotting down notes as a partner asked questions. To both the client and the partner, nothing would seem amiss about her. Even today, Merrill would be as she always was: poised. If Paul had been there, he immediately would have picked up on how hard she was bearing down on her pencil, almost to the point of breaking its tip on the page, and the hint of tears that had formed in the corners of her eyes.

The second call was harder. Paul could feel his heart pump hard as he dialed; he closed his eyes and tried to slow it with long deep breaths. When David Levin answered—he picked up quickly after only one ring—Paul realized suddenly that he had no idea where to begin.

# WEDNESDAY, 4:47 P.M.

She had called twice, once late the previous evening and then again early in the morning, before he had even left the house. When the first call went to voice mail, she hung up. When the second did, she left a message. This was unusual for her. The message was short and without detail, but her voice was thick with urgency.

The missed calls collected on his BlackBerry like impatient taps on the shoulder, raising his blood pressure. He resolved to call her the following day, and not to give her a thought until then. This, of course, proved impossible. He was thinking of her constantly now: at work, running in Central Park, in meetings with clients. Even at home, with Ines.

Carter had always prided himself on his ability to compartmentalize. Lately, though, his thoughts about her were uncontrollable, bubbling to the forefront of his consciousness at random, inhibiting his work. He was sleeping poorly; he would go for days now without more than an hour or two of continuous rest. Because he feared they would dull his thinking, he refused to take sleeping pills. Instead, Dr. Stein had prescribed Xanax to help with the anxiety. He had resisted at first, but it was reflexive now; he couldn't imagine life without it. He popped one as he waited for the garage attendant to pull the station wagon around from the underground lot.

As he waited on the curb, Carter felt his BlackBerry vibrate in his coat pocket. Reluctantly, he pulled it out. If it wasn't important, he decided, he would let it go to voice mail. If it was her, he would answer, but only to tell her that he couldn't talk during the holiday weekend.

When he saw that it was Sol, Carter answered straightaway.

"Are you sitting down?" Sol sounded agitated, but then, Sol always sounded agitated.

"No," Carter replied. "I'm standing on the curb at the garage. They're pulling my car around. What do you need?"

There was a momentary silence. Carter wondered if he had lost reception. He held the BlackBerry away from his ear to check the signal. When he put it back, Sol was saying, "I take it you haven't turned on a television lately."

"Why? Don't give me bad news about Lanworth."

"No, no, nothing like that." Sol paused again. "Look, something's happened," he said. "Morty . . . Carter, Morty's dead."

Carter felt his legs buckle out from under him. Without thinking, he flipped his suitcase on its side and sat down on it, his knees rising above his torso like an adult at the kid's table. He was having trouble breathing. He pulled a few shallow breaths in through his mouth, but it didn't feel as if it were enough. The garage air felt suffocatingly hot. Carter knew that the attendant behind the desk was staring at him, but he didn't care.

"I'm sorry to have to tell you. It's just that it's all over the news. His car was found this morning. They're saying it was a suicide. There was a note. And a bottle of pills." Sol's voice had a hollow echo, as if he were calling from an airport terminal. When Carter stayed silent, Sol offered, "I'm so sorry. I can imagine this is very difficult for you to hear."

For a moment, Carter wondered if this was actually a real phone call. Perhaps it was an elaborate hoax? *What a cruel, strange pointless prank*, he thought. Yet somehow more plausible than the proposition that Morty Reis, the Morty Reis he knew so well, had driven himself outside the city limits before it was yet light, parked his car, taken pills, and jumped off a fucking bridge.

The Morty he knew never drove himself anywhere. He was a terrible driver. Carter didn't even know Morty *had* a car in the city. That was the irony of his car collection. Carter used to kid him about it: *You collect them, but can you drive them? A car like that, don't you think it deserves a real driver at the wheel?* Morty didn't give a shit what anyone thought about him. He loved his cars—his favorite was a 1963 Aston Martin DB5—and it gave him pleasure just knowing that they were his. He kept them in his garage out in East Hampton, sleeping peacefully beneath their canvas covers. Except, perhaps, one.

"Which car was it?"

"What?"

"You said they found his car. Which one was it?"

Sol paused. "I don't know. They may have told me, but I don't remember."

It made more sense, Carter supposed, than any of the alternatives. Morty was too squeamish to slit his own wrists. He was terrified of blood. And he was terrible with guns. Carter had taken him shooting once, a pheasant hunt with clients, and Morty had managed to injure his shoulder from the kick of a 20-gauge Remington. He had spent the rest of the afternoon back at the lodge, making phone calls and drinking Diet Coke and eating jellybeans by the fistful. He never would have kept a gun in his house.

A minute went by, maybe thirty seconds, and then the front of Carter's black Mercedes station wagon appeared over the ramp and pulled up beside him. The attendant got out of the car, leaving the driver's side door open. He walked toward Carter, his extended hand offering the key. He was a young kid, and his pants were slung too low, revealing a slice of his boxer shorts. With irritation, Carter noticed that he had left the radio in the car tuned to a rap station. Ordinarily, Carter would have said something disapproving. Instead, he got up from his suitcase and stood there, frozen. He had forgotten he was on the phone.

"I'm sorry," Carter said finally to Sol. "I just need to be sure I understand this." He paused, glaring at the garage attendant. *Go the fuck away.*

When the attendant didn't move, Carter cupped the phone and hissed, "You're going to have to give me a minute here." Then he turned his back to him and said in a low voice: "You're telling me that Morty has taken his own life. Just now, just today. Am I hearing this correctly?"

"Yeah, it's all over the news, Carter. Turn on any channel. I spoke to Julianne about an hour ago. We're trying to get her on a flight back from Aspen, which is proving to be something of a challenge."

"Jesus Christ. This cannot be happening."

"I know. I feel the same way. Morty, of all people."

"I mean, *Jesus fucking Christ.* He was supposed to be at Thanksgiving with us. Did I tell you he was coming? I'm on my way out to East Hampton now." Carter realized that his voice had risen; he was becoming hysterical. From across the garage, the two attendants were staring at him, whispering now in Spanish. They were gesturing. His car was blocking the garage entrance.

"You sure you want to go? There's going to be . . . fallout."

"I have to go. We have to go. It's fucking Thanksgiving, Sol. Ines will lose it if we ruin Thanksgiving." He had to get off the phone. He had to get out of there. He was yelling, and sweating like a pig. He mopped his brow on his shirtsleeve.

"Carter, look. I know you're upset. We'll play this however you want—however you're comfortable. Listen, please let me send a car. I'll send my guy Tony. He can take you out to East Hampton. I'm not sure you should be driving right now. Okay?"

Carter was shaking his head, *no no no*, against the phone. *No. Unfucking-believable. This wasn't happening.* And there was no fucking way he would be answering his phone. At least, not until he talked to Ines. "No," he said, "No. I have to go. I need to go pick up Ines. Give me three hours and I'll call you from East Hampton. Get in touch with Julianne. Tell her we'll get her back here as fast as possible. Call the Marshalls, or the Petersons; if they aren't out in Aspen, they'll know someone who is. Tell them we need a plane for her, and we need it now."

"Okay. Look, drive safe." Sol said. "Don't worry about Julianne; I'll take care of her."

"How can I not worry about Julianne? No one else will."

"I know. You're a good man. Listen, we're driving out to East Hampton tonight. I'll be on my cell. Marion drives, so I can be on the phone the whole way. Okay? And Carter?" Sol's voice had taken on a softness that Carter wasn't used to hearing from his lawyer. "My heart goes out to you. I know how close you guys were. You'll be in my thoughts."

"Thanks," Carter said. "That means a lot." His voice cracked. He realized that his face was wet; he wasn't crying exactly, but his eyes were running, and he felt a strange mix of anger and deep affection for Sol thick in his chest. He cleared his throat. "Go home to Marion, please. I need three hours. Then we'll figure out what happens next. Take care of yourself."

"Be well," Sol said, but Carter had already hung up the phone.

Carter drove for exactly one block before he pulled over. He turned off the ignition and looked at the clock on the dashboard. It blinked 4:59; he was two hours behind schedule. Ines would be annoyed. She hated rush hour traffic. If they got stuck on the Long Island Expressway, it undoubtedly would now be considered his fault. This seemed unfair, given that it was Thanksgiving and there was inevitably traffic on the Long Island Expressway. And also, his business partner had just taken a swan dive off the Tappan Zee Bridge without so much as a fucking phone call. All that said, fairness was rarely a compelling argument with Ines. Lately, this had been particularly true.

Driving, however, would be impossible until his hands stopped shaking. That was the first order of business. Carter reached into his pocket and fished out the bottle of Xanax. He swallowed it dry. He closed his eyes for a second, and pressed all ten fingertips against each other, waiting for the rush of calm to sink in. He checked the bottle for another Xanax but it was empty.

As he sat in the driver's seat on the corner of Seventy-first and Lexington, Carter shuffled illogically through the events of the past few days.

He had spoken to Morty the previous Friday. Or was it Thursday? Morty had called about redemption requests, which was unlike him. He seemed stressed out, *who didn't these days*, by the topic of redemption requests, but by the end of the conversation, they were talking about Thanksgiving dinner in the Hamptons.

Then there had been dinner at Café Boulud—that was Saturday night—with Leonard Rosen, a major investor. No call from Morty. Frederick Fund team meeting on Friday, over breakfast. They had discussed RCM's redemption request situation. Shrink appointment after the meeting. Drinks on Sunday evening at Roger Sinclair's place. That was it. That was all he could come up with. What the hell had happened since last Thursday? Why hadn't Morty called him? They could have worked it out together. Hell of a solution.

Of all the ways to go, there was something so unnatural, so unseemly, about electing to die. Carter's father had, if only indirectly. Charles Darling Jr. drank himself to death by age forty-five. He was found dead in his bed, wearing only a dressing gown and reading glasses. A highball of scotch was on the bedside table, and under that was a letter. The letter was addressed to a Mr. Sheldon Summers at One Christopher Street in the West Village. Who, as it was later explained to Carter, had been his father's lover for over a decade.

Carter never forgave him for it. For years, Carter lied about how it had happened, telling teachers, friends, and colleagues that his father had died of stomach cancer. To Carter, stomach cancer sounded less self-induced than cirrhosis of the liver. The Darlings were of good New England stock, well educated and well-bred, not Irish peasants who drank themselves to undignified ends. It never occurred to Carter that his mother, Eleanor, might say otherwise, or that everyone already knew that Charlie Darling was an alcoholic and a homosexual. Everyone who was anyone, anyway. Carter said "stomach cancer" for so long and so convincingly, that by the time he met Ines, he himself believed it. Ines knew only that Charles had been sick for a great many years before he had died, and that his sickness had rendered him unable to work, and that this had caused the Darlings to lose what was left of their family fortune. Carter was a self-made man. Ines liked to put a pleasant spin on it, saying things like, "Well, he was a reminder of why you should live every day to its fullest." That was Ines, stubbornly positive, unfailingly able to bend the world's contours to her own.

It was the dead of winter when Charles Darling died, just four days before Christmas. The presents remained beneath the tree, entombed in gold wrapping paper, forgotten about. Carter was too shy to ask for them. Eleanor's sisters, Hilary and Cathy, came down from Massachusetts for the funeral and had stayed at their apartment for what seemed like an eternity. To make Hilary and Cathy more comfortable, Carter had been asked to give up his bedroom. Told, really: No one ever asked Carter anything. He'd slept on a foldout couch in the den, the one with needlepoint pillows, hard and square. Eventually, he was told that he had been withdrawn from the Buckley School in Manhattan and would be sent to Eaglebrook, a junior boy's boarding school in Deerfield, Massachusetts.

Cathy had been the one to drive him up to Eaglebrook. His mother, Cathy said, was too tired to make the trip herself. The other students were still on winter recess, and the dorms were empty but for a few international students whose parents didn't care enough to send for them. Before she left, Cathy told him that he was a very lucky boy to enroll in the middle of the school year. An exception had been made just for him because he was a Darling. Cathy gave him a hug and checked her watch. Carter wondered if she had played a game of rock-paper-scissors with Hilary and whoever lost had to be the one to drive him there. They both had curly blond hair but Hilary was prettier, more outgoing, more authoritarian. Cathy seemed like the type who always lost at rock-paper-scissors.

Eventually, the house master appeared and helped them with his suitcases. Carter didn't feel like a very lucky boy. As Cathy drove away, he felt only the nauseating pain of loneliness.

---

Outside the car, the light was fading to black. Night had set in. A few cars passed on his right, but the traffic was thin and the city felt empty. Carter restarted the engine. He would go get Ines. He would drive to Long Island. He would figure it out from there. Minute to minute, as his crew coach used to say. Take each minute as it comes.

Carter managed to get the car down to Sixty-fourth Street without incident. A parking spot was open just in front of the apartment. Ordinarily, he would have considered this lucky, a good sign. When the doorman came to open the car door, Carter rolled down his window and said, "Please let Mrs. Darling know I'm here."

The doorman nodded. "She's been waiting for you," he said neutrally, a statement of fact and not a judgment. Still, Carter wanted to say something in his own defense; what kind of man leaves his wife sitting in the lobby on Thanksgiving eve? As he was turning off the engine, Ines emerged carrying two suitcases. Bacall trotted behind her wearing a charcoal-gray cable-knit sweater. His leash was looped loosely around Ines's forearm. Ines was bundled in a shearling coat and her leggings were tucked into Hermes riding boots, the kind with a silver buckle gleaming at the calf.

Though Ines was, as always, impeccable, Carter could see that she had heard. Her face was pinched with worry. Ines looked ten years older when she was worried; her forehead creased with sharp lines that even Botox couldn't erase. *Jesus. She really needs to eat something,* he thought as she approached the car. The tendons in her neck would have been visible were it not for her scarf, and her thighs were mercilessly thin. She moved purposefully, without a wave or a smile.

As he watched his wife stride from the lobby, Carter had the soul-deadening thought that everything was ending. He sat on his hands and tried to breathe deeply as Ines and the doorman put the suitcases in the trunk, *thock thock thock*, and she slid into the passenger seat. It was unlike him not to help her, but he found himself unable to move. Ines didn't say hello, but simply reached over and kissed him hard on the cheek. The air between them felt stiff and cold. For almost an hour, they sat in the parked car with the seat heaters on and a compact disc of opera playing quietly on repeat. As they talked, the windshield began to steam up. Eventually, Carter started the car again and they began the long drive to the country.

That night he dreamt of the first time he had her. He could feel her under his rib cage, her chest heaving against his, her legs spiraled tight around him as though no amount of contact between them would ever suffice. She was still wearing the tailored, tweedy skirt of her suit, pushed up around her hips. His hands covered her body, sliding up it and then down again, over and over, unable to find a single flaw or imperfection. She covered her mouth with her hand when she came, stifling a scream.

God, it had been incredible.

Though he always enjoyed her—*and Christ, did he enjoy her*—no night would ever be like that first night. Years of flirtation, at first harmless, then casual, then overt, then desperate, had built up like pressure in a steam pipe. They had had a few near misses; once, he had drunkenly leaned in to kiss her but she had turned away at the last moment, so his lips just grazed her cheek. Another time, they arranged to meet for a drink at a hotel bar (there was really no reason she would agree to this, he knew, if she didn't want him; but still she made him so nervous he couldn't quite be sure) but after only ten minutes or so, an acquaintance of hers walked in and she panicked, leaving him with a flimsy excuse about a phone call and the overwhelming feeling that he was a terrible person for pushing things as far as he had. But he couldn't help himself . . . When he was with her, he felt understood. She genuinely cared about his work, she wanted his opinions on real things . . . she made him feel as important and powerful and interesting and dynamic as he did when he was at the office. And then he would go home to Ines, who would be fretting about something so inane and trivial that it was almost laughable. So when finally, finally he had her, panting and sweating and pulling at her earlobe with his teeth, her high-heeled pumps abandoned in the sprint to the bed, that incredible voice of hers moaning how much she wanted him, how desperate she had been for him all along, the rush was unimaginable.

Though it had happened nine years ago, he still dreamt about it. Though he had never told a soul this (not even her), it was the reason he kept that stupid hotel ashtray on his desk at work. He had taken it from the room, not as some sort of juvenile trophy, but simply as a physical reminder that such a magnificent, raw night had actually occurred at all.

"*Well*," she said, when they were done, "*that* was sex." She laughed, a throaty, full laugh.

"That was more than sex."

"What was it then?" She teased. She was playing with him, but he wasn't in the mood to play. She flipped over on her stomach so that she could look at him. "Oh, God," she said suddenly, frowning. "You aren't crying?"

"I think I'm in love with you," he said.

"Don't start with that."

"I'm serious. You're brilliant and beautiful and funny and poised . . . but there's something else. I've just never felt like this before. I mean, Christ, I just cheated on my wife. I don't take that lightly, you know. I swear, this has never—"

"You don't have to say that."

"I know, but I just need you to understand this." He sat up, and wiped his eyes with the back of his hand. It was humiliating, talking like this . . . humiliating but also strangely cleansing, liberating, sensational . . . he couldn't seem to stop it . . . "Honestly, I think I would do anything for you."

She nodded slowly. He was gripped with the fear that she would burst out laughing—it would be so easy to do right now—but instead she just lay her head gently on his thigh.

"I'm not asking for anything," she said.

"I know you aren't. But I would. I just . . . I just want you to know that."

"Just spend time with me," she said. "When you can. Let's keep this simple."

---

Always, when she said this the dream would end. Then Carter would lie awake with his thoughts. The unbearable heaviness of having stayed married to the wrong person was most acute, he found, late at night. Some nights, he thought it might kill him. But his regrets would always lift when the sun began to rise, and the day would seem new again. Over time he had learned how to lie still and to wait for that.

# WEDNESDAY, 5:03 P.M.

The thing about Champion & Gilmore, the white-shoe law firm where Merrill worked, was that everything was always in order. Founded in 1884 by Lorillard Champion and Harrison Gilmore IV, C&G, as it was called on Wall Street, had long been known as a WASPy firm that represented other WASPy firms, the JPMorgans and Lazard Freres and Rothschilds of the world, and employed mostly WASPy lawyers who, like Merrill Darling, had fancy academic pedigrees and appropriate-sounding surnames.

Though the work at C&G was—like at any law firm—often stressful, combative, and emotionally fraught, the office was always pin-drop quiet. Clients exited the elevator bank into a soothing, sun-filled reception area with white carpets and walls. The conference rooms were immaculate and had sweeping views of midtown Manhattan. On clear days especially, Merrill found it hard to focus when she was seated facing one of the conference room windows. The city rolled out before her, impossibly dense, silent, magnificent in scale. Only the flow of traffic on the grid below, and the sweep of the clouds overhead, reminded her that what she was looking at was real.

Merrill was currently spending much of her time in Conference Room C, which, for the foreseeable future, had been converted into a workroom for the attorneys staffed on the Gerard case. Elsa Gerard, the firm's client, was a portfolio manager at Vonn Capital. Elsa had become something of a celebrity in the hedge fund world. She had started at Vonn in 1985 as the executive assistant to Mark Vonn, the fund's CEO. She was twenty-two years old and a newly minted graduate of St. John's University in Queens, New York. After putting herself through business school at night, she persuaded Vonn to take her on as an analyst. She worked her way up slowly and eventually became one of Vonn's star portfolio managers. Despite her success, Elsa had never made apologies for her humble beginnings, and she had never tried to fit in with the industry establishment. In fact, she seemed to take pleasure in standing out. Her suits were now designer (she favored Versace and Dolce and Gabbana), but they were just as tight, just as short, and just as loud as they had been when she had first started at Vonn. Her hair was still the same bottle blond. ("All T and A," as one rival manager had crassly put it in an e-mail that had "somehow" ended up in the hands of the press). Unquestionably, Elsa had once been a knockout. At forty-seven, she looked a little brash and worn, but there was still a sexiness about her that was undeniable.

Predictably, Elsa Gerard was a polarizing personality. She seemed to inspire either reverence or hatred (sometimes at the same time) wherever she went; rarely did someone meet Elsa and not have something to say about her. Regular adjectives and labels didn't seem to suffice; in the past few months, Merrill had heard Elsa described as a genius, a slut, a fame whore, a rock star, a rising star, a prima donna, a role model, a liar, and the future of Wall Street. Unfortunately, she had also been called a criminal. Elsa had been implicated as a member of what the press had dubbed "the Ring": a sophisticated group of hedge fund managers, consultants, lawyers, and pharmaceutical industry executives who allegedly conspired to exchange and trade on inside information. Six indictments had been issued, and everyone knew that more were to come. Elsa, who had not yet been indicted, vehemently denied any connection to the Ring, but refused to say much more in her own defense.

With her lawyers, Elsa was candid. Though he was married, she and Mark were lovers. Occasionally, he had given her instructions to buy or sell a particular stock, and she had done so without questioning him, both because he was her boss and also because she was in love with him. It had never occurred to her that Mark was instructing her to trade on the basis of information that he had obtained illegally. It had also never occurred to her that when the time came, he would sell her up the river.

Criminal or victim: Even Elsa's lawyers were split. An internal debate now raged at C&G as to whether Elsa's story held water. Half the team thought she should just plead guilty and cut a deal; she was simply too smart to have been used by Mark Vonn, no matter what their relationship. The other half of the team either believed her or at least thought that a jury might. As of yet, no one had found any evidence of a connection between Elsa and any member of the Ring. Mark Vonn, however, had a personal relationship with a high-level executive at OctMedical, the stock that Elsa had purchased just days before the company had unveiled a revolutionary new diabetes drug.

Merrill had been tasked with overseeing the document review process for the case. "Doc review" (as it was known in-house) was a necessary but tedious process, reading through every single e-mail sent or received by a particular group of hedge fund employees over a seven-year period before turning them over to the SEC. This was part of the pretrial litigation process known as "discovery." Of course, before C&G turned anything over to the SEC, they were painstakingly reviewed themselves. Twelve hours a day, seven days a week, attorneys took shifts clicking through CDs of e-mails. After reading an e-mail, the attorney would label it with the appropriate tag. A Responsive tag meant that the e-mail was "responsive" to the SEC's subpoena request and therefore needed to be turned over; Privileged meant that the e-mail contained information that could be withheld from the SEC on the basis of client privilege; Hot meant that the e-mail contained information that could be potentially harmful to the client if turned over; and Second Review was used if the contract attorney wasn't sure how to categorize the e-mail. Merrill's job was to review all the e-mails labeled Hot and Second Review. The work was exceedingly monotonous but terrifyingly crucial. If an incriminating (or exonerating) e-mail somehow slipped through the doc review unnoticed, it could cost C&G the case.

For this case, the document review was so large in scope that a team of contract attorneys had been brought in to complete it. Contract attorneys were not permanent employees of C&G but rather attorneys who were paid by the hour (on contract) to work on specific cases or transactions. On-staff attorneys saw them as cheap reinforcement labor, not unlike the army reserves. Though some of them were quite experienced, the Gerard case contract attorneys had been sternly advised that if they had even a flicker of a doubt on any given e-mail, they were to bring it to the attention of one of the other midlevel attorneys immediately. Of course, the midlevel attorneys had plenty of work of their own, and most of them weren't all that keen on being regularly pestered by the contract attorneys. Merrill, however, was always happy to help. Unlike most associates, who treated them with mild derision and occasional downright hostility, Merrill was unfailingly polite to the contract attorneys, appreciative of their work, and respectful of their time. She often stayed late to pitch in when they had fallen behind, even though she hardly had the capacity to do so. Everyone on the Gerard case was overworked and overwhelmed. The associates were barely sleeping and the partners seemed short-fused and increasingly unreasonable. Underlying everything was a current of unspoken desperation that was picking up speed as the case progressed.

Merrill happened to like Elsa, and had thrown herself headlong into the case with an almost fanatical zeal. She was crass, sure. God, Ines would absolutely hate her. But she had fought her way to the top without help from anybody. And she seemed honest—if anything, maybe a bit too honest—a real "what you see is what you get" kind of woman. From Merrill's perspective, the guys on the team were too quick to judge her based on her appearance. This really got under Merrill's skin; wasn't Elsa Gerard, just like anyone else, innocent until proven guilty? Didn't she deserve to be believed, especially by her lawyers?

Today had been a big day for the Gerard team. Elsa's former assistant had given a very favorable deposition, and the team seemed charged with new energy. Merrill tried to muster enthusiasm, but inside she was numb. Everything that had happened since she had heard the news about Morty had simply gone by in a blur. By 4 p.m., she had decided it was better to just go home. She had put on her coat, but couldn't seem to find the energy to leave.

"Merrill, could you take a look at something?" A timid voice stirred Merrill from her thoughts. She sat facing the window, staring out into the darkening night sky. She had no idea how long she had been sitting like that, just staring. "Oh, I'm sorry," the voice continued. "Are you on your way out?"

Merrill swiveled her chair around. In her doorway was Amy, a diminutive redhead who always looked vaguely nervous to be speaking at all. Amy was one of the hardest working contract attorneys on the Gerard team, and Merrill went out of her way to help and encourage her.

Merrill mustered a smile. "Hey, Amy. Come on in."

Amy hesitated. "It's just—are you sure you weren't on your way out? I can ask John or Mike instead."

Merrill shook her head. "Really, I wasn't. I mean, I was going to eventually, but this is more important." She gestured for Amy to come into her office. "So what's up?"

"I think . . . I think I found something in Elsa's trash."

"Her trash?"

"Her deleted e-mails. We had them pulled off the server. I've been reviewing them since yesterday."

Merrill felt her stomach clench. "Okay . . . is it bad?" She knew from the look on Amy's face that it was.

"Umm . . ."

"Let me see it."

Amy proffered a thin sheaf of paper, which she had secured with a binder clip. It appeared to be a long e-mail chain between Elsa and Mark Vonn. "If you start from the back . . . I've highlighted the parts that I think are, uh, relevant." Merrill was already reading. As her eyes skimmed the page, the knot in her stomach grew and grew until it was so large she could feel it pushing on her throat. For a moment, she thought she might throw up. She closed her eyes and pressed her palms against the chill surface of her desk. They were damp even though the offices were kept at a cool 68 degrees.

"Are you all right?" Amy's voice sounded far away. Merrill felt as though she were at the bottom of a swimming pool and Amy was shouting at her from above the surface . . . the words seemed garbled from where she was . . .

"Merrill?" Amy said, this time clear as a bell. Merrill looked up. Amy was standing in front of the desk, leaning in toward her. Her watery blue eyes were filled with concern.

Merrill snapped back in her chair. "I'm so sorry," she said, her face flushed with embarrassment. "I just . . . honestly, I'm just not feeling all that well today." She put her hand against her forehead and realized she was sweating.

"You, uh, you don't look that great. Maybe you should go home?"

Merrill bit down hard on her bottom lip. She had never—not once—taken a sick day. And now, of all times . . . "You know, I think I need to." She handed Amy back the e-mails. "Listen, you were right about these. They need to get seen right away. Take them to Phil. If he's not there or he tells you to wait, tell him it's urgent. I'm going to send him an e-mail, actually I'm going to send all the partners an e-mail, telling them what you found."

Amy nodded frenetically. Her red curls bounced against her shoulders. "Okay. Don't worry Merrill, I'll take care of it. Really, please go home. You don't look well. This is totally, totally under control."

Merrill offered her a weak smile. "Thanks, Amy. You did a great job."

"Well . . . I don't know. I'm not sure anyone's going to be all that psyched to see these."

"Don't worry about that. Just take it to Phil."

Amy was already halfway out the door. Before she closed it, she spun on her heel. She paused, hesitating. Then she said, "It's sort of disappointing, isn't it?"

"What's that?"

"Well . . . I liked Elsa. I dunno. I wanted to believe her." Amy shrugged, her face shrinking into an embarrassed smile.

"I know," Merrill said sympathetically. "Me, too."

"Do you think she'll have to plead?"

"I don't know. Maybe. I honestly don't know."

"She shouldn't have put this into an e-mail." Amy shook her head disbelievingly. "You really never can tell with anyone, can you?"

"Well. Don't give up so fast." Merrill smiled, but it was a thin smile. "See what Phil has to say."

"Okay. Go home and lie down. I'll keep you posted."

After Amy shut the door, Merrill stood, her mind racing. She threw a few files in her bag and headed for the door. She reached for her coat, but the hook on the back of the door was empty. With her free hand, Merrill patted her side. She had been wearing it the whole time.

# WEDNESDAY, 5:27 P.M.

Yvonne found Patrick in the kitchen, setting out place mats for dinner. She could smell garlic bread in the oven. In the background, the 5 o'clock news was playing; she hadn't realized how late it was.

"I'm so sorry," she began, before she had taken off her jacket. Her cheeks were flushed red, from adrenaline and from the cold. "Where are the boys?"

Patrick smiled, his eyes tired. He put down the last place mat and gave her a hug. He wasn't angry, which made her feel even guiltier.

"I sent them up to their rooms. Pat got suspended."

"Oh, Christ."

"Yeah. It's not good." He shook his head. "I gotta say, though, I think the kid was right. I don't know what we do now."

Yvonne sank onto a kitchen chair, her bag dropping beneath it. "What happened?"

"Pat and Chris were supposed to meet after school to walk home, but Pat was late. When he got there, that kid from down the street, Joe Dunn, was picking on Chris. That's been going on for a while. So Joe called Chris a pussy and Pat decked him. The teachers were all leaving because school had just let out, so a lot of people saw it."

Yvonne let out a sigh. “How many days?”

“Three. Starting Monday. It’s a stupid punishment. The kid’s getting a seven day vacation.” Patrick joined her at the little round table, set for four. He always sat next to her at a table instead of across, which she loved. Even in restaurants. He had done it on their first date (the place was loud, he said) and had never stopped.

Pat was dressed in what had become his daily uniform, work boots and cargo pants. A year ago, he wore chinos and a button-down every day, a requirement of his position as manager of the Operations department at Bear Stearns. It was a stable job, replete with health care and stock options, which now, of course, were worthless. For six months after the bank shut down, Pat pounded the pavement, looking for a comparable position at another financial institution. He was qualified, everyone said, but no one was hiring. By August he was desperate. He took a part-time job as a security guard for a local bank, “until there was something better.” He was still saying it was temporary, but with less conviction. From what Yvonne could tell, he had stopped looking for jobs in the financial sector. The bank offered him extra hours—four days a week instead of three—but still, it wasn’t enough. Even with Yvonne bailing as hard, their little boat was sinking, faster than she ever imagined.

“Chris okay?”

“Yeah, he’s all right.” Patrick glanced away. He scratched his head reflexively. This was an uncomfortable topic. Whenever they talked about it, they did so with eyes averted, like strangers in an elevator. “I don’t know. I think he’s embarrassed. He was shaking like a leaf when I got there.”

“We need to do something.”

She had said this before.

Usually, Patrick said: “Like what?” She had no answer for that, so the conversation would stop there. “I know,” he said instead, his eyes meeting hers.

“Thank you for getting the boys, I was going to do it myself, but—”

"It's okay. I knew what was going on. Must have been crazy at the office."

She frowned. "It wasn't really. Sol just needed some wires set up. It was just bad timing; he called right after I talked to the school."

Patrick nodded. He sat back into his chair, stretching his legs out beneath the table. "Yeah, I just figured with the Morton Reis thing, you know. Stuff got busy. It was no problem getting the boys."

Yvonne paused. The news blared in the background. "What Morton Reis thing?" She said, perplexed.

His eyebrows peaked in surprise. "The . . . the—you know. I saw it on the news. That's why I called; I was worried about you." Suddenly, he was looking over her shoulder at the television. "See!" He said. His eyes were alight with recognition. He pointed at the screen. "It's on again. That's Morton Reis."

Yvonne pivoted, following the line of his finger. The picture was fuzzy, but there was a shot of Morty on the television, in a tuxedo standing next to Carter Darling.

"And that's—"

"Carter Darling." Yvonne finished other people's sentences sometimes, a nervous tic. She was quiet for a moment, and then said, "Oh, God," as the headline began to sink in, "when did you hear about this?"

"When I called you. Around lunch." Patrick sounded confused. "But it's been on TV all day."

"I don't have a TV on my desk." She said numbly. She felt as though someone had poured a glass of ice water down her spine. *Morty's dead?* She stared at the television screen. *How could Sol not have said anything?*

"Sol didn't tell you?"

"He just wanted me to set up some wire transfers."

"You seem . . . you okay?" He flicked off the television.

The static silence of the room felt almost unbearable. From upstairs, the *whump* of a chair leg ricocheting off the floorboards reminded them both that the boys were home, confined to their shared bedroom.

"I think—" she said and halted. Then she slipped the sleeve of her coat back over her arm, buttoning it at the neck. It was night now, and she shivered thinking about walking all the way back to the subway. It would be empty, heading in the wrong direction back into the city, away from dinner tables and toward darkened office buildings. "I think I have to go back to work."

Patrick's eyes widened. "Now?" he said, frowning. "Yvonne. It's six. It's dinner time."

"I know," she said, nodding. "But there's something wrong with the wires."

She stood up and grabbed her purse. "Feed the boys, all right? I'll be back as soon as I can."

Patrick inhaled deeply. He released it slowly; he was counting to five. She thought he might snap at her—he had every right to—but she didn't have time to waste.

"Please be safe," Patrick said resignedly, kissing her on the cheek. "It's nighttime."

As the subway car rumbled its way into Manhattan, Yvonne closed her eyes. Data rolled through her head in waves. There were so many things she knew: things she shouldn't know, things she was supposed to have forgotten, things that no one thought she was smart enough to piece together on her own. She was a dangerous woman, in that way. And yet, it was the things she didn't know that were the most dangerous.

As she emerged from beneath ground, the cold air hit her square in the face. Yvonne sped up, walking at a fast clip past the glistening doors of the office buildings, a closed coffee shop, store windows barred shut for the night. When she reached the offices of Penzell & Rubicam, she flashed the night watchman a smile and held out the laminated badge that hung from her neck on a silver-balled string. She thought he gave her a suspicious look, but then he yawned. *I'm just a little jumpy,* she thought. *He doesn't know a thing.*

Questions about the night watchman were quickly replaced by the two questions that had been plaguing Yvonne since earlier in the day. Now, they would keep Yvonne in the office for the next several hours.

*What were the wire transfers for?*

*And why had Sol asked her to backdate them?*

# WEDNESDAY, 8:03 P.M.

After he released Marina, Duncan sat at his desk for a little longer. He knew he ought to go home; there were groceries waiting for him—the ice cream was melting, probably—at his service door. But God, some nights he really hated an empty apartment. He had sworn to himself that he wouldn't drink alone anymore, but he already knew that tonight would be an exception. The nights before holidays were the worst. The junior staffers seemed invigorated all day, charged with fresh energy, suitcases beneath their desks. They left quietly, slipping out one by one. Where were they going? Did they all have the big meal to look forward to, a long table with aunts and uncles and children in tow? How was that possible? Even as a child, Duncan had never experienced that. There had been the drunken Mommy/Daddy Thanksgivings, then just the drunk Mommy Thanksgivings. College, well, college he didn't remember. As an adult, he had bounced from house to house, leeching family off his significant other like a parasite. And the last three years he had been alone, and knee-deep in scotch by 4 p.m.

But tomorrow would be different. A week ago he had gotten a call from his favorite niece, who lived in the city and had too much work to go home to visit her mother for the holiday. Some issue or other with her boyfriend, she had said. She didn't know if he would be up for celebrating. "Come over," he had said. "We're having a party." She sounded as though she needed that.

Overnight, Duncan had rounded up six friends so that it wouldn't seem to her as though Thanksgiving dinner had been thrown together on her account. He gave each one an assignment to bring something, wine or a side dish or apple pie. *Like a tradition*, he thought. His niece would enjoy that.

The news was awash with reports about Thanksgiving Day Parade balloons, stuffing recipes, and predictions of snow. One story caught Duncan's eye: the suicide of billionaire Morton Reis. Duncan had met Reis once, at a *Vanity Fair* party in the Hamptons. He came across like an old codger, friendly but out of place. He had been terribly dressed, in ill-fitting chinos and a plastic watch. A strange pairing with his flamboyant wife, who had, as Duncan recalled, parked him at the bar so that she could go mingle. Duncan had found Reis intriguing. In his experience, it was usually the least assuming guy in the room who turned out to be the most interesting. After a few inquiries, someone told Duncan that Reis was a billionaire and a bit of a recluse, something of a car aficionado, and that Julianne, unsurprisingly, was his second wife.

*I wonder if she killed him*, Duncan thought, as he scrolled through a gallery of photos that CNN.com had posted of Reis. *Shot him and dumped his body off the bridge to make it look like he jumped. Wouldn't have been the first time. They always say it's the spouse.*

Only one photo was with his wife; it showed the couple at a benefit for the Metropolitan Opera. They were turned away from each other, each chatting with other partygoers. At Reis's right shoulder was the dapper Carter Darling. Carter was leaning in, as though whispering something into Reis's ear. Each man held a glass of champagne. *Carter Darling looks like Cary Grant*, Duncan mused. *What a pity he isn't gay.*

As he walked home, Duncan tried to remember every detail he could about Morton Reis and Carter Darling. There was something there; he could feel it in his fingertips. After twenty-five years in this business, he had a nose for a story. Though it had led him down a few dead ends, it had sniffed out some ungodly messes, too. This was how it began: an offhand comment, the recurring thought that the newspaperman in him couldn't dismiss. He walked faster and faster down Sixth Avenue, moving past the corner where he typically found a cab. Something was coming, hard and fast. He had to steel himself for its arrival.

# WEDNESDAY, 8:45 P.M.

The walk home was blisteringly cold. The wind ran in currents across Park Avenue. Paul hunched into his turned-up collar, hands stuffed deep in his pockets. He shivered uncontrollably and cursed his decision to wear the Barbour. By the time he reached the front door, his eyes stung with tears. Merrill opened it and fell into him, wrapping her small warm body against his. He could tell that she had been waiting for him. She had changed into sweatpants and her red cashmere socks, the ones that were too thick to wear with shoes. Her smile was fleeting and beneath it, her face looked drawn.

They hugged. "How are you?" Paul said gently.

"I'm sad," she said, her voiced muffled against his lapel. She sounded like a child. "I can't believe it. I've known him since I was a kid."

"I know you have."

They retreated to the couch. There was an imprint on its cushions; she had been lying there for a while, he thought. They lay down together, her body snug beside his. Her head rested on his rib cage. Paul kicked off his shoes and they clattered over the couch's arm. His body ached with tiredness.

"How're your parents?"

"Mom's upset. It's strange, she seems angry, more than anything. No sympathy for Julianne whatsoever. I don't know. They never had a particularly solid marriage, I guess."

"That doesn't matter. This must be terrible for her."

"That's what I said. Did you talk to Dad?"

"No. I called his cell but he wasn't answering."

"He's trying to get Julianne home from Aspen. It's Thanksgiving, of course, so there are no flights at all. He's trying to get a friend to fly her home on a private plane or something, but now she's saying she wants to stay out there, for the holiday at least. They're talking about having a service early next week. Dad thinks it should be sooner, but so many people are away for the holiday weekend." She sighed, realizing that she rambled when she was tired.

"We'll be there, whenever it is."

"Of course."

"Paul?" Merrill lifted her head off his chest. "What's going to happen at work?"

Paul stared at the blank whiteness of the ceiling. It was a relief from the walls, which were painted dark green, like a British racing car, and cluttered with paintings and photographs. The richness of the room, the overlay of so many hanging things felt grand to him; at times, mildly claustrophobic. The far wall was dominated by two antique maps, given to them by Carter and Ines as an engagement present. One was an early map of New York, back when the Upper East Side was nothing but open farmland. The other was a nautical map of Cape Lookout in North Carolina, from 1866. Cape Lookout wasn't anywhere near where he was from, but—according to Ines—it was the only antique map of North Carolina available.

Beneath the maps was a slim mahogany table, selected by Elena and Ramon, the Darlings' decorators, to "complement" the maps. Merrill hadn't told Paul how much it cost, and though he wondered about it every time he walked into the apartment, he really didn't want to know. Some days, the apartment felt disorientingly ornate, like something out of *Architectural Digest*. This was one of those days.

Paul looked down at his wife. Her hair was pulled into a messy bun, her face stripped bare and slightly ashen. Still, she was beautiful, her eyes a luminous blue flecked with gold. Her hair smelled as it always did, and her body felt familiar next to his. It was only because of her that he lived here. Sometimes, he wondered if he would have stayed in New York at all, if it wasn't for her.

"Is Dad going to lose the business?"

She looked at him in that way of hers, loving him and needing him all at once. He felt a rush of sadness fill his chest; he wanted so much to make everything okay.

"Come here," he said, and wrapped her up tight in his arms. His body was just beginning to feel warm again. "Your dad's going to be fine. We're going to figure everything out."

"I love you," she said simply. "Things like this just make me realize how much I love you."

Paul decided not to bring up his conversation with Alexa until later. Maybe when they were in the car, on the way to East Hampton. This was mostly out of cowardice, but then it would be quiet in the car, with no distractions. And, for a couple hours, she wouldn't be able to get up and walk away from the conversation, which Merrill sometimes did when she was angry or upset or frustrated. Paul had a sense that it was very likely she would be all three. Not necessarily with him, though that was a possibility.

For the moment, Paul held her on the couch and let her talk. She needed that, to talk and have someone just listen. What she said didn't really matter, and she was so tired that it didn't make much sense anyway, but Paul sensed that it was a relief for her to let it out. She rambled on about how Morty had been like an uncle to her and Lily, how after a few drinks he would tell them stories about her father as a young man that they weren't supposed to hear and how he took them both to get their ears pierced after school, when Ines didn't want them to. How he never bought himself new clothes but would lavish the Darling girls with presents around the holidays. How it felt, to her, like the world was coming slowly apart at the seams.

Merrill started to cry as she talked, the hard kind of crying, with snot slipping down her face. Paul held her as her body shook. When she was done, they ordered from the Chinese place down the street.

"I haven't eaten since breakfast," she said to the delivery boy as he wordlessly peeled off singles, making change. As though she owed everyone an apology.

She ate ravenously, straight from the cartons. Usually he would have enjoyed being with her like this, informal and cozy. But she looked so pale and thin in his oversized UNC T-shirt . . . She worked so hard, always putting everyone—her colleagues, her family—ahead of herself. Lately, it seemed to be taking its toll on her physically. She had lost weight. She was sleeping badly. She had developed a cough that she couldn't seem to shake.

"Do you want to play Scrabble?" she asked when she was done eating. They always played Scrabble after Chinese food.

"I think you should get some sleep," he said.

"You always win, anyway," she said, and smiled.

"You let me. Go brush your teeth."

Paul tucked her in. Her body disappeared beneath the duvet and her eyes shut as soon as her head hit the pillow. After he turned off the light, he stayed for a while, watching her in the amber twilight of the unlit room until her breathing became shallow and rhythmic. When he kissed her, she stirred lightly beneath his touch. Her brow rippled as though she was consumed in a dream.

After the leftovers were packed away in the fridge and the trash had been taken out and his face had been scrubbed clean in the bathroom sink, Paul padded into his home office to look through old e-mails. There was one in particular that he wanted to read. He did so again and again, until its words blurred across the page and he was no longer reading it but simply reciting its memorized contents in his head. Finally, he printed it out and put it in a file. Though he was tired, the pieces of the last shattered day were coming together like a Rubik's Cube.

Eventually the world behind the semitranslucent window shade brightened, and the room came alive again with the pink light of morning. It was Thanksgiving. He had been waiting for it for weeks, though now that it was here it certainly didn't feel like a holiday. He heard Merrill stirring in the bedroom. He went to put on coffee.

The coffee brewed gently on the counter, filling the kitchen with a familiar, rich scent. Paul reached up into the cabinet to pull down a mug. He had to dig behind the china coffee cups they had gotten off their registry in order to find the big, chipped Harvard Law School mug that was his favorite. If Merrill were awake, she would try to steal it from him. It was the biggest of the mugs, and she was even more of a caffeine fiend than he was. He smiled. He put it out on the counter for her, and pulled the slightly smaller Dean & Deluca mug down for himself.

Sometimes he wondered how much stuff from their apartment they would take if they ever moved. Did they need sixteen eggshell-thin coffee cups with matching saucers? What about the perfect window treatments with the matching pillows that Ines had so painstakingly picked out and Merrill secretly loathed? The porcelain vase and the cut crystal ice bucket and the set of good silver, all of which lived in the storage unit in the basement of their building? They never used any of it. Would Merrill even notice if one day it was all gone?

What they needed was a plan. By the time they arrived in East Hampton they would have one, he told himself. It wouldn't be over—in fact—it was all just beginning. But at least, he hoped, they'd be in it together.

# THURSDAY, 5:06 A.M.

Carter was up early. He dressed quietly in running pants and a Harvard sweatshirt and carried his sneakers into the bathroom so as not to wake Ines. As he brushed his teeth, he stroked his day-old beard. It was more silver now than black. Beneath his fingers was the wobbly neck skin of an old man. He couldn't remember when they had lost their battle with gravity, but his jowls had surrendered. He decided to shave later. It was a holiday, after all.

He padded down to the kitchen where Bacall thumped his tail against the tiles, happy that someone was awake. Carter felt the cold stone floor through his socks; the temperature had dipped into the twenties overnight. After a cup of coffee, Carter poured Bacall a bowl of kibble and went outside for a run. Snow hadn't yet fallen, but the air felt primed for it, chilled and wet. No one had been out to the house in East Hampton in more than a month, but the caretakers had wrapped the hedges in sackcloth to protect them from frost.

Running was one of Carter's greatest pleasures. He liked to follow Apaquogue Road to Georgica Beach before circling home on Lily Pond Lane. Though he had run the route countless times, the beauty of the area always improved his mood. Apaquogue was a charming street with well-kept hedges and traditional, shingled houses. An open expanse of land had been preserved just before the beach and residents enjoyed an open skyline. The colors in East Hampton were muted—olives and browns and blues—but richer somehow than the colors of Manhattan. In the autumn, the trees exploded in a symphony of crimson and burnt orange. The air felt crisper, too; a welcome change from city smog.

The turn onto Lily Pond Lane was the run's crescendo. Some of East Hampton's most moneyed residents lived on Lily Pond Lane; the homes were among the most expensive in what was already an expensive town. For the most part, they were tucked discreetly behind high hedgerows. An occasional iron gate afforded passersby a glimpse of the rolling lawns and estate homes. Carter always slowed his jog to take in the view. There were few times in life when he allowed himself to feel as though he had made it, but a jog down Lily Pond was awfully close. Even more than the Sixty-fourth Street apartment, Carter's home in East Hampton brought him endless pleasure, a sense that he had been rewarded for years of hard work.

The Darlings' home sat on the north side of Lily Pond Lane. The less prestigious side; it didn't enjoy the oceanfront views and beach access to the south. Despite the once-removedness of the shoreline, Ines had still insisted on naming the house "Beech House." She thought this was a particularly clever play on words, referring to the indigenous beech trees that graced the edges of Lily Pond Lane.

As a young man, Carter had accepted that there would always be a bigger house, a richer neighbor. Though the Darlings were a venerable New England family, several generations of irresponsibility had reduced the family fortune to nothing. Regardless, Carter's father had maintained a lavish lifestyle for them, one that had far exceeded their means. Carter had been raised as an only child in a classic six on Park Avenue. They had a nanny (Gloria), a cook (Mary), and a revolving stable of housekeepers and other help. Carter's earliest memories were from summers spent in a gabled house in Quogue, an old-guard community just down the shore from East Hampton.

"As a boy," Carter once told Paul, "I assumed that everyone spent the summer on the southern shore of Long Island. I actually thought that Christmas only happened in Palm Beach. Not that we celebrated Christmas there, but that it actually *happened* there. The year Father died, they told me he was too sick to travel to Florida. And that was what I was upset about. I thought that meant there wouldn't be any Christmas that year."

Carter was right. After his father died, everything changed.

Eleanor hung on to the Park Avenue apartment as long as she could, but eventually was forced to move to a charmless condominium on Second Avenue. The Quogue house was sold without comment. During the summers, Eleanor and Carter found themselves at the mercy of wealthier friends. July and August were a patchwork of invitations: visiting cousins in Nantucket, staying in a guest cottage in Sag Harbor, sailing in Newport with Eleanor's latest gentleman friend. Carter rarely enjoyed these seasonal jaunts. He usually slept in a back guest room, the kind with a rickety twin bed, a decoupage wastebasket, and faded floral drapes. Worse yet was when he had to share a room with the child of the house, who always resented the intrusion.

At least one weekend every summer was spent with the Salms in Southampton. Eleanor and Lydia Salm had been roommates at Vassar. Lydia had dropped out during their junior year to marry her father's business partner, who at the time was thirty-seven and according to Eleanor, "very dashing." Carter assumed something unfortunate had happened in the intervening years, because Russell Salm was extremely fat and coughed chronically as though his throat were made of phlegm. He smoked cigars by the pool and wore a ring on his pinky finger that bore the Salm family crest. The Salms had only had one child, which Carter thought was just as well.

Russell Salm Jr. was three years older than Carter and preternaturally large for his age. In the afternoons, he would invite his friends over to eat potato chips and sneak cigarettes behind the pool house. They fashioned wet towels into weapons, which, when appropriately snapped, raised flesh into red welts in an instant. At night, Carter was forced to sleep in a trundle bed that pulled out like a drawer from beneath Russell's bed.

At the end of the weekend, Mrs. Salm would pack a paper bag filled with Russell's hand-me-downs and force Carter to look through it in front of her. It was, Carter later realized, the greatest humiliation of his young life. Russell would sulk behind his mother during this ceremony, his silence occasionally pierced by a protestation that something "still fit." Once back at home, Carter would write Mrs. Salm a thank-you note on his sailboat stationery. He was careful to address it only to her and not to Russell, who he felt deserved no acknowledgment of any sort.

As much as he hated boys like Russell, Carter reserved a special type of vitriol for their mothers. More than cruelty or disdain, he hated pity. It would dog him throughout his young life. He was often cast in the role of the earnest boy from modest circumstances. While the Darlings were not poor by conventional standards, they were in the company they kept. Carter suspected that Eleanor never doubted that she belonged anywhere but among the very rich. The Darlings were people of privilege, and people of privilege was what they would remain, no matter what the cost.

Hence the cobbled-together summers, the endless rotation of weekend visits to the right places. And, of course, the schools. Carter was never once reduced to applying for scholarships. He never knew how his mother managed his tuition, but instead was left to imagine what she had cut back on to provide it. Though it was never far from his mind, he inquired about it only once, when he had been accepted by Harvard College.

Carter was admitted to Harvard's class of 1966, but without financial aid or a scholarship. About this, Eleanor said simply: "All Darling men go to Eaglebrook, and all Darling men go to Groton. But not all Darling men have the smarts to go to Harvard. I'm so very proud of you."

"Mother, can we afford this?" Carter said. He had just turned eighteen and was feeling assertive. He was, after all, now the man of the house. "If we can't, I can take a scholarship to Williams or Bowdoin. Both of them have offered, and I would be happy enough rowing crew for either."

Eleanor's face went cool and blank. "Carter," she said, her voice as smooth as a gimlet, "Harvard is something you don't turn down. You'll find your way after that, but leave the next four years to me. I won't have it any other way." Carter felt momentarily bested, but also deeply relieved.

Eleanor was right, of course. Harvard College was where Carter ought to have been, where he deserved to be all along. He was a Darling, and a hardworking one at that. Unlike his father, who had whiled away his years at Cambridge studying literature and attending parties, Carter concentrated on economics. He spent most of his time in the stacks of Widener Library, determined to graduate at the top of his class. When he socialized, he considered it a form of networking. Unlike his father, Carter chose not to join the Porcellian Club, where most of his classmates from Groton became members. Instead, he joined the Delphic Club, a gentlemanly, if slightly less selective, final club.

Even at eighteen, Carter knew the Groton boys would never be his friends. They had always kept him at an arm's length while in prep school. They accepted him out of respect for his family, but recognized, some more politely than others, that he didn't have the resources to be part of their inner circle. He didn't have the house in Palm Beach and so he wasn't invited to their New Year's parties. He couldn't fly to Gstaad for spring skiing. "To be jealous of money is uninspired," Eleanor would say with a dismissive wave of the hand. "You can only be jealous of someone who has something that you can never have. More style, for example, or wit. Money is easily earned."

One of those Groton boys was now Carter's neighbor on Lily Pond Lane. Nikos Kasper (Kas to his friends) lived directly across from the Darlings in an eleven-thousand square-foot compound, discretely, if somewhat misleadingly, named "Endicott Farms." Carter found Nikos's touted genealogical connection to the Reverend Endicott Peabody, the founder of the Groton School, dubious at best. It had long been whispered that Nikos's grandfather, to whom the family fortune was owed, was in fact a self-invented entrepreneur of Greek Orthodox descent who had grown up in a working-class community somewhere deep in the Bronx. Nikos, along with his fear-inspiring twin sister, Althea, now ran the family's multibillion-dollar real estate company. Nikos was especially proud of the group's investments in luxury properties in California and Florida, though their main business was developing low-income residential properties in Mexico. In private, Ines had christened Nikos and Althea "those glorified slumlords."

Like many real estate companies, the Kasper Group had recently taken a few public blows. Over Labor Day, the *Wall Street Journal* had run a front-page article titled "Strapped for Kas?: Kasper Group's Desperate Search for Financing." The article had precipitated a wave of negative press that had, in turn, sent the stock price into a tailspin. Privately, Nikos was hurting. Most of his net worth was tied up in the family company, and in 2007, he had made the poor decision to guarantee a highly risky development project in Mexico City personally. Rumors of bankruptcy had dogged him for years, but this time Carter knew the threat was real. Adding to the ignominy, Nikos's wife, Medora, had recently filed for separation.

Endicott Farms showed no external signs of turmoil. The window boxes brimmed with white geraniums. Carter slowed to a fast walk when he reached the edge of Nikos's property and came to a stop in front of its gates. After only five miles, his breathing was sharp and labored.

*I'm getting old*, he thought, checking the timer on his sports watch. *This is ridiculous.*

He walked up to the Kaspers' gatepost and held on to it as he stretched his quadriceps. Beyond the gate was a sweeping expanse of lawn. Even in November, the grass was as manicured as a golf-course green. The only farmlike thing about the property was a small, meticulously maintained apple orchard.

Endicott Farms wasn't so much a house as a collection of them. Nikos and Medora had purchased two eighteenth-century saltbox houses from Vermont, a barn from New Hampshire, and a stone schoolhouse from upstate New York and had, beam by beam, taken them apart and reassembled them on the parcel of land at the corner of Lily Pond Lane and Ocean Avenue. Together, the buildings formed a sprawling compound that bore little resemblance to any of the original structures. In Carter's opinion, it looked more like a boarding school than a home. There was something campuslike about Endicott Farms: It boasted an indoor squash court and an outdoor tennis court; a swimming pool and a croquet pitch; and though the main house had eight bedrooms, two stand-alone guest cottages dotted the lawn. "For the help . . . and for Medora's parents," Nikos like to joke at parties.

Carter couldn't see it from the gate, but behind the compound was a large slate terrace overlooking the ocean. Every summer, the Kaspers had a Fourth of July cocktail party on the terrace for three hundred of their closest friends. Carter and Ines always attended. Though the Kaspers threw a great many parties, this one was definitively referred to as "the Kasper Party." Ines claimed the Kasper party was one of the highlights of her summer, but Carter quietly loathed it. Though they had known each other for fifty years, Nikos still introduced Carter as "my banker." He usually threw in a complimentary tagline, but Carter resented the intonation. It seemed to imply that he should step around the bar and start mixing martinis with the rented bartenders.

At the end of the day, both men were aware of the fact that a good banker was more valuable than a good friend. If Nikos wasn't yet bankrupt, he had Carter to thank for it. Carter had been managing Nikos's money since his days at JPMorgan. At the start, their professional relationship was as uncomfortable as it had been at Harvard. It had been an unpleasant coincidence that Carter was put on the Kasper account as a junior banker at JPMorgan. At the time, the account was too big, and Carter was too junior, for him to protest the arrangement. Carter had done what he did best: swallow his pride and put his nose to the grindstone.

Long ago, Carter had accepted that he held only a guest pass to the world of the very rich, and, unlike men like Nikos, he would have to earn his keep in order to stay. But that changed when he went into business with Alain Duvalier. Alain was a great investor, but he was difficult to work with, hotheaded and always right. He liked his cars too fast and women too young, just generally a little "too too," as Ines liked to say with a roll of the eyes, for a white-glove place like JPMorgan Private Banking. He had more than one enemy in the upper echelons of senior management.

Carter moved in on him the moment he heard Alain had been passed over as head of asset management. Everyone was talking about it. Carter knew exactly how to play it. Alain had expensive tastes and a well-developed ego; he would operate best in an environment where he could be his own boss. At Delphic, Alain could have everything he wanted: an office in Geneva; a big cut of the equity; and best of all, total freedom to do business as he pleased. Carter would bring in the clients and stay out of his hair. They would make perfect partners.

Alain was expensive, but worth every penny. Among other things, he was the reason Delphic was in business with Morty Reis. Carter was never quite sure of the connection, but it had something to do with their sisters being friends. Whatever it was, Carter was grateful for it. If delivering Morty was the only thing Alain had ever done for him, it was enough. In their first five years of business, RCM knocked it out of the park. On average, the fund returned 14 percent annually, an untouchable record. The press began to call. Clients turned up on Carter's doorstep. Many of Carter's old JPMorgan clients who had originally been too risk averse to put money in a new venture came to him, hat in hand.

Nikos and Althea Kasper didn't, but they agreed to have lunch with him. They met at the Four Seasons. At the time, Carter could barely afford the lunch tab much less conceive of moving the Delphic headquarters to the fancy offices just upstairs. Carter remembered vividly how cool Nikos had been at that initial lunch. While Althea was enthusing about the fund's performance (the only thing that ever animated Althea was the prospect of more money), Nikos took a call in the lobby. When he returned to the table, he offered a tepid congratulations, as though he was talking to a sixth grader who had won the science fair. He picked at his steak tartare as though it bored him. It was half eaten when Carter paid the bill.

No matter. Carter walked away from that lunch two million dollars richer. Over the next ten years, Nikos and Althea migrated 60 percent of their combined net worth over to Delphic. They brought their father in and several friends. They invited Carter to dinners, for golf, for Fourth of July.

As Carter stood stretching at the Kasper gate, pain radiated down his left side. He couldn't identify its locus. At first he thought it was a cramp, but as he stretched, the pain rolled upward like a wave. Soon it filled his torso and he found it difficult to breath. His head spun from the lack of air and he could feel tears forming at the corners of his eyes.

*I'm having a heart attack*, he thought, and lay down in the grass by the side of the road.

He closed his eyes and felt the grass shoots pricking at the back of his neck. The ground was wet and hard. He wondered how long it would be before a car passed by. A driver would stop if he saw him like this.

A plane passed overhead. Carter wondered where Julianne was, if they had gotten her home from Aspen. He would have to call Sol and check. Ines had been merciless about Julianne the night before. Carter winced as he replayed their conversation. Ines was disarmingly direct. She said what others were thinking but dared not say (Recently: "Oh please, Althea Kasper is more than a man-eater, she's a bull-dyke lesbian"; "I didn't get to where I am by being nice."). Ines could be callous, even cruel, but she was almost never wrong.

About Julianne, Ines said: "Tell me it wasn't your first thought."

She was right. The possibility that Julianne had killed Morty had occurred to Carter right away. He had dismissed it, admonishing himself for even considering it. Julianne wasn't capable of that, and in her own way, she did seem to care for Morty. Carter wouldn't allow himself to think anything else. Still, while Carter would never say so out loud, there was a certain cold logic to it.

"And if he did kill himself, she pushed him to it," Ines had said. "Their marriage was empty. You know that as well as anybody."

Again, Ines was right.

Eventually, the pain in his side subsided and all Carter felt was the numbing cold of the air around him. When he heard the sound of car tires on gravel he popped to his feet. He brushed dirt from his leg. Thirty yards away, a car pulled out of a driveway. The driver turned to the left and disappeared down Lily Pond Lane, unaware of the man who had been, for the past ten minutes, lying by the side of the road. Charged with embarrassment, he sprinted to the house, not stopping until he had reached the safety of his own front porch.

Carter's BlackBerry was vibrating against the kitchen counter as he swung open the screen door. Bacall let out a yowl and barreled toward his knees, his nails clicking against the tiles. Carter shushed him halfheartedly and rubbed his head, just behind the ears, while he tried to scroll through his e-mails.

"Everyone is asleep, kiddo, except for you and me," he said affectionately. He loved this dog. Their loyalty to each other was absolute. Ines would never love Bacall the way Carter did; at her core, she wasn't a dog person. Bacall knew which side his bread was buttered on. His leg thumped furiously as Carter hit the exact spot behind the ear that sent him into throes of canine ecstasy.

Carter retreated to his office, allowing Bacall to follow before he shut the door behind them. Bacall nested in his tartan dog bed while Carter turned on his computer and plugged his BlackBerry into its dock. He looked at the clock: 7:30 a.m. on the dot. He had about twenty-nine minutes before Ines began banging things inexplicably in the kitchen. She hated it when he closed his office door.

When she answered the phone, he said, "Is it too early?"

She said, "Where the fuck have you been? I've been calling you." Then she chuckled, reprimanding herself. "I'm sorry," she said, her voice softened. "Forgive me. It's early."

He had intended to be cold with her. She should be expecting that; he hated it when she called him repeatedly. And yesterday, a three-ring circus of a day. If she had given it twenty seconds of consideration, she would have come up with a hundred reasons not to call. He would be with Ines. He would be with his kids. He would be driving to East Hampton. He would be frantically wrapping up preholiday business. He would be fielding calls from Sol, the media, portfolio managers, Merrill, Lily, Ines, clients, clients' wives, his secretary, Sol's secretary, Morty's secretary. He would be calling emergency meetings and scheduling flights and setting up wire transfers. He would be alone in the bathroom, shedding private tears for his friend.

But then he had heard her voice, and his anger had lifted like fog. She always did that to him, which is why he kept going back to her for more.

"How are you?" she said. She was the first person who asked and meant it. Everyone else, including his wife, meant: "How is the fund?"

"Well, not good. I don't begin to know how to answer that question. How are you?"

She said, "I'm a fucking mess. But that's obvious. The hardest part of this is knowing I can't be with you."

"I know. I hate that, too."

"Look, let's just avoid platitudes. I know you're probably at a loss here, too, but what do we do?"

Carter leaned back in his chair and inhaled deeply. Eyes closed, he stopped breathing; the world went pleasantly blank. For a moment, he wondered if he could will himself dead.

Then Bacall let out a yowl and Carter's eyes opened. *No,* he thought, *still here. Just barely.*

"We still don't know why he killed himself," he said. "All I can think is why the fuck would he do this to me? Not to himself, but to me. I know. I'm a selfish bastard."

"Everyone's a selfish bastard. And God forgive me for saying this, but Morty's the most selfish bastard of all. It's a very selfish thing to do, suicide."

Suddenly, Carter realized he was angry. He hadn't been able to identify it before, but the furious surge of energy that had been coursing through his body since yesterday was anger. Not at the situation, but at Morty himself. How could Morty have done this? Morty never made a move without a cost-benefit analysis. He would have precisely calculated the collateral damage of this decision. To Julianne, to Carter and Alain, to countless others whom Carter couldn't even begin to name. He would have weighed it against whatever demons were driving him. And then Carter saw it: Morty was on one scale; everyone else was on the other. He had decided in favor of himself. *Selfish fucking bastard. I was your friend.*

He sat up, feeling impatient with the conversation. "Look," he said, "I feel like the world's come down around my ears. I know it has for you, too, but I'm just going to have to take things minute to minute, and make decisions one at a time so that I don't do anything stupid. It's going to be intense for a while. For how long? I don't know. Let's say the foreseeable future. And I don't think it's smart for us to talk during this period. Much less be together, which is out of the question."

He stopped and took a deep breath. There was a quiet pause. His words had tumbled out, emotional, uncontrolled. She had this effect on him. He spoke more freely to her than to anyone else. Some days this felt amazing. He loved the release, the heady rush of being with her. Now, any interaction with her seemed dangerously stupid.

"What does Ines know?" she said. She sounded matter-of-fact.

"Ines knows nothing. Well, I don't know; I think she has her suspicions. But she knows nothing from me. And it'll stay that way. I need her support right now, to be frank. Morty just turned a big spotlight onto the fund and onto me. I already have everyone from the *Wall Street Journal* to the attorney general's office knocking on my door and it's fucking Thanksgiving. I can't afford to be sloppy."

"She may be more supportive if you're honest with her. I agree it's best not to tell her now. If she starts getting angry and asking questions, you may just want to come clean with her. She's a rational woman."

As ever, she was gracious, poised. Despite the situation, he was aroused.

"Has the press called you?" he said.

"Yes. But I haven't spoken to anyone. Screw them. I'll make a statement when I'm ready."

"Will you talk to Sol before you do that? I mean, just let him help you manage things. He knows how to deal with public attention."

"I know. I'm not stupid. But right now there's no need for me to say anything about it, so I think my best strategy is to just stay quiet."

"You're right. I'm being paranoid. I'm sorry. I want to be with you so badly. I know that's wrong, but I can't help it."

She didn't respond right away. He wondered where she was. When they spoke, she was always on the cell phone so he never really knew. It was hard not to be able to picture her. He hated thinking that she would be spending Thanksgiving alone. The thought of it hurt him so much that he didn't dare to ask. *I'm a selfish bastard*, he thought.

"I don't know," she said, finally. "I only know that what's moral is what you feel good after and what's immoral is what you feel bad after."

He smiled. "Fitzgerald?"

"Hemingway, actually."

"Clever girl," he said. "Don't ever let anyone underestimate you."

"I never do."

"Clever, beautiful girl."

"I have to go, Carter."

"I know. I love you," he said and hung up. It was, he thought, one of the only true things he had said in as long as he could remember. It had been true for years. He looked over at Bacall, who was asleep on his bed. Above him, an antique nautical clock ticked away with maritime efficiency. The house was waking and the children would begin to arrive soon.

The next call he made was to Sol.

# THURSDAY, 7:50 A.M.

She hung up the phone and let her forehead drop into her palm. *Please don't ring again,* she thought.

For a few minutes, it didn't. The office was disarmingly quiet. She sat, eyes closed, face still, for as long as she could. Beneath the desk, her feet lay limp, neatly crossed at the ankles. She was wearing her old moccasins, the camel-colored ones that were scuffed around the heels. They were suede, soft as socks, the soles peeling at the edges. She only wore them with jeans, to walk the dogs in the morning or to pick up coffee at the deli, never to the office.

This morning, she had been too overwhelmed to change. What did it matter anyway? No one else would be in. It was Thanksgiving. The bleary-eyed security guard had seemed surprised to see her. He had reluctantly set down his coffee to turn on the bag scanner. He gave her a look that read *You're the reason I'm working on Thanksgiving.* Jane gave him a brisk nod, and for a second felt her eyes prick with tears from the cold.

Upstairs, the whole floor was dark. The printers hummed, still asleep. When she switched on the overhead fluorescents, they flickered for a few seconds, then filled the hallway with the a buzzing sound and threw off a dingy yellow light.

Her office was just as she'd left it, stacks of papers overwhelming the plastic in-box at the left-hand corner of her desk, Post-it notes stuck haphazardly to the frame of her computer screen. Each one insisted that she do something: Call someone back, review the division budgets, buy the special dog food the vet had recommended. She couldn't face them. She sat with her head cradled in one hand, cell phone still in the other, as though one small movement would break the silence and the office would spring back to life again. The only thing moving was her pounding, adrenalized, overcaffeinated heart.

When the phone rang again, a small wash of relief passed through her.

The only thing worse than being in the office on Thanksgiving was being in the office with nothing to do. She was used to the tightrope walk of work. One foot in front of the other; deliberate, measured movements under stress. All she had to do was not look down. Because if she did, she would see the chasm beneath her, empty and lonely, threatening to swallow her whole. Best not to stop moving.

"This is a helluva situation," the voice barked when she answered.

"Happy Thanksgiving to you, too, Ellis." she said.

"Give me a break, Jane. Happy Thanksgiving."

Ellis Stuart. Ellis was Jane's counterpart in D.C. Technically, he was Jane's superior, but most days, they worked side by side. The power balance between them, always tender, was more delicate now than ever. In January, a new SEC head would be named, and Jane was the frontrunner. Ellis was slated to retire. Because this made him impartial, Ellis had been tapped to advise the president-elect on the nomination.

This was Ellis's swan song. Ellis had spent his entire career at the SEC, law school to retirement, "cradle to grave," as he liked to say. While he had been grandfathered into a senior position, Ellis had been, for years, discounted by his colleagues as a dinosaur. The longer he stayed, the more restless the office had become with him. The junior attorneys greeted him like day-old bread, not palatable but not quite appropriate to chuck altogether. He had never really fully grasped e-mail and sent out missives with spelling errors or in all caps. He made the occasional off-color joke. And he hadn't run his own cases in years, which put him out of touch with the daily ins and outs of investigation and trial. At one time, Ellis had been a rising star, hungry and sharp, with the winningest record of any trial attorney at the SEC. But those days were long gone. They were remembered only dimly by the most senior attorneys, paid the same due as the playing victories of a college quarterback.

Now in his last months, Ellis found himself with the ear of the president-elect and the ability to shape the agency's future. Anyone with an outside chance of a promotion kowtowed to him, and the ones who didn't acknowledged him with a dutiful respect. The change in tenor wasn't lost on Ellis. He relished it. He talked louder, demanded answers sooner, made his presence known in meetings. He walked the halls with an infused swagger. Especially with Jane, Ellis took on a dictatorial tone. He took every opportunity to remind her that he was evaluating her, and that he would be up until the day the new chairman was announced. Nothing was certain.

Recently, Ellis had become the king of the status update. "Calling to check in on the status," he would say, or more irritatingly, "Just a friendly status call!"

"I'm trying to manage it as best I can," she said. "What can I tell you?"

"Tell me what's going on. Update me."

Jane took a deep breath and fought the urge to smash the receiver against the side of the desk.

She said, "Ellis, it's 8:30 a.m. and it's Thanksgiving."

"You told me to call you. You left me a message last night. Didn't you?"

Jane sighed. She had called him, but she hadn't told him to call her back. It was a preemptory strike voice mail, apprising him of the situation with just enough color so that he would feel looped in. She had hoped this would be enough to satiate him, at least through the weekend.

He wasn't going to let her off that easy.

"All right," she said. "Here's what we know. We believe that Reis was running some kind of Ponzi scheme. We're not sure how long it's been going on, if RCM was ever a legitimate operation. We looked into it briefly in 2006, but nothing came of that. David Levin began an informal investigation a few months ago, but it wasn't well handled. Everyone in our group was focused on the mutual-fund sweep and the ball got dropped. So now, yes, it's a situation." She was repeating what she had said in the voice mail, but she would be doing a lot of that over the coming days. Everyone was going to want to hear her version of the RCM investigation: the press, the attorney general's office, her superiors, her staffers, her friends. If she had to think every time she told it, it would exhaust her. She would tell it again and again until the words themselves lost their meaning. Might as well get it down pat now.

"When you say the ball got dropped, by whom? By Levin?"

"I don't think David handled the situation appropriately, no," she said carefully. "He didn't convey the urgency of this investigation, to me at least. So I thought it was best to keep him staffed on the mutual-fund sweep. What he was doing on his own time with respect to RCM was outside of marching orders, and again, it wasn't properly elevated to senior management." She hoped this came across as contrite but unapologetic.

"Would he say he dropped the ball?"

"What's that?"

"David Levin. If I asked him, would he say he dropped the ball?"

Jane squeezed her eyes shut. Her head hurt. Every time she pictured Ellis, he still had that ridiculous white mustache, even though he had shaved it off over a year ago. There was a part of her that pitied him. Their paths had crossed in the sky for a brief moment, before her star continued on its meteoric ascent upward and his slipped off into cosmic obscurity. He reminded Jane of a supernova, the brief and overwhelming burst of radiation that occurs shortly before the star itself fades to black.

Still, his support was crucial to her promotion, and they both knew it. For the moment, she was at his mercy.

"I don't know what he'd say. I don't know why he didn't push harder. I got the sense that he was a little territorial about the investigation. It's not appropriate, but it happens, particularly with career-making cases like this one. He also may have simply misgauged the magnitude of it. He's got a lot on his plate right now."

"Seems like you guys are stretched pretty thin."

"We are," she said curtly. "We're managing it as best we can."

Ellis grunted. She heard what she thought was his feet swinging up onto the desk. She had seen him sitting like that before, feet on his desk, headset on, hands folded behind his head—like a telemarketer.

"It just seems to me," he said, "that we're really going to look like assholes if we had someone on the case and it got lost in some sort of administrative black hole."

She knew where this was going.

Her eyes bounced off the surfaces of her office: the industrial black shelves lined with case binders; the dismal putty-colored rug; the depressed-looking ficus in a wicker basket in the corner. Her Harvard Law School diploma hung slightly off-kilter, flanked on either side by her Harvard College diploma and a photograph of a young, dewy-eyed Jane with Justice O'Connor, for whom she had clerked in 1986. The tops of the frames were dusty, like everything else in the office. Her desktop hummed in front of her. Outlook was actively collecting unread e-mails. The light on her second line had gone on twice, pushed to voice mail. Jane's standard breakfast—a large black coffee and a cheese Danish from the twenty-four-hour deli—was churning angrily in her stomach.

"I know you're swamped up there," Ellis offered. "I'm not saying anything's your *fault*. I'm just saying how it *looks*."

"You're saying it looks like my fault."

Ellis made a lip-sputtering noise, like a car exhaust. "It looks like *someone's* fault. I just think we have to be clear on what happened before the press comes knocking."

"The press is already knocking. A statement doesn't need to be made until Monday, I don't think. I thought that was the consensus. I'll have one prepared by the weekend."

"That's fine. I just think—I think everyone's going to be looking for someone to blame. I think very highly of you Jane, always have. I'd hate to see you take the fall for something like this."

"Why don't you just say what you're going to say, Ellis?" Jane snapped. The little hairs on her arms stood at attention.

"Whoa there, Jane. I'm just saying protect yourself. What you do over the next few days—what you say and what you do in response to this situation—is gonna matter. You've got a lot of people who would like to see you succeed here. We need a real leader. Someone who's going to instill real confidence in the Commission. I think you'd be great. But you've got to make it very clear that what happened with the RCM investigation wasn't your fault."

---

After she hung up the phone, Jane went to the bathroom and let the cold water run over her wrists. She stood with her eyes closed, hands turned upward, the delicate blue veins exposed beneath the frigid tap.

*Get ahold of yourself,* she thought.

She was taking this David Levin business harder than she had thought. She had never much liked David. He was dating a woman in the office, and this bothered her. Admittedly, they were discreet about it, but it was still a distraction, for them and for everyone else in the office. Also, he dressed too casually. Jane had come across him wandering the hallways in jeans or scuffed Converse sneakers, not just on weekends but in the middle of the workweek. He never looked sheepish about it. Jane felt he was too old to be getting a lecture on either dating in the workplace or appropriate office attire. He was smart enough, she thought, to pick up on her tacit disapproval.

She thought about his Converse sneakers as the chill of the water began to set in. She thought about his relationship with Alexa Mason, and how she had come across them holding hands at a movie theater on the Upper West Side. It had been embarrassing and awkward, particularly for Jane because she was alone.

Then she thought, *This is neither here nor there. David is a good lawyer, one of our best.*

*You don't need to like or dislike him to fire him.*

*You need to fire him because it has to be done.*

She had sacrificed so much already for her career. Years of perfect grades, of ninety-hour workweeks, of missed dates, of missed dinners. Years spent fielding questions about when she was going to get married and have kids. Worse still, the years after when the questions stopped because the answer was always the same. She had earned the position of chairman. Finally, it was right there for the taking. Whatever had to be done now, so be it.

David Levin would do the same, she thought, if the positions were reversed. Any man would. David Levin would sell her down the river without a second's hesitation if it meant he could save himself.

She imagined he would try to, if he hadn't already. But it was too late for him.

She turned off the tap. Flicking the drops from her wrists, she pushed back her shoulders and stood tall. She caught her reflection in the bathroom mirror. Her black hair came to a practical, blunt edge beneath her ears. Her cheekbones, once elegant in their definition, now read as gaunt.

*You've earned this,* she said to herself.

She forced a smile in the mirror and thought about the call she would get from the president when it was all decided.

Her nerves steeled, she went back to her office to fire David Levin.

# THURSDAY, 9:30 A.M.

"What are you thinking about?" Merrill asked as she closed the trunk of the car. It made a satisfying *thunk*, the sound of a weekend away in the country. She looked up at Paul inquisitively, her hands stuffed into the pockets of her parka. The garage was freezing, almost the same temperature as outside.

He had let her load the bags without really helping. That was unlike him. "I'm sorry," he said, flustered. He gestured at the bags in the back of the car. "I got distracted. The coffee hasn't sunk in yet."

She smiled, a half-watt smile. She was tired, too. "That's okay. Want me to drive?"

"No," he said, and opened the passenger side door for her. "Let's go. I'm fine."

As he slid into the driver's seat, he noticed that his left hand was shaking. He adjusted the rearview mirror, checking it twice as he always did before he pulled out of the garage and onto the street. "So we need to talk about something," he said, flicking on the blinker. He turned onto Third Avenue. The street was wide and empty. "Something's happening with your dad's business."

Merrill had already settled in on the passenger side, her feet folded beneath her, Indian-style, on the seat. She had been fidgeting with the radio dial, but she stopped. King sensed the shift in tone and perked up, his ears alert.

"Come here, sweetheart," she said, and scooped the dog out from the backseat and onto her lap.

Paul took a deep breath. "I found out yesterday that Morty was under investigation by the SEC. He was about to be indicted when he died. It looks like all of us—all of the officers, anyway—are under investigation."

Merrill's eyes widened slightly. She reached out and put her hand on top of his, her fingers finding their way, familiarly, into the grooves between his.

"Okay. Tell me everything."

As he talked, the city unfolded like a paper doll against the white winter sky. They drove north past Ninety-sixth Street, the doorman buildings turning into bodegas and gas stations, then housing projects. They came to a full stop at the light. Three teenage boys passed in front of the car and Paul fell quiet. There had been stories recently about all the carjackings and muggings at the edges of the city. Crime was on the rise. One of the boys held a basketball tucked beneath his arm. He was the biggest of the three. He made eye contact with Paul through the windshield, and he dragged his hand along the front of their car. It lasted a second, but Merrill silently pulled her hand away from Paul's knee to check the lock on the car door.

When the light turned green, Paul gunned the engine and caught the lights all the way to the FDR Drive. Once they were moving, Paul picked up where he had left off, speaking quickly, telling Merrill about the meeting with Alexa, and then the call with David Levin. Though he felt the absence of her hand he knew he had to keep going if he was going to get through everything without completely losing it. They both forgot about the boy. Eventually, the sound beneath the tires changed to a higher pitch as the car transitioned from the cement highway to the bridge, suspended above the river.

---

They passed the sign for Long Island. Usually, it promised a weekend at the beach or apple picking or playing golf on a crisp Sunday morning. Paul spoke for what felt like a very long time, and Merrill listened. He spoke quietly and efficiently, trying not to editorialize. She was a lawyer, after all. She would want only the facts. Still, when it came to his conversations with David Levin, Paul faltered. He wanted to explain his actions away.

"I wasn't trying to lie to him," he said, chewing hard on his lower lip. "I just wanted him to stop asking questions. Not because I thought there was something to hide. We were all just so busy . . ." His voice trailed off.

Merrill covered her mouth with her hand and began to cry. King put his paws up on her shoulders and tried to lick the tears from her cheeks.

"Stop it, King," she said. Her voice cracked. She pushed the dog to the backseat of the car with a firm hand. "Stop it."

She released the seat belt and drew her feet up beneath her. Her shoes were on the floor in front of her and they clunked together as the car hit a pothole.

"Ask me anything," he said. "Please."

"You saw Alexa yesterday and didn't tell me about it." She coughed fiercely.

"I know. I know that's complicated. But she's trying to help." Paul reached for her hand but couldn't find it.

"Help who?" Merrill said. Her voice was loud and Paul flinched. King barked; he hated it when they fought. "Help you? She comes to you with this insider trading bullshit, or whatever it is, which she doesn't even know for sure, by the way, because she's not the one running the fucking investigation, and tells you what? That my dad's a bad guy and you should go be an informant for the SEC? That *they're* going to save you? And you think she's helping you?"

King paced frenetically in the backseat. Paul could hear the sound of his paws against the leather as he tried to make the jump by himself.

Merrill ignored the dog and he began to bark. For a minute, Paul thought that he ought to pull over and stop. Talking in the car now seemed like a very bad idea. He couldn't even look her straight in the eye, talking this way. They had another hour before they reached East Hampton. But the traffic was running by on the right and there wasn't much of a shoulder. The only option was to keep driving, straight ahead, as fast as he could.

"I know it's a lot to take in," he said, trying to stay calm. "It's a lot for me, too."

"Yeah, it's a lot." Merrill paused and stared out the window. She grew quiet, but tears still flowed down her cheeks. She wiped them away and made a snuffling sound. Fumbling in her purse she said, "Damn it, I don't have any tissues left. Okay, forget what Alexa told you. Do you have any reason to think Morty was doing something wrong?"

Paul hesitated. "It doesn't make any sense. The performance is statistically perfect. And there are other things, undeniable stuff that doesn't add up. They won't let us look at their accounts online, for example. They send trade confirmations by mail, these hard-copy printouts that could be anything."

"What do you mean, hard-copy printouts?"

"Just lists of what they traded. But it comes straight from them. And they don't have an outside broker, so there is no way to verify their trades with an outside party's books. Basically, we just rely entirely on the information they provide, which isn't much."

"I've never heard of that."

"I haven't either. No one else does it. Frankly, I don't think we'd let anyone else get away with it, but RCM has always had a sort of favored status at Delphic."

"So you have no idea what they're trading, really, how they're doing it, or with whom."

"It seems that way."

She closed her eyes and shook her head. "The lawyer in me really hates hearing this kind of stuff."

"Trust me, the lawyer in me isn't thrilled, either. I mean, Christ. It's our job to run diligence on these funds before we invest our clients' money in them. We should know everything about every fund we're invested in."

Paul hated to talk about it, but Merrill seemed calmer now that they were getting down to brass tacks, and that encouraged him. She had always been coolheaded in a crisis, always focusing on what logically could be solved, never letting her emotions run away with her. In law school, Paul was sure she'd make a great lawyer. She would make partner one day, if that was what she wanted.

"You said the performance was statistically perfect? What does that mean?"

Paul pointed to the backseat without taking his eyes of the road. "Get those folders back there. Open the top one—it shows the performance. You'll see what I'm saying. It's a perfect curve."

The car fell silent. The exits were growing farther and farther apart. They had passed the suburbs, Glen Cove and Jericho and Syosset and Huntington, strung together as if on a low-slung clothesline, the local traffic thinning out on the highway. They were close to Exit 70, where they usually got gas and sodas at the 7-Eleven. Paul kept driving, his knuckles white on the wheel.

Merrill studied the folders' contents intently, the crease of her brow fixed. Paul resisted the impulse to ask questions. All he could hear was the undulating *chunkachunkchunk* of the highway's pavement beneath the car, and the quiet hum of the radiator.

Finally, she glanced up and said, "It's not insider trading. Is it."

*Smart girl,* he thought. "I don't think so."

"Right. Inside information would enhance their performance, but there would still be variability in the results. No one earns the same amount every single quarter." She shook her head, thinking of Elsa Gerard. "I just don't understand how they did it."

"I don't think they did. It's an illusion. Don't you see? It has to be. They weren't investing the money at all. And I think I have a way to prove it.

The SEC hasn't quite connected the dots, but they don't have access to all the information that I do."

"You think it's a Ponzi scheme?"

"I know it sounds insane. It's a multibillion-dollar fund. It's fraud on such a massive scale, it seems inconceivable. That's what I kept thinking, too, all day yesterday."

"What about the trade confirmations? I mean, you said Alain has drawers of them. They just made them up? That's crazy."

"Look in the second folder. There's one trade confirmation, at the very back. Just pull it out. Do you see it?"

"Yes, here. Okay. I've never seen one of these. So I don't know what I'm looking at. It's just a list of trades . . . oh! March twenty-first. My birthday."

"Right, your birthday, last spring. It was Good Friday. Remember? We went to the inn in Connecticut for a long weekend to celebrate. And we took the day off because the markets were closed, so we figured it would be slow; I remember it exactly. I was still at Howary. We left on Friday morning, I'm sure of it."

"Right, so—" she started. Then it clicked. "Oh, my God. You're right. The market was closed."

"Right. So there was no way these trades could have happened that day."

"Do you think it's a mistake? It got misdated, or something?"

"Do you think so?"

Merrill paused. "No," she said. "No, I'm starting to think I don't."

They were quiet for a minute. When she spoke again, her voice faltered. "They think Dad knew. Or that he was involved, somehow, in all of this."

"I think they'll try to say that, yes. They'll say that about me, too."

"Do you think he knew? Dad, I mean. Alain probably had to."

"No, I don't." Paul said. He was momentarily grateful that he could answer that question honestly.

He had thought about it, of course. Carter and Morty had been so close, and worked together for so many years, that part of him said, *How could he not know?* But Paul knew Carter. He had spent his life providing for his family. The scheme Morty had been running was so incalculably perilous that no rational investor would undertake it. The risk simply outweighed the return. Why would Carter spend a lifetime building on such foundationless ground? It didn't make any sense.

"Your dad's a salesman, Merrill. He hasn't been involved with the investment side of the business for a long time. It was Alain who should have seen it. To be frank, I think Alain had to have seen it. The only thing your dad's guilty of is placing his trust in the wrong people."

"He doesn't have it in him. Did you tell them that? Dad's so ethical. He works now because he enjoys it, not because he has to. He'd never get involved in something like that."

"I know. But it's possible they won't see it that way. Or maybe it doesn't matter. The fact is that if there was any kind of misconduct at RCM, Delphic should have seen it. That's our duty to our clients. If it's a Ponzi scheme, we're talking millions of dollars that we've lost, of other people's money." As he said it, Paul's jaw clenched reflexively. "Hundreds of millions. Fuck."

"And if you cooperate with them, what happens then?" Merrill's jaw was set at a hard angle. She was asking a question, he knew, not condoning an option.

"I'm not sure. I think it means I bring them internal files—memos, e-mails, voice mails. That sort of thing. To help them build the case against RCM, but also against Alain and other members of the Delphic team, for diligence failure." Paul paused, momentarily weighing how she would respond to the concept of a wire. No good would come of telling her, he decided. He wasn't supposed to, anyway. Levin had warned him against it; Merrill might tell her father in an effort to protect him.

It was the part of the deal with which Paul was most uncomfortable. Turning over e-mails and documents was passive cooperation. But wearing a wire felt like an act of disloyalty. There was something insidious about it, like an inside job at a bank robbery. Paul wasn't sure he had it in him, even with someone like Alain, who, he was certain, had betrayed the rest of the firm. There was also the alarming possibility that someone other than Alain could be drawn into this unwittingly. An offhand comment on tape, taken out of context, could be deadly. "If they have nothing to hide, they have nothing to hide," Levin said. But they both knew it was more complicated than that.

"It's possible they'll pursue criminal charges, too. They want to."

Her face crinkled up like a used tissue. "For *what*?" she wailed. "How can this be happening to us?"

"I don't know, Mer. I really don't."

"You can't cooperate with them. You can't. They'll use whatever you give them against Dad. They're going after him, don't you see that? It's him they want."

His heart softened the second he felt her small hand wrap itself around his. She pulled it off the wheel and kissed it, soft lips pressed hard against the inside of his palm. "You have to fight it," she said, her voice hard and resolute. "You can't help them. We have to fight this as a family. If you give them anything, it will destroy us."

He knew she was right. If he cooperated, it would destroy the Darlings. That was certain. The question, horrible and unclear, was what would happen if he didn't.

# THURSDAY, 9:57 A.M.

There were days when Duncan was close, *this close*, to calling his broker friend at Sotheby's and saying, "That's it, I've had it. Put the apartment on the market and find me a little cottage in Connecticut where I can have some peace." Lately, even small things triggered the impulse: a nauseating cab ride, a fourteen-dollar martini. The things that once infused him with energy now wearied him. The billboards around his office were too bright and the talk in restaurants was too loud. Fifth Avenue was too packed with holiday tourists from Iowa. And since last summer, negative economic news had saturated the city. Friends were losing jobs, restaurants were closing, and everything, *everything* was on sale.

For twenty-seven years, Duncan had been fiercely loyal to this 22.96-square-mile cement block of an island. To his London and L.A. and even Brooklyn friends, he swore countless times that he would leave Manhattan only feet first, in a pine box. But lately he couldn't shake the sensation that his cement island was sinking slowly beneath him.

He had felt worse than usual since Monday, when he had awoken with a rush of foreboding and it dawned on him that Thanksgiving was upon him. He hadn't done a damn thing about it, either, probably because on some subconscious level, he had been hoping that it simply wouldn't happen. Of course, that was childish and irresponsible, and now it was here.

He called Marcus because he didn't know what else to do. Duncan had been doing that a lot lately, calling Marcus, about small daily details like seating arrangements or whether he ought to buy an iPhone. Marcus was currently his most stable friend. This was, to some extent, by default; historically speaking, Duncan's most stable friend was Daniel. But Daniel and his wife Marcia had both been laid off in the past six months, and Marcia had gotten herself pregnant by accident sometime in July. So Duncan felt that, at least for the time being, it was probably best to lean on Marcus instead.

"You sound like Chicken Little, Duncan," Marcus shouted over the roar of a contractor's drill. Duncan could see him standing in the middle of his Tribeca loft, BlackBerry pressed to one ear, hand clamped over the other so he could make out what Duncan was saying. "Even your column is starting to come off as vaguely alarmist. If I didn't know better I'd say you sounded like a fucking bankruptcy attorney."

"We should all be so lucky," Duncan muttered back. He was walking to work because he had promised himself that he would only take cabs if he was running late or if the weather was inclement.

"What's that?" Marcus shouted. "Sorry, my contractors are finishing up the bathroom renovation. We're two weeks behind already. What a nightmare renovation is, you know?"

"No, I don't."

"I can't hear you."

"Nothing."

The drill stopped. Marcus said, "Look, don't worry for one second about Thanksgiving. Just order up some stuff from Citarella, Pieter and I will take care of the wine, and Leonard is a pastry chef for chrissake so I'll call him and make sure that he knows he's in charge of the desserts. We'll all come over early and help you set the table. Okay? It's going to be simple, I promise. Just like Mom used to do, except with only very well-dressed men."

"Well dressed, yes. Thanksgiving in Chelsea." On the corner of

Twenty-third and Eighth a twentysomething couple stood wrapped in an embrace that seemed excessive for 10 a.m. One's mouth enveloping the other's until the light changed. Duncan glared at them and then looked away, feeling a bad taste on his tongue, a cocktail of acrimony and loneliness. "I want Marcia and Daniel to come," he said. "Did you speak to them?"

"They may have to go upstate to be with Daniel's family, love."

Duncan sighed. He had no idea why it embarrassed him suddenly that all his friends were gay. "I just don't want my niece to be the only woman at the table. I don't want it to be awkward for her."

"She knows you're gay, Duncan. This isn't *La Cage Aux Folles*."

"I know she knows I'm gay."

"Then why do you care if she's the only woman? She won't care. We'll give her lots of undivided attention."

"I know. I've been dying for you and Pieter to meet her. She's adorable, you'll see. Nothing like her crazy mother."

"Her mother is your sister."

"Right. Now don't you feel sorry for her?"

"Is she seeing anyone?"

"I don't know. I think she might have just broken up with someone; she seemed down when I spoke to her. Sanders are all doomed to spinsterhood."

"Stop missing Henry."

"I can't help it."

"We're going to have fun on Thursday. Pieter and I will be over around eleven, booze in hand."

"Have you spoken to him?"

"Who, Pieter? Or Henry? No, of course not. I hope you haven't, either."

"No. I don't even know where he's living."

"Better that way. I'm hanging up now. Go call Citarella and order a turkey."

Thursday morning, 9:57 a.m., right on time. *Thank God*, Duncan thought, when he was interrupted from reading the morning paper by the insistent blare of the service entrance buzzer. As hard as holidays were in Manhattan, at least everything could be catered. He was still in his fluffy house shoes and had barely lifted a finger except to set the coffee to brew.

At one time in his life, Duncan had been a decent cook. He had gone through an entertaining phase in his late thirties, and found it was far less expensive to cook than to continue to order in. He had signed himself up for Fine Cooking I at the Institute of Culinary Education on Twenty-third Street. He enjoyed it so much that he briefly considered enrolling in one of their degree programs. Instead, he satisfied himself by taking as many weekend and night courses as he could: Essentials of Tuscan Cooking, Knife Skills I and II, French Bistro Fare, the Art of Artisanal Bread Baking. It was in the latter class that he had met Leonard, a pastry chef and instructor at the ICE, and it was Leonard who introduced him to Henry.

Henry was an investment banker at Morgan Stanley. He was from an old money family and had gone to Exeter and Princeton. He was pale and thin and wore bespoke suits and little round glasses. His main interests were the foreign currency market and the slightly obscure sport of court tennis. In short, not at all Duncan's type. Their first date had gone badly. Henry was twenty minutes late and kept checking his BlackBerry, and Duncan was recovering from an allergic reaction that had caused his cheeks to swell up like balloons. They had parted ways after a quick dinner and no dessert. Duncan had called Leonard on his way to the nearest subway station to complain about his swelling, and to make it clear that while he had no interest in seeing Henry again, Leonard should at least let Henry know that Duncan had been suffering from an allergic reaction and was, in fact, a very handsome man.

"I'll tell him, but why on earth do you care," Leonard replied. "You said you weren't interested. You're not in the same circles. You'll probably never see him again."

Three weeks later, Duncan and Henry ran into each other while both were reaching for fig jam at Murray's Cheeses on Bleecker Street. After a few minutes of slightly stilted chatting, they discovered that they were both headed to the same dinner party and had both been given the task of bringing something other than wine. The coincidence catalytically melted the ice between them. All of a sudden the mood was warm and slightly flirtatious, and they decided to split the cost of manchego and fig jam and Marcona almonds. Henry noticed how attractive Duncan was when not swollen, and Duncan thought that Henry wasn't nearly as uptight as he originally supposed.

A year later, they traded Duncan's one bedroom in London Terrace Gardens for a two bedroom directly upstairs. Duncan became the managing editor of *Press* and Henry was promoted to managing director at Morgan Stanley. They rented a house in Sag Harbor for the month of August; they adopted two Jack Russell terriers and named them Jack and Russell; they sent Christmas cards from the "Sander-Smith Family." Over the years, they took several classes at the Institute of Culinary Education (Sushi for Couples, Sunday Night Suppers, Cheese and Wine Pairings) and went on a Tuscan cooking tour for Duncan's forty-fifth birthday. Then, just after Duncan's forty-seventh birthday, Henry moved to London, alone.

This was Duncan's third Thanksgiving without Henry, but it was his first without *anyone.* After Henry left, there was a parade of progressively younger men, each more attractive and less interesting than the last. No one was a substitute for Henry, and indeed, Duncan didn't intend for any of them to be. They kept Duncan treading water at a time when his friends became concerned he might allow himself to drown in his own misery. And for a long time, that was enough.

Duncan learned quickly that there was no shortage of young writers and artists and designers who salivated at the opportunity to hang off the arm of *Press's* managing editor. He could exchange them one for the next, or play around with more than one of them at a time, and no matter how poorly he behaved, he never seemed to suffer any real consequences because, he knew, they were using him just as much as he was using them.

He found these relationships to be not altogether dissimilar to cocaine, his youthful vice of choice. He felt exhilarated and powerful at first, then paranoid, and eventually nauseatingly empty. And so, as he had with cocaine, he eventually quit cold turkey.

As he laid out seven places at the table, Duncan recalled the toast he had given the previous May, at his fiftieth birthday party: "One is never alone if one is among friends." At the time, he more or less believed that statement to be true. There had been fifty guests at his fiftieth birthday (there was an elegant synchronicity to this, he felt) and they had all raised a glass and nodded, smiling, when he made this declaration. He had rented out Le Bilboquet for the occasion, a tiny French bistro on the Upper East Side. The space could barely contain all of his guests. They sat nestled shoulder to shoulder, neighbors' forearms grazing against one another in pleasant intimacy, and the room glowed from the company and the wine. Duncan went to bed that night thinking the evening a great success.

In the morning, he had woken up alone and sorted through the photographs and felt profoundly depressed. It dawned on him that nearly all the guests had been work colleagues, if not people with whom he worked directly, people whose professional lives were entwined in some way with his. Duncan's business, of course, was knowing people. He knew socialites and fashion designers and social entrepreneurs and politicians. Great dinner company. But while they would come to his birthday party and sometimes invite him to theirs, it was clear in the bright, hungover light of Sunday morning that almost none of these people were really his friends.

Daniel and Marcia, of course, were dearly loyal, though now that she was pregnant (finally, at forty-one), and he had lost his job (shockingly, at forty-six) they had slipped quietly away into connubial isolation. There was Marcus, his roommate from Duke, and Marcus's longtime partner Pieter; constants, both. And Leonard, of course, who had squarely taken Duncan's side when Henry left, was the sort of friend who would come bail him out of jail at 4 a.m. without asking questions. Duncan spoke to his mother once a year on Christmas, and to his sister as infrequently as possible. He was unaware of any cousins, aunts, uncles, though he suspected there were a few floating around down in North Carolina. His father, not unfortunately, was dead.

Duncan had never much liked children. In fact, they made him nervous. Any paternal instinct was quickly squelched by his fastidious distaste for mess, and his skittishness around random, unpredictable movements. Anxiety had been a lifelong problem for Duncan, and he found that he was most comfortable in pristine, light-colored environments. His home, much like his office, was appointed primarily in beige. The furniture was minimal—clean lined and sharp edged—and the windows opened to a glorious terrace overlooking the Hudson River. Decidedly not childproof.

On the best days, light poured into his apartment and music was kept to a quiet, soothing minimum, Nina Simone, perhaps, or Ella Fitzgerald. Anyone who had ever lived with Duncan, or who had been a guest in his home, was required to remove his shoes at the door, to speak quietly, to return books to their given spot on the shelf. The dogs were notably well behaved. Henry had taken them with him, of course, along with the Barcelona chairs, the Frank Stella lithograph, and worst of all, the Le Creuset six-piece cookware set they had bought together at the conclusion of their culinary adventure in Italy.

People with children were rarely, if ever, invited over. As a result, Duncan didn't have occasion to get to know his niece until she was a grown woman. There were other reasons for this, more pertinent but less palatable. His sister, Roxanne, was difficult, and from an early age, disapproved of Duncan's sexuality. He left North Carolina the day after his eighteenth birthday and never looked back. In New York, he received the occasional phone call or birthday card from his sister, and offered the same to her, and later, to her daughter.

This mode of operation was suitable for both parties until a crystalline Tuesday in September. Duncan was enjoying coffee from his new French press on the terrace. Henry was out with the dogs. Though he should have been at work, Duncan was indulging; the air was crisp and the sky was a brilliant shade of azure. Because his face was buried in a book—he remembered it to be John Irving's *The Fourth Hand*, which he wasn't particularly enjoying but which was on the bestseller list at the time—he didn't see the plane that hit the north tower of One World Trade Center. The rolling, booming sound jerked his head and ricocheted throughout his chest cavity like a collapsing mine. He stood up, and could see a wall of black dust billowing upward. It wasn't until nineteen minutes later when Henry burst through the front door, the hysterical dogs gathered like laundry in his arms, that Duncan realized that they probably knew someone who was dead.

Alexa was grown by then. She had just graduated from Harvard Law and was traveling through Europe when her father was killed. After a few hours, once the phone lines were partially restored, Roxanne had finally gotten through to Duncan. Michael, her husband, had been on American Airlines Flight 11 bound from Boston to L.A. Michael was traveling for work; it had been a last-minute trip; he had added L.A. to the schedule only the day before; there was still a small chance he wasn't on the plane, but safely in Boston. Unable to speak of any larger ramifications, they focused on how to get Alexa home. It was hours before they were even able to reach her because the circuits were jammed in New York and Alexa was in Prague without an international cell phone. Henry was able to get through first by having his secretary dial her hotel from an open line at Morgan Stanley. Alexa answered cheerfully, strangely unaware of how the world, and her world most specifically, had changed.

Because her mother was unable to speak, Duncan was the one to tell her.

"Your father, you see . . . well, something's happened," he said, and the rest of the conversation was a blur.

Duncan remembered standing in his kitchen, pouring the dregs of the French press coffee down the drain and thinking: *When I brewed this, the world was still whole.*

In their first few conversations, Duncan and Roxanne told Alexa that her dad might be in the basement of the tower. They were telling themselves that, too. It was a myth that people were allowing themselves to retell, like a bedtime story or fairy tale, for nearly a week. No one knew from where that information had originally come. During those first days, information was passed through the news and Web sites and neighbors, bouncing around like a cue ball on a pool table, the words losing momentum with each retelling. Still, to say anything else felt sacrilegious.

Afterward, Duncan had tried to be more present for Alexa. He took her for an occasional drink, met her for breakfast at a coffee shop near her law firm. He found that he liked her, not as a niece, but as a person. And after a short while he realized that he looked forward to their meetings as eagerly as he did dinners with his closest friends. She was exceptionally bright, and had an implacable vivacity. She liked dark chocolate; she possessed as sharp a wit as he had ever seen on a southerner; she read the *New Yorker* religiously; she got her friends to try Greek restaurants in Astoria and Russian cabarets in Brighton Beach. Worst of all, she looked like Duncan. She had his round eyes, luminous as buttons, and her hair was so black that it read nearly blue. In restaurants, people mistook her for his daughter.

"Oh, spare me your narcissism!" Henry would moan when Duncan came home from a visit with Alexa, breathlessly extolling her virtues. "You love her because she's exactly like you!" Finally, he understood what it might be like to want children.

---

*Where, where would he put her?*

After an internal debate and several rotations of the silver-rimmed place cards he had bought for the occasion, Duncan sat Alexa between Daniel and Marcus. He didn't want her to think he was trying to fix her up with Leonard, who oftentimes came across as straight, and he didn't want to monopolize her by seating her next to himself. Marcus, he reasoned, could talk with her about the law. And Daniel was straight and had a lot of straight friends in finance and could, perhaps, think of someone new for her to date. Duncan placed himself at the head of the table, flanked on either side by friends. He felt rather regal as he did so, like the king of his own small fiefdom.

When he was done, he stepped back and surveyed the table with a critical eye. It had been a long time since he had entertained. The silver napkin rings and good china had to be exhumed from the storage boxes at the top of the linen closet and dusted off. At the last minute, he splurged on white orchids for the centerpiece; the expensive ones from L'Olivier that came potted in square vases filled with black pebbles. There had been a time when he and Henry had kept orchids around the house, even when they weren't expecting company. "They're for us," Henry would say. "Why should we have them just for guests?" That was a bygone era, the heady days of two incomes and a buoyant stock market.

Though Duncan found round dining tables visually displeasing, he found himself resenting the large rectangle in front of him. Rectangles were so unforgiving when seating a number other than ten or eight or two. There would always be two heads to the table. Across from his place was a blank slate, an unused chair. It felt as awkward as a gap-toothed child. Though he thought for a moment to remove it, he concluded that it was less significant somehow to allow the chair to stay where it was. Then the bell rang, and as he went to answer it, the thought was lost.

---

Alexa arrived first. Right away, he could sense her nervousness.

"Am I too early?" she said from the doorway, craning her neck like a goose into the silent apartment. A brief scan turned up no evidence of other guests.

Duncan reached for her coat, which she tendered with slight reluctance. She had grown thin. Nervously, she forked her fingers through her mass of curls, fluffing the tendrils. "I know I'm early," she said, "Is that all right?"

"Of course. I'm thrilled to get you to myself for a while."

She was too early in fact; it was just past 10 a.m. and no one else would arrive until noon. Duncan was quietly glad. He hadn't seen her in months, and while he had waved off her periodic apologies and cancellations with cheerful iterations of "It happens!" and "I'm swamped, too!" the distance had saddened him.

Duncan set some fresh coffee to brew and turned on some jazz, so that she wouldn't feel as though she was intruding on a house unprepared for visitors. As he fussed in the kitchen, she opened the sliding door and walked out onto his balcony. He could see her through the kitchen window, her smooth, white hand on the railing as she looked out across the Hudson River.

"Gorgeous day," she called. "Cold, but beautiful."

He joined her on the terrace, handing her a mug of coffee. He had prepared it with a dash of soymilk and Splenda; he had bought both for her, for this specific purpose. He took his own coffee black. "A little gray, no?" he replied. "Looks like snow."

She nodded. "A little gray. But I kind of like it this way. It's so peaceful before it snows. The sky feels empty." A sharp wind blew across the terrace. They stood side by side, each tilted slightly forward against the cold. His button-down shirt felt thin against his chest. Out on the river, the wind ruffled the water into tiny crested waves, like the tops of a meringue. A single sailboat was tacking to the west, its prow aimed at Ground Zero.

"Let's go in," Duncan said after a minute. "It's too cold to stand out here."

The sliding door made a hearty *thunk* as it closed behind them, sealing them in. The apartment felt warm by comparison.

"It's still strange for me to see the empty space," she said, tracing a circle around the dining room table. Her voice didn't register any wistfulness, and for a moment, he thought she was referring to the single unused chair. Her slender fingers dragged lightly across the chair backs as if they were piano keys.

Duncan nodded. He understood what she meant. "You can still feel them on the skyline, can't you? The city's phantom limbs."

"Do you miss him?"

"Who, your dad?"

"No, Henry. I mean, I'm sorry. I know that's a weird question. You probably don't even think about him anymore. I didn't mean to open old wounds."

"It's all right. I do, and you're not."

She inspected the names on the place cards. When she found her own, she took a seat, slumping down into the chair. Her feet splayed out in front of her in first position, like a dancer. "I just really tried to steel myself against missing Dad during the holidays. Happens every year. Last night I couldn't sleep. So eventually I turned on the television and ended up watching—don't laugh at me, I know you're going to laugh when I say this—I ended up watching *Sleepless in Seattle* at two in the morning and I just lost it." She laughed at herself; Duncan could see her eyes glass over with tears. "I mean, I had snot running down my face. It just bowled me over, this intensely overpowering feeling of loneliness and failure and sadness and hurt. It felt like when you get hit square in the chest by a wave and pulled under into the surf. I could barely breathe."

The timer *dinged* in the kitchen; the oven had reached 400 degrees. Duncan turned and went to put the turkey in, trying to think of what to say.

"They should ban that movie from the airwaves," he called from the kitchen. "In fact, they should ban every movie Meg Ryan has ever been in. At least during the holidays. I mean, my God. *You've Got Mail*, *When Harry Met Sally*? Please. I don't need that. No one needs that."

Then Alexa laughed and her shoulders trembled. "Sorry if I sound a little melancholy," she said. She pushed her chair back and joined him in the kitchen. Wordlessly, they began to unwrap the cheeses and place them onto a cheeseboard.

"You all right otherwise?"

"Work's been tough," she said, spooning fig jam into a small bowl.

"I mean, the pay's shit, but I knew that going in. It's something else. I'm thinking about leaving."

Duncan's hands stopped moving. He lay the cheese knife down on the cutting board. "Talk to me."

"I don't know if I can."

"Quitting's a pretty big decision, especially for you."

The cracker arranging ceased, and she sank onto a kitchen stool, one foot still on the floor. She stared blankly at the counter, avoiding his gaze.

"You have to promise that you won't look at me like I'm crazy, even if you think I am."

Duncan turned off the music with a remote control. The apartment fell silent. "I'm always here for you," he said. "Whatever you need. My job aside, I'm an excellent keeper of secrets. Decently good adviser, too."

Alexa frowned, thinking. She trusted Duncan implicitly, perhaps more than anyone else, but she felt her heart pounding in her rib cage. Telling anyone, even Duncan, felt wrong. It felt wrong, she knew, because it was wrong; speaking about an investigation with someone outside her office was a clear breach of confidentiality. Even if she didn't use names, her toe was on a cliff edge and she could feel the earth giving way beneath it.

They sat down together at the kitchen table, the half-assembled cheeseboard between them. The air was filled with the potent scent of roasting turkey and tuberose candles.

After a moment, she said, "David—he's the guy I've been seeing, but he's also, well, my boss—has been investigating a hedge fund for a few months now. Without going into specifics, he's built a really strong case for fraud. In our office, the next step is to submit a memo requesting that the investigation be elevated to formal status. That allows you to issue subpoenas, that sort of thing. So he did that, and never heard back. At first, he blamed it on bureaucracy; you know, the usual government office complaint. But weeks passed. He got totally obsessed, he was working all the time, and he became really vocal about needing the office's support. I thought he was going a little crazy, to be honest. And when he told me what he was involved in . . . well, it's massive. Billions of dollars. Literally, these people have stolen billions of dollars from investors."

"Goodness. Why wouldn't he get the office's support? I can't imagine they have bigger fish to fry."

"Hardly. The numbers are staggering. To put it in perspective, it's the largest financial crime that I've heard of during my entire legal career. He finally appealed to Jane Hewitt last week, hoping she'd cut through the red tape so he could get the indictments out."

"I am guessing she didn't."

"Worse than that. David said she was angry in their meeting. He said he felt like he had offended her in some way. She gave him a speech about how a number of factors go into the resource allocation process, there were budgetary issues at play, blah blah blah. She didn't like his 'renegade attitude.' He left feeling like he'd been fired. It scared the shit out of him. It was the exact opposite response from what he thought he'd get."

Duncan's brow furrowed. "Maybe she doesn't like having her authority questioned. Or maybe she's embarrassed that if this blows up, it will reflect poorly on the SEC."

"That's what I thought, too, at first. I mean, we've looked into these guys more than once in the past few years, and no one ever followed up. It's been, actually, a pretty egregious failure on our part. That's a whole other part of the story. At the end of the day, it's just too risky to sit on a fraud of this magnitude."

"I would think she'd want to pursue it full tilt. We see it all the time: over-eager DAs and judges surge into action right before an election or a promotion. But she's not." Duncan drummed his fingers against his lips. "Odd, I agree."

"I know how this sounds, but do you think it's possible that she's being bribed? There was a lawyer—Scott Stevens—who was the only other person at the SEC to ever investigate this fund. One day, he just quit the SEC altogether, and the investigation was shut down. This money manager whom David spoke with said Stevens basically disappeared. He thought that he had been pressured to walk away from the investigation, just like David."

"Have you talked to him?"

"No. We tried a basic search but didn't have time for much else. We should."

"I can find him," Duncan said.

Alexa looked up, hopeful. Then her face grew dark again, like cloud cover over the sun. "I haven't told you the worst part of the story. The principal of the firm—and please, you can't breathe a word of this to anyone—is Morton Reis. Or was, I guess. And when we found out yesterday, Jane went right to David. She wanted to know whom he talked to over there, what he had been doing, as if he had caused it. David said she was irate. She told him she was going to get him fired, that he was out of line, that he was causing more damage by raising this than he could possibly understand. Then on the way out, she told him she was aware of us. Him and me, I mean. The way she said it, well, it wasn't good." Alexa's hand shot to her forehead, massaging her furrowed brow. "I never thought that our relationship would be used against him. Not like this. He's a mess."

Duncan's heart was pounding, but he tried to appear calm. "I'm so sorry you are going through this," he said slowly.

"Either way, I'm scared for him, Duncan. Even if David just drops the investigation and walks away, the fraud will get uncovered at some point. Some point soon, now that Reis is dead. And when it does, David could take the fall."

"Shouldn't Jane Hewitt take the fall?"

Alexa shook her head. "No way. She's too popular with the new administration. They want her to run the Commission. So they'll find someone else to take the fall, someone less senior, but still important."

Duncan watched her as she stood and began to rearrange the cheese plate. Her hands moved quickly as she lined up the crackers just so, placing them with nervous precision, then the grapes, washed and full, splayed out against the plate's lip. "Are you sure about that?"

"He's the head of the department. He'll have to explain why the SEC dropped the ball on a multibillion-dollar fraud. But if he pushes the investigation, Jane will fire him. It's clear that she wants to bury this. The only thing he can think to do is to prepare the case and hand it to a friend at the attorney general's office. We've been talking to someone we know over there. That way, David stays out of the line of fire at work, at least until the AG breaks the story. Then he plans to resign, but at least his name will be clear. But it needs to happen now. Like, this weekend. Before the newspapers get ahold of the story and beat us to the punch."

Duncan nodded, mentally running through his Rolodex to figure out whom to call first. "Let me see what I can find out about Jane Hewitt. I know her, you know. Interviewed her for *Press*. Made of steel, that woman. If she's involved in the case, I have some journalist friends who will get to the bottom of it. They live for this stuff."

"I hate involving you. I don't even really know what I am asking you for. But I don't know where else to go."

"Well, I'm not sure what I can offer, yet. But we've got to understand whom you're up against. If she is being bribed or if she's connected in any way to RCM, we need to know."

Before Duncan could respond, the intercom buzzed through the kitchen, jarring them both.

"You can just send everyone up," Duncan told the doorman. "No need to ring up again."

They walked to the front door. "It's all gone so far off the rails," she said.

"We're going to get it back on track. I promise." He pressed his hand firmly on the small of her back. Though she knew his face would light up the moment the doorbell rang, his voice was deadly serious. "No one is going to get away with anything. A lot of people owe me favors in this town. More than you think. If there's anyone I would go to the mat for, it's you."

She put her hand in his, and held on tight as he opened the door for his guests.

# THURSDAY, 11:16 A.M.

Quiet was Marion's gift to Sol. She had been asleep when he crawled into bed beside her the night before—it must have been 2 or 3 a.m.—and she was asleep when he went back to work a few hours later.

Sol was sure she had been up for at least a few hours. But she was lingering upstairs, reading maybe or taking a long bath. Staying out of his hair, basically, so he could work. It was this sort of gesture, so subtle that any other person would have missed it entirely, that made him love her after thirty-six years. Not just a warm, familial love, but a deep, rare sort of love. Her body was a mass of lumps and veins, and her hair was like an overgrown shrub most of the time, no longer really worth tending. But still, Sol thought Marion was beautiful.

When he heard her softly padding around in the kitchen, he couldn't wait to see her. Though they had been together since the previous evening, he hadn't really *been* with her. The Morty situation had swallowed him whole.

He hoped she was making coffee. It was less acidic somehow when she made it. Sol made a mental note to thank her for driving last night and for the coffee, if there was any. He never remembered to thank her for coffee.

He found Marion in front of the open refrigerator, her spandexed body sticking out from behind the door.

He patted her on the rear. "Sol!" she exclaimed. "You scared me half to death. I thought you were working."

"I am," he said, feeling unusually affectionate. "But I wanted to say good morning."

Marion's chocolate-brown eyes softened as she smiled. The little crow's feet that sprouted from their corners were so kindly, he thought. He couldn't imagine why she kept threatening to erase them.

"Well, that's nice of you," she said, leaning in for a kiss. "I hope you got some sleep last night. What time did you get to bed?"

He smiled and wrapped her in a hug so that she couldn't see his face. Marion could always tell when he was lying to her. "I'm fine," he said. "I got a few hours. You know me. I'll sleep when I'm dead."

"That's what worries me!" she said and laughed a little. "You need to take care of yourself. You work too hard."

"No such thing."

She shot him an admonishing look. "I know," he conceded. "I know."

"I'm meeting Judith for spin class this morning," Marion said, changing the subject. She closed the fridge. "We might go for a bite after, but everything's probably closed."

Usually, when Marion went "for a bite" she returned home with a shopping bag or two dangling from one arm. She was unable to walk through East Hampton's main drag without buying something. She shopped with heightened abandon in East Hampton. Sol assumed this had something to do with feeling relaxed. She would come to her senses later in the day but by then, it was too late. On principle, Marion almost never returned anything. She didn't like to upset anyone, even salesclerks. Every time Sol went into the closet, he found something else with the tags still on.

Sol usually kept his mouth shut. If he saw it as part of the cost of doing business, he would accept the thirty-dollar spin class, and even the post-class shopping spree.

"There are spin classes on Thanksgiving?"

"There are always spin classes in East Hampton," Marion said drily. "We're supposed to be at the Darlings' at 6 p.m.?"

"Yes, 6 p.m."

"Okay, I'll be back by then. I hope everything goes okay today. I set a fresh pot to brew." She kissed him on the cheek. "How's Julianne?"

"She's holding up. Considering."

"Have they . . . any word?"

"No," Sol said. He shook his head sadly. "They're still dredging the river. The storm's making things very difficult, they say."

"And the memorial service?"

Sol sighed. "It's complicated. Julianne doesn't want to move forward until they've found the body. We're preparing her for the possibility that they may not."

"Oh," Marion said. "That's just awful." Her eyes shone with tears. "When you speak to Carter, tell him they're all in my thoughts."

"I will." Sol said. Marion ducked her head respectfully. She offered him a sad smile then turned. Through the open door, he watched her descend the porch stairs to the gravel drive.

"Thank you for the coffee," he called after her.

"Anything for you, my love," she called back, and was gone.

Sol never spoke to Marion about his clients. He was naturally circumspect, but his job—and client list—demanded the utmost discretion. Marion knew some of them; some she even considered friends. They had family dinners together and weekends in the Hamptons. She sent gifts for birthdays and children's graduations. But she never pried about their business.

Marion was the listening type. She had been a family therapist for fifteen years. She was retired now, but she still continued to volunteer as a grief counselor at Beth Israel Medical Center. Though Sol never spoke of his own work, he was quick to praise Marion's at parties, or to clients. He was happy whenever she came up in conversation.

Her practice had put him through law school. Their first years of marriage had been a struggle, a constant flow of work and bills. She never complained. Sol often marveled that she had stayed with him all that time. Part of the joy of making as much money as he did now was watching Marion thrive in her volunteer work. By the end of the year, construction would be completed on the Marion and Sol Penzell Wing of Beth Israel Medical Center. They had been working on it for five years, and talking about it for nearly fifteen. It was their baby, she said. The baby they couldn't have themselves. He liked it when she bought herself nice things; certainly she deserved them. She had given him so much, and he wanted to give her back everything he could.

It had been many years since he'd left life at a large law firm to form Penzell & Rubicam LLP, a small boutique firm that specialized in securities enforcement and litigation, white-collar defense, and government relations. His partner, Neil Rubicam, ran the firm's Washington, D.C., office, which, if you asked Neil, was the firm's headquarters. Neil was more of a showman than Sol. He took pleasure in being interviewed on the courthouse steps, and he favored custom-made suits and bold ties that photographed well. On the wall behind his desk, Neil had framed clippings that mentioned the firm, or more specifically, mentioned him. Sol thought this was an amusing and somewhat juvenile practice. The only things on Sol's wall were a photograph of Marion and his certificate of admission to the New York State Bar. Most of Penzell & Rubicam's real successes were by their very nature unknown to the public. The high stakes court battles were important, of course, and served to garner the firm's sterling reputation. But keeping their clients out of court—and out of the limelight—was the firm's forté.

The most lucrative of Penzell & Rubicam's victories were the ones about which no one, except the client and a small handful of attorneys under Sol and Neil's management, would ever know. These were settlements negotiated in the shadows, the kind where money simply disappeared into numbered offshore bank accounts. Sometimes no money exchanged hands at all, except of course to Sol, who was compensated handsomely for the representation. Instead, billion-dollar relationships were forged, debts of gratitude incurred, favors curried. The fact that he received no recognition for this work, not even from his wife, was, to Sol, a small price to pay for the privilege of doing the work he did. While he loved the practice of law, his work now was far more sophisticated than a traditional legal practice. It was negotiation at the highest level, a form of extralegal deal brokering that made him a very powerful man.

They ran the two offices like two discrete firms. Neil was in charge of the high-visibility litigation practice in Washington, and Sol spearheaded a hybrid advisory business that served the biggest names on Wall Street. While functionally independent, the arms were complementary; Sol and Neil often worked in tandem on different aspects of a client's business. Sol looped in Neil when a client looked as though he might be headed for litigation, and Neil called Sol for behind-the-scenes negotiations, M & A advice, and crisis management. Publicly, Sol was happy to let Neil be the firm's front man. To the firm's most valued clients, discretion was mandatory, and Sol was their guy.

Carter kept Sol on retainer, consulting him on everything from dealings with FINRA and the SEC to dealings with Ines. Admittedly, Sol often found the latter to be stickier. Over the course of their thirteen-year business relationship, Sol had seen Carter through marital peaks and valleys. There were times when Sol had braced himself for Ines to leave, but she never did. This was different. Ines was tough as hell, but this would be a test for the strongest of wills. Sol wasn't sure that Ines could withstand the coming storm. He wasn't sure any wife could.

"Let's hope she's got some Silda Spitzer in her," Neil had said the night before. He had been shooting hoops in his office with his mini basketball; Sol could hear it as it bounced off the rim.

"Take me off speaker. Did you get PR lined up?"

"Relax." Neil's voice came in clearer now. "I have Jim working on it. I think his firm does the best work in corporate damage control. I've been using them a lot lately."

"I can imagine."

"He's the best."

"We'll need it."

There would be more than rumors about Carter this time. In a matter of weeks, maybe days, the Darlings would be exposed to immeasurable intrusion from the press, the authorities, friends, and strangers. Their personal lives would be on display. Many would relish the fall of such a privileged family. The baseline assumption, Sol knew, would be that Carter was guilty.

He was trying to cut a deal as fast as he could so that wouldn't happen. He had made some headway with Eli Sohn, his contact at the attorney general's office, but they weren't there yet. A deal couldn't be cut until tomorrow, at the earliest. Carter would have to show up in person, hat in hand. Unfortunately, Carter wasn't great at hat in hand.

# THURSDAY, 12:56 P.M.

There were already four cars in the driveway. Paul wondered if they were the last ones to arrive. Adrian and Lily's black Porsche Cayenne was parked at the apex of the curved drive, blocking everyone else. The front door of the house was ajar. When Bacall heard the rumbling of the gravel beneath the tires, he burst out through it, barking happily and wagging his tail like a windshield wiper. It felt like a standard-issue late fall day. Paul pulled to a stop just behind Adrian and Lily's car, trying to keep his eye on Bacall, who was skirting the edges of the drive. King sat up and pressed his dappled paws against the window, panting in anticipation.

"We're here, honey," Merrill said. She spoke in the singsong voice she used when addressing the dog, but it was halfhearted. "Are you excited?"

King let out a yelp as Merrill opened the door and set him down on the drive. Steam rose from his nostrils and his feet crunched on the ice-crusted grass. He and Bacall went about sniffing each other while Paul and Merrill got out and stretched. The air was colder out here than it was in Manhattan; clean and bracing. Paul shivered through his wool sweater. It wouldn't be a pleasant weekend, but it still felt momentarily nice to be out of the city.

The house had taken on that stark New England quality that shingled houses do in the fall. Ines's prized window boxes stood empty; in the summer they overflowed with pink geraniums. The house's façade was an aged nut-brown. Though the Darlings had built the house in 2001, it was traditionally designed, fading seamlessly into the Island's patchwork of farmhouses and saltboxes. At the back of the house was a small formal English garden, the hedges of which were clipped neatly into a rectangular maze. They were covered now to protect them during the winter.

The house was, as ever, eerily perfect. The outside had white-trimmed gambrels and a porch that caught the breeze just so. The footpaths were constructed out of brick, eaten away at the corners, the colors as varied as the back of a tabby cat and faded by the sun. Inside, the house had all the trappings of a family estate. Ines favored old silver for meals, the kind that was supposed to be passed down, never purchased, and was slightly worn around the handles. A painting of Carter's grandfather hung on the library wall; across from it was a framed car company's stock certificate that supposedly bore his signature. Everything that could be personalized or monogrammed or customized was: the crisp white sheets, the soft blue towels, the L.L.Bean canvas bags that were lugged everywhere, from the beach to the golf course to the farmer's market. Yet there was something manufactured about it, as though Ines had opened the pages of *Architectural Digest* and said, "Give me this."

All of the heirlooms and old photos were from Carter's side of the family; his stories were the family's communal history. Paul never once heard Ines speak about her childhood in Brazil. Paul knew all about the summers in Quogue, the cousins back in Grosse Pointe, Michigan, the winter recesses from boarding school. He knew that Charlie Darling had been an equestrian and an expert marksman, that Eleanor had had a tent for her debutante ball that had been made entirely of white roses. Once, when she was drunk, Merrill told Paul that a lot of her father's stories were embellished. "They were never really all that well off," she whispered, after her father finished a story about childhood Christmases in Palm Beach. "My grandfather was just a showman. Dad is, too, I guess."

You were with them or you weren't. Paul and Merrill spent every weekend at the Darlings' house in the summer, and every holiday. After they were married, it was often said to Paul that "he was a Darling now." He was glad about it; he wanted nothing more than for his wife's family to accept him. Still, it felt a little strange, as though he had joined a preexisting family instead of beginning one of his own. Sometimes, less now than in the beginning, Paul wondered how Patricia and Katie felt about his relationship with the Darlings. He tried not to have an ego about it—his family was in North Carolina after all, and the Darlings were here—but there were moments when he was troubled by it.

And then there was the issue of the name. At their engagement party, Adrian had jokingly asked Paul if he was going to take her name after they were married.

"No, but I'm keeping my own," Merrill had replied before he could answer. She turned to Paul. "Lily goes by Lily Darling Patterson, but only socially," she added, as though that bolstered her cause.

"Socially? As opposed to what?" Paul said, sounding snarkier than he intended. Merrill raised a quick eyebrow in Adrian's direction, a reprimand and a warning.

"Professionally," she said coolly. Conversation over.

"How do you feel about that?" Adrian asked, winking at Paul.

"Just fine," he said, but felt his face flush with embarrassment. "I'm going to get a refill," he said and nodded toward the bar.

As Paul walked away, he heard Adrian say to Merrill, "You girls have to maintain your brand equity, huh?" They both laughed. It felt like a slight, though Paul knew it wasn't meant as one. It was a joke, nothing more.

It had never occurred to Paul that his wife wouldn't want to be Mrs. Ross. "Why didn't you tell me?" he asked her later, clumsily, after too much scotch.

"I'm sorry," she said. "I just thought you'd understand."

---

They unpacked the car in silence, the wind stirring up the leaves along the edges of the drive. Eventually, Adrian appeared at the door, Sam Adams in hand. He whistled at Bacall and both dogs bounded into the house. Paul was momentarily irked by the fact that his dog responded so willingly to Adrian's whistle, and then felt childish for caring.

"Welcome, kids," Adrian said. He meandered down to the car to give Merrill a hug. "Need a hand?"

"Looks like you guys just got here," Paul nodded his head toward the open trunk of Adrian's car.

"Yeah, we got a late start. Because of the Morty thing. Lily's a little shaken up." Adrian's throat sounded dry, as if he had been up talking late into the night. On first glance Adrian was his usual, relaxed self: hands stuffed in his pockets, errant shirttail emerging from the waistband of his corduroys, a page from the J. Crew catalog. But Paul knew Adrian well enough to sense a heavy chord in his voice. The men locked eyes. For a moment, Adrian looked older than Paul had ever seen him.

"I'll go find her," Merrill said.

"Everybody's in the kitchen, except Carter. He's at the Penzells', I think."

Merrill nodded and disappeared into the house without acknowledging Paul. Not wanting to follow her, he took their suitcases to their bedroom.

Upstairs, Paul began to unpack his suitcase and then closed his eyes for a moment, succumbing to a bone-deep fatigue. He knew he needed to go say hello to the family; he was simply delaying the inevitable. But once he left the bedroom, the weekend would begin in earnest. That overwhelming thought kept him pinned down to the bed.

There was no real need to unpack, anyway. Closed suitcases left on luggage racks at Beech House were silently and miraculously unpacked by Veronica, the housekeeper, the clothes withdrawn, steamed, and hung neatly in rows. Like many details about the Darlings, Paul found this practice unsettling. It created a strangely intimate association with Veronica. She folded his undershirts; she placed his spy novel by the bedside and his Dopp kit on the bathroom counter; she left his work files untouched in his duffel, as if to say that *some things, work things, are still private here.* But they weren't, really. She touched his toothbrush and saw his condoms under the sink. It seemed inequitable, a streaming one-way channel of information. He didn't even know her last name. Some days, it felt to Paul as though the staff knew the Darlings better than the family knew themselves.

He was hanging a button-down in the closet when a voice behind him said, "You don't need to do that. Veronica's here today."

Merrill was slouched against the doorjamb in a manner that was simultaneously alluring and standoffish. Her arms were crossed tightly over her chest.

"Hi," Paul said. "I was beginning to worry you were never going to speak to me again." Paul realized that she hadn't spoken directly to him since the Milk Pail, a farm off the Montauk Highway in Water Mill where they sometimes picked apples and pumpkins in the fall. When they had pulled into the parking lot, Merrill was sitting tight-lipped; her face a mask of tears and anger. They had wordlessly picked up two pies and a dozen cinnamon donuts and a jug of cider: their agreed-upon offering to the Thanksgiving table.

She proffered a taut smile, but didn't budge from her post at the door. A look crossed her face as if she wanted to say something, but thought better of it, and bit her tongue. "Why would you say that?" she said instead.

They stood looking at each other.

"I haven't heard a peep out of you since the Milk Pail."

"Dad loves those donuts. I'm glad we stopped."

"Everyone loves those donuts."

"Are you coming downstairs? The football game's on in the den. Veronica will unpack you."

"Are we not going to finish the conversation from the car? I'd like to talk before I see your dad."

Merrill sighed, a heavy guttural sigh, her whole body wilting beneath the weight of it. Shutting the door behind her, she went to lie across the bed. Horizontal, her face took on a smooth, blank expression. Her eyes blinked up at the ceiling. They faded in color when she was tired or when she cried, more silver than blue.

"You dropped a lot of information on me," she said finally. "I'm not trying to ignore you, but I need a little time to process everything."

"That's fair. That's understandable."

"I'm not angry with you," she said, though he hadn't suggested that she was.

"I hope not. Did you read the e-mails?"

"Yes. It's not that I don't understand your concern."

"But?"

"But nothing." Her voice was calm, but Paul could tell she was suppressing her anger.

"Look," she said and sat up. "I'm just never going to tell you, yes, go talk to the SEC about my dad's company. You'll ruin him. You know that. And I have zero confidence that it would save you, either. It's like walking directly into a lion's den."

Paul shifted away from her on the bed and they both stared at the walls, robin's-egg blue and cream striped like everything else in the room. The stripes hurt his eyes if he looked too long at them.

There had always been a nascent fear in Paul that when it came down to it, Merrill might choose her family over him. He had never said this, of course, though they had danced around it countless times, during stupid fights about scheduling or the Hamptons house or whether she would ever move out of New York. Some of the fights were real and others weren't. He thought he had gotten over it, after six years of marriage. But it held him now so tightly in a vice grip, he thought his heart might explode.

"Merrill," he said. "What choice do I have? Sit and wait for them to come for me? I lied to the SEC. That's a pretty big fucking deal."

She was silent. The edge of her thumb was in her mouth and she bit at the nail.

"It wasn't lying," she said quietly. "You were just saying what the firm told you to say. People do that all the time."

"Don't you get it? *We never asked RCM who their counterparties were.* I wasn't outright lying, maybe, but I wasn't being honest, either. I shouldn't have been out there saying, 'We're on top of it; they're all triple-A rated or better.' All that shit. We were all lying to our investors when we said it to them and I lied to David when I said it to him. And the worst part is, I put it in a fucking e-mail. So now they have me. Don't you see that? Now they have me if they want me."

Merrill got up off the bed, and Paul was seized by the fear that she was leaving. Instead, she crossed the room and picked up the folder atop his suitcase. He watched as she reread the e-mail, the one he had read a million times since the day before, the one where he gave David Levin the party line about counterparties, and then told him to fuck off, basically. To stop asking questions. He hadn't thought he was lying when he sent it. That was the scariest part to him, how easily it had slipped off his fingertips. The e-mail, he could see now, read with such arrogant dismissiveness that Paul could hardly believe that he had written it. He felt as though he were reading a stranger's e-mail, some cocky prick who worked at a hedge fund, the kind who ended up at his wife's office shortly before being indicted for misconduct. That wasn't him. At least he had never thought that was him.

Merrill put the e-mail back in the folder. She sat back down on the bed, the folder in her hand. He reached for her thigh. It felt tense and cold beneath his palm. He hated himself for losing his temper with her, and for cursing, which she hated.

"I feel like there are two teams here," she said deliberately, her face pinched. "And it's clear to me which one you're on. And so hearing you talk about switching teams, well, it upsets me."

When he didn't respond, she continued, "Obviously, stuff went wrong at Delphic. But at the end of the day, this is about Morty and RCM. Just because he's not here, that doesn't mean you guys should pay for it. It's easy to Monday-morning quarterback and say, 'You should have known' or 'You shouldn't have let this happen.' But really, that misses the point. This isn't about Dad, or you, and it's not really about Delphic. They're just looking for a sacrificial lamb, because they need someone to blame for what happened. If you go to them now with your hands up and surrender, you're justifying what they are doing. But if you stand behind the firm, and behind Dad, it sends a very clear message. This is about family now."

There was a certain kind of comforting logic to what she was saying. More than anything, Paul wanted everyone's interests to be aligned: his wife's, his father in law's, his own. He had always wanted to be one of them. Not because of the money, or the status. Not even the education and worldliness. It was their closeness he craved, their tribal clannishness. They were fiercely loyal to one another, even in times likes this. Especially in times like this. It all seemed so simple when she explained it. Family comes first. Family is unconditional.

Until he met them, Paul didn't know that kind of family existed. His own was a loose affiliation of people bound by genetics. They had been a full family once, but it was so long ago that Paul no longer remembered the touch and feel of it. There had been five of them. Casey was four and half when she had drowned in a community pool. Paul and Katie were eight years old. They had been at a friend's birthday party when it happened. No one had picked them up from the party. Instead, the sky had gone gray behind the trees and they were the last guests to leave, sitting at the picnic table with paper hats and noisemakers while the birthday boy's mother placed calls to locate their parents. Paul remembered feeling cold as the breeze picked up; he was still wearing a damp bathing suit and there was water in his ears and he worried that Katie would get sick from having wet hair. He had given her his towel. It was draped across her shoulders, her tiny body shivering beneath it. The streamers that had been tied to the trees fluttered nervously around their heads, and at their feet candy wrappers from the piñata lay empty on the grass.

The Ross house had gone silent after that, like a radio unplugged from the wall. It was a matter of months after the funeral when their father left, happier to start again than to live with Casey's specter. He was the one who had been in charge that day, taking them to the party and Casey to the pool while Patricia worked the weekend secretarial shift at the office. He remarried quickly, to a woman from Savannah. Paul and Katie went to visit them a few times. They would sit awkwardly in the living room of his new home, eating ice cream on the sofa out of orange plastic bowls and trying to be polite, as Patricia had told them to be. A year later, the stepmother was pregnant, and the new family moved to New York.

Patricia told Paul and Katie that their father was a banker. She said he was successful, and that he had moved away from them because it was the right thing to do for his career. He called them on their birthdays, on Christmas, and told them he loved them, that he was very busy with his new job and the baby. Paul would try to keep him on the phone for as long he could, peppering him with questions about New York, the Yankees, the weather up north. Paul imagined him in a big house with a silver car out front, and an office that had windows overlooking Central Park. He would tell his friends that his father was *a banker in New York* whenever possible. Whatever success his father enjoyed never translated into child support for Patricia. The bank foreclosed on their house the month after Paul and Katie turned thirteen. Paul never took his father's birthday call again.

Patricia was only twenty-one when she had gotten pregnant with Katie and Paul. She had met their dad in high school; he was three years older, and according to Patricia, "going places." Young as she was, she was sometimes more of a friend than a mother. She and Katie developed together, like the trunk and branch of the same tree. On her better days (or Katie's worse ones), they could pass for sisters. Both were the type of woman who had never been entirely pretty but instead had always looked as though they might have been pretty many years ago. Their features were plain and unrefined, like oatmeal.

Paul hadn't seen either of them since his wedding. This worried Merrill; she felt as though she was in some way responsible for the separation. He knew that she wasn't. To Paul, there was no rift, just a natural separation that had occurred over the course of many years. The movement had been slow enough that it felt almost imperceptible, like a continental drift.

He felt guilty, of course. Patricia wouldn't take money from him, so instead he sent presents for the holidays that were overly expensive and inappropriate for their daily lives: Hermes scarves, Tiffany bracelets. The only real thing he could offer them was financial advice. A few years earlier, he'd set up small nest eggs for them both at Vanguard. Before that, they had only savings accounts, and mortgages that were unmanageably large for their incomes. It gave him a reason to call them at least once a month, and it gave him something to talk about when he did. Both women were overly grateful for his help. Katie sent him cards at the holidays, updating him on the kids' lives and thanking him profusely for "everything he did for them" in her loopy, childlike script. Katie's kids, too, sent letters: "Thank you, Uncle Paul, for the PlayStation" or "Thank you so so so much for the tickets to the UNC game." The letters kept coming even though he told Katie they were unnecessary. He was their uncle, after all. Family never needed to send thank-you notes.

The truth was that he hated their letters. It worried him how much so little money meant to them. They seemed so helpless, so unable to make even small financial decisions without calling him first. Of course, what was a small financial decision to him was often monumental to Patricia or Katie. They had no idea how much money Merrill had, nor did they know that the Darlings had access to all kinds of resources they couldn't imagine: private equity investments with half-million dollar buy-ins, money managers, tax attorneys, estate planning advisers. *That doesn't take away anything from them,* he told himself. *It's not a zero-sum game.* But still, the guilt was pervasive some days, seeping into his chest like rising tidewater.

---

Now it all seemed inverted. More than once in the past twenty-four hours, Paul had felt an impulse to disappear to Charlotte, taking Merrill with him. Charlotte, or somewhere new altogether—Hong Kong, London, Paris, São Paulo. Somewhere that belonged to them, not to the Darlings.

His phone was ringing. They could both see it light up on the dresser.

"Are you going to answer that?" Merrill said.

"No. Let it go to voice mail."

"Is it Alexa?"

"I don't know." Paul rolled toward Merrill and took her in his arms. Her body felt stiff at first but then she relaxed into him. He buried his face in her neck, kissing it, his eyes closed tight. "I love you," he said. "I'm so sorry I saw her and didn't tell you right away. I'm trying to do everything right."

She squeezed him back, her torso pressed to his. "I know," she said, kissing his hairline gently. "I know. You would do anything for me, I know that." From the way she looked at him, it was a statement and a question and an affirmation all at once.

"I would."

"Please talk to Dad before you decide what to do. Please."

As they held each other, they heard the sound of a car pulling down the driveway.

"We should go," she said.

"I love you," he said again. "More than anything." But she was on her feet already and didn't answer.

---

Downstairs, the table was being set. Ines's Thanksgiving china, rimmed in gold and emblazoned with tiny turkeys, had been unsheathed from its muslin coverings and laid out on an antique lace tablecloth. Candles flickered against the glittering silver. In the center of the table was a cornucopia overflowing with apples, pears, grapes, oranges, and chestnuts. All temptingly vibrant, but in fact, made of wax. Carmela had to place each fruit out with precision, as she did every year, striving to achieve what Ines referred to as "casual elegance." Veronica had failed at this the first year—she had stacked the fruits too uniformly—and Ines had been forced to rearrange them frantically before anyone was allowed to sit down. The task had been reassigned to Carmela after that. John had removed one chair from the nine-person table. He had been instructed to bring it all the way down to the basement, completely out of sight. No one, Ines had told him sternly, wanted to be reminded that there was one person who wouldn't be at dinner. Anyway, the table was really meant for eight chairs; the extra had been brought up just for Morty. It was slightly different from the others.

On the sideboard was a stack of name cards for Ines's arrangement. She was already thinking about how to place them.

# THURSDAY, 5:00 P.M.

Marina was in Brooklyn, of all places.

She hated Brooklyn; hated taking the subway, hated how low all the buildings were. She hated how Brooklynites made it seem as though their decision to live there made them edgier or morally superior. What she hated about it most of all was how dislocated she felt from Manhattan whenever she stepped off the subway platform. It made her feel as if she were moving backward, away from the rotational center of the earth. Marina had come to New York straight from college, with nothing but a thousand dollars in her checking account, her possessions packed into a few brown boxes neatly labeled with a Sharpie, and a conviction never to live in an outer borough. She was proud of herself for sticking to it. She had ended up with two roommates in a Chinatown walk-up that inexplicably smelled like curry. But it was worth it because she was living in Manhattan.

Max had, evidently, elected to live in Brooklyn. Marina knew that six-figure apartments existed in Brooklyn Heights and Williamsburg and Park Slope, but until now, she had never actually been in one; only crappy tenements in Prospect Heights and Fort Greene. This, as she realized later when she was good and drunk, was because all of her cool friends were poor, and all of her rich friends were too boring to live in Brooklyn.

Max was neither poor nor boring. This surprised her. She had met him only a couple of times, usually at loud parties where she couldn't hear anything, but he hadn't impressed her. She had thought that Georgina could do so much better. After all, George was fabulous; she had that perfect, effortless, enviable sense of cool that rich city girls seemed to inherit, like long straight hair and perfect teeth. George had the metabolism of a whippet. Everything looked good on her: couture dresses, sweatpants, men's button-down shirts. She had grown up in a town house on Eleventh Street that had a back garden and a Cy Twombly hanging above the mantelpiece. She was the love child of a former model-turned-photographer and a guitarist who had once played with Bob Dylan. She was twenty-four. And she was at least an inch taller than Max. Still she was crazy about him, absolutely head over heels.

What George had failed to articulate was that Max wasn't just a software designer, he was a super-rich, super-successful thirty-six-year-old software designer who basically invented the iPod (or something like that). And his father was a billionaire venture capitalist who had a house in East Hampton next to Carl Icahn's.

So now it made more sense.

But when Marina had called George the night before, bawling and recounting every horrible detail of the Morgensons' Thanksgiving Eve party, she knew none of this. Max was simply George's chubby, curly-haired boyfriend, with his little paunch and scuffed red sneakers, the kind of guy who laughed awkwardly and one second too late, and probably still played video games. So when she accepted the invitation to spend Thanksgiving at his apartment, it was clear what a desperate, defeated state she was in.

The problem was that she had not made a backup plan. This was unlike her. Marina was typically extremely organized, methodical, risk averse (these were the characteristics that were most often cited by her parents in their on-going campaign in favor of law school). Clever as she was, Marina was also sadly prone to bouts of hopeless romanticism. Just as she had romanticized the job at *Press* (stylish co-workers, fabulous parties, mentorship from of a journalistic icon), she had also romanticized Tanner.

Slowly, she had fallen deeper and deeper into the throes of infatuation with him, the youngest grandson of William Morgenson. As she had done so, Marina had quietly turned down the volume on each of Tanner's shortcomings. It happened insidiously, over the course of many months, until one day all she could hear when he walked in the room was beautiful music.

Despite her admitted pedigree consciousness, Marina no longer cared that Tanner had gone to fair-to-middling schools. She had made peace with his decision to quit the analyst program at Morgan Stanley after only four months, as well as his decision to spend the subsequent two years "searching for the right opportunity." Sometimes, though she would never admit it aloud, Marina actually relished Tanner's unemployment. He was always available to take her to art openings and dinner parties and benefit galas, which was refreshing in a city full of men who lived at the office. And if he could afford the tickets and the tux, really, what did it matter? Tanner was perfect.

Marina's friends had become quietly concerned. It was clear to everyone but Marina that Tanner had no intention of marrying her. In fact, word had gone around that they were on the outs and Tanner was on the prowl for someone more suitable. While Marina was very pretty and very well educated, she wasn't really marriage material for a Morgenson. She had attended Hotchkiss because her parents were on the faculty; she had gone to Princeton on a partial scholarship because she had been the valedictorian of her class at Hotchkiss. Her parents were lovely people with no social connections. As much as Marina had done her best to gloss over these subtle distinctions, they hadn't escaped the serpentine tongues of her competition. Marina wasn't unaware that a few of Tanner's female friends thought he could do better, and told him as much.

Marina's parents taught at Hotchkiss so that they could give their daughter the very best education available. They had achieved this end, but with an unfortunate side effect: they had unwittingly exposed Marina to a world of obscene privilege and excess of which she wanted nothing more than to be a part. Because she was pretty, she was popular, and because she was popular, the majority of her friends were very rich indeed. She vacationed with them at their homes in Aspen; she borrowed their Chanel jackets for parties at the Ivy Club; she watched as they took glamorous, impractical jobs (jewelry designer, novelist) instead of worrying about their salaries. Somewhere along the way, Marina became determined that she, too, was worthy of all this. She would simply have to go out and get for herself the life her friends had been given. It would require careful planning and execution, but Marina always accomplished everything to which she put her mind. She made a lot of spreadsheets.

Law school was out. It was a reasonably sound next step for a liberal arts major, and the promise of $160,000 starting salary was certainly appealing. But after some consideration, Marina concluded that relegating herself to seventy hours a week of document review among schlumpy, poorly socialized colleagues would be an underutilization of her talents. She was smart, yes. And diligent and logical and all the other things that made for a good lawyer. But Marina knew what truly set her apart from the pack: her looks, her wit, and her innate sense of style. And those she had in spades.

What Marina saw, that her parents failed to see, was that law school was just too provincial an aspiration for her. She loved her parents deeply, but for reasons she could never fully understand, Richard and Alice suffered from limited horizons. They had chosen to live out their lives in quiet anonymity, settling in a pleasant Connecticut town, teaching high school European History (Richard) and French (Alice) when both could have easily gone on to tenure track professorships at major universities or even careers in consulting or law. They wore duck boots and polar fleece, and were almost always covered in dog hair. Their ancient yellow station wagon (fondly dubbed Old Yeller) had, for several years, wheezed like an old accordion when the key was pulled from the ignition. It had ferried the family everywhere, from Marina's middle school soccer games to her college graduation. Periodically, Richard and Alice revisited the idea of replacing Old Yeller, but Alice would get misty-eyed, as if they were discussing putting down one of the actual dogs, not a seventeen-year-old station wagon with gummy seats and no CD player. Marina knew they would drive it until it literally died on the side of the road.

Her parents were happy, and Marina knew that was all that really mattered. Yet she felt strongly that her own life would be something of a grander and more cosmopolitan construction. She didn't want to look back on her life choices; her career; and, most of all, her marriage and feel that she had settled.

For a year or so, everything fell into place. Marina landed a coveted spot as Duncan Sander's assistant, a job for which most socialites would pull out their eyeteeth. She finagled her way onto a few benefit committees, turned up at the right kind of parties. Most impressive, she had snagged Tanner.

Tanner Morgenson was, on a number of metrics, a catch. He wasn't handsome, but he wasn't unhandsome, either. He was well liked. He dressed well. No one would say Tanner was funny, exactly, but he was lively and had entertaining friends. He was fun. He took socializing very seriously. It wasn't uncommon for Tanner to spend whole days drifting from one private club to the next: a long lunch with his father at the Knickerbocker Club; a squash match and a steam at the Racquet Club; a dinner dance at Doubles. Tanner ran with a fast crowd, almost all native Upper East Siders who had known one another since birth, all rich and well connected, but because his grandfather was William Morgenson Sr. (founder of Morgenson Gas & Electric) and his mother was Grace Leighton Morgenson (heir to Leighton & Leighton Pharmaceuticals), very few were as rich or as well connected as Tanner.

Marina had had her eye on Tanner since college. He would come to visit his sister Clay now and again up at Princeton, usually with the aim of hitting on her friends. One dewy spring evening on the cusp of graduation,

Tanner appeared on campus without warning. By midnight, he was standing on a table at the Ivy Club, his arms entwined with two swaying lacrosse players who had successfully goaded him into singing "You've Lost that Loving Feeling" into a beer bottle. His Nantucket reds were stained and he looked wild-eyed. Clay confided to Marina that Lily Darling, Tanner's on-again, off-again sweetheart, had married an older guy who worked for her father. Though Tanner had never been able to fully commit to Lily, he was devastated. Smelling blood, Marina had moved in for the kill.

By the end of the summer, Marina had moved to New York and Tanner was hers. Well, almost hers. She learned quickly that Tanner wasn't a subscriber to the concept of commitment. She tried not to take this personally. After all, Tanner was universally noncommittal. He had dropped out of two summer camps as a child (hockey camp in Maine; squash camp in Newport), owned but couldn't play a multitude of instruments (a guitar, a saxophone, a paddle-tennis racquet). He had never stuck with a job for more than four consecutive months (JPMorgan held the record). Dinner reservations were often canceled at the last minute; weekend trips to Aspen or Palm Beach were penciled in on a whim. Marina spent her first fourteen months in New York engaged in an elaborate form of romantic brinkmanship with Tanner, a delicate, diplomatic operation involving seduction, feigned disinterest, patience, impatience, bikini waxing, ultimatums, open flirtation with others, and one extremely drunken couples weekend in the Napa Valley.

By the end, Marina had lost all perspective. Never before had she failed to achieve something, and she wasn't about to start with Tanner Morgenson. So desperate was she to believe that her affections were reciprocated that she broke a cardinal rule of courtship. She had (eagerly, blissfully) believed Tanner when he said that she was more than welcome to spend Thanksgiving with his family. Immediately, she called her parents and announced that she would not be making it home to Lakeville this year, much to their disappointment. This was an unfortunate misstep, and one that could have been avoided if only she had remembered never to take to heart the words of a drunken man.

"Never, ever, *ever* believe anything a man says when he is drunk!" George shook her head vigorously after this proclamation, her honey-colored ringlets flying. "And definitely don't when he's drunk and about to get laid. I mean, that's *rule number one.*" She glared sternly at Marina, who looked away and busied herself rearranging the rack of leather pants and bustiers that they were supposed to be bringing downstairs for a shoot. A moment earlier, Marina had felt effervescent. Then George had come along and uncorked her.

"I know," she said feebly. "But he wasn't that drunk. And things are going so well! I think he really wants me there."

"Were you naked?"

"What kind of a question is that?" Marina scanned the hallway to make sure they were out of earshot.

"Well, were you? Just answer the question."

"Fine. Yes. So what?" she hissed.

"And he said it before, right? Before you slept with him."

"I get the point."

"I'm just *saying—*" George raised her eyebrows in a way that made Marina want to slap her. "Just be careful. Weren't you going home to see Richard and Alice? They're going to be *so* disappointed."

"Let's drop it," Marina said coldly, and pressed the elevator button twelve times in rapid succession.

"Dropped," George said. She raised her palms in surrender.

Marina stewed for the rest of the day, trying to decide what annoyed her more: that George liked to call other people's parents by their first names or that George was right about Tanner.

So Marina's humiliation was complete when she was (1) made to suffer through the Morgensons' Thanksgiving Eve party, during which time it became slowly but excruciatingly clear that the Morgensons not only had no idea that Marina was dating their son but also that they had no intention of hosting her the following day, and (2) forced to call George to admit what had transpired. She had no one else to call.

"He introduced me to his mother as 'Clay's friend from Princeton'!" she said. "*His mother.* You should have seen her face. Totally blank. No idea who I was."

"Oh, my God, don't say another *word.* You're dumping him immediately. In fact it's done; he's been dumped. You're coming out to Brooklyn to have Thanksgiving with Max and me. It is going to be fabulous and by the time it is over you will have completely forgotten Theo Morgenblatt the Third or whatever his name is. Fuck him. *You can do so much better.*"

In the background, Marina could hear Max's voice, entreating George to get off the phone and come to bed.

Through her snorting, hiccupping tears, Marina thought to protest but couldn't muster the strength. "Are you—*hic!*—sure? I don't want to impose."

"Please. Max doesn't even know who's coming anymore. It's going to be great. Wear something cute. Oh, and can you bring a pecan pie? I was supposed to bake one, which means I was going to buy one and pretend I baked it, but I forgot." Max's snorting in the background was silenced by a *thwump* that Marina identified as a pillow colliding broadside with his head.

"I'll bring pie," she said miserably. "Thanks, George. Love you."

---

That was how Marina ended up on the 4 train on Thanksgiving day, having spent the morning wandering aimlessly through SoHo in search of an open bakery. She had slept in and once awake, tried to go to the gym, only to find it was closed. Now she tried to make herself as compact as possible in her subway seat, her purse and a pie competing for prime real estate in her lap. The pie was blueberry, because it was all the bakery had left. She figured that no one would notice. In fact, she figured no one would even notice her.

She had been too depressed to put any thought into what she was wearing, and had settled on an amalgam of black items that disappeared into one another in an indistinct, forgettable way that she knew would not score her any points with anyone. On her way out, she pocketed gold hoop earrings; her thought was to slip them on at Max's if everyone else looked more festive than she. As she walked to the subway stop, the idea that hoop earrings could, like little lifesavers, rescue her from obscurity became laughably, almost unbearably depressing. She looked awful and there was nothing to be done about it. Not awful, actually; worse than awful. She looked ordinary.

People pushed past Marina on the subway platform, causing her to grip the pie with the protectiveness of a squirrel with a nut. New York had a strange way of making her feel simultaneously claustrophobic and lonely. People surrounded her all day long: on the street, in the subway, in the office. The thumps of the downstairs neighbors wafted into her bedroom every night; her roommates' laughter reverberated through the paperthin walls; her window looked directly into the bedroom of a young Chinese couple with a newborn. There was a certain kind of intimacy to this physical closeness. But it was no substitute for family or for the friendships she had shared with her college roommates and boyfriends. The proximity of so many strangers made her feel unmoored. New York, she realized, was a sea filled with ships, slipping silently by one another on their way in and out of port.

Marina stared at the people with whom she was currently sharing Thanksgiving. Across from her was a homeless man talking to himself and rocking slightly, his ebony hands so chapped that they looked as if he had rolled them in white chalk. A kid in baggy pants and a backpack slouched next to him, wholly absorbed by his iPod. The only people who occasionally made eye contact were a tourist couple (midwestern, Marina guessed) wearing matching sweatshirts. They were overweight, and because they were holding a map, she made a bet with herself that they would be mugged before their trip was over.

Marina closed her eyes and tried to conjure her parents, alone for the first time in their house in Lakeville. The house would be quiet except for the creaky swinging of the dog door as Murray and Tucker darted in and out of the kitchen. Her mother would be wearing mom jeans, a turtleneck sweater embroidered with autumn leaves. She would have put the dogs in their "festive" collars because it was a holiday. Or maybe she wouldn't have, because Marina wasn't there to share it with them. Her father would be in his study while dinner was prepared, his stomach growling because, as he would tell them every Thanksgiving, he was accustomed to eating at specific times (7:30 a.m., noon, 6:30 p.m.), and not just one big meal in the middle of the afternoon. His glasses would have slipped to the tip of his nose by now and he would be squinting through them, grading papers primarily through his left eye because the right one was weaker. For years, Richard Tourneau had relied on cheap drugstore glasses, insisting they worked just fine. Alice had finally gotten him to the eye doctor five years ago, and though he had acquiesced to prescription glasses ("A hundred and fifty dollars!" he had sputtered, but looked so distinguished in them), he hadn't been back since. His eyes, of course, had weakened; he was turning sixty this year. Instead, he had affected a strange habit of reading and watching movies with one eye closed, like a pirate.

When she emerged from the subway station, it occurred to Marina that nothing would make her parents happier than a surprise visit on Thanksgiving. George wouldn't mind; Max wouldn't even notice. She knew better than to hope for a phone call or a last minute invitation from Tanner. Her parents were, she realized with sudden and violent acuity, the only people in the world who actually cared about her. As she stood on the corner of Montague and Henry streets trying to orient herself, Marina felt her face grow hot with tears. *Was it possible to turn around and go home?* Her chest was wracked with a very deep sort of pain, a hideous feeling that she identified only later as homesickness.

No one would notice if she gave up on New York and went back to Connecticut, tail between her legs. Her friends would miss her, of course, but only for a minute, like that sigh at the end of a good movie. She could live in Lakeville, study for her LSATs (*was registration for the December test still possible? She'd have to check*). Maybe her father could get her a part-time job tutoring students at Hotchkiss. Knowing this option existed no longer made her nauseated but instead filled Marina with an odd and liberating sense of relief.

Instinctually, she dialed her parents' number.

The moment her mother answered the phone, Marina knew she could never actually go through with it. At least, not today.

"How was the Morgensons' party last night?" Alice Tourneau asked enthusiastically. "Did you see the balloons all blown up? Did you get all dressed up?"

"It was nice," Marina replied vaguely."There was caviar and blinis," she added, for color.

"That sounds lovely, darling. Your father's just beside himself this morning because I decided to make only the apple pie this year and not pecan, too. But one pie is always more than enough, and this year it is only the two of us! Everyone always prefers the apple." Behind her, Murray and Tucker were tussling on the kitchen floor, yowling fitfully. "*Stop it, you*!" Alice's voice sounded distant as she scolded one of them, her face turned away from the receiver.

"How are Murray and Tucker?" Marina asked, feeling as though she might cry. "Do they miss me?"

"Oh, they're fine. Well, Murray ate something he wasn't supposed to just now and he's bound to throw it up any minute, but other than that, they're fine. They're seven this year, you know! Big boys."

"Mom and Dad's empty-nest dogs."

"Yes, well. The house is quiet without you in it! These rascals keep us on our toes." Though she was trying to sound chipper, Marina knew her mother well enough to hear the shakiness in her voice. They fell silent for a minute, each savoring the sound of the other.

"How's Dad?"

"Oh, just fine. Harumphing his way through the semester, as usual.

He misses you, you know. I know he's not a big phone talker but it would mean a lot if you gave him a buzz now and then."

"I miss him, too," Marina said. She felt overcome with sentimentality, as though she wanted to slip through the phone wire and into her mother's arms. "I miss you guys so much. I was thinking maybe I would come up for the weekend, sometime soon."

"Oh, we would just love that! It's so pretty up here this time of year. You missed apple season, unfortunately. This year's crop was pitiful. Worst I've ever seen, I think. The weather was just so erratic. Our little orchard really suffered." Alice sighed. "We just had the last of them fall off the trees. I canned what I could. But you know what? Those little apples were delicious. We made applesauce and a pie, and I made strudel for my students. They were just the sweetest apples. Or maybe we just appreciated them more because there were so few of them." Alice laughed, and Murray let out a single bark.

"Maybe even this weekend," Marina said. "Maybe Saturday."

"Maybe Saturday! We would love that. Look at the train schedule and call me anytime darling. Oh! I have to go now. Murray's just thrown up all over kitchen floor. *Murray!*" And then she was gone, and Marina was alone in Brooklyn.

---

Over dinner, the conversation quickly turned to the declining state of the magazine industry and, more generally, the world. To Marina's left was a perfectly chiseled man named Franklin who she at first assumed was gay. His silk button-down shirt was open one button too many, revealing a slice of muscled pectoral. As it turned out, Franklin was living with Isabelle, the exquisitely fair woman at the far end of the table. Both were photographers. Franklin was from Trinidad and had the slightest lilt of an accent. When he laughed, it sounded honey coated. He looked Marina directly in the eye when they spoke, as if mentally taking a picture of her.

Marina ate little but drank heavily. As she drifted into drunkenness, she began to find Franklin deeply attractive. His teeth were perfect, Hollywood white against his clean dark skin. He spoke about things foreign to her: contemporary Caribbean fiction, his brother's recent wedding in Mumbai. He had baked the bread for tonight's dinner himself. It was being passed around in a wicker basket, slightly misshapen and enticingly sweet and wrapped in a paper napkin. It was served with mango chutney, which a number of guests were smearing on the turkey in lieu of cranberry sauce. Marina took seconds, even though she usually made a point of staying away from bread.

The dinner was haphazardly constructed. George had tasked her guests somewhat whimsically and had lost track of who was bringing what. There were three kinds of potatoes (mashed sweet, mashed Yukon, scalloped Russet), but only one vegetable (candied beets). Marina had brought the only pie, not enough for all sixteen guests. A bearded writer named Tom had brought three dozen gluten-free sugar cookies that had crumbled on their journey from Astoria. And instead of salad, Isabelle had brought an offering of pureed pumpkin (delicious) and a crimson amaryllis, which stood at the center of the table, its petals opened like trumpets.

Soon, Marina was leaning in, her thigh pressed against Franklin's, she could feel the thick fabric of his jeans brushing against her tights, and she pushed her hair back from her shoulders to expose her clavicle. He was polite but declined to engage with her flirtation. As the dinner wore on he glanced more often at Isabelle. Marina had never before been attracted to a black man, and she had never openly hit on another woman's boyfriend. But the steady flow of wine emboldened her, everything she thought she knew was dissolving, and the world felt raw, as if its skin had been turned inside out. Today felt like a day for firsts.

"Marina would never move to Brooklyn!" George was exclaiming across the table. "Never. But I might! I like it out here. I thought you would have to drag me feet first from the Village, but I've reconsidered. Anything's possible." She smiled coyly at Max, who downed a glass of wine and dropped his hand into her lap.

"Uh-oh, Max," Franklin said. He shook his head, chortling. "Manhattan may lose its It Girl thanks to you. What will happen next?"

George rolled her eyes, but Marina could see that she was reveling in her coronation as Manhattan's It Girl. She picked up a bottle of merlot and began to refill the empty glasses. *She thinks she wants to marry him,* Marina thought bitterly. *She thinks he'll marry her because he's thirty-six and probably wants to get on with it.*

"Nothing to do with Max," George said grandly. The bottle in her hand was kicked. She stood behind him as he opened another, and stroked his cheek with the back of her hand. "Really, I've fallen for Brooklyn. Or maybe I've just fallen out of love with Manhattan." She began to pour again.

"Oh George, no you haven't!" Marina said. She was aware of a slight slur in her voice.

"Don't you find it so depressing? All the restaurants are empty. All the good stores are closing. I hate it."

Isabelle laughed. "I thought it was depressing until I went into Barney's last weekend. Everything is like forty percent off! It's the first time I have ever been able to afford anything there."

"Any price tag that says forty percent off should have a disclaimer that reminds you that your 401(k) is forty percent off, too," said Malcolm. Malcolm was a lawyer, the only corporate type present. Laughter rippled down the table, bouncing off the double-height ceilings, the faint shadows of treetops discernible through the darkening wall of glass windows. "And no one's getting a year-end bonus, either."

"None of us expected to, counselor," Franklin said, smiling without a trace of resentment. "We're all artists and writers, remember?"

"Or self-employed," Max said. He raised his glass. "If anyone sees my boss, tell him I deserve a raise!"

Everyone was merry, clinking glasses and toasting their sorry fate.

Marina found this vein of humor surprisingly refreshing. All of Tanner's friends were hedge funders or trust funders, and they were taking the downturn seriously indeed. It was an oft-discussed topic at dinner parties. Trips to Aspen were being canceled; summer homes were on the market; there were fewer holiday parties than ever before.

"I have trouble feeling sorry for the bankers in your neighborhood, George," Isabelle said. "Yes, their hedge funds are closing and they're getting laid off. But the same thing's happening in the magazine industry."

"And they were *responsible* for what's going on. There's a big difference between an ailing magazine and Lehman Brothers. Lehman deserves to go under. They created the problem," a writer named Elise offered. The mood was turning somber. Brows furrowed around the table and more than one person nodded in consent.

"I'm not sure that's entirely fair," Marina countered cautiously. "I mean, an analyst at Lehman is no more at fault than an editor at *Press.* They aren't making the high-level decisions. They're just doing what they're told. Sure, some of them were getting paid too much. But why turn it down if it's being offered?" What she was saying might not be well received by liberal company, but the alcohol had eroded her judgment. Her head was spinning slightly, and the dim candlelight and brightly painted walls made her feel vaguely as though she were trapped in the middle of Mardi Gras. She was, she realized, dead drunk. Through the fog, she heard a distant ringing.

"I think your purse is calling you," Franklin said gently into her ear. He reached behind her and unhooked her handbag from the back of her chair.

"Thanks," Marina muttered, embarrassed. She stood up abruptly and fumbled for her phone, which had found its way to some hidden corner of her bag. No one noticed as she slipped through the nearest doorway, away from the din of the party. She closed the door behind her. Glancing around, she realized she was standing in Max's home office. Unsure of whether it was okay for her to be there, she stood awkwardly in the center of the space, lights still off.

She didn't recognize the number. It was from area code 212, a Manhattan landline. For a fleeting second, her heart fluttered. It was Tanner, calling from his parents' apartment.

"Hello?" she said. She tried to sound as casual as possible. For a second, she thought to reopen the door, letting in the ambient noise of the party.

"Marina? It's Duncan." He paused and the line went silent.

Marina's heart stopped. *Duncan.* What on earth could he want?

Unable to speak, she simply remained, phone pressed to her ear, her lips slightly parted.

"So, happy Thanksgiving," he said. He cleared his throat. He sounded nervous. "Hello? Did I lose you?"

"No, I'm here," Marina said hoarsely. "Happy Thanksgiving to you as well. I'm sorry. I'm out in Brooklyn and the reception isn't very good."

"Brooklyn! Why? You don't live out there, do you?"

"No," Marina said quickly. "Just at a friend's for Thanksgiving dinner."

She thought: *if he's calling to ask me to do something, I'm going to quit on the spot.* "Can I do something for you?"

"Oh goodness, you're in the middle of dinner. Terribly sorry. I shouldn't keep you." He sounded uncharacteristically chastened, and Marina instantly regretted the sharpness of her voice. He didn't want anything; he was calling to wish her a happy Thanksgiving. Of course. It was so thoughtful of him to think of her, and here she was snapping at him.

*You're becoming a bitch,* she thought. *And you're drunk.*

"There is actually something I need from you. Now that you mention it."

Marina was silent.

"It doesn't have to be done today, just when you get the chance. Maybe tomorrow."

There were few turns of phrase Marina hated as much as "when you get the chance." Duncan employed it often, tacking it onto any request that he had otherwise indicated as urgent or time sensitive.

"Certainly. Happy to."

"Can you pull the interview I did with Jane Hewitt this summer, as well as any notes, *et cetera* that I used to prep for it? I also want to see my schedule from the day she came in; you can pull that off my Outlook. I'm thinking of doing a sort of follow-up piece on her, so I want you to get me the names and general hierarchy of the SEC. Don't rely on the one we created this summer; it's out of date."

Marina had begun to cry. Tears slipped silently down her face, but they were thick and fast and she knew that soon she would be outright sobbing. She cupped her hand around lower half of the phone in an attempt to muffle it, wiping her nose on the back of her hand as she did. Through the wall, she could hear the muted roar of laughter and the sound of someone clinking a fork against a glass as if in preparation for a toast.

"That sounds interesting," she said. It was the best she could manage for someone who was being dictated to in the middle of Thanksgiving dinner.

"Oh and pull what you can on Morton Reis and his firm RCM and also Delphic—that's Carter Darling's firm." After a half-step pause, he exclaimed, "My dear. Are you crying?"

She had thought she had been quiet, but it was possible she had let out a small whimper.

She sniffled. "I'm sorry," she said. She felt reckless and numb and like she had nothing left to lose. "I am crying. I know that's terribly inappropriate. It's just that my boyfriend broke up with me yesterday, and I had already canceled Thanksgiving with my family to spend it with him, so I'm at a friend's instead. And now I'm working. Anyway, I'm sorry."

A silence ensued. Marina tapped one foot nervously against the plush carpet.

"Well, nothing like a little wanton honesty," Duncan said, finally. He chuckled, his strange little nervous chuckle that had an unusually high pitch. "What's the name? Your boyfriend?"

"Tanner," Marina said. She now felt very sorry to have brought it up. "Tanner Morgenson."

"Well. Marina. I know a lot of people and I have to say I consider myself a good judge of them. This may be out of line—but hell, I think we lost sight of the line a few minutes ago—Tanner Morgenson sounds like an absolute idiot. You're beautiful and clever, and poised for someone your age. You're going to do well here, Marina, I'm sure of it. Not many people can put up with me, you know. You've got a certain confidence and thickness of the skin, which are absolute necessities in this town."

"Thank you. That really means a lot to me. Especially from you."

"Well," he said, and she imagined him turning slightly pinkish, "I think you should see this as a blessing. A release from a lifetime of mediocrity. No doubt you outshine this young man in most every way. He isn't the grandson of William, son of Bill, is he? If you don't mind my asking."

"Yes." Though she imagined he was about to let loose some scathing criticism about the Morgensons, Marina felt a blush of pride to be affiliated with so grand a family. She might go up a half tick in Duncan's social register.

"Well, Marina, I'm going to tell you a little secret now, which is perhaps a poorly kept secret, but most of them are, anyway. The Morgensons are absolutely, completely, and utterly bankrupt. Have been for quite some time. I have it on the very best authority."

Marina's eyes grew wide as pumpkins. "No. That can't be! I've been to their home—to several of their homes! Just last night, in fact. Their apartment's beautiful."

"Well, that may be true, but young Tanner has another thing coming if he expects to get a dime. His grandfather made a killing, but gave most of it to charity and what was left he split between four children. Tanner's father's a complete moron. Bill Morgenson's never worked a day in his life, except getting himself tangled up in the occasional get-rich-quick real estate investment. He reduced his small fortune to virtually nothing over the years, and has gotten a bit desperate. Eighteen months ago, at the height of the market, he sank whatever he had left into that big glass building in midtown—you know the one I'm talking about, the name will come to me in a minute—which was a complete bust. I have a very dear friend who happens to be close to the deal who told me the three main investors—Morgenson being one—personally guaranteed it. Which of course is absolute idiocy. So really, the family's in the ground. It's only a matter of time until Tanner's tending bar."

"But the mother!" Marina said. "Doesn't Grace have money? That's what everybody says."

"Oh no, none at all. Her father couldn't stand Bill. Didn't go to their wedding, I'm told. Cut her off entirely."

"Amazing." Marina was stunned. "They certainly put on a good show."

"That they do. Now what do you say you finish your dinner and then you help me do some research on Jane Hewitt. And Morton Reis. And Carter Darling. And after that, we will see who really holds the cards."

"Happy to," she said. She grabbed a pad off Max's desk and wrote down the names as quickly as she could.

"Call Owen Barry at the *Wall Street Journal*, too. Tell him I need to talk to him and it's urgent and I'll be in touch shortly. Give him those three names. He knows everything about everyone. Also, see if you can track down the contact information for Scott Stevens. He used to work at the SEC down in D.C., and at one time oversaw an investigation into RCM. My understanding is that he left there rather abruptly—in late 2006, I think—and the investigation was shut down after that. It would be interesting to speak to him."

"Owen Barry. Scott Stevens. Okay. Is there anything else I can do?"

"Not for the moment. If I think of something, I'll ring you. This will be a fun little project for us, Marina. Think of it as vigilante justice."

"Do you want me to call him, maybe? Scott Stevens?"

Duncan paused. "Let's not get ahead of ourselves. Just the contact information will be fine."

She bit her lip. "All right," she said. "Let me know if I can be of help with research or anything. This is the kind of thing I really like to do."

After she hung up the phone, she took a look around Max's home office and smiled. Here was someone who had actually done something, despite having been born privileged. His desk was overflowing with papers, and his computer glowed in the semidarkness, as though alive with ideas. Suddenly, she found herself liking Max immensely. As she slipped back into the party, her hand instinctively brushed her cheek; it was now dry. She had stopped crying.

# THURSDAY, 6:02 P.M.

"Let's all sit," Carter said as he ushered everyone into the dining room. Carmela was standing nervously at the back, waiting for instructions. The table was perfect; soft candlelight lit up the peach-colored walls. The china sparkled. Stomachs began to growl, mouths moistened as everyone took their seats. Outside, the wind had picked up, setting the porch lamps swinging in the night air.

When everyone had found his place, Carmela said to Carter, "Everything's ready. Do you want me to serve?" They both glanced at the sideboard. A feast had been laid out. Carrots glazed in brown butter; steaming mashed potatoes; roasted autumn vegetables shimmering with olive oil; Carmela's famous stuffing—all presented in terra-cotta serving dishes, a symphony of fall color. In the center was a perfect, plump turkey. Whenever Carter gave the word, Carmela would whisk the turkey back into the kitchen for John to carve. Then Carter would serve it, placing pieces delicately on the plates with silver tongs, and everyone would tell him how beautiful it looked this year.

"Not yet," Carter said brusquely. "Just make sure everyone has a drink." Carmela nodded and began to pour the wine.

Sol turned his glass over before Carmela reached him. "Just water for me," he said. "Or whatever he's drinking." He pointed to Carter's ginger ale.

"Of course. Would you care for some?" Carmela said quietly, holding out the bottle for Marion's approval.

"Oh yes, please. This is beautiful," Marion said apologetically, gesturing at the spread. "You always do such a lovely job."

Carmela nodded in acknowledgment and then glanced around, as if unsure the compliment was rightly hers. As soon as the glasses were full, she disappeared into the kitchen. The table fell back into an awkward lull. From behind the swinging door came the sound of pots banging on the stove. A strain of classical music wafted through and then stopped abruptly; Carmela had switched off the radio.

Adrian yawned loudly, breaking the silence. He reached forward and took a roll out of the breadbasket. He nudged Lily for the butter. She glared at him as she passed it, her ears flushing red with annoyance. Adrian pretended not to notice and began slathering his bread.

"Do we think she's coming down soon?" Merrill said to her father.

Carter's jaw tightened. "I imagine so." To the table, he announced loudly, "Let's talk about something." He was trying to keep things light, but it had come out wrong and he sounded angry. Merrill looked down at the floor like a reprimanded child.

"Has anyone spoken to Julianne?" Adrian asked.

"Something else." Carter snapped, cutting him off.

Carmela reentered the room with a pitcher of water. "Let's just start," Carter said to her. "The turkey's getting cold."

"Who won the game?" Marion offered, trying again. She smiled at the group.

"Lions got crushed," Adrian said. He pulled off a piece of crust, crumbs skittering across the tablecloth. He shrugged. "Decimated. We lost forty-seven to ten."

"Oh my. Against whom?"

"Tennessee Titans."

"Now remind me why it is that you all root for Detroit every year."

Like spectators at a tennis match, the rest of the family glanced back toward Adrian. No one else dared to touch the bread. "Damned if I know," he said. He shrugged, and with pointed disinterest, jammed a bit of roll into his mouth.

When he was done chewing he wiped the edge of his mouth with his napkin and turned to Lily, who was actively glaring. "What?" he said, rolling his eyes. "He said we were starting. I'm starving."

"Why don't you wait until everyone's served?" Lily said crisply. She was sitting up perfectly straight, fingers laced primly together at the table edge. She looked eerily like Ines. Any trace of the erection which had plagued Adrian earlier in the evening was instantly gone.

"My grandfather was one of the original owners of the Lions," Carter announced, drawing attention back to the head of the table. "He was friends with George Richards, who brought the team to Detroit in 1934."

"Oh, *that's* interesting," Marion said, even though everyone had heard this story before. "Do you still have family in Michigan?"

"Is that story even true?" Merrill asked suddenly. Her voice was laced with an acidity that Paul had never heard her use with her father. Only Paul could see that she was picking ferociously at the cuticle of her thumb beneath the table. It had begun to bleed. Paul reached out to stop her but she pulled away, wrapping her finger discreetly in a napkin.

"Of course it is," Carter said. He seemed disarmed by Merrill's tone. Their gazes locked intently. For a moment, it was as though the rest of the table had fallen away and only Carter and Merrill existed. Paul and Adrian both sat frozen in their seats, unsure of what would happen next.

"Because you always say that half the things your dad said weren't true, and that sounds like the kind of story he would make up."

"*Merrill,*" Lily said sternly from across the table. "Stop." She widened her eyes in the direction of the Penzells. The sharpness of her voice, the angle at which her pale eyebrows had knit themselves furiously together, conveyed an urgency that Adrian evidently found amusing. He let out a sharp, barking laugh that was met with silence from the rest of the table.

The Penzells stared off into space, brutally aware that they had happened upon a private family moment. All evening, they had been trying with limited success not to draw attention to themselves. Sol, unfortunately, had made the mistake of wearing a tie. His was the wrong sort of shirt for a tie, however, soft collared and plaid, and it gave the impression that there had been a last-minute squabble with Marion over the dress code, which Sol had lost. Sol now pulled at the tie, loosening it around his neck, and pretended not to sense the tension between the Darlings.

He sat back in his chair and it rocked a little too far on its back legs, startling everyone.

"Careful!" Lily squeaked reflexively. She reached forward as if she could snag him from across the table. Sol snapped his chair back into place and readjusted his tie.

"Sorry," he said to Lily. "Didn't mean to scare you."

"For God's sake, Lily," Merrill said, exasperated. She turned to Sol and Marion. "I'm sorry," she said. "But I don't think we should start without Mom." She put her napkin down on top of her plate and rose to her feet. The napkins were linen and lace, like tiny little tablecloths. A red spot of blood about the size of dime was visible at its edge of hers.

"Sit down, Merrill," Carter said. "Your mother will come down when she's ready. We have guests."

"I'm going to go check on her," Merrill said, and walked out, the door swinging gently in her wake.

---

"Mom?" Merrill's voice skipped off the bathroom walls like a stone. "Are you up here?"

Ines paused, her body still for a minute while she decided whether or not to reply. Ines wondered how long they had been waiting for her to come down. Could it already be 6 p.m.? No one cared if she watched the football game. She thought she had heard the Penzells pull up in the driveway, but she wasn't sure. Outside, the sky had grown dark, and the drive up to the house was dotted with lights.

Dinner must be ready. Ines imagined what was going on downstairs; she could see it exactly. Adrian was probably hungry. Lily was fretting with the place settings, or buzzing nervously around the Penzells, impatient with Adrian and embarrassed that her mother was being an ineffectual hostess. Carter would be hungry, too, but he wouldn't allow them to start without her. The girls must have discussed it quietly and agreed that someone should check on her. Merrill might have volunteered, but more likely, they had drawn straws for the job. When they were little, the girls used to put their pointer fingers up against their noses when an unpleasant chore was suggested—taking the trash out or helping with the dishes—and whoever was slower to the draw would be responsible for it. Merrill, older and quicker, usually won.

*Merrill must have lost this round,* Ines thought. Or maybe she had volunteered; Merrill the diplomat, Merrill the peacekeeper.

Ines imagined her trudging dutifully up the stairs, wondering why her mother was being difficult. The conversation among the others would be stilted in her absence. They would talk in circles about football and the coming storm, avoiding anything that had to do with Morty or the business. Or Julianne. Or Ines. Ines felt a pang of guilt, but it was passing.

She had been trying to pull herself together all day. Her makeup bag had tipped over and exploded across the bathroom floor. Shards of powdered bronzer and a fractured mirror had skittered across the tiles. Her expensive foundation had splattered like beige paint. Broken glass from the bottle glistened between the fibers of the bathmat. Ines kept trying to clean up the mess, first with tissues and then with her hands, but it was everywhere. Now she was kneeling on the bathroom floor, trying hopelessly to pick the glass out of the rug before she hurt herself. The fine bones of her feet felt unprotected from the hardness of the tiles. Small red dents had begun to appear on her kneecaps where the edges had dug into her flesh, like the lines that appear on one's calves when kneesocks are too tight at the top. It wasn't an altogether unpleasant sort of pain. It reminded her of being in church, kneeling on the unforgiving surface of the wooden beam that folded out from beneath the pew.

The shower was running. Ines had turned it on to drown out her crying. Tears rolled down her face in salty, hot drops. Her nose ran, too; clear mucus that stung at her chin. Because the trashcan was just out of reach from where she sat, crumpled Kleenex bloomed like flowers across the bathroom floor. Just listening to the shower felt cleansing. Its constant, steady pounding against the marble felt reassuring, too, there was something infinitely practical about it.

She was too tired to bathe herself today. The thought of drying her hair and applying makeup overwhelmed her. No one would notice, anyway. Carter certainly wouldn't. It had been months since he had looked at her with any kind of sexual interest or even casual physical appraisal. It was as though he no longer saw her at all.

Ines wasn't a fool. She was practical enough to recognize that her inherent value was depreciating. Her once boundless energy was now diminished. She could hardly keep her eyes open past 10:30 p.m., even at the ballet or a dinner party with friends. She was more forgetful than ever. And worst of all, her body was deteriorating at a rate that felt unbridled. This drove her to distraction. Every year, it seemed, she had to explore increasingly drastic options (facelifts, juice fasts, liposuction) just to maintain the status quo. It wasn't that she didn't understand her husband's waning interest. But that didn't make it easier to accept.

Ines knew that she had lost him as a lover a decade ago. It could have been longer than that, though she didn't like to consider this possibility. She had spent the end of her forties and the beginning of her fifties conceding that struggle. She had arrived at a place where she no longer craved that sort of attention from Carter. Instead, she settled for a platonic strain of admiration, the kind Hollywood bestows upon older actresses. It wasn't sufficient, but it sustained her. Maybe it was a bad patch, she told herself. Maybe it was temporary.

At the very least, Carter had never resented her. The money had always been theirs, not his. For that, Ines was grateful. She couldn't stand to be monitored as some of her friends were, submitting credit card receipts to their husbands like a member of the household staff. It always shocked Ines to hear her friends complain of their husband's resentments about money. It seemed to have gotten worse with age, despite the fact that many of these men were only growing richer by the year. It was as though, once past childbearing age, wives became functionally useless. They lunched and threw parties and bought clothes, but they were no longer sexually appealing. Their children required little if any maternal attention. Their husbands saw them as cash drains, an extra person on the payroll.

Perhaps it was she who had strayed first. It had happened insidiously, sometime between the births of Merrill and Lily. Ines's focus, once on Carter, shifted to her children. She wasn't one of those women who romanticized motherhood. There were days that she hated it, all the feeding and the ear infections and the lack of adult conversation. But she tried to do it well, and the girls were hers, in a way that no one, not even Carter, had ever been. A lot of nights she was asleep by the time he got home. In the midst of it, her marriage slipped out of focus, the backdrop behind a portrait of the girls.

On bad days, Ines told herself that she had stayed in it for Merrill and Lily, so that they would have everything she hadn't. Not just the schools and the houses and the tennis lessons and the perfect dresses but the full family, a father who adored them. Ines's own father had passed away when she was eight. Her mother fell into a deep depression and was deemed unable to care for her, so Ines was sent to Rio to live with her grandparents. Ines recalled little from her childhood except that her grandfather was kind and forgetful, and their house was silent, and furnished in austere dark woods and stone tiling. She spent her teenage years lost in American fashion magazines and cinema, and resolved to get out of Brazil as soon as she was able. At seventeen, she came to New York to model. After a year, Ines realized that she was neither tall enough nor striking enough to sustain that sort of career. She was, however, stylish and smart and willing to do whatever it took to get where she wanted to go. She found herself a job as a secretary at *Women's Wear Daily.* By twenty-five, she was a junior fashion editor at *Harper's Bazaar*, working elbow to elbow with Anna Wintour.

She went to a lot of fancy parties in those days, and it was at one of those fancy parties that she met Carter Darling. After their first date she thought that he was a bit of a snob, and also that it was inevitable that she would fall madly in love with him. She did. They got married at City Hall, and afterward went for a long, champagne-soaked lunch at La Grenouille with friends. She wore an elegant white shift and matching jacket from Valentino that she thought made her look like Mia Farrow at her wedding to Frank Sinatra at the Sands. There was no honeymoon because Ines was already pregnant with Merrill and feeling too nauseated to travel.

For a time, she worried that she might eventually fall out of love with her husband, or he with her. They had married so quickly, and so young, and were from different worlds altogether. Yet over the years, they were able to form a partnership that felt more functional and aligned than any of their friends' relationships. They never fought about money or where they would live or how the girls would be raised. Perhaps they should have, Ines thought sometimes, because then they might have felt more like lovers than business partners.

When he did ultimately fall in love with someone else, Ines didn't consider leaving as a real possibility. Where would she go? And how could she ever do that to the girls? They were a family. Staying with Carter was a selfless decision, and the right one. Or so she told herself. The fear that it was neither cut her to the core.

---

"Mom?"

Ines shut off the shower.

When she emerged from the bathroom, Merrill was perched on the edge of the bed like a pigeon. Her face was fresh, a clean-scrubbed pink. Her golden brown hair was pulled back from her face in a ponytail, clean and girlish. Though Ines imagined she wasn't, Merrill looked rested, as she would on any other weekend in the country. It was an illusion, of course, but Ines was grateful for it. Seeing her children suffer was more than she could bear at this point.

By contrast, Ines looked like shit.

"How are you doing, Mom?" Merrill blinked at her expectantly. She looked concerned but not disapproving. "I think dinner's ready."

Ines sighed and disappeared into her walk-in closet. From inside it, she said, "I know. I'll just be a minute."

"Are you going somewhere?"

"What?"

"Your suitcase is out here."

"I haven't decided," she said. She could sense that Merrill was on the verge of saying something but thought better of it.

"Where would you go?" Merrill said, after a minute of silence. "Back to the city? Or somewhere else?"

When there was no reply, Merrill said, "Mom, could you please come out of the closet? Have you spoken to Dad?"

Ines emerged from the closet. In her hand was a cashmere turtleneck. They both stared at the open suitcase, which was lying on the rack beside the bed. The lid was propped against the back wall, revealing a half-hearted attempt at packing. Absently, Ines pulled the sweater over her head without bothering to put on a bra. In the naked sunlight, her body looked old, like some external force had been sucking at her skin until it had started to come lose off her.

The truth of it was that she was terrified to leave Beech House. Carter would return to Manhattan in the morning, and both he and Sol had expressed how important it was for her to go with him. "I need you, Ines," Carter had said. It had been so long since he had assigned her any importance that she found this almost heartwarming. Then Sol had said: "It will look bad if you're apart. Anyway, what would you do out here all by yourself?" The two of them stood there like a team. They had rehearsed their pitch beforehand, she realized, her heart hardening. She was just part of the plan's execution.

The more relevant question, to Ines anyway, was what would she do with herself in Manhattan? She couldn't visualize it. Should she stay home and watch television, waiting for Carter to return and tell her their life was ending? That the lawyers' fees would bankrupt them? That he was going to disappear to some country with no extradition treaty, and she would see him again only on the television screen?

She would go to the gym or to the deli or to Starbucks, where undoubtedly she would see an acquaintance who would stop her and ask after the family and, if they were particularly tactless, express sadness over Morty's death. Or, after Carter's mistress was inevitably interviewed on television, they would say nothing to her but simply duck their heads and pass by as though they hadn't seen her. That's what she would do if she were they. What could she possibly say to anyone now?

She realized, as she considered these actualities, these threads of what would now be her life's fabric, that there wasn't a single person in the world she wanted to see. She would make a lifetime of avoiding the people she had once worked so hard to befriend. Even getting coffee at the deli around the corner would be a gauntlet run. She would have to wear a hat and slip in and out, unnoticed. She'd be embarrassed to be anywhere—*even the deli*—like some sort of Hester Prynne. And this was all before the press got wind of everything. This was the beginning.

It would be easier to avoid all that in the country. Days could be whiled away at Beech House, checking on the temperamental boiler, instructing the staff, inspecting the hedgerow. Ines always felt purposeful when she was there. It wasn't that the tasks were important or could only be accomplished by Ines herself (most of it, admittedly, could and often was delegated to a third party: Carmela or John, an interior decorator, a gardener). But rather, their value lay in the fact that Ines was good at them, and it brought her pleasure to be able to look back on the day and see tangible evidence of what she had accomplished. The apartment in the city, contained as it was within a fully staffed building, ran itself. A relief on most days, but on other days, days when she was alone, the apartment's self-sufficiency made her feel obsolete, like an outdated coffeemaker relegated to the back cupboard.

Beech House was a place of suspended reality, filled with manicured lawns and porticos and putting greens. Like all summer homes, it had no real purpose. During the summer season, its residents could pretend that the question that pressed most heavily upon their minds was *Golf or tennis this morning?* Weather discrepancies—impending rainstorms, unseasonable chills—sent everyone into frantic caucus. Even the tasks that Ines clung to as purposeful were, for the most part, manufactured. No one needed an arbor by the swimming pool, for example, and the mudroom furniture didn't need to be repainted nearly as often as it was. These banalities were merely meant to occupy her, allowing the time to pass gently. Ines could lose herself for days there, even weeks, like Alice down the rabbit hole.

Also, Carter had bought it just for her. Back in the days when he would do anything for her. She could have had a less expensive house, or one requiring far less work. But this was the one she wanted. And what Carter wanted, or so he had said at the time, was to see her happy.

If Ines had a choice, she would stay there in perpetuity.

"Your father's going back into the city tomorrow morning," Ines said. She sat down at her glass-topped vanity table. Its triptych of mirrors reflected her features, dark and defined, at three angles. She looked at herself, and then at her daughter, and they locked eyes. "He wants me to go with him."

"I think that's probably a good idea."

Ines sighed. She glanced away from the mirror and out through the darkened window. "I was hoping we could all enjoy the weekend out in the country," she said. She began to brush her hair. "It's so rare that we're all together."

"Mom," Merrill stood up. She crossed her arms over her chest. She was all elbows and eyebrows, sharply impatient. "We can't just pretend this isn't happening."

"That what isn't happening?"

"This whole mess with the firm. I'm not a moron, Mom. I'm a lawyer. There's going to be media attention soon, and indictments and all the rest."

"Yes, thank you, Merrill, for bringing your legal expertise to bear." Ines's eyebrow arched as she pulled her hair back into a severe knot at the nape of her neck.

Merrill's eyelid's flickered, but she didn't take the bait. "We have to rally behind Dad," she persisted. "There has to be some kind of family unity."

Ines stopped fussing with her hair. "Don't you dare imply that I haven't stood behind your father. There's a lot that you don't understand."

"Then explain it to me," Merrill said, her eyes large and plaintive. "Please, Mom. If you don't come into the city, where will you go?"

"Are you asking me if I'm leaving your father?"

Merrill glanced away. "I guess. It's not like I wouldn't understand."

Ines felt a welling up of guilt, the way she used to when Merrill was young and she and Carter had had a row. Whatever frustration she had felt for her daughter had subsided, and was replaced only by a tender sadness. "You know I love you all very much," she said, "but I'm not sure—I'm not sure I can get through what he's putting me through right now."

Without warning, Ines started to cry. Though Merrill was startled, she tried not to show it. She realized that she had almost never seen her mother cry, except during old movies. Ines didn't cry for personal reasons. She was too efficient for it. She had buzzed through Merrill and Lily's weddings with greater equanimity than the caterer.

Ines also rarely confided in anyone. Merrill often wondered if her mother saw a shrink—God knows the rest of them did—but knew better than to ask. If ever she needed to see one, now was the time.

Ines rose and came over to the bed. They sat side by side, mother and daughter, not looking at each other but feeling the other's closeness. Ines wiped back her tears with one hand and then patted Merrill's thigh. "I promised myself a long time ago that there were two things I wouldn't do to you and Lily. I wouldn't talk badly about your father, no matter what, and I wouldn't leave, no matter what. He's not always made it easy, you know. Your father's a great father. He's not always been a great husband."

"Why did you stay with him then? Please don't say for us."

"Of course for you."

Merrill wiped at her eyes with her sleeve. "Mom, all I want is for you to be happy. And I know Dad hasn't always been a great husband. Honestly, there were times where I expected you to leave him and I was surprised you didn't. But right now . . . well, it seems like a really bad time to hold him accountable for some of his, you know, his indiscretions. There's going to be so much bad press when the news comes out about Morty's fund. If you leave him, it won't look good."

Ines stiffened. "If I left your father, it wouldn't have anything to do with the firm. Not really." She hesitated, but couldn't help but continue. It had been so long since she had been able to speak about this to anyone. "He should have told you this. Will you promise to keep this to yourself? Lily doesn't need to know about this unless it becomes an issue. But I want you to understand it. Maybe that's selfish, but I want someone to understand. I don't have anyone to talk to."

"Understand what?"

Ines paused. When she spoke, her eyes were closed and her hand floated to her mouth, as if her words embarrassed her. "That your father is having an affair. It's been going on a very long time."

"I know, Mom," Merrill flushed uncomfortably. They had never spoken of it, never even alluded to it, before now.

"Do you understand who the woman is?"

"I always . . . to be honest, I've sometimes wondered if it was Julianne." Merrill paused. "Oh, I see," she said, nodding. Her face opened up as though she had just realized something important that had been eluding her for years. "I see why that makes this more complicated."

Ines snorted. "Oh, sweetheart," she said, shaking her head. "It's so much more complicated than that."

What struck Merrill most about the conversation that followed was her mother's tone. It was neither angry nor hurt, but simply pragmatic, as though she were explaining the order of the world to a child.

When she finally appeared in the dining room, Ines looked radiant. Her hair was pulled neatly back and her makeup had been carefully done. Her cheekbones had been stenciled in with blush and bronzer, and she looked full of life. She wore a scarf tucked neatly around her neck, its crimson folds lending color to an otherwise black outfit. If she had been crying, no one could tell. "I'm so sorry to have kept you waiting," she said graciously to Sol and Marion.

Everyone was so relieved to see her that conversation resumed with a new buoyancy, as though it were any other Thanksgiving. Ines talked the most, engaging Sol and Marion in chitchat, pulling her chair around to talk with Lily and Adrian. The only person she didn't speak to directly was Carter.

At the end of dinner, Carter rose to his feet and clinked his glass. "Thank you all for being here," he said, looking at Ines. She was staring away from him, into a mid-distance. She smiled faintly, tartly, like an actress aware that she was being photographed from afar. "I would like to take a moment to remember those who are not with us tonight, and to thank God for those who are." He bowed his head. "During times like these, it's easy to forget how blessed we've been. But Thanksgiving is a time of reflection. More than ever, I'm grateful for the blessing that is my family."

Carter breathed in and glanced around the table. His children stared off in different directions. Only Sol looked directly at him, and offered him a kindly smile. Carter acknowledged it with a nod and then slipped silently back to his chair. Soon, Carmela appeared with a pie, and the room grew loud again with chatter.

# THURSDAY, 9:20 P.M.

Finally, Ines was in bed, the kids were upstairs, Marion was pulling out of the driveway. The distant sounds of Carmela and John picking up the dishes, clinking the pots against the steel sink rim as they set them to soak, had stopped. Sol closed the library door behind them and looked at his friend. Carter looked as though he had aged fifteen years overnight. It made Sol tired just to look at him. He was fighting off exhaustion himself, it filled his body, settling in his temples, his joints, his chest cavity like groundwater. It was hard to believe that after twenty years in business together, they might have reached the end of the line, but it was beginning to feel that way.

"Any update on the body search?" Carter said, once Sol had taken a seat.

"No. I spoke to the chief of police before coming over. They haven't found anything. The storm's made it nearly impossible for them. The wind's creating some kind of cross current in the river."

Carter nodded. "Are we moving forward with the memorial service?"

"Julianne's coming around to it. She still wants it to be a proper funeral, but—" He shrugged, the gesture finishing off the sentence. They were all doing a lot of that lately: shrugging, gesturing, implying, alluding their way around the indelicate realities of the situation in which they now found themselves. "But realistically, we may never find anything. Especially the way it's going. We're now talking about Wednesday of next week."

"I should call her."

"You don't need to. She understands you have a lot on your plate."

"This must be horrific for her."

"Of course. But I think you're better off focusing on yourself for now."

Carter fidgeted in his chair, unable to relax. After a moment he said, "Did you get ahold of Eli?"

"I did. We've spoken a few times. Not to say he owes me a favor, but—you know. He's going to be actively involved."

"All right. Good. That can only help." Carter settled back into the chair.

Sol frowned. The way Carter relaxed, his arms behind his head, irked him. Eli could help, but he wasn't a miracle worker. "Here's the situation," he said gruffly. "We know Robertson's going to make a run for governor. And he's under heavy pressure to crack down on the financial industry. Someone's head's going to end up on a stake."

Carter sat up again. "So they're going to make an example of me."

"They're going to make an example of somebody. They can't afford not to. RCM investors are going to lose billions of dollars, and at a time when the country is enraged about Wall Street corruption. Not to mention the government's systemic failure to prevent it."

"I'm not a fucking moron, Sol. I'm aware of what's going on. Morty caused this, so they would go after him, but since they can't, they're going after me. Is that the gist?"

Sol sighed and pushed his glasses on top of his head. They kept slipping off the bridge of his nose; either they had stretched out from overuse or he had actually lost weight in his face. He had lost weight everywhere in the past few months. He usually wore sweaters to cover his paunch, but now the paunch was gone and his sweater was awkwardly large, collecting in rolls around his midsection. "Not just you. That's my point. You and anyone at the firm who may have had any involvement. And the folks at the SEC who should have paid more attention."

"Eli said this? Without you pressing the point?"

"Yes. He mentioned Adrian and Paul by name."

Carter bristled. "Paul got there two months ago. He barely knows where the printer is."

"It won't matter what their actual involvement was. It's a family firm, Carter. They'll go after the family in any way they can. Look at the Adelphia trial. They went after the father and both sons. John Rigas got twenty years. The good news is that the NYAG's office isn't aware of any"—Sol searched for a benign word—"*relationships* at the SEC. If it were, however, to, hm, come to light that there was any connection between Delphic and the SEC that wasn't entirely above board, quite frankly, all hell would break loose. I don't think this is something I need to explain, but I think we're at the point where we need to speak frankly, here, no?"

Carter offered a silent nod, glancing away into the fireplace.

"Look, in a nutshell, here's what Eli can offer you. Our side is maintaining the position that Alain was the one responsible for the RCM relationship, and he was responsible for any due diligence failures on Delphic's end. You're just a sales guy, and Eli gets that. Still you're the CEO, so we've got to work this so that you're playing on their team. I've expressed to them that you're just as shocked and outraged as they are by the situation. You've spent years building this business and it's devastating to your investors. Blah blah blah. And you're happy to facilitate their investigation in any way, even into members of your own firm. Understood?"

"Where the fuck is Alain?" Carter said. Suddenly, he was seething. He rose to his feet. "I mean, tell me. On holiday with his girlfriend? He hasn't returned one fucking phone call."

He wandered over to the fireplace. At his feet was a brass bucket that Ines decoratively filled with firewood every autumn. He picked up a twig and began to pull the bark from it, allowing small brown shards to litter the carpet. He stripped it bare, exposing its smooth, creamy interior and then tossed it into the fireplace. "He's such a fucking coward to disappear."

"He's in Switzerland somewhere, where he'll stay, if he's smart," Sol said. Carter's pacing had always irritated him. It was like watching a zoo animal, caged and restless. "I imagine he's under advisement from counsel not to speak to you. From my perspective, you're better off not having any contact. He's the adversary now."

"When did his flight leave, do you think? An hour before the news broke? Two? It's like he knew. Somehow, he knew."

*I am losing him*, Sol thought, as Carter dismembered another twig. Carter's mental state had deteriorated since the previous evening. He looked terrible. He seemed not to have slept, which was unfortunate. Sol worked backward in his head; Carter had likely been awake for over forty-eight hours. The fatigue combined with the emotional toll of Morty's death had begun to eat away at his reasoning capabilities. They would have to move swiftly now, and at some point, before they met with Eli, Carter would have to get some rest.

Sol had seen this before. When faced with indictment or bankruptcy or guilty verdicts, clients became emotional and erratic, shifting from anger to quiet acceptance and then back again, sometimes in the course of minutes. Physical and mental exhaustion only exacerbated it. Over years of practice, Sol learned how to stay in control in highly stressful situations. He often thought it was this that allowed him to be a great negotiator. It wasn't always easy. Clients often lashed out at him, even though it was, of course, the client who had brought them there in the first place.

"It doesn't matter," Sol said. "The point is, he's in Europe. Which is fine for us. In fact, it's better because it makes him look guilty as hell." There was a small part of Sol that felt bad about ramming this plan through without giving Carter the time to reflect on it. By the time it was over, Carter would have sold Alain, his friend and business partner of twenty-plus years, down the river, and there would be no looking back. Other casualties were possible, too; Paul, for example, wasn't outside the strike zone. But Sol quieted these thoughts. There was only one person whose interests he had to protect, and that was Carter. The call was tough, but it was clear.

"So that's it, then. We don't wait to hear from Alain, we don't even consider approaching this as a partnership."

"Listen to me. You're the CEO of Delphic. Either one person is going to take the fall, or several will. But if it's just one, that one is you. So it's you or him. Start getting used to that."

Sensing Carter's hesitation, Sol sighed and took a seat on Carter's desk, one foot swinging off the edge. "As a kid," he said, "we used to drive down to the Jersey Shore for the day. My brothers were bigger than me, so I usually wasn't allowed to go in the ocean with them unless it was a white flag day, you know, completely calm. I was a pretty husky kid, totally unathletic, so I was actually perfectly content to stay under the beach umbrella with a book. But pride's a pretty powerful propellant. So I used to beg and plead with my mom—*I'm old enough, let me go, too, let me go, too*—until one afternoon, she gave in. So then I was stuck. My brothers used to just jump right in and swim out to the breakpoint, and then they would ride the waves in on these body boards we had. But I was scared, so I stayed close to the shore. When a big wave finally came, I just froze, totally paralyzed. I ended up getting pulled into the vortex at the center of the wave and it held me under until I blacked out. I washed up on shore like a dead crab. It took the lifeguard three minutes to revive me. Scared the shit out of my mother. After that she used to say to me, 'Inaction is action, Sol, inaction is action.' I like to think about that every time I'm making a tough call. Diving in is no fun, but it's a hell of a lot better than drowning."

Carter didn't respond. Instead, he put his face in his hands. For a moment, Sol wondered if Carter was crying. He had to keep talking. One thing they couldn't do was stop and let paralysis set in. If they stopped moving, it would be over. "Look," he said, "this story will break in less than sixty hours. I'm not throwing those hours away, and I'm not going to sugar-coat things for you in order to lessen the blow."

Carter wasn't accustomed to getting told what to do by Sol or anyone else. Ordinarily, it would have angered him to be spoken to this way, but today he felt only crushing exhaustion. He fell back into the soft leather of the chair. For a few minutes he allowed himself to remain with his head propped up against it, unmoving.

He closed his eyes and saw Merrill. It was she who had, somewhat unexpectedly, haunted his thoughts these past few months, when everything was going to hell. Merrill, age six, her tiny face crumpled with determination as she begged him to remove the training wheels from her bicycle. Middle School Merrill, crying in the cab on the way home from an interschool dance, because the boy she liked had liked someone else. Merrill making pancakes in the kitchen in her Spence uniform. Merrill standing outside the courthouse after her swearing-in ceremony, looking impossibly adult in her crisp black suit. Like no other woman, Merrill had captivated him wholly since the day she was born.

He had been dying for years, he thought now, slowly, insidiously, without really even realizing it. This feeling had come over him once before, last spring. He remembered the exact date: May 2. The Dow had rebounded to 13,058 from a low of 11,900 or so fewer than sixty days before. And he had thought to himself when he heard that number: *That's it, that's the dead-cat bounce.* And then he thought, for no particular reason: *I'm dying. I know it.* Which was strange, because just that morning he had received a clean bill of health at his annual checkup. But he was right, at least about the first thing, because after that, the market unwound into a complete freefall, never again hitting the 13,000s. Ever since, he had behaved like a dying dog, sneaking off into the woods to be alone whenever he could. He had heard once that dogs did this so as not to show fear. He did it, he thought, out of cowardice.

"What is it you want me to do, then?" Carter asked. His voice had grown stronger, the tiredness washed away on a tide of determination. "How do we get this done?"

"They haven't committed to this. This is me and Eli talking. No one else."

"I understand."

"The plan right now is containment. We have to move with the NYAG's office so that by the time it comes out in the media, the ink on the deal is dry. Then you can at least rest easy knowing that they aren't going to go after you. The media still will. It's going to be a firestorm. They'll be outside your building, they'll run old pictures of your family. Pictures of the girls, riding horses, at their deb balls, that sort of thing, whatever they can find. And they'll dig up any dirt—and I mean any—that they can find, whether or not it is relevant to the case. We're thinking this will happen by Monday. Tuesday at the latest."

"We have to prepare Ines."

"Ines will get it. She's a businesswoman; we will have her prepped so that in the short term, you two will come out as a unified front. It won't be easy for her, but it's better in the long run. Neither of you want allegations of an affair out there in the press. Think about how that will make her look."

Carter cut him off. "Quite obviously, I've thought about that. I'm not a complete boor."

Sol shook his head. "I'm sorry, that came out wrong. All I meant to say was that you two have aligned interests on this one."

The two men paused. After a second, Carter's shoulders dropped; it wasn't Sol he should be fighting. In fact, he should not be fighting at all. "All right, so Alain first," he said. "I imagine they want his records, anything that shows he was the one running the relationship with RCM."

"Yes, and I have associates working on that already. It shouldn't be hard to establish; we'll pull some things that really highlight what a long leash Alain was giving RCM. That he didn't even have access to their accounts, that he never cross-checked anything with their counterparties or with an outside broker. Basically, he handed them money and didn't ask questions. We've gotten RCM's accountants to tell us that Alain and his team never once went out to see them, so that's helpful, too."

"Okay, and what about me? Where was I during all this? Not paying attention?"

"You were semiretired. Which is accurate. You were maintaining some high-level relationships and that's about it. You assumed, as anyone in your position would, that your investment team was handling the diligence work on the outside advisers. It will be helpful if we could find some correspondence between the two of you—Alain and you—that supports the case that you were just relying on him for information."

"I'm sure there's some of that. There may also be correspondence that, well, perhaps isn't as favorable."

"Right, there always is. If there's stuff you can remember specifically, let me know; it will make my associates' lives easier when they comb through your e-mails. Look, no one's subpoenaed your records. And I hope no one will, if we cooperate. So we show them what we want to show them, for the time being."

"What about the rest of the firm? I don't want any of my junior guys getting pulled into this. That's not right."

Sol nodded. "They want a sacrificial lamb. They may want a sales guy, you know, one who used particularly loose tactics."

"Not Markus. He pushed back on Alain, all the time. Pain in my ass."

"Not Markus, then."

"Richard?"

"Maybe. Let's talk to Neil first, and to Jim. Jim's handling the PR spin."

Carter nodded thoughtfully. He furrowed his brow. "What about Jane?"

Jane. Finally, someone had said her name.

Sol clenched his fists in and out before answering. "I can't negotiate for her, Carter," he said, shaking his head. "If I tell them about your relationship with Jane, it's game over. She's too important. She's about to become the head of the Commission. But here's what I came up with. We offer them someone else at the SEC. That way, we preempt an investigation. Again, we play offense so we don't have to play defense down the road."

Carter paused. His eyes met Sol's. "I'm not sure I understand," he said haltingly. "You want to volunteer the information that we're in bed with the SEC? Excuse the atrocious play on words."

"Here's why: Then we control the information flow. That's what the game is about. We go back to the NYAG and say, 'We've realized Alain wasn't only not doing his homework but he was also actively bribing authorities so that he wouldn't get investigated.' We give them a name, we show them how he did it, they thank us profusely for doing their homework for them. Then we say, 'Look, we're handing you the whole case on a silver platter. But that is all you get. After that, you stop investigating so everyone can move on.' I promise you, they will."

Carter shifted uncomfortably. "Isn't that pretty risky? I mean, why would they stop there?"

"Because they want this to be over quickly, too. They want a quick, easy, cheap win. If we cooperate, that's what they get. If we don't, this thing will drag on for years. They can't afford that. They don't have the resources for it, and frankly, the media doesn't have the patience for it. A ten-year trial—can you imagine? They'll look like inept morons. This way, everyone goes home happy; they have their victory, we have ours. It's like tossing a dog some scraps so he won't see the sirloin steak on the kitchen counter."

Carter felt a chill run down his spine. It was all a chess game to Sol; he saw this now very clearly. It was a brilliant play. Highly risky, of course, and totally illegal. But if successful, they gained much while giving away little. It was a classic deflection sacrifice: Offer up the pawn to save the king.

"Do you have someone in mind?"

"Yes." Sol said simply. "His name's David Levin. He's a director in the New York office. He was conducting an informal investigation into RCM." Sol sounded calm, but then Sol knew it was the right move. At least, the tactically correct move. This was the kind of move that got him paid.

"I've never heard of this person," Carter said. He shifted uncomfortably in his chair. For a moment, he wished he hadn't asked the question.

Obviously, there would be collateral damage. But knowing his name made Carter uneasy. "Does he have any connection to anyone at Delphic?"

"No. But he's the person directly under Jane and so he had the ability to quash an investigation. He's the logical person we would have talked to, you know, if we were engaging in that type of thing. We also ran a profile on him and determined that, if push came to shove, he was someone who might be willing to cooperate with us. He's practically bankrupt. His wife died of cancer a few years back, and the medical bills nearly cleaned him out. So it won't be hard to manufacture. There's already a numbered bank account in the Caymans, traceable to him. We give them the routing number, and its exact balance. We'll fund the accounts, but make it look as though they were paid up a few months ago. The transfer records are already in place, they've been backdated. It'll be a number substantial enough to have bought someone off, but not exorbitant. I've got the numbers, just not with me right now. I think we should actually put the money in the accounts for the time being. Even if we never see that money again, it's a worthwhile investment."

Carter looked quietly shocked. Sol crossed his arms and said, "This is not exactly the time to get moralistic."

"How did you find him? This David Levin?"

"We've been aware of him for a while," Sol said. He shrugged. "He started asking questions a few months ago. I know Jane is on top of it from a high-level standpoint, but we were always cautious that someone more junior might get overly inquisitive about the fund. I think Paul may have spoken to him, in fact, on a few occasions."

Carter nodded. "Ah yes, his name rings a bell." He frowned. "Let's keep Paul out of this."

"I'm not sure that's realistic. Or possible."

"I know Paul, Sol. This isn't going to sit well with him. He's a loyal kid but he's—well, forgive me here—but he's a lawyer. He doesn't have the killer instinct. You know what I'm saying."

"I know what you're saying. What I'm saying is that may not be realistic or possible. Paul's not stupid. He has access to a lot of valuable information, whether he realizes it or not. Information that could be damning for you. God forbid he cuts his own deal. He'll take us down."

"He wouldn't do that. Do you know how much that kid owes me?" Carter shook his head. "He's not got it in him."

Sol gave a quick nod. "I'll talk to him. But he better be a team player."

"Let's just cross that bridge when we come to it."

"Fine. But I'm going to need to talk to him about his conversations with David Levin. For starters."

"I understand." Carter took a deep breath and was quiet for a moment. He knew when to back away from an argument with Sol. "Won't he fight it? Not Paul. David Levin. Accusing an SEC lawyer of bribery and fraud seems a bit like throwing water on a hornet's nest and sticking around to see what happens next."

"Well, yes. At first, I imagine so. But he'll realize quickly that he has neither the time nor the resources to do so, and he will be offered the opportunity to walk away with a slap on the wrist. There's something else about him. He was let go from his law firm before he came to the SEC. It happened just before he made partner. The firm never pressed charges but we understand from a source that there was an incident involving marijuana possession. Suffice to say, he's very lucky to still have his bar license at all."

"He's a pothead? Fantastic. And people wonder why the SEC can't get anything done."

"Well, it's a bit more complicated. He claimed it was medicinal, for his wife. Anyway, a few of the partners went to bat for him, and he was allowed to leave quietly."

Carter's head bowed when he heard this. He was about to ruin this man's life. It was cowardly to paint him as someone who deserved it. Whoever he was, Carter was certain that he didn't.

"He's also dating a woman in his office."

"What does that matter?"

"Gives him a reason to resign. I suggested that to Jane a month or so ago, when he was asking too many questions. Anyway, the point is that David Levin's got skeletons in his closet, too. He got away with something that perhaps he ought not to have, many years ago." Sol fell silent as he watched Carter absorb what he was saying. This was a part of his job that he disliked. Typically by the time Sol was pitching an exit strategy, the client was already so far into the woods that they had lost sight of any ambient light long ago. Sol's job was to lead them out of the darkness. This was why he had been hired. Sometimes this required cutting down a few more trees.

"Can I sleep on it?" Carter looked stubbornly childlike, as though perplexed by the weight of it all.

*You're too smart for that,* Sol thought. *You know exactly why we're here and what needs to happen now.*

"No. You can think about it as you sleep, but the decision has to be made now."

"What if I fight it? I let them press charges, if that's what they are going to do, and we take them all the way to court?"

Sol shrugged. "You'll lose."

"Because the jury will hate me."

"Because the jury will hate you, yes."

"They'll have seen pictures of my house in East Hampton or of Ines and me at some charity benefit or of the girls riding horses, and that's what they'll judge me on. They'll look at me and see a guy in the custom-made suit and the John Lobb shoes with the team of lawyers and want to throw rocks at me."

"I wouldn't recommend the John Lobb shoes," Sol said drily.

"Remember those photos of Martha Stewart showing up to court with her Birkin bag?" Carter's face was stonily serious, but for the first time in days, Sol could hear a glimmer of levity in his voice. "And the fur. I mean, Jesus. Show some fucking humility. Her lawyers should have been shot."

"Yes, no one ever accused Martha of being well advised." They both broke into laughter. For Carter, the laughter came out from behind the wall of a very thin dam, which, once broken, overflowed with tears. It felt good, as though his whole body had become a stagnant pond and for the first time in days it was flowing again. He wiped the tears back with an unsteady hand. Shaking his head, he said, "I'll talk to Ines about her wardrobe choices if we go to trial."

Sol smiled. "Let Ines wear what she wants. Let's talk about the deal."

Carter nodded. "Right," he said. "Eli's sure I'll walk away then?"

"Yes. If we play it right."

"And Paul and Adrian."

"Adrian doesn't matter. He's just on the client service side, no one would expect him to know anything. Paul, well, Paul we'll have to see about. Let's worry about you first. You're a big fish, Carter. We're going to have to trade a lot for you."

"I'm not giving them Paul. That will crush Merrill. No."

"I said we'll talk about it later. I need more information before I can have that discussion. I'm sorry, but that's all I'm going to say about that now. It's just too early."

Carter paused. He said, quietly, "What happens after?"

"After what?"

"I assume I'll be barred from the financial industry. That would be part of it, right?" Carter's voice broke. "What the hell am I supposed to do with myself?"

"I don't know if that's part of it. But if it is, you have enough money abroad that you'll be fine; they won't touch that. And you and I will work something out."

"It's not a financial issue."

"Well, yes, in fact, it is." Sol said, his patience worn thin. "Bankruptcy is a real issue here, Carter. I know that's hard to hear, but it's something you should factor in to your decision making, not just for yourself but for your family. There's a possibility that you could end up in prison for the rest of your life, and lose everything in the process if you choose to fight this."

"Forget the fucking money, Sol. I'm sick of talking about money."

*Typical,* Sol thought. *Believe me, it'll be about the money as soon as you don't have any.*

"I'm talking about what I do with myself, on a daily basis. I wake up in the morning, and I do what? What would be left for me? My friends will be gone. I won't be able to show my face on Wall Street. Half of the members of the Knickerbocker Club are invested with us."

"You're being overly dramatic. People have a shorter memory for these things than you might imagine. And you'll have your kids. Become a grandfather. Buy a house in Gstaad where you can teach them to ski."

"*Maybe* I will have my children. What if they turn on me? What then?"

"I don't think they would."

"You don't know that," Carter said hoarsely, and cleared his throat. He shook his head, thinking about his own father.

"I know your kids. They're great kids. They won't walk away from you. I've almost never seen that, even in far worse situations than this."

Carter's eyes darted nervously around the room. "I can't lose my kids," he said firmly. "And I'll lose Merrill if anything happens to Paul."

"You won't lose your kids."

"Ines will leave. I mean hell, she ought to after what I've put her through."

"She looked well tonight. I was very impressed with how she's handling things."

"She was missing an earring. Did you notice that? She only had one earring on. She was missing the left one." Then, more softly, he said, "I hate what I've done to her."

"I didn't notice the earring," Sol said quietly. "Look, it's getting late. And you need to get some rest. Let's take this one step at time."

"When do we meet with Eli?"

"Saturday. We'll drive into the city as soon as you're ready to go. Neil's flying in from D.C. He pushed up his Thanksgiving dinner actually, so he could come up sooner. Wife's pissed. Anyway. We'll meet with him first, then with Eli in the afternoon."

"I should talk to Jane. I spoke to her this morning, before coming here."

"You shouldn't be doing that. For now."

"She's involved, Sol. She deserves some clarity."

"Let's get this done first, Carter. One thing at a time. All right?" The men rose to their feet. Sol clapped his hand across his old friend's shoulders. "You spoke well at dinner," he said, "about Morty."

Carter nodded. "I didn't know what to say."

"None of us do."

As Sol turned to go, Carter said, "I appreciate everything you've done for me, Sol." Sol nodded and extended his hand. Rather than shake it, Carter leaned in and embraced him quickly. It was a rare moment for both men. Both were silent, aware that they needed each other now more than ever before.

When Sol pulled away, Carter cleared his throat and said, "Listen, I know you've done great work here, especially under the circumstances. Really, I mean that. But I think at this point there's no such thing as a good deal. For any of us."

And though he was content with the work he had done, Sol was inclined to agree.

# FRIDAY, 6:03 A.M.

Paul was having trouble determining whether he had woken up early or simply never gone to sleep at all. Merrill was curled up in a fetal position, like an infant. Her hand lay atop his thigh, its soft palm open in surrender. He felt strangely trapped by the small weight of flesh. He had tried not to move so that he wouldn't disturb it. Eventually, he had slipped into a twilight state, somewhere between sleep and consciousness.

It was still dark when he snuck out of bed. He wasn't sure of the time, but it was close enough to morning. Anyway, it seemed senseless to lie awake and do nothing but stare at the ceiling, particularly given how much work there was to be done. The dogs thumped their tails eagerly when he entered the kitchen. Someone had been there not too long before; one light was on and the smell of recently brewed coffee lingered. Paul poured himself a bowl of cereal in the semidarkness.

The lights flickered on above his head. Carter appeared in the doorway, clad in running pants, polar fleece and sneakers. He had on a thin skullcap and gloves, the kind worn by serious runners. His cheeks blazed from the morning air. Rubbing his hands together, he didn't look particularly happy to see Paul.

"You're up early."

"Couldn't sleep."

Carter pulled up a kitchen stool next to Paul and took off the gloves and hat. His fingers were stiff from the cold, and he fumbled with the laces on his shoes. Bacall came over and rubbed himself up against Carter's calf, as if to warm him. Instinctively they both dropped a hand to pet him.

After giving Bacall an affectionate scratch, Carter said, "Is Merrill sleeping?"

"I think so. She was when I left."

"How is she?" He got up and poured himself a mug of coffee, which was no longer hot. After a sip, he grimaced and dumped it into the sink. He turned back to the counter and began to prepare a fresh pot.

"It's hard to say. It's been a long few days."

"She seemed upset when you two arrived."

"Yeah, well. It's a lot to take in. Not sure what I can say right now that won't upset her more."

Carter nodded. "They're always upset with us, son. About something."

Carter's back was to Paul as he worked at the counter. He measured the coffee exactly, holding it up to eye level like a scientist. As it began to percolate, he slipped a teaspoon of sugar each into two mugs, pouring the coffee just as it finished brewing. He gripped the mugs' handles in one hand as he brought it over to the table. He always does everything so efficiently, Paul thought.

"Thanks," Paul said, accepting a mug.

Carter was quiet as he let Paul take a sip. Then he said, "Did you speak to Sol before dinner yesterday?"

Paul felt Carter's eyes on him. He couldn't meet his gaze; instead he looked away, drinking his coffee. He felt like a double agent deep in enemy territory. He hadn't committed to anything with David Levin, he reminded himself. Not one thing. Still, the betrayal was there, ripe for the taking. How could he be expected to sit at this man's table and encourage his confidence, knowing he had a call with David in less than an hour? Paul wanted to flash Carter some kind of sign, like a lighthouse warning a ship off its rocky coast. *Be careful what you say now. You can't trust me with it.*

"I spoke to Sol briefly," Paul said. "Mostly about my interaction with David Levin at the SEC. He gave me a thumbnail sketch of what to expect from them in terms of an investigation into RCM."

Carter nodded. "Our investors won't be pleased."

"No, I wouldn't expect they would be."

"We're all at risk here, Paul," Carter said. "I mean, this was Alain's relationship. And Sol's going to do his best to insulate the rest of us from the fallout. But they're going for blood. CEOs, general counsels; taking us down makes for good press."

"Sol was clear on that." Paul shifted uncomfortably.

"What does Merrill know?" Carter asked. His tone softened slightly.

"I gave her a general outline. I tried not to upset her."

"Did she ask about what it would mean for the firm? And for the family?"

"Honestly, sir, she was pretty quiet. I'm sure she's aware of what it could mean. She's entirely supportive of you, though."

Carter replaced his mug carefully on the table. Staring at its rim, he snorted.

"Meaning what, Paul? She knows her dad's not a crook?" The first light of morning had crept its way across the countertops, and they could see each other more clearly now. Carter's benevolent face had contorted; Paul could see it, buried beneath his brows, the question that was brewing: *Who the fuck do you think you are?*

"I'm sorry," Paul said, taken aback. "I didn't mean to imply that anyone in the family wouldn't be supportive. We all are, of course."

Carter was staring out the window at his lawn. On it stood four deer, their dappled bodies fading at the edges with the autumn grass. They looked well fed, though they always did this time of year; they would have to be in order to survive the winter. Unaware of their audience, the smallest of the four wandered off on its own, nose to the ground. The stag raised his head to watch him but returned to feeding after a moment. It looked like work, finding sustenance at this time of year. Though thick in the summer, the lawn had shrunk to a sparse brown carpet, glazed over in patches with frost. The deer worked their way across it in silent unison, their bodies nimble, alert. Paul knew if they were to move even slightly, the deer would sense that they were being watched and scamper off beneath the hedgerows.

"You love Merrill, I can tell," Carter said finally. The edge was gone from his voice. "That was what I always wanted for her. Someone who would see her for who she is, and love her for her. I hope one day you two have children, Paul. Because no matter how much you do love her, I promise you it's a different kind of love from what I have. You probably think that you would do anything for her. But you wouldn't. Not like I would."

Paul opened his mouth to disagree but said nothing.

The first time Paul had met Carter, Paul had beaten him in tennis. He had been dating Merrill a few months, since the beginning of their 2L year in law school. It was July and they were both working in the city. He was a summer associate at Howary, and Merrill was clerking for a judge in the Southern District. They weren't living together yet, but they had started spending more nights together than not, always at her apartment because it was nicer. The invitation to stay at her house in East Hampton for the weekend had come very casually over a dinner with Merrill's friends; the friends were invited, too. It didn't occur to him that her parents would be there. Not that it mattered. He would have spent the weekend in a Motel 6 in Hoboken if she had asked him to.

The weekend did not begin auspiciously. When he had arrived at Merrill's garage, Paul saw that he was already doing everything wrong. He stared awkwardly at the laces of his New Balances and hated the fact that he was wearing jeans. Josh, the other male houseguest, was dressed up. Not dressed up, exactly, but dressed: Nantucket reds, a button-down, and loafers with no socks. An expensive, bright blue cashmere sweater was tossed across his shoulders. Rachel, Josh's wife, and Merrill were in white pants and nearly identical cotton tunics. It was as if a memo had been circulated with the attire for the weekend, and Paul had missed it.

And then there were the three tennis bags that Josh was packing into the trunk.

"Where's your racquet?" Merrill said. The three weekenders looked at him inquisitively. "I thought I told you to bring it. We've got a court at the house."

Paul was sure she hadn't told him, but he didn't want to seem combative. Before he could respond, Josh piped up: "He can borrow one of mine." He threw Paul a little wink, which made Paul want to punch him.

"You have stuff to play in, right?"

"Sure," Paul said casually, thinking of his Patagonia bathing suit and T-shirt. "Sure I do."

"You'll be great," Merrill said. She hopped into the driver's seat of her Mercedes sedan. "Ready to go? Dad will be dying to play by the time we get there." She still had that new-girlfriend glow, that *you're perfect, why didn't I find you sooner?* vibe that women radiate in the early stages of a relationship. If the jeans bothered her, she didn't say so. But they bothered Paul. The weekend already felt off-kilter.

When they arrived at the house, Carter opened the front door and waved. Bacall had burst from behind him and ran down to the car, where he danced happily about Merrill's feet, all paws and slobber. Paul recognized Carter, of course, most recently from his picture in *Barron's*. Paul had always been careful not to say anything to Merrill that implied he knew who Carter was, outside of being her father. He didn't want to seem like some kind of creepy celebrity hound. He wasn't sure if that kind of thing existed for finance people. But even at law school, he saw how other students whispered about her family: Her dad was a rock-star fund manager, her mom was a socialite, her sister, Lily, was an It Girl, always in the society pages of magazines.

He couldn't tell if Merrill politely ignored the chatter or simply didn't know about it. Beyond gossip, Carter Darling was hard to miss for anyone who read the financial news. Paul figured Merrill would either think he was a moron for not knowing who her father was, or worse still would suspect he was more interested in Carter than in her if he did. So mostly he just nodded when she mentioned him.

In the beginning, Merrill painted her family only in broad strokes. Paul admired this about her. The way she dressed, the friends she kept, most of all, her warm, honest smile: All were both practical and refined, bespeaking good breeding but also a genuine kindness toward all people. Unlike nearly everyone else in New York (Paul knew himself to be among this flawed majority), Merrill was neither impressed nor embarrassed by where she came from. Some of Merrill's friends flaunted their wealth, but there was a smaller group that hid theirs, too. Paul found both unsettling. It was the easy way Merrill carried herself that made her so appealing. She was fluid in her own skin. When he had met her, Paul thought he would have to fall in love with her despite her family. But later, he came to see them as she did: neither a blessing nor a curse, but simply a fact.

Carter was already dressed for tennis when they arrived, in a polo shirt tucked cleanly into matching shorts. To Paul's surprise, Carter greeted him with warm familiarity. "I need an opponent," he said. "Mine just canceled on me. You wouldn't mind keeping an old man on his toes for an hour or so, would you? Merrill tells me you used to play for UNC. She can help you find some clothes upstairs if you're up for it. We have plenty."

Josh and Rachel said a quick hello, then retreated upstairs to the guest bedroom, leaving Paul to fend for himself.

Paul had never seen a home this nice. Not in person, anyway. The proportions, more than anything, were disorienting. All the things in the house felt oversized and grand: the Viking range that looked as though it belonged in a restaurant kitchen; enough plates and glasses to cater a wedding. Carter himself dwarfed Paul. They stood awkwardly together in the kitchen, Merrill's suitcase still in Paul's hand, and the screen door propped open with a wrought iron doorstop shaped like a dog. The kitchen itself was patterned in tiny white and blue tiles, liked the inside of a teacup. It smelled of fresh cut grass and tennis balls, the smells of summer. On the lawn, Paul could hear the far-off buzz of a landscaper's lawnmower.

"Shall we?" Carter said, gesturing to the outside. "Let's go hit some."

Paul beat him, but not without thinking about it first. Carter seemed to him like the kind of man who would rather lose an honorable fight than win a fixed one. Paul let him take a few points here and there, but only on the occasionally excellent serve or volley. By the second game, they had gathered a crowd, Merrill and Ines and Josh and Rachel, who cheered with equal enthusiasm for both sides. The girls had changed into bathing suits and shorts, and they drank Bloodies out of plastic cups, swirling their celery stalks and laughing.

When it was over, Carter and Paul shook hands across the net.

"Great game," Carter said, bowing his head without a trace of bitterness. "You weren't ever thinking of letting me win, were you?"

"No sir," Paul said.

"Good. Good man. You seem like the kind of fellow who understands that even an old dog like me likes to win his own fights."

---

"Paul?" Carter looked up from the window, as if suddenly struck by a thought. "I know we've never talked about this, but do you get along with your dad? Merrill mentioned to me—this is a long time ago now—that you don't speak much about him."

"Haven't seen him since I was eight."

"Do you talk to him? Know where he is?"

Paul got up and poured himself more coffee. "Want some?" He held up the pot.

Carter nodded. "We don't have to talk about it if you don't want."

"No, it's fine." Paul put the pot down on the counter. "We spoke just after the wedding. He saw the announcement in the *Times*. He's a bank teller out in Westchester, actually." He paused, took a sip of coffee. "When he left us, my mother told Katie and me that he was going to be a banker in New York. She made it sound really impressive, like it was a big opportunity. That was what I told all my friends: My dad's a banker in New York."

"With your brains, I would've thought he was a mathematics professor."

Paul shrugged. "Well. The apple fell far from the tree."

"Trust me, I get that." Carter leaned backward and stretched. "It must have been hard for you. Growing up without a father."

"It was, especially in the beginning. After a while, you learn to cope. I know you understand."

"I do. It's a formative experience, losing a parent. Particularly at a young age. It sets you apart from your peers. I was ten when my dad died. And twenty-one when I lost my mother. I had hoped she would have been there to see me graduate from Harvard."

Paul nodded. "It was hard on my mom, not having my dad there for my graduation. It was one of the few times she cried about him."

"We have a lot in common, you and me," Carter said. When the light hit his face, Paul could see the pronounced bags beneath his eyes, and the delineated sagging of his cheeks. He looked tired. Carter stared out at the now-empty lawn, the brightening sky, and the sleeping trees. It didn't seem as though he was looking at anything in particular.

"I never asked you what went on at Howary, Paul," Carter said. "I could have, when you came to see me about a job. I could have pressed you on it. But I didn't. You know why? Because I knew you were like me: Family would always come first. To me that meant you would never do anything stupid; you would never have done anything to jeopardize your position. You couldn't afford to get fired. For Merrill's sake, if not for yours. So you played it safe, never skirting the edge of common sense. Which is why you lasted as long as you did, all the way through this fall. Am I right?"

"I think so," Paul said. "I'm glad to hear you know I didn't do anything wrong. A lot went wrong, certainly." Paul wanted to say more, but didn't. He had suffered silently through months of questions: from friends, from his mother, from those incidental acquaintances like Raymond, his doorman, and Leo, the guy who shined his shoes.

*What had happened at Howary?*

*They all had to know, right?*

*How could you work there and not know?*

It didn't matter whether the questions were concerned or accusatory, gossipy or well-meaning; Paul couldn't answer any of them. It wasn't that he didn't want to, though most of the time, he didn't. But he simply couldn't. A simple, "I knew" or "I didn't know" didn't suffice. The lines of what he knew, and what he had relegated to some shadowy place of semirecognition had blurred long ago.

And what should he have known? Well, who could answer that? Though he was closer to all the players than anyone—he had been Mack's junior guy, after all—he still couldn't identify who was responsible and who wasn't. Really responsible, not just "look the other way" responsible. They all were, in some larger sense. And yet, while he knew this was a wholly indefensible position, he felt that somehow none of them were, either. Just like the guys at Lehman or Bear Stearns or AIG. Just like the guys at Delphic. They just went with something. They rode the bull as long as they could. It became a game, a contest; the only rules that governed were what made you money and what didn't. All Paul did was hang the hell on and try not to get thrown.

It was such a delicate web of decisions. He remembered the big ones, of course. Those he revisited again and again as he was falling asleep, and when awake, chastised himself for not doing differently. But Paul knew that it was the small decisions, those tender tipping points as inconsequential as what sandwich you ordered for lunch (*your boss ordered the same one; you spoke of it; later, he became your mentor*), whom you e-mailed that day (*e-mails remain forever, lingering on firm servers just waiting to be taken out of context*), or what route you took home from work (*you were running late that day and so you decided to split a cab with a co-worker instead of taking the subway*), these were the fibers of the noose with which they had hanged themselves. Not just Howary. Everyone on Wall Street.

"Well, now," Carter said. "I never said you did nothing wrong."

"What?"

Carter gave Paul a disquieting look. Paul felt the way he did the second after a bad deal went through; he wasn't sure how, but he knew he'd been had.

"I never said you did nothing wrong," Carter repeated. "I said that you would never do anything stupid. There is a difference."

Paul bristled. "Forgive me, but what's the difference?"

"Don't get defensive. You and I are cut from the same cloth, Paul. We put our family first. That means we play by the rules."

"Right," Paul said, trying to understand where this was going.

"We stay in the game so that we can provide for our family. That's the smart thing to do. The problem arises when the game is being played with rules the rest of the world doesn't understand. The mortgage business, for example. Everybody in the business knew the rules. Everyone was playing by them. Problem was, the little guy on Main Street didn't, so the little guy got burned. Same story for tax pass-throughs in the Caymans. Right?"

"Well," Paul said, crossing his arms, pulling back from the counter. "There were rules that weren't being followed. There were shell companies that no one was even writing down. Money getting moved just to move it, to make it disappear. That kind of shit shouldn't have happened."

"Fine. But you weren't doing that. Right?"

"Never. I wasn't crazy enough to be doing that."

"But you saw it. And there was an unspoken code that, well, you turn a blind eye. Right? I mean, what would be the point of challenging the system?"

"That's just it," Paul said, slightly exasperated. "You can point to Deal A and say, 'that shouldn't have happened,' or Deal B, and say 'that shouldn't have happened,' but what does a guy in my position do? Challenge one? I'd get fired. Challenge them all? I'd get banished from the industry. Then what? Nothing has changed."

Now Paul was fired up, cylinders blazing. "You want to ask me if I knew?" he said. "Sure, I knew. Some of it. Not all of it, but yeah, some. But at some point, you put your head down and say to yourself, if someone else wants to go off the reservation, that's his fucking problem. And you know what? I was wrong. Because now it's everybody's problem. So that's what you wanted to hear: I knew. Think less of me?"

Carter chuckled. "No, son. I think more of you." He grinned at Paul. He looked sort of wild-eyed and delirious, and it crossed Paul's mind that he might be having a breakdown. Maybe they all were. Carter hopped to his feet and paced across the kitchen floor, and Paul could hear the faint pulsing sound of music—*was that the B-52's?*—emanating from the pocket of Carter's running pants. His iPod had been playing this whole time, Paul realized, so faintly that he had edited it out as white noise.

"You do what's right for your family. You do it even if down the road the rest of the world is going to chastise you for what you did. I told you son, we're the same. I had a shitty father growing up, too, and as soon as I was able I took one look at him and said, 'That's not the kind of man I want to be.' And I haven't been. I provided for my girls. I've given Merrill and Lily the world. The fucking *world*. They're going to call me greedy: the media, the lawyers, all of our so-called friends. Starting tomorrow or Monday. Maybe for the rest of my life. But they won't get it. Greedy? I was *selfless*. One hundred fucking percent."

The words hung in the air, and the kitchen felt cold and silent. The sun was almost up now, but it still felt like twilight, an in-between hour. For the first time since Paul had met him, for the first time since he had heard his name, in fact, Paul didn't want to be Carter Darling. He didn't want to be a Darling at all.

And yet, with a sinking feeling, he knew Carter was right. They were the same. One hundred fucking percent.

"What are you going to do?" Paul asked. He spoke as quietly as he could, as if they were inside a china teacup. The world felt so fragile that the very reverberations of his voice might crack it. "What are we going to do?"

"It's very simple," Carter said, and they both took a seat at the kitchen table.

---

When Alexa picked up the phone, she sounded bleary. It was still early.

"You awake?"

"Barely. Shit. Stayed up late last night."

"Crazy Thanksgiving festivities?"

She laughed wryly. "Hardly." She paused. "They suspended David," she said. "He's not supposed to go into the office. He's shell-shocked and we've been scrambling. So it's been an, uh, busy morning in our house."

Paul was silent. Finally he said, "On Thanksgiving? That's very . . . unchristian." He had a tendency to make jokes when he was nervous.

She laughed again, her voice was rough and raw. If he hadn't known better, he would have thought he had woken her. "Yeah, well. They basically told him to take an extended holiday. You know, until they've done an internal investigation into him. It's not looking good. They're already teeing it up so that they can blame him. I told you these weren't nice people."

"Did they—did she—did she say for what, exactly?"

"Not really. Something to the effect of his mishandling the RCM investigation. 'Operating outside of marching orders': I think that was the exact phrasing. Which he was, of course, because his marching orders were to shut the thing down. Whatever. You can tell I'm still seething." She sighed loudly. Then she said, "Are you going to come in and talk to David today? He's meeting with Matt Curtis, our guy at the NYAG, later on today. You should be there. David's working on his resignation statement now."

Paul paused and closed his eyes. Then he dove in, knowing that what he was about to say was something he would reflect on for the rest of his life.

"I'm coming into the city," he said. "But to be with the family. I'm sorry, but I'm just not in a position to talk to David. Particularly if he's not with the SEC anymore."

He was met with silence, which wasn't surprising. For a moment, he wondered if Alexa had hung up. "You have to understand," he said. "This is about family."

Then she said, "Don't be stupid, Paul. If you come in and talk to the NYAG with us now, you won't go down with the rest of them. You know that."

"I understand what you're saying. But I'm standing behind my father-in-law. You can't take a whole firm down based on the mistakes of a few people."

"You're making a mistake."

"I have to go, Alexa. Good luck to you, and to David. Try to stay focused on the real enemy here, all right?" His heart was pounding wildly in his chest. He wanted to leave the door open, just a crack, but he was out of time.

"I hate thinking of you among them," she said. "I hate it."

But he had already hung up.

---

Paul headed straight back to the bedroom. He wanted nothing more than to crawl into bed beside his wife and hold her. But when he opened the bedroom door, he saw that the sheets had been pushed back and Merrill was gone. He sat on the edge of the bed and put his face in his hands, wondering if he had made the wrong decision. The stress of the last three days poured over him and he felt submerged in it, as though he were being carried, like flotsam, off on a great tide. The shore looked farther and farther away.

# FRIDAY, 7:50 A.M.

Paul was gone.

Merrill felt a rush of nerves when her eyes blinked open and took in the empty pillow. She ran her hand twice across his side of the bed, wondering where he was.

*He's just down in the kitchen,* she thought. *He didn't want to wake me.*

She slouched back against the headboard, desperate for sleep but knowing it would elude her. The house had been alive all night with constant, nervous motion. Someone had moved about on the floor below until dawn, the distant creaking of floorboards stirring her from restless half dreams. At one point, she thought she heard voices on the porch outside; later, car wheels turned on the gravel drive. Both times she had sat up in bed and glanced out the window, but all she could see was darkness. The wind, too, had been coming strong off the water since the previous afternoon, battering the house with blustery gusts. Oddly, Merrill was grateful for the commotion around her. Without it, the house would fall silent and she would be left alone with her thoughts.

After a minute she pushed herself out of bed and went to the bathroom to wash up. She moved quickly through the motions of flossing and brushing her teeth, washing her face, putting in her contacts as though she was needed somewhere urgently. At the top of her suitcase was a pair of jeans and a turtleneck sweater that she pulled on without consideration. As she dressed, she tried to focus her thoughts on something outside Beech House—a friend's upcoming wedding in Connecticut, a securities litigation case at work—but her mind felt like a closed-circuit television, looping around and around to thoughts of her father, of Paul, and back again.

*Where had Paul gone? Maybe out for a run?* She didn't allow herself to indulge in the fear that he had left altogether.

She peered out the bedroom window. If she stood on her toes, she could see the strip of road leading down to the beach. It glistened in the sun, dusted with a crystallized frost. Before the perimeter hedge was the open expanse of the back lawn, the frozen grass as brown and prickly as a doormat. The pool lay sleeping beneath a dark green tarp. Metal lounge chairs were lined up along one side of it, their bare backs stripped of cushions for the winter. From October to June, the cushions remained stacked inside the locked pool house like a giant pillow fort. Bone-white snow had collected in the elbows of the trees overnight.

Only three months ago, Merrill had been sitting on those chairs with Lily, drinking Diet Cokes and feeling the hot sun on their browning skin. They laughed and called out scores as Adrian and his brothers showboated on the diving board. Carter and Paul played backgammon on the glass-topped patio table, their serious faces breaking into the occasional smile or grimace as they took turns besting each other. When the sun dropped below the hedge, Carmela and John had come out to light the mosquito torches around the pool. Everyone smelled of sunscreen and bug spray and salt water and chlorine. Dinner was outdoors—barbequed chicken and corn—and the girls' hair dried in the warm night air, the sound of ocean waves rolling in the distance. Nights like that felt far away now, like stories about someone else's past.

Merrill saw the silhouette of a jogger drawing closer to the house, his face obscured by the shade of the trees. He was tall and broad, like Paul. Her heart quickened a little and she leaned in to look, her eyelashes nearly brushing the windowpane, her palms leaving prints on the ledge.

When she met Paul, she hadn't thought much of him, except that his answers in Corporations class were remarkably articulate and that he had a warmth about him that put people at ease. He wore blue button-down shirts and stuffed his hands in the front pockets of his jeans with an aw-shucks honesty that made Merrill trust him despite his handsomeness.

Merrill had always been quietly guarded, particularly with men. Before Paul, there had only been two boyfriends of any consequence, and she had avoided casual dating in between. Ines and Carter had raised both girls to be cautious of everyone. *This is New York*, Ines would say about anything from taking the subway to going on a blind date. *You never really know who anyone is in New York. You have to be careful.* Merrill and Lily had many acquaintances but few friends, and typically dated men who they met through friends and family.

Sometimes (more often after she met Paul), Merrill wondered what she would have been like if she had grown up outside New York. Would she be herself but more open, less circumspect? Sunnier? Less sarcastic? Manhattan children were like armadillos: sharp clawed and thick-skinned, deceptively quick moving. They had to be. Manhattan was a Darwinian environment: only the strongest survived. The weak, the nice, the naïve, the ones who smiled at passersby on the sidewalk, all got weeded out. They would come to New York for a few years after college, rent shoebox apartments in Hell's Kitchen or Murray Hill, work at a bank or wait tables or audition for bit parts in off-off-Broadway productions. They would meet other twentysomethings over after-work drinks at soulless bars in midtown; get laid; get their hearts broken. They would feel themselves becoming impatient, jaded, cynical, rude, anxious, neurotic. They would give up. They would opt out. They would scurry back to their hometowns or to the suburbs or secondary cities like Boston or D.C. or Atlanta, before they had had a chance to breed.

The ones who stayed long enough to raise children were the tough ones, the tenacious ones, the goal-oriented ones, the gold-digging ones, the deal-closing ones, the "kill or be killed" ones, the ones who subscribed to the philosophy "whatever it takes." They looked out for themselves and slept with one eye open. Being born in New York wasn't enough to make someone a true New Yorker; it was in the blood, like a hormone, or a virus. Merrill often doubted whether or not she had it in her to stick it out in Manhattan with kids. The older she got, the more she wondered if she wouldn't be happier somewhere quieter, less stressful, less competitive. Were they really willing to fight tooth and nail the way her parents had, toiling away at hundred-hour-a-week jobs to live in their fifteen-hundred-square-foot apartment with its troublesome electric stove, shelling out thirty-four thousand dollars—*thirty-four thousand!*—a year for a single tuition at Spence. Not to mention what they would have to spend on clothes and nannies and gymnastics just so that their child didn't feel wildly behind her peers . . . and could they possibly bear to spend every summer weekend with Carter and Ines once they had children? That seemed unreasonable, but of course you couldn't keep a child cooped up in an apartment in August when all her classmates were playing tennis or riding horses . . . so in addition to the million-dollar mortgage they were already carrying on their apartment, not to mention the appallingly high maintenance charges that they forked over to the co-op each month, they would need to consider at least a small summer rental in the Hamptons . . . what would that run them what, fifty thousand dollars for the season? A hundred thousand? And was it true that a top SAT tutor cost a thousand dollars an hour? Who had the stomach to run these kinds of numbers? For even the very rich, this sort of daily calculus required a steel nerve . . . a ruthless will to succeed. Merrill would see schoolchildren on Park Avenue, golden-haired cherubim in pinafores and Peter Pan collars, and she would think: *These are the offspring of killers.*

Now Lily was different. Lily was a New Yorker through and through. Lily had never (Merrill was certain of it) wondered if she might end up anywhere else. Maybe a year in Paris just for fun, or a stint in London with a husband who was sent abroad for career advancement. But Lily would always return. For her there were only two places on the map: Manhattan and everywhere else.

*How enviable,* Merrill often thought, when she listened to her sister talk about the future. *How inexplicable and enviable, never to want to be anywhere other than where you already are.* Merrill had always felt the explorer's itch. In school, her curiosity had propelled her to the top of the class. Outside of school, she was often lost in the world of one book or another, or dreaming of places that her parents had yet to take them: Paris or Prague or Istanbul or the pyramids of Egypt. She had wanted to study Shakespeare at Oxford more than anything in world, but Ines wouldn't hear of it. "Too far away!" she was told, and "Your father would just be so proud if you went to Harvard . . ."

Life would be easier, Merrill realized, if she could just stop wondering what else was out there.

Dating, for example. Lily had always appeared content with men who regularly crossed her path. The shaggy blond Buckley boys with their blue blazers and untucked shirts; the lacrosse-playing prep schoolers who drank scotch and sodas at Dorrian's Red Hand on the Upper East Side; the Patagonia-wearing Dartmouth frat brothers with ACK Airport stickers on their cars and bongs beneath their beds; the Racquet Club boys and the Union Club boys and the Maidstone Club boys; the future investment bankers, private wealth managers, hedge funders, and M & A lawyers of Manhattan. The sons of fortune. Lily's boyfriends had always looked the same, interchangeable with one another and with nearly every other boy with whom they had grown up. Adrian was no different. Merrill agreed that he was probably the best of the lot; the top-of-the-line edition.

Merrill, on the other hand, never much cared for New York boys. Most of them, she found, were arrogant. Many were charming but not funny, or polite but not kind, or well traveled but close minded. They drank too much and read too little. They had grown up in cold, WASPy households where hugging felt awkward and overly intimate. Merrill would sit through dinners with them at Orsay or J. G. Melon's, listening to their stories about rowing crew for Exeter or their summer analyst training at Morgan Stanley. She would nod and smile. She would try to remember her friends' effusive squeals: "He's so cute!" or "He's such a catch!" Inside, boredom would incubate and then flower into disgust, coating her insides like mold. She would begin to squirm. She would signal the waiter and try to steal a glance at her watch as her wrist bounced into the air. She would plot an exit strategy; anything to get her home to a nice warm bed and a good book. The handsomer they were, the more quickly her interest seemed to dissipate.

The first time Paul smiled at her, she felt her cheeks flush like a schoolgirl's. *Oh my God*, she thought, *he is handsome.* Then: *Does he know who I am, or is he just being friendly?* All the women at Harvard Law knew who Paul was. He was just too charismatic not to be noticed.

When Paul stopped her after class and asked her for coffee, Merrill balked. She had trained herself to believe that good-looking men were typically afflicted by the same maladies—arrogance, dullness, self-centeredness, and an appalling sense of entitlement—and so bothering with them was never worthwhile. Also, she was mortified. The fact that Paul's face—his piercing eyes—and broad shoulders featured heavily in what could only be described as the occasional highly sexualized in-class daydream reduced her to a throbbing lump of awkwardness in his presence. She said no, citing a flimsy excuse.

He asked again. Twice more, until she finally said yes.

Grudgingly she went, refusing to wear anything more provocative than a white button-down and jeans. She calmed herself by thinking that, maybe as they sat uncomfortably across from each other at Starbucks, or later over dinner and a bottle of wine, or maybe even after third-or-fourth-date drunken sex, Paul Ross's charm would begin to fade like all the rest of them. Only a tiny, hidden part of her dared to hope that the opposite might happen . . . that as time went on, she might discover how earnest and tender and goofy and open Paul was, and how he made her feel beautiful even when she was sick or stressed or grouchy, and how he would bring her her favorite black-and-white cookies instead of flowers, and knew exactly how to rub her feet, and what questions to ask about her family so as to appear interested instead of nosy. And most impressive to Merrill, was how hard Paul worked for everything that came to him, while never expecting anything in return. He was unlike any man she had ever met, which was exactly why she loved him.

*So why, then, had she put so much pressure on him to be like her father?*

She hadn't meant to, of course. But she had—*she knew she had!*—in a million small ways. She couldn't stop tallying them up now . . . Why had she pushed Paul to play more tennis at the club or to learn backgammon or to take up skiing? Why had she suggested that he join the Racquet Club? And then there were the stupid matching sweaters that she had gotten him for Christmas . . . and of course, the job. The fucking job, which would be the undoing of them all . . .

The jogger darted out from the shadows, crossing over from one side of the street to the other. His hair glistened gold in the light: It wasn't Paul. Merrill's shoulders dropped. She slipped away from the window, her heart heavy with worry.

*Maybe he was in the kitchen?*

Merrill stole down the stairs, trying not to make a sound. The house was quiet, which she hoped meant that everyone was still sleeping.

As she drew near to the kitchen door, she heard men's voices from behind it. Her fingertips pressed against it but she hesitated, listening first before she pushed it open.

---

"No, son. I think more of you," she heard. She moved closer to the door, the edge of her ear grazing the wood.

The voice was muffled, and gruffer than she was used to, but it was unquestionably her father's.

"You do what's right for your family . . . ," he was saying, "You do it even if down the road the rest of the world is going to chastise you for what you did. I told you son, we're the same. I had a shitty father growing up, too, and as soon as I was able I took one look at him and said, 'That's not the kind of man I want to be.' And I haven't been. I provided for my girls. I've given Merrill and Lily the world. The fucking *world*. They're going to call me greedy: the media, the lawyers, all of our so-called friends. Starting tomorrow or Monday. Maybe for the rest of my life. But they won't get it. Greedy? I was *selfless*. One hundred fucking percent . . ."

Merrill recoiled from the door, her heart racing. Unable to think, she began to put one foot in front of the other, heel then toe, silent against the carpet, until she had retraced her steps back up the stairs and into their bedroom. Only when the door was shut behind her did she allow herself to burst into tears.

Her father's words swirling in her head, she became a firestorm of motion, pulling clothes from drawers, folding, packing, pushing things deeper into her suitcase . . . she couldn't slow down long enough to think through what exactly she had heard, or what he might have meant . . . but she knew she didn't trust him.

*They're going to call me greedy . . .*

Her father was going down. She was sure of it. He was sinking like a stone, and if she didn't get them out of there, he would take Paul with him.

---

Paul found her outside on the gravel drive, packing up the car. When Merrill looked up and saw him, she shook her head, frustrated, and hunched her shoulders against the cold. The engine was running to defrost the windshield, and King was riding shotgun, lulled asleep by the seat warmer. He was breathing in that labored canine way, his body twitching periodically as if in the throes of a dream. The dogs could sense the tension in the house. They had been cowering all weekend, as they did when a storm was coming. King hadn't strayed more than ten feet from Merrill since yesterday.

"You okay?" Paul said. "I thought you were still sleeping. Why didn't you come find me?"

"I was going to. I just need to get the hell out of here."

"Did you pack up everything?"

"Yes. You can go check but I'm pretty sure it's all in the back."

"Do you want me to drive?"

"Yes," she said simply. She slipped into the passenger seat and shut the door. Paul followed her lead. He wanted to go get his scarf—*it's just hanging in the foyer,* he thought—but was afraid she might leave without him.

Inside the car was quiet and a little cold.

"Do you want to say good-bye?"

"No. I just want to go."

Paul nodded and slipped the key into the ignition. The car lurched slightly forward as he shifted it into drive. His hands vibrated against the hum of the steering wheel, but he couldn't take his foot off the brake.

"What's going on?" he said, biting his lip. He wasn't sure he wanted to hear the answer.

"This is my fault," she said. Her voice was hollow. She looked straight ahead, her eyes boring holes into the side of the house. "I forced all this on you. We're out here every weekend; you're working for the family company; we spend all of our time with my sister and my cousins and my friends from Spence. We live in an apartment that looks exactly like theirs, for chrissake. I did this, Paul. I did this to both of us." She took a deep, quaking breath. "I never even asked you what you wanted."

"All I've ever wanted was to be with you." He released his seat belt and reached across the car to kiss her. When she didn't look at him, he kissed her shoulder instead, and pressed his nose against the quilting of her olive-colored coat. "I love your family," he said, because he wanted to believe it, and saying it might make it so.

"I love my family, too. And I know Dad loves us . . . but this . . . he betrayed Mom for sure. What he did to Lily and me might be just as bad, in a way . . . Nothing we have is real. He raised us believing that all of this was ours." She gestured at the house with a sweep of her arm. He knew she meant all of it: the house, the apartment, the city—everything. "That it would *always* be ours. It never even occurred to me that everything could get taken away from us. It certainly didn't occur to Lily—" Her voice broke. She knew she was working herself up, but she couldn't help it.

"No one will blame you for any of this, Mer. Whatever your father's done, those are his choices, not yours." Paul paused. He wasn't sure if he should say what he was about to say, but *hell with it*, he thought, *it just might make her feel better.* "And he made those choices because he loves you. You know that."

"I'm angry at Mom, too, you know," she said. "We're all so worried about her because of what Dad's done. But did she know? Maybe she did and she just didn't care. She wanted us to have everything so badly. That's Mom. More is more. "

"Isn't that what everyone wants for their kids?"

Merrill made a muffled snorting sound, and wiped her nose on the back of her hand. Paul fished a tissue out of his coat pocket and offered it to her. It was wilted and old, but it was all he had.

"Thanks," she said, snuffling her nose into it. "I'm sorry. I'm losing it. I just mean that we all should take some responsibility here. In our relationship, I certainly should. We could have done things differently, you and me. We still could; we're different from them. We don't need as much."

Paul chuckled. "Not sure I have much of a choice there."

She smiled a little. "Well, good," she said. "Let's just get away from here for a start."

---

They drove in silence most of the way home, fingers intertwined. There hadn't been any traffic, and they made remarkably good time. As they reached the edge of the city, a light snow began to fall, coating the tops of the buildings with a thin film of white. Even Queens looked beautiful.

"I want you to talk to David Levin," she said, breaking the silence. "Tell him you're willing to work with them, if they can promise you a deal."

"Are you sure? You have to be sure about this."

"Yes," she said. "I'm sure. I don't care what you promised Dad or what Dad wants from you. Okay? But I'd like to go with you."

"Okay." They didn't say another word until they were home.

# FRIDAY, 9:10 P.M.

"I found Scott Stevens!" Marina exclaimed when Duncan finally called her back. She realized that she sounded giddy, perhaps overly so for so small an accomplishment. It wasn't like Scott Stevens was in the witness protection program. But still, she found her own resourcefulness satisfying, and she was flying high from her first experience with investigative journalism. "I met him actually, in person. At his office in Connecticut." She grinned against the phone.

The search for Scott Stevens had begun badly, in fits and starts. The woman who had answered the phone at the SEC had been of no help. The SEC had no forwarding information for him on file, she informed Marina rather crisply, then hung up the phone. A name search on the Internet turned up nothing; or rather, it turned up so many things that the search was fruitless. Marina tried to modify the name with "attorney" or "lawyer" or "SEC" but nothing. It seemed like a simple task: Get Duncan the contact information for Scott Stevens. How could she fail so quickly?

She almost gave up, but then decided to call her cousin Mitchell. He was the only lawyer she could think of, and the type of cousin who was nerdy and eager and grateful to be included. Marina guessed that Mitchell might have access to resources at his law firm that she didn't, and also that he'd be in the office even though it was the day after Thanksgiving. She was right on both counts.

Mitchell was the cousin Marina's parents made her invite everywhere because he had no friends of his own. He sat behind her and her friends at the movies, with his own bucket of popcorn. He trotted alongside her on foot, his backpack bouncing against his fat-padded back, as she biked slowly around the neighborhood. His grades were perfect. Marina thought he was exactly the type to become a lawyer.

It took Mitchell only eleven minutes to find that six Scott Stevens were currently admitted to practice as attorneys in the United States. Of those six, only one was a member of the D.C. Bar. There was no contact information listed for him, Mitchell told her apologetically, but his profile also showed that he had been admitted to practice in the state of Connecticut in 2006. Right around the time the Scott Stevens she was looking for had been forced out of the SEC's D.C. office. Armed with this information, Marina returned to the Internet. It wasn't long before she came across a listing for Stevens & Cohgut, LLP, based in Greenwich, Connecticut. She went ahead and called, just to be sure it was the right Scott Stevens before she got Duncan involved.

It threw her off a little when Scott Stevens answered his own phone.

"Stevens and Cohgut."

"I'm looking for Scott Stevens," she said nervously.

"This is he."

"The Scott Stevens who used to work at the SEC?"

"Who is this?" he said, his voice now gruff and guarded.

Marina was quiet. She hadn't thought through what she would actually say to him.

"Fantastic!" Duncan said. "Where is he?"

"Out in Greenwich. He has a small legal practice, just general corporate stuff. He started it after he left the SEC."

"That sounds dull. You actually met him?"

Marina paused. It had occurred to her only after the fact that Duncan might not appreciate her zealous proactivity. What was done was done, though. She took a deep breath.

"I did," she said, as confidently as possible. "I got the sense over the phone that he wasn't going to talk to a reporter he didn't know. So I asked if I could come out and meet him. I said it was urgent."

"And he met with you? How did you get out to Connecticut? Where are you now?"

Marina was in her father's office now, in sweatpants. They were old and faded, the Hotchkiss *H* barely discernible on the upper thigh. She had taken them from a drawer in her old bedroom and they smelled faintly of pine and mothballs. Her hair was tied back in a messy bun. It had been a long day. She had walked all the way up to midtown to borrow Mitchell's car. By 3 p.m. she was on I-95, driving as fast as the law would allow out to Greenwich. She had told Scott Stevens she could be there before 5 p.m., which was, he said, the latest he liked to be in the office on a Friday.

She had planned to drive back to the city after meeting with him. But instead, she had sat in the parking lot, behind the offices of Stevens & Coghut, watching the sun dip behind the trees. She called Duncan again, but he didn't answer. Then she called her mom.

"I'm on my way home," she said, when her mother answered. "I hope that's all right."

"Of course it's all right, darling!" Alice exclaimed. It was nice to hear such exuberance in her mother's voice. Marina felt wanted. "This is your home, too. Are you staying the weekend?"

Marina hadn't yet made up her mind, so she ignored the question. "I'm in Greenwich now," she said. "But I should be there soon."

"Your father and I just had dinner, but we have leftovers. I'll have them ready for you when you get here. Can't wait to see you."

---

Marina drove the whole way in silence, radio off, so she could think. She thought so clearly in the car, even in traffic. Some of her thorniest problems had been solved while driving. There was something particularly soothing about the road home to Connecticut. Maybe it was the gentle familiarity of the route's details: the shape and color of the signs, the distances between exits. The way her body reflexively knew when to shift and turn, out of instinct and not recollection. New York felt so chaotic and noisy sometimes, and her apartment was crammed with roommates and their things. The car gave her space to be reasonable. It was her suburban upbringing, perhaps. Driving was like riding a bike: You learned young and never forgot. Tanner and his city friends had never really acquired a taste for driving. As a consequence, Marina ended up chauffeuring him out to his house in Southampton any weekend they were together, even though the car was his. She didn't miss that.

Even though the leaves were off the trees now, the drive up Route 22 was still a pretty one. She tried to think whether she knew anyone still out here, besides her parents' friends. The lawns grew bigger as she drove farther out of the city, the trunks of the trees more solid. Twice, she saw a column of smoke rising from a backyard where someone was burning leaves or had a fire in the fireplace. It was peaceful. She thought about what it would be like to live here again. What would people think of her if she moved back home with her parents? It would only be for a little while, while she was studying for her LSATs, maybe, or after her lease ran out in January. Would anyone even notice? She wasn't sure.

The reality of it was that she had been living beyond her means in New York, carrying on with the subconscious assumption that she would soon be Mrs. Tanner Morgenson. All the girls she knew lived that way. New York was ungodly expensive. Marina paid just over half her salary for her shared walk-up apartment on Orchard Street; it was the cheapest she could find that was reasonably clean and on a well-lit street. What was left had to be carefully apportioned for food and utilities, then for cab fares and new clothes and all the things that dating required of her. God forbid if she were to get sick or break the air conditioner. She couldn't afford unforeseen expenses like that. Every single month was a juggling act. Her credit card was sometimes maxed out, her checking account periodically overdrawn. At twenty-two, there was a sport to it, making it all come together. But she couldn't live that way forever. She could either wait for a white knight to come and rescue her, or she would have to learn to fend for herself.

She caught herself. This wasn't how she had been brought up. She was supposed to be a self-sufficient woman. Why else had they sent her to Princeton?

There was a practicality to Richard and Alice, but they were also tenderhearted parents. They wanted her to be her best self, they always said, to do what made her truly happy. Had she taken the job at *Press* for the wrong reasons? Had the parties seduced her? Was it the cachet? Or the proximity to the gilded class? Perhaps all of these things. But as she drove out to Greenwich to talk to Scott Stevens, she felt an effervescence that she knew she would never feel about law school.

---

"I drove myself out to Greenwich," Marina said to Duncan. "It's on the way to my parents' house, and I figured he would be more willing to talk to me in person. I told him about David Levin. Not a lot of detail, just what you told me on the phone this morning. I thought his story might resonate. Also, I fibbed a little."

"Fibbed how?"

"I told him Alexa Mason and I were family. I just thought it might, you know, help him get comfortable."

Duncan smiled against the phone. "And is he? Willing to talk?"

"I think so. He was nervous at first, really nervous. But he asked for your contact information, and also for the person at the attorney general's office that David and Alexa were talking to. I don't have that name—I'm sorry—so I told him he could get it from you. He said he needed to think about it, but that he would call you directly."

There was a long pause. Marina's stomach flip-flopped. "He remembers David from the SEC, by the way," she added quickly. "He said that David was a good man and a good lawyer. He seemed upset that this is happening to him."

"Did he seem to know what you were talking about?"

"Yes, right away. I could see it in his face."

When he didn't answer, she said, "Duncan, I really hope I did the right thing. By coming out here, I mean. I just wanted to be helpful."

"My dear," he said quietly. "You have been spectacularly so."

Marina felt a rush through her whole body and she shivered. They shared a quiet moment, each reflecting on what it would mean if Scott Stevens could corroborate David Levin's story. The tide was turning, slowly, in their favor. She relaxed into the sofa, rubbing her feet against each other.

"Are you out at your parents' house now?" he said, after the moment had passed.

"I am. But just for the night. I'm planning to drive back early tomorrow morning. So if I can be of use—"

"Don't come in on my account, please. It's a holiday. You should be with your family."

"Thank you. I'd really like to help out, though. That is, if you'd like me to."

"Why don't you call me when you're back in town? I don't know where I'll be tomorrow, but if you want to, you can come along for the ride. I don't know what I can do with you exactly, but we'll figure something out."

"Thank you," she said breathlessly. "Thanks so much. I'll do that."

"Have a good night, Marina. And enjoy the evening with your parents."

Marina was doing research on Morty Reis when she heard a gentle knock on the door.

"Come in," she said, swinging her feet off the desk.

Her father peeked into the room. He had one pair of reading glasses on top of his head and another dangling from the pocket of his button-down shirt. The collar was frayed, and the light blue plaid was softly familiar. In one hand, he held a plate of apple pie, a napkin, and a fork. When he saw her at the desk, a proud smile played across his lips.

"I thought you might like some brain food," he said, holding out the pie. "Your mom made it. How's it coming along?"

"Good," she said. "Thanks, Dad."

"Well," he corrected, and then blushed reflexively at the floor. "Sorry," he said.

She smiled. "No, you're right. It's coming along nicely."

"Can you talk about what you're working on, or is it top secret?"

"No, not top secret. But I'll tell you about it when it's finished. It's an interesting piece."

"You're working very hard," he said. He paused, looking momentarily embarrassed as he often did when he got sentimental. With slight sheepishness, he added: "I probably don't say this enough, but your mom and I are so proud of you. You seem to be doing such a great job."

Marina stood up and went to him, hugging him full around the chest. He held the pie in one hand, cradling his daughter in the crook of his elbow. Eyes closed, his cheek pressed softly to the top of her head, he said: "I don't worry about you, Marina. Well, maybe a little. But you've always accomplished everything you set your mind to, and you're really a wonderful writer."

"Thanks, Dad." She pulled back from him, allowing him to hold her at arm's length for just a second more. Then she took the pie, offering him her sweet smile.

"Are you staying the weekend?"

"Just the night, I think. I have to help Duncan out with this story."

"Okay. We always love to have you."

"I love being here. But I do need to get back. This is my first chance to work on a real story. You know, something other than lipstick shades for spring. And I think it's going to be great."

When he left, she devoured the pie. It was perfectly sweet and crumbled in that way that only homemade pie can. When the last trace of apple had been scraped off the plate, she sat back in her father's chair, satisfied. It had been, for the first time in a long time, a good day.

# SATURDAY, 6:15 A.M.

"We're coming back into the city now," Sol said. He adjusted the rearview mirror and stepped on the gas, the monotony of suburban Long Island rolling out beneath his car tires. He hated this part of the island, not yet city but no longer country. All car dealerships and office complexes and people putting gas in their Honda Civics. The kind of people who either couldn't afford to live in Manhattan or chose not to. Sol couldn't decide what was worse. All the houses looked the same, stacked ten deep around cul-de-sacs. It brought back bad memories.

As he passed a furniture warehouse with fluorescent green "Sale" banners fluttering from its windows, Sol thought, *I can't believe I grew up here.* His sister and Marion's two brothers still lived within ten miles of the next exit, but Sol had successfully avoided visiting any of them for more than three years. Instead, the family came to them, for birthdays and Seders and the occasional casual visit. "Sol has to work," Marion would say. "But we'd *love* to have you over to the apartment." Sol suspected that Marion's brothers took quiet offense at this pattern, but he didn't really care. If they thought he was being selfish, they were right. If they thought he had a superiority complex, they were also right. The reality was that he and Marion had a cook and staff, and set the table with cloth napkins instead of paper, and at the end of the night, no one had to take out the dogs or the trash. To pretend Passover with the Schwartzmans in Great Neck would be equally nice required theatrical capabilities that Sol didn't possess. Also, he usually did have to work. He wouldn't say that his time was too valuable to spend it in transit, but it was too valuable to be spent in transit to his in-laws' house.

Sol felt as though he had been in the car for two days straight. Thanksgiving had passed in a blur, more a pause than a holiday, with long stretches of highway gating it on either side. How many times had he spoken to Eli in the past few days? He had lost track. He had spent the whole car ride out to East Hampton on the phone with Eli; now the whole car ride home, too . . . Driving was becoming synonymous with unpleasant conversations with Eli. Sol didn't want to seem desperate, but they were now operating on borrowed time. Hours mattered. Fewer than seventy-two hours had elapsed since Sol had gotten the news of Morty's death. Sol imagined they had, at most, another forty-eight until rumors began leaking into the media about what was going on inside RCM. The only reason it hadn't started already was because of Thanksgiving. Which, Sol realized gratefully, the rest of the country seemed to recognize as a holiday, even though lawyers never had. It wasn't a head start, but it was something. A head step, maybe.

"Carter's driving back on his own," Sol said, his foot fused to the gas pedal. He was cruising at just over 80 mph; reflexively, he checked the mirrors for cops. "We'll both be back in the city within the hour. When can you meet?"

Eli paused. When he spoke, his hesitancy was apparent. "Listen, why don't you guys come in tomorrow morning? We need to get our house in order first. I'm not sure we're prepared enough to make it worth your while."

Sol snorted in frustration. "Eli, we've got to get this worked out. He's willing to cooperate, but he's going to need some assurance that he's not going to get burned if he does. This is extremely stressful for him and for his family. Everyone wants to see this resolved, right?"

"Of course. But you came to me with this forty-eight hours ago."

"More like sixty."

"I'm doing the best I can. It's a holiday. And I gotta be honest, here, this isn't the kind of deal I can get done on my own." Eli's voice had gotten high and nasal, which wasn't good. He was annoyingly close to whining. Sol had known him long enough to know that he didn't like feeling pressured, but Sol didn't have the time or the patience to hold Eli's hand on this one.

"This is a high-profile case, Sol. Robertson's not going to be thrilled at passing up the opportunity to go after a CEO who had thirty-three percent of his fund invested in a Ponzi scheme. Does Darling understand that he's about to have a horde of angry investors on his doorstep?"

"Yeah, of course he does. Look, Robertson will get his win. We're not saying that Delphic shouldn't be held accountable. Just hold the right people at Delphic accountable. Don't go after Carter simply because he's CEO. Any involvement they had with RCM was one hundred percent the fault of his partner and the investment team."

Eli sighed. In the background, there was the piercing sound of children's voices, and Sol realized that Eli was taking the call from home. This annoyed him. Why wasn't Eli at the office? *This is what happens when you leave private practice*, he thought. *No sense of urgency.*

Sol wondered where Eli lived. It was probably pretty dismal. One of those white brick buildings on Second Avenue, with a cookie-cutter layout and low ceilings. Parquet floors, a dishwasher that leaked, a superintendent who wore a wifebeater under his work shirt and looked as though there was a game on somewhere that you were keeping him from watching. Eli had three kids. Sol had gotten all of them into a private school in Manhattan. The school cost forty thousand dollars a year, but all three were the quiet beneficiaries of a scholarship fund underwritten by a client of Sol's, who at the time was being investigated for options backdating. Sol wondered if there was a number that would make Eli move faster, but he bit his tongue. Unfortunately, Eli was one of those people who preferred to get paid off in favors. More than likely, he would balk at the suggestion that taking cash wasn't really too far from what he was doing already. Everyone had a line in the sand. Sol just wished Eli's line was a little closer to his own.

It didn't take much to convince Eli of Alain's accountability. Beyond the rather obvious point that Alain was, in fact, guilty, he also played the part of the corporate villain perfectly. He was the embodiment of Wall Street at its worst. His e-mails would read well in the *Post* (Sol reminded himself to call the associate who was combing through them now); Sol could have one on the front page by Monday, if that was what Eli wanted. And Alain would inevitably do something flamboyant—drive his black Lamborghini to the courthouse, or tell a reporter to fuck off—in just such a way as to fan the flames of public resentment. He would, in all likelihood, be arrested at his weekend home in Gstaad, where Sol suspected he was hiding out. It would be a slam dunk for the feds, and a splashy one. It was exactly the kind of preelection press Robertson was looking for, and Eli's main goal in life was pleasing Robertson. The trickier question was whether Alain alone was enough.

"The thing is," Eli whined, "it's not really an either-or situation. I mean, we have to justify to the public why we aren't prosecuting Carter, too."

"Justify to the public? Or justify to Robertson's campaign staff?"

"Both, I guess."

"I told you what to say publicly. Carter was semiretired. End of story."

"Okay, justify to Robertson, then."

"Tell him what I keep telling you. My client talks and this case gets handed to you on a silver fucking platter. And then some. The work's done for you. You'll have him in handcuffs by Monday and you'll have barely lifted a finger. How's this not an easy "yes" for you?" Sol snarled. Between

Eli and the traffic, Sol was getting irritable, and he really had to pee. He reminded himself that if Eli had any tolerance for risk, he wouldn't be a government lawyer. He tapped his fingers furiously on the steering wheel and then honked as a Honda Civic cut him off in the middle lane. *Fuck you,* he thought, channeling all his frustration at the driver of the Honda. *Fucking cretin.*

Eli was silent.

There was one card that Sol was still holding, and though he would have preferred to play it later, it seemed Eli was in need of a nudge.

"There's one more thing," Sol said. "Better discussed in person, but it seems that my associates came across some unusual communication with the SEC. We'll have to confirm some things on our end, but it seems like Alain thought of everything, including how to get the SEC off his back, and Morty's. The information is yours. That is, if you're willing to work with us."

"Are you saying he bribed someone?" Eli said quickly. His voice had brightened noticeably. "I mean, what kind of communication are we talking about here? Do you have a name?"

Sol smiled. Usually he preferred to do business face to face; the eyes gave away so much more than the voice. But he knew exactly what Eli was thinking now. The possibility of bribery charges against an SEC official would be a career maker for Eli. If he could bring that home for Robertson, well, the sky was the limit.

"Well, now I said we were going to have to confirm some things," he said casually. "We're moving as fast as we can on our end, too. Let's not forget that we're not under subpoena here, either. Why don't we talk about this when we get together?"

Eli cleared his throat. "Yeah, okay. Sunday morning okay for you guys? First thing?"

"How's seven tomorrow morning?"

"Mmm, let's make it nine."

Sol rolled his eyes. "All right, nine. But let's get this done, all right? It's going to be a lot easier to work together once we're all playing on the same team."

"Yeah, I'll see you both tomorrow. Call me if something comes up."

"Will do. Likewise."

"Come ready to talk about this SEC situation, okay?"

"Come ready to sign something. Have a good night, Eli."

*Got him,* Sol thought, and clicked off the call. "Call office," he articulated into the empty cabin of the car. He fiddled with the Bluetooth as he waited for the cool greeting of the Penzell & Rubicam central receptionist. There was something about unsecured phone systems that made him vaguely nervous. Sol had expressed this concern to the guy at the Mercedes dealership when he had traded in the car last year; the guy had looked at him as though he were either paranoid or very old. Old and paranoid. He was both, he realized, as he adjusted the speaker volume again. And this Morty thing wasn't going to improve either. He felt as if he had aged five years since Wednesday.

Central reception picked up after one ring. "Penzell & Rubicam. How may I direct your call?"

Sol breathed a calming sigh. "This is Sol Penzell. Could you get me Yvonne, please? At home?"

"Just a minute."

Sol didn't feel guilty about what he was about to do, but he felt that he ought to feel guilty, which was the next closest thing. Yvonne hadn't taken a vacation day in more than two years, and she sorely deserved this one. But Yvonne never got upset with him, and he imagined she would take this as she always did: in stride. He would buy her something nice when it was all over.

"For the record, I am upset with you," she said, when she picked up. "I do have a life, you know."

"I know. I need you to meet me in the office in an hour or so. I promise to make it up to you. I feel very guilty for asking."

"No, you don't. I haven't taken a day off in four years."

"I thought it was two."

"It's been four. And-a-half. Not that anyone's counting."

"You know I wouldn't ask if it wasn't important," Sol said, tired of apologizing.

"I have the wire confirmations for you." Her voice was flat and hollow. He was testing her patience. If he pushed her on it, she would say what she always said: *Sol, I'm in no mood.*

Sol felt flushed with a warm sense of relief. This was the first thing that had gone right in days. "You're sure, everything's in place? Set up no problem?"

"It wasn't 'no problem.' I mean, they weren't excited about backdating them. But yes, there are now two wire transfers of cash, out of account A into account B, in the amounts specified; the first is recorded as taking place on September 5, 2008, and the second on October 31, 2008. Both Fridays. The accounts are numbered accounts in the Cayman Islands; you have to go through two levels of security, but you can ultimately trace both back to an original signatory. If you do that, you see that account B is registered in the name of David Levin. There's a slight issue with account A, though. There need to be two names signing off on it because it's technically a Delphic Europe account and transfers of that size require two signatures."

"Put someone else from the Geneva Office down then."

"It has to be a corporate officer. We used to list Alain and Brian, before Brian quit as CFO."

"Fine. Put Paul's name, then."

"Paul Ross?"

"Yeah. He's a corporate officer. He's the general counsel. Also, he's talked to David Levin before. It makes sense."

"But Paul just got there. I'm not sure he was at the firm on September fifth."

"Fine, change it to the twenty-sixth, then."

Yvonne paused. "Who is David Levin?" she said.

"That's not something you need to know." Sol's voice was sharp. A light snow was misting against the windshield; he flicked the wipers on high and they darted back and forth with a rhythmic flourish, like chef's knives across a cutting board. "This is a formality anyway, Yvonne. These are transfers that should have been made in the past; now they've been made. I apologize for asking you to record them on a previous date but sometimes things like this need to occur in order to keep business flowing productively. Whether or not Paul signed off on this transfer is not of consequence. I know I can trust you, I always have, but I'm telling you that right now is not a good time to test me on that."

"I'm sorry."

"Don't apologize. Just please do your job."

When she was silent, Sol sighed. He said more gently, "I know I sound like an asshole today. This is a very pressurized situation. I just need everyone to get things done right now and not ask questions."

"Jane Hewitt called again last night. They were still rolling your line to my home phone. She seemed upset. I told her you were in Long Island and tried to give her your cell, but she said she had it already. She didn't want to leave a message."

"Thank you. Could you call her back for me please, and let her know that we're managing the situation and I'll be in touch soon. Also let her know that I've advised Carter not to reach out to her, and that if she needs to speak to someone to call me instead. I have my cell phone and she has the number."

"She was really upset."

"I understand that."

"I'll call her now."

"I know you're thinking I should call her myself. But she'll understand. It's business."

"I said 'I'll call her now.' I wasn't thinking anything."

"I know you, Yvonne," Sol said. "And I know when you're judging me in your head." He was friendly Sol now, big bear Sol, with his ruddy cheeks and grandfather beard, jovial *"I'm going to swipe all the M&M's from the dish on your desk"* Sol.

He chuckled. "Just trust me here and hopefully we can get this thing under control. It's been like a goddamn runaway freight train since Wednesday. Did you check on Julianne? Did she get in okay? Thank you for getting her on that plane, by the way."

"She gets in tomorrow. Not the best way to spend Thanksgiving, alone in that house. I'll call to check in on her, just to be sure."

"You're a good woman, Yvonne."

"I know. I'll see you in the office," she said, and hung up the phone.

Already he felt better, knowing that Yvonne would be there. It was her rare absence that made Sol appreciate what a useful creature Yvonne was. He couldn't imagine existing without her. She ran his life. She typed his correspondence; she answered his phones; she told him when to go to the dentist. She made dinner reservations and booked flights and proofed legal agreements. She bought Marion's birthday and anniversary presents every year. She reminded him to say something nice when someone in the office had a baby or got married. Sol paid her more than most of the junior associates, but she was well worth it. Yvonne had access to more information than anyone: every client file, every e-mail, his calendar, even the password to his voice mail. She was his vault. Next to Marion, she was the most important woman in his world.

Yvonne was the only person, other than Sol, who knew that Sol had two sets of just about everything, from his calendar to his accounting log to his address book. There was the set that would be found if anyone was to subpoena him, and then there was the set that only he and Yvonne knew existed. Around 90 percent of the content overlapped—on any given day it might be 100 percent—but it was the other 10 percent that really mattered. After-hours meetings with Senate Finance

Committee members, the numbers and content of offshore accounts, wire transfers to government officials, all existed within the margins of this 10 percent.

As he passed through the tollbooth on the bridge, Sol realized he hadn't wished her a happy Thanksgiving.

# SATURDAY, 10:02 A.M.

The room was uncomfortably hot, particularly for November. A knob had broken off the radiator and it was spitting out steam like an angry teakettle. Paul glanced around, hoping to open a window, but there wasn't one; instead, there were four walls and a low ceiling all painted a leaden gray, the slapped-on kind of paint that was standard issue in government offices. He wondered if this was in fact the kind of place where interrogations happened. He had never been to the New York Attorney General's office before, but he imagined that some unpleasant meetings had taken place in this room. He hoped this would not be one of them.

Paul gripped Merrill's hand. He was aware that his palm was beginning to sweat and he was crushing her fine knuckles, but he couldn't let go. He was grateful she was there. She had been quiet on the cab ride over. He couldn't tell whether she was angry; she seemed only contemplative, the surface of her face betraying nothing. Maybe she was just tired. They were all tired. Even King seemed spent. That morning, he had turned around and headed home after only two blocks, his ears flopped like wilting lettuce. Paul was thankful: he didn't have the energy or the time for a long walk in the park.

The door opened, revealing Alexa and two men, all dressed in jeans. As he stood to greet them, Paul wondered if the custom-made button-down with his initials on the cuff was a mistake. He had tried to spiff himself up a little bit, showering and shaving for the first time in days, just to feel human again. But the last thing he wanted was to come off like an arrogant hedge fund guy. The loud purple check of the shirt hadn't even occurred to him until now; he had just grabbed the first clean one off the hanger. Now it seemed louder than the siren that was wailing in the street outside. When had he started dressing like this? He had forgotten. Now it was all cable-knit sweaters and Ferragamo loafers. There were still a few Brooks Brothers shirts in the back of his closet, but he never wore them. Why would he, when the custom-mades fit so well?

"Thanks for coming," Alexa said, closing the door behind them. The sound of the siren muted, then drifted away into silence. "Do you all know David?" The taller of the two men nodded and extended his hand. "And this is Matt Curtis, our friend from the NYAG's office."

David cleared his throat and pulled his chair back on the carpet. "Please take a seat. I know, this is moving at light speed here, and we're all just sprinting to catch up. Matt has been incredibly generous with his time, and so has Alexa, of course, but basically, you're all here because of me. So this started because I tried to open an investigation into RCM. As an ancillary matter, I was also poking around into RCM's feeder funds, Delphic included. I was closing in when Morty Reis's death was announced and everything spiraled out of control."

"When did you start the investigation?" Paul asked. He had been wondering this ever since David had called him a few weeks ago.

"About two months ago. I think Alexa told you, but I started with an inquiry into an accounting firm, which was funneling business into RCM without being properly registered as an investment adviser. It struck me as strange that one of the world's largest hedge funds would be doing business with this two-bit accounting shop, so I took a harder look at RCM itself. At first, I thought we were dealing with insider trading. Something was illegally boosting RCM's performance, but I figured that was probably just a few rogue guys getting greedy inside an otherwise legitimate fund. Honestly, it took me a while to wrap my head around the idea that the entire thing was a Ponzi scheme. Fraud on that massive a scale involves many, many more people than just the guys inside RCM. It's widespread system failure; outside law firms, accounting firms, feeder funds, even the SEC."

Paul leaned forward to interject, but then pulled back, restraining himself. *Keep your mouth shut,* he told himself sternly. *Keep your mouth shut and let them do the talking.* Merrill, he noticed, was much better at this than he was. She was sitting still but alert, her face betraying nothing. They made eye contract for a fleeting second and her lips flickered in a small smile, as if to say, *It's okay. We're all right.* Instead he gave David a quick nod.

"So now I've got a huge investigation on my hands, but no support from my office to pursue it," David continued. "In fact, I was getting pressure to drop it altogether. At first I thought I was just being paranoid, that my appeals were probably just getting lost in a bureaucratic black hole. But then the pushback became overt. Things got so bad that I called Matt, who's an old friend and at this point, one of the few people in the world that I trust."

Matt smiled tightly at Paul, and leaned into the table in acknowledgment. He had a pad in front of him, and Paul fought the impulse to try to read the scribblings on it upside down. A few words were underlined and in caps. Paul wondered if that was good or bad.

"The long and the short of it is that some very senior folks didn't want me poking around. When I continued to do so even against their recommendation, they started fighting dirty. I was suspended from the SEC yesterday morning on an indefinite basis. Everything in my office is gone—my files, my desktop, everything. I have no access to the building. So now Matt here has got three cases on his hands. There's the case against RCM that I was building, which I've handed off to him. There's the secondary case against the funds, like Delphic, that were heavily invested in RCM, and also the accounting firm and the attorneys who looked the other way. And then there's what we've been calling Case Three."

David took a breath and sat back in his chair. He had been twirling his pen in between his fingers with perfect dexterity, but he stopped and placed it in front of him on the table. There was something cool about him; this surprised Paul. Government lawyers were rarely cool. David had tan skin and slightly silvered hair. He was tall, maybe six foot two or three. He had a charismatic smile and a firm handshake. The kind of guy women went crazy for. The kind of guy who should have been in television maybe, or advertising. Alexa was smitten, that much was clear. Though they were treating each other with only professional courtesy now, Paul could feel a palpable electricity between them.

Paul shifted in his chair. "So Case Three . . ." he prompted.

"Yeah, Case Three. The last few days have felt like a moving target, but right now that's our major issue. Case Three is the case against the SEC. The one thing that everyone can agree on at this point is that someone at the SEC was bought off. Most likely by someone at RCM, or at Delphic."

Paul frowned. "Why do you say Delphic?"

"Here's the problem," Matt said. "Yesterday, a colleague comes to me with a story that is nearly identical to yours. He claims that there's an insider at Delphic who's already talking to someone in our office. Not only that, but this insider has hard proof that Delphic was in bed with the SEC. That there're wire transfers to an account in the Cayman Islands coming out of a Delphic corporate account into an account of someone inside the SEC. My colleague didn't have much more information than that because it's not his case. But he heard about it because it has apparently been elevated all the way up to Robertson. When the AG gets involved, word gets around."

"Sorry." Paul shook his head. "You already have an insider, someone at Delphic?"

"Who?" Merrill injected, sitting forward. "Bring them in now, to talk to us. Maybe between Paul and this other person we can piece together what actually happened at RCM. And if someone at the SEC is to blame, too, let's just get it out on the table. I think we could all use a little clarity at this point."

"It's a little more complicated than that," Matt said, looking nervously at David.

Alexa's eyes were on the carpet, which made Paul's stomach lurch uneasily. She couldn't even look at him.

"At first, I thought there might have been some miscommunication, and that the insider my colleague was talking about was you, Paul. I thought maybe you had come directly to someone else in our office, someone you know and feel comfortable with. It seemed unlikely to me that there would be two insiders at Delphic. So I did some digging last night, to find out what was going on. Turns out there *are* two of you. Insiders, I mean." He cleared his throat. "The other person—well, it's Carter Darling. He's talking to someone at the NYAG's office through his lawyer. The complicated part is that he's apparently implicated both Paul and David as part of some scheme to get the SEC to look the other way."

There was a moment of silence in the room. Matt's words buzzed in the air like static electricity.

"What?" Paul stammered. Then he slammed his fist on the table, hard, startling the two women. It surprised him to hear such a violent sound but he couldn't help it, and it felt good, as if a small and necessary valve had been opened and a little bit of steam had been released.

"Are you saying that Carter is accusing me of bribing David not to investigate RCM and Delphic? Are *you* accusing me of bribing David?"

"That's insane," Merrill muttered. She was staring at her hands, which were folded in her lap. "I'm sorry, but it's insane."

"They're being set up," Alexa said evenly to Merrill. "They had nothing to do with this. Your dad's cutting a deal. Don't you see that?"

Merrill looked up and met Alexa eye to eye. "Of course Paul didn't have anything to do with it," she said. Her voice was as steady as her gaze, but her lip was quivering. "He's my husband."

Alexa nodded and looked down at her BlackBerry, which was vibrating on the table. She stared at its screen for a second, before rising to her feet. "Excuse me," she said. "I have to take this." To David she said, "It's Duncan." When she closed the door behind her, the room fell still again, except for the persistent whistle of the heater.

"No one here is accusing anyone of anything," Matt said. "We're all on the same side here. I'm just presenting the facts as they are. We've got a serious problem."

"There must be some kind of mistake," Merrill said quietly. She had started to cry. David stood up and offered her a box of tissues. She blew her nose and then crumpled the tissue in her fist.

"Thank you," she said. She slid the box back across the table. "Look, Dad wouldn't implicate Paul in anything. It just doesn't make sense."

Matt looked at Paul uncomfortably. "It's possible that there's been a mistake," he said. He shrugged, but Paul could tell from his voice that he didn't believe that for a second. "Or some kind of misinterpretation. But as of right now, Carter Darling is cutting a deal. And that deal seems to include selling out you and David. The question is, why would he do that? Besides simply to save himself."

"David," Merrill said. Her cheeks were burning red, and she looked as small as Paul had ever seen her. Everyone in the room was looking at her with pity. She kept her eyes on the table in front of her so she didn't have to look at any of them. "Your boss is Jane Hewitt, is that right?"

"Yes," David said. "Or was. She's the one who suspended me."

"And she was the one pushing back on you all this time."

"Yes, that's right."

"I think"—Merrill glanced sideways at Paul and reached for his hand—"I think I have to say something then." Her face was wrought with worry.

Paul squeezed her hand hard three times. Usually, this meant *I love you*. This time he was thinking, *Are you okay?*

Before she could speak, the door swung open and Alexa appeared. She held her BlackBerry up with one hand and smiled triumphantly. The other four stared at her.

"I think we've got something. Duncan's on his way over here now, with someone he wants us to speak to."

# SATURDAY, 11:01 A.M.

The *Wall Street Journal* offices were humming. Duncan was now accustomed to the slower pace of magazine work, and found the atmosphere overstimulating, like children's television or the floor of a casino. Fluorescent track lighting and the omnipresent glow of double-screened monitors lit the large, open bullpen. Televisions hung from the ceilings, streaming information from multiple channels. It had the energy of a young persons' office, though nowadays, all the young people wanted to work for blogs or online news aggregators or social media outlets that Duncan didn't know about. Newspapers were becoming dinosaurs, too large and slow moving to keep pace with the changing environment. Duncan related. He felt like a dinosaur himself, a wooly mammoth loafing about on a glacier somewhere, waiting for the onset of the next ice age.

The thought of Owen working here made Duncan smile. Owen had been Duncan's protégé during the early days at the *New York Observer.* He was like a puppy: endearingly untrainable, endlessly energetic, always with his nose in something. "You're either going to end up in jail, or winning a Pulitzer," Duncan used to tell him. "Maybe both."

They had stayed in touch over the years. They met for drinks before industry dinners, grabbed the occasional diner hamburger or dive-bar drink, and every once in a while Owen would introduce Duncan to whichever young thing he was dating that month. Owen still deferred to Duncan for periodic professional advice, though he had long since established himself as a star journalist. This was the first time Duncan had ever asked him to return the favor.

All around the bullpen, journalists were talking on the phone, clicking away at their keyboards. Still, Duncan spotted Owen immediately. He always stuck out like a sore thumb. Even after a decade at the *Journal*, Owen still looked as though he belonged at *Rolling Stone*. His reddish hair hung shaggily around his eyes. He wore cowboy boots and a Marlboro Man belt buckle. Duncan wondered, not for the first time, how he got anyone to take him seriously.

"Come sit," Owen said, after the two men embraced. He pulled up a couple of chairs around what Duncan gathered was his desk. It was by far the messiest on the floor. "Sorry for the short notice. There's someone I want us to talk to together, so I thought this was the easiest way to do it."

"Listen, you're helping me here. I really appreciate this, especially given the holiday."

"Please, you know me. I don't do holidays," Owen said enthusiastically. It was true; Owen had worked nearly every day that Duncan had known him. "Holidays are for the weak."

"So what have you got for me?"

"Sol Penzell," Owen said, leaning back, his hands folded behind his head, "is Carter Darling's lawyer. He's the signatory on all the Delphic offering docs, you know, the stuff they file and send out to investors. And his firm does business with RCM, too. The two of them and Morty Reis are thick as thieves. Anyway, he was my first thought when we talked. I've wanted to do a piece on that guy for God knows how long. Never got enough on him, though. Runs a firm called Penzell & Rubicam. Firm's more like a lobbying firm than anything else. They do a lot of high-level brokering work, connecting high-profile corporate folks to government, that kind of thing. They have some pretty slippery clients."

"Like who?"

"Remember that DOJ investigation into Blueridge, the private security company that allegedly was stockpiling automatic weapons down in Texas to sell overseas? There was a big brouhaha about it in the media. Some military people came forward and said they were selling weapons to Afghan resistance fighters."

"That was last fall, no? Whatever happened?"

"Nothing happened. And Penzell is Blueridge's lawyer. Go figure. Here's another one: BioReach, the world's largest agribusiness? I've got a friend who's a journalist for *National Geographic*. Leslie Truebeck. Very cool lady. Nice legs, too. Anyway, she's doing a piece on corporate humanitarian efforts in East Africa. BioReach is the big story over there; they've been partnering with the World Bank to distribute free grain to farmers. They've gotten a bunch of positive PR for it. Long story short, Les does her homework and ends up finding an exec at BioReach who talks off the record. He admits the company's been cooking its books. And worse still, they've been purposefully giving out grain that can't reproduce. So anyone who takes the free stuff cuts down their fields—which is irreparable, basically—and then the next season finds that the grain won't grow back. So now they are hooked on BioReach's grain. Pretty nasty idea, right? Hooking aid recipients on your product? Sort of like big tobacco. Anyway, Les starts to write the article, but she never finishes it. Want to know why? Because the exec disappears. Not just from her radar; I mean, literally. The guy *disappears*. No one's seen him again. Not even his wife."

"Let me guess: Penzell is BioReach's lawyer."

"You got it. And even though Les has been screaming bloody murder for a year now, nothing's ever come of it. No investigation, nothing. Maybe he's just super good at his job, I don't know. But I think there's a whole lot more going on below the surface. I mean, guys with briefcases of cash and bodies at the bottom of the East River, that kind of stuff. I could talk about it for hours. Penzell & Rubicam is, shall we say, a pet project of mine."

"Let's talk about RCM and Delphic instead."

Owen held up his hands. "All right, all right," he said. "Just giving you a little of the backstory. I'll cut to the chase in a second. You're going to thank me later, though, so just bear that in mind."

"Listen, I'll thank you now. All I can say is, I'll get you the exclusive."

Owen laughed. "Damn straight. Or just get me a date with that lovely young assistant of yours, the one you had call me in the middle of Thanksgiving dinner. Where do you find these women? Craigslist?"

"I'm sorry about that."

"You never need to apologize for sending pretty girls my way," Owen said, his blue eyes laughing at Duncan's discomfort, which had appeared in his cheeks in the form of an awkward purplish blush. "Plus, this is a hell of a story."

"I just wish my niece weren't in the middle of it."

"Well, listen to this: Yesterday afternoon, I lob in a call to Sol Penzell. I thought maybe I could shake him up a little. I leave a message with his secretary saying that I'm with the *Wall Street Journal*, and would he like to comment on the article that I'm writing about allegations of fraud and conspiracy at RCM and Delphic. You could tell that really took the wind out of her. Twenty minutes later, I get a call from a random cell phone number. It's Yvonne Reilly, the secretary."

"That's interesting," Duncan said. "The secretaries always know everything, don't they. What did she ask?"

"She starts peppering me with questions. Who's running the investigation? Is Delphic under investigation, or just RCM? What about Penzell & Rubicam? She was nervous as hell. Anyway, I did my best to scare the shit out of her, you know, without really saying much of anything."

"Gentlemanly of you."

Owen rolled his eyes. "Oh please. If anyone taught me how to pressure a source, it was you. Took a little cajoling, but I worked the Barry magic on her. Anyway, she agreed to meet with me. She wouldn't really say much over the phone, but I got the sense that she has a serious story to tell. I thought you might like to come along."

Duncan whistled. "I think I owe you more than an exclusive. Is she coming here now?"

"I'm going to meet her in twenty minutes. Ready for a walk down Wall Street?"

"More than ever."

---

Later, when Duncan sat down to describe Yvonne for the article in *Press*, the first word that came to mind was *nondescript*. She was of medium height and build, with hair that was neither orange nor yellow, but a sort of faded, fried in-between. She could have been thirty-five or fifty. She had spent too much time in the sun. It showed on her face and on the backs of her hands. Tanning was perhaps her only real act of vanity. Her nails were short and bitten to the quick, working-girl fingers. Duncan always noticed everyone's hands. He thought they said a lot about a person, whether they were vain or nervous or practical or well taken care of, which is why he still got a manicure twice a month. Yvonne looked like any other secretary, one of the herd that crossed over through the tunnels, across the bridges, twice daily on their way in and out of Manhattan.

Nondescript, but he knew exactly who she was the moment he saw her.

Because it was the Saturday after Thanksgiving, the Financial District was thinly populated. Duncan was relieved to see that Fraunces Tavern, a pub Owen frequented and Duncan was sure he had suggested, was open. It was a watering hole during the week for Goldman Sachs bankers, but on the weekends, it wasn't highly trafficked. Particularly before noon. The lights were on but there didn't seem to be any patrons. A good place for an anonymous conversation.

Yvonne was finishing a Camel outside on the cobbled street. The wind had picked up off the river and felt piercingly cold against the skin. Her shoulders hunched up around her ears. It was too cold to be outside for long. She was either a serious smoker or very nervous; Duncan suspected both.

"Are you Yvonne?" Owen said, when she looked up. She had smoked the cigarette down to the filter. She took a last drag and stubbed it out beneath her toe.

"You didn't say you were bringing a friend," she said, and cocked her head to one side. Her hands were stuffed deep into her pockets. She withdrew one reluctantly to shake hands with them both, but returned it with the speed of a card dealer in Vegas.

"Duncan Sander, Ms. Reilly," he said, holding open the door for her. "After you."

"Duncan's a friend but also a colleague," Owen said. "He's an exceptional journalist. He's been working on this story with me, so if it's all right with you, he'll stay for our talk?"

Yvonne's eyes darted across Duncan's face, assessing him. "I know who you are," she said. She dropped her *R*'s almost imperceptibly, so that *are* sounded more like *ahhhh*. Duncan saw the flash of a gold cross, tucked into the collar of her blouse. It was the only jewelry she was wearing besides her wedding band. *Boston Irish*, Duncan thought. *I bet she has five kids at home. Goes to Mass every Sunday.*

"You're that magazine guy, I forget which one." She didn't sound impressed, but Duncan nodded his head humbly anyway.

"Yes, ma'am. Can I get you a drink from the bar?"

She hesitated and then said, "Water's fine."

"I'll have a Sam Adams," Owen said. "You sure you don't want one of those? It's noon somewhere in the world. As my father used to say."

"What the hell. I'll need a drink after this."

"Three Sam Adams, coming up," Duncan said.

When he returned, Yvonne was picking apart a cocktail napkin and rolling its remains into tiny white balls with her fingertips.

"I want you to understand Sol," she was saying to Owen. She paused as Duncan pulled up a chair. Her voice was low and tense, and Owen was leaning in on his elbows in order to hear her. "I know what you must think of him. Or of me, for that matter, working for him for so long. But he's a good man. Or he can be. He cares about the people in his life. He's taken care of me for over fourteen years. Not just paying me well. Though he did that, too, and I've been able to give my boys more because of it, more than I ever thought I could. I have two, you know." Her eyes darted inquisitively between them like a bird's, sizing them up. "The younger one, well, he was a real premie. A lot of complications. I went into labor while I was in the office, right there at my desk. It was real touch and go, you know, from the beginning. I almost died from losing so much blood. Sol got us in with the head ob-gyn at Mount Sinai. Private room, whole nine yards. I was pretty out of it but all I could think was, 'We can't afford this!'" She laughed, her eyes softening. "I had never stayed in a room that nice, not even on our honeymoon. Anyway, at the end of it, the hospital wouldn't charge us. The doctor, he wouldn't either. Someone told us that the office had taken care of it, but I knew it was Sol. I asked him about it, but he just kept saying that the insurance picked it up. Course that wasn't true. We both knew it, but that's just the thing about Sol. He does some really incredible things for people, and he doesn't even want the credit."

"You called me, Yvonne," Owen said. "Let's talk about why."

She took a deep breath. "You got kids? Either of you?"

They shook their heads in unison.

"Well, I'd do anything for mine. I've seen a lot of stuff come across my desk, you know, in the last fourteen years. But some of the stuff that's been going on lately, well. And if what you're saying is true, that there's an investigation and all that, I'd rather not be caught in the middle of it."

"Have you thought about going to talk to the attorney general's office directly? Or getting yourself a lawyer?"

Yvonne winced. She had a turned-up nose covered in freckles like a speckled egg. It wrinkled slightly as she sat back in her chair. "Listen, you're way ahead of me. Your call was the first time I heard about any investigation. I hadn't really thought about going to the authorities or anything. I can't just run out and get myself a lawyer. Lawyers are expensive. I should know. I send out their bills."

A smile flickered across Owen's face. "I understand."

"Also," Yvonne leaned into the table, nervously fingering the cross around her neck. "Look. I've got to look out for myself here. My husband got laid off nine months ago. He worked at Bear, doing investment operations. It's been hard; there aren't any jobs. He's working now, but it's not enough. Everyone talks about these bankers and fund managers losing their jobs, but people like us are getting hit pretty hard, too. We live paycheck to paycheck."

Owen's face was impassive. "Your boss is about to get indicted for fraud, malpractice, bribery," he said. "The best thing you can do is blow the whistle before that happens."

Yvonne nodded, her eyes cast down at her shoes, and dismembered the last napkin. It came apart easily between her fingers, and she rolled it slowly into a series of long twists, like little white cigarettes. "Sol took care of me," she said simply. "Now I've got to take care of myself. I'm not talking to the media out of the goodness of my heart."

Duncan pulled a pen out of his pocket. On a napkin, he wrote a number. He pushed it across the table. "Your story has value. I get that. What we want to do is a piece in the *Wall Street Journal* now, then a longer follow-up in *Press*. An exclusive. You only talk to us."

Yvonne stared at the napkin. "How do I know someone won't offer me more?"

"They might," Duncan said. "But time is money. Every second you wait, your story depreciates in value."

"And the investigation? You're sure it's happening?"

"We're sure." Owen said. They both nodded.

She looked at the number, then back at them. When she spoke, her voice was heavy with resignation. "There's a guy named David Levin. At the SEC. They're setting him up. Sol and Carter, I mean. Or they have, it's done already. They wire transferred to an offshore account in his name, and made it look like he was on the take. The wires are backdated so it looks as though it happened a few months ago."

Duncan could barely breathe. "How do you know this?" he said. "Are you sure what you're saying isn't some kind of mistake?"

"I'm sure," she said, "because I'm the one who set up the transfers."

---

Later, when it was over and Duncan had paid the tab at the bar, he asked her what made her do it.

"Set up the transfers?" she said.

"No, agree to talk to us."

"I told you. I've got kids. If I'm going to lose my job, well, I've got to take care of them somehow. You guys better be ready to pay me pretty quick."

She took a fresh pack of Camels out of her pocket, and pulled the gold cording so that the wrapper came off in two expert halves. She withdrew a cigarette from the pack. Owen offered a light and waited as she took a long drag. "What kills me about this whole thing," she continued, "what really got me about it, was that they set up Paul. You know, Carter's son-in-law. I don't know him real well; no idea if he's a decent guy. I met him a couple times, at firm Christmas parties and baseball games, that kind of thing. Seems nice enough." She shrugged.

"Why would that upset you more than their setting up anyone else?"

"Because he's family. They were willing to sell out family, to save themselves. That's a line," she said, "that I just don't ever want to cross."

"You ready to talk to the AG's office now? I know it's been a long day."

"It's been a long fourteen years," she said.

After he spoke with Alexa, Duncan stared at his phone, debating. "One more quick call," he said to Yvonne. Marina answered on the first ring. "I'm in a cab on the way to the NYAG's office. How quickly can you get there? I can pick you up on my way, if you'd like to join us."

"I'm already there," she said.

# SUNDAY, 8:58 A.M.

A black Escalade pulled up in front of 120 Broadway and out popped Neil Rubicam, looking fresh as a daisy. Carter had never seen Neil looking anything but. He was always slightly tan and seemingly well rested, which irritated Carter even though he knew the man hardly slept and never took vacations. There was a slickness to Neil that made him come off more like an actor playing the part of a big-shot attorney than an actual attorney.

Most lawyers whom Carter knew cared little about their appearance, but Neil cultivated his. He liked his power tie and his custom-made suit; he made a show of checking the time whenever he had a new watch. Neil wasn't exactly handsome but he was well groomed. He had the kind of kinetic charisma that people took notice of. Women loved him. The last time Carter checked, he was divorcing Wife Number Three and had already tee'd up Wife Number Four. Carter wondered how he had time for it all.

As he strode toward him, Neil flashed Carter a brilliant smile. One thing that always struck Carter about Neil was his height. At six foot four, Carter wasn't used to meeting anyone eye to eye. Also, Neil's teeth were improbably white and he smiled easily, even when someone was trying to screw him. Today, Carter found his smile oddly reassuring. For better or worse, Neil always seemed in command of the situation.

"Great to see you, Carter," he said, with an easy handshake. He clapped him on the shoulder and gestured toward the building. "Let's get started?"

"Thanks again for coming up for this, Neil," he said. "Are we not waiting for Sol?"

"Sol's on his way. We can start the meeting without him." Seeing Carter's hesitation, he added, "Not to sound ominous, but I'll be the one running the conversation today. Sol's close with Eli, but everyone understands that you'll be coming to the table with a litigator. It doesn't mean anything, except that we mean business."

Neil seemed to be enjoying himself. That was the thing about lawyers, Carter realized. On corporate deals, the lawyers worked twice as hard and got paid a quarter as much; they handled all the unpleasant tedious details that bankers didn't have the patience to address; they did it all with a smile because at the end of the day, the bankers were the ones paying their bills. Lawyers were the team goalies. If the team won, the guys who scored got all the credit. But if they lost, the goalies got all the blame.

But in the rare situations where the deal went horribly off the rails and the ball got handed to the litigators, the tables turned. Carter may still be paying Rubicam & Penzells' bills, but he was no longer running the show. There was no going back: What was once a corporate matter was now a litigation matter. Carter couldn't have prepared for how it felt. In fact, he didn't really feel anything at all, except for an odd sense of dislocation, as though something had gone very wrong and he had been mistaken for someone else, and all he could do was feel helpless and wait for things to play themselves out.

"I understand," Carter nodded.

They passed through building security, emptying their pockets of keys and change and wallets, removing their belts and shoes and putting them into a plastic bin as though at the airport. The halls had a dingy, depressed air about them, as though everything was coated in dust. Carter remembered them viscerally; he had been in this building years before, when Merrill was still in law school. She had interned in the Civil Rights Bureau while studying at NYU. He had met her for lunch a few times when he was downtown for meetings. She would bounce out of the dank elevators with her eyes shining, bubbling over with what she was working on that day, and the whole lobby would light up with her energy. Merrill had always wanted to be a prosecutor. She took the job at Champion & Gilmore because it was a feeder to the U.S. Attorney's office. She had promised Carter it wasn't about the money—he could give her as much of that as she needed—but rather, the right approach to the career she wanted. That was Merrill, always willing to work hard and play by the rules. As far as Carter knew, coming to work here was still her objective, though he wondered how she would feel after all of this was over. He was so proud of her, his shining star. He wondered if she would ever feel that way about him again.

The thought of what he was about to do unleashed a wave of queasiness. He blinked hard against the fluorescent lights. The room started to spin. Carter nodded when the guard asked him if he had a BlackBerry, and turned it over wordlessly for inspection. He thought if he opened his mouth he might throw up. Neil was talking, but Carter couldn't hear him. He began to feel as though he were floating. He was present, but not fully so; it was as if he had drifted out of his body and was bouncing up against the ceiling like a balloon, watching himself down below.

Carter wondered if this was how it felt before you died. If it was, it wasn't so bad. He felt light, nearly weightless, as if the fatigue and stress that had been weighing him down for the past few months had somehow evaporated. He should have been scared, or at the very least concerned, but he wasn't that, either. Instead he felt relieved. Perhaps because in some back corner of his mind he felt as though the end was finally here. He had been waiting for it, and the anticipation was worse than anything else.

The elevator lurched slightly when its doors closed, a nauseating jolt to the body.

"Jesus Christ," Neil muttered. "Fucking government buildings. Nothing works." He turned and looked at Carter. "How're you feeling?"

"I'm okay," he said, stuffing his hands in his pockets so that Neil wouldn't see the slight tremor. "I'm ready. Let's just get it over with."

Neil stared at the floor numbers as they slowly ascended. "Well. Nothing's gonna be over today. But let's get the deal locked up so we can start moving forward. Okay?"

"Yeah."

The doors *ding*ed open. "You'll feel better when today is over," Neil said, leading the way. "I promise you that."

Down the hall, a door was propped open with a rubber-tipped kickstand. Sun came in through it and played on the hallway floor; then a figure emerged and blocked the light. It was Eli. There were other voices in the conference room behind him, but Carter didn't think any of them belonged to Sol.

"Thanks for coming," Eli said, as they approached him from the elevator bank. They all shook hands in the hallway. Eli held the conference room door open for them and two other men rose to their feet. "This is my colleague, Matt Curtis. And I think you both know Bill Robertson."

Robertson's face was instantly recognizable. He was all over the media; speculation of his gubernatorial bid had been simmering at a low boil for months. Carter had met Robertson a handful of times, but doubted Robertson would acknowledge that now. Though Robertson was slightly younger, they moved in the same social circles. Robertson's daughter was a senior at Spence, Merrill and Lily's alma mater. Both men had, at different times, sat on the school's board. They had several mutual friends.

Delphine Lewis, Ines's bridge partner, had thrown a cocktail event for Robertson back in September. Ines had forced Carter to stop in for a drink, not because she had any real interest in the attorney general but because she was eager to see the Lewis's Rothko, which was said to be worth around $28 million. Carter wanted to stay at the office; they had sparred about it and he had lost. Truth be told, Carter hated Robertson's guts. Everyone on Wall Street did. Robertson was a wholly political animal, in it for personal gain rather than a sense of the greater good. He used his position as attorney general to curry favor with people who would back him when he eventually ran for governor, and in the meantime, invite him to dinner at their Park Avenue apartments. But when appearances demanded it, he would take one of them down. Carter couldn't understand why someone like Peter Lewis—a fellow hedge fund manager—would allow his wife to host a party for Robertson. It was like letting a fox into the henhouse.

Still, at that moment, all Carter could think was how glad he was that he had attended that party and taken the time to shake Robertson's hand.

Robertson looked slighter and less imposing now than at the fundraiser. His hair was thinning at the temples and needed to be cut. His teeth were slightly too long, imparting his signature ratlike smile. Thin lips and limbs. Up close, his cheeks were mottled like a tufted chair, war wounds from an adolescent battle with acne. He looked thin. Perhaps the stress of the fall had caused him to lose weight. Carter wondered if Robertson was thinking the same about him.

"Sorry we weren't able to meet with you yesterday," Eli said, when the door was closed.

"It's my fault," Robertson said, extending his hand to Carter. "I wanted to be at this meeting myself. It's nice to see you again, Carter. You too, Neil."

"Nice to see you, Bill," Neil said. He was smiling casually but Carter could tell he was surprised. "Glad you could join us."

"Ines well?" Robertson gestured for them to sit.

"She is, given the circumstances. Thanks."

"And the girls?"

Carter paused. *How long was social hour going to go on?* "Also well. And your family? Martha is a senior at Spence now, isn't she?"

"Well, that's good to hear," Robertson said, ignoring the question. "I can only imagine how tough the past few days have been. First Morty, then the investigation. Are they here with you in the city? I heard you were spending the holiday out in East Hampton."

"Yes, we all came in. Well, Ines stayed to close up the house, but the girls are here with their husbands."

"Their husbands, right." Robertson nodded. He was still standing, his arms half folded across his chest. He crooked one finger and pressed it thoughtfully against his lip. "Paul and Adrian. Adrian Patterson. I've met his parents. And Paul Ross. Paul's your GC?"

Now Carter was uneasy. Neil was, too; he could sense it. The energy in the room had shifted, but its direction wasn't clear. "You have a good memory, Bill," he said. "I didn't realize you had met them."

Robertson smiled. "Oh, I haven't. Just know their names. Well, Paul's especially. In fact—" He didn't finish the thought. He reached into his briefcase and pulled out a manila folder. From it, he withdrew some papers. He kept them in front of him and said, "I imagine you'd like me to just get to the point."

"Yes, why don't we," Neil said, his impatience obvious.

"From the sound of things, your partner, Alain Duvalier, was the one overseeing Delphic's investments with RCM on a day-to-day basis. Is that right?"

"Alain oversees all of our outside managers."

"But you had a personal relationship with Morton Reis, did you not? I think I met him with you, actually. At a benefit last year."

"Morty was a personal friend. But I wasn't any more involved with the day-to-day management of that relationship than I was any other outside manager. I was given diligence reports and performance updates on RCM by Alain or members of his team on a periodic basis. My job is and has always been client relations. That's a full-time job unto itself." This was a rehearsed speech, and Carter tried to deliver it as earnestly as he could. He watched Robertson's face closely, gauging his reaction.

"Of course, of course." Robertson said, nodding. "My father was in your business, many years ago, as you may know. Lots of golf games and client dinners, right?" He threw Carter a wink and let out a good-natured laugh.

"Something like that." Carter said, as evenly as he could manage.

"All right. So it seems like all of this came as a surprise to you. I have to say, you did a very good job of mobilizing the troops to get to the bottom of it. Particularly given the holiday. And without the help of Mr. Duvalier, who I understand is out of the country and has not been reached." He turned to Neil. "Your office has been very responsive to mine. Sol's provided us with a lot of very useful information."

"We've done what we can." Neil said. "There's no choice in the matter. Reis is all over the news. They have clients to answer to."

"Yes. And this issue with David Levin at the SEC. Obviously, there are serious implications. Fraud at RCM is one thing. Bribery of an SEC official is another."

Carter opened his mouth to speak but Neil cut him off. "That came as a surprise to everyone," he said. "At least, it helps explain why the SEC failed to investigate for as long as they did."

"Were you aware that David Levin was in touch with members of your office? Alain Duvalier and Paul Ross?"

"No." Carter said. "Well, yes. I know that he called our offices. I wasn't aware that he was also in contact with Alain. And I don't believe that Paul was, either. And I certainly wasn't aware of any wire transfers to anyone until Sol brought it to my attention."

"Right." Robertson slid the slim stack of papers in front of him toward Carter and Neil. "Sol provided these to us earlier this morning. These are the records of payments out of a Delphic Europe corporate account into an account that was traced back to David Levin. I know you said you weren't aware of the transfers being made. There're two copies there—take a look. Have either of you seen these before?"

"What's this about, Bill?" Neil said. He and Carter flipped through the pages that were in front of them. "He said he hadn't heard about the transfers. When did you get these from Sol?"

"Oh, I understand, Neil. I'm asking if either of you had seen these actual records, before just now. Had Sol shown these to you?" Robertson asked. He stared intently at Carter.

*Arrogant prick,* Carter thought. *He's getting off on this, watching me squirm in his grasp.*

"I've never seen these before in my life," Carter said. "Look, I built my business from the ground up. I've always trusted Alain to manage the firm's investments so I can focus on the client side of our business. That has never changed. My plan had always been to retire at the end of this fiscal year; anyone at the firm will tell you that I've been consciously reducing my involvement with firm's management for several years now. I regret—now very deeply—having put my trust in my partner, but it's ludicrous for me to have to defend myself against the actions of a single rogue individual. We have over fourteen billion dollars under management. It's a big operation. There has to be some sort of division of labor."

"Well, it wasn't a single individual. That's the thing."

"If other members of the firm were involved with either mismanagement of our assets or Alain's dealings with this David Levin at the SEC, clearly that is unfortunate. But as of this time, I'm unaware of it. And I like to think I employ ethical, upstanding people. For the most part."

"How about Paul?"

"Paul?"

"Were you aware that he was involved? With these, as you say, 'dealings' with the SEC?"

"Paul wasn't involved in this. He came to the firm two months ago. And I resent the suggestion."

"I'm not suggesting it," Robertson said. His voice was at once cold and victorious. "I'm stating it." He pushed the papers back across the table.

"From the looks of what you've provided here, Paul was one of the signatories approving these transfers."

Carter felt his heart plummet. Suddenly his body was cold and he shivered inadvertently. He snatched up the papers.

"Turn to the last page. See there? Right under Alain's signature."

"There must be some mistake," Carter said, turning to Neil. "I need to speak with Sol. Why is Paul's name on this?"

Neil glared at him with eyes that demanded silence. "Sol needs to be here," Neil said, addressing Eli and not Robertson. He was visibly unnerved. "We need to at least get him on the phone."

"He won't be joining us," Robertson said. "And you won't be able to reach him. We arrested him this morning."

Neil stood up, his palms flat on the table. "What did you just say?" He looked so angry that Carter wondered if he was going to physically attack Robertson.

Now everyone was standing and the room was spinning again. Carter thought he might pass out. He was blinking hard over and over behind his glasses, trying to stay focused, but everything was happening quickly, as though someone had pressed fast-forward on a movie he was watching, and he was having trouble processing the rapid movements of the actors on the screen.

"It's not a nice thing to do, set up your partner," Robertson said to Carter. "It's even worse to set up your son-in-law. Don't you think?"

"I didn't—"

"Not another word, Carter. *Not another word*." Neil tried to sound commanding, but there was desperate shakiness in his voice.

There was a knock at the door. "Come in," Eli said, and made a move to open it.

"I need to talk to Sol," Carter said to Neil. "Paul wasn't involved with this. He didn't tell me that."

"Are you challenging the validity of these documents?" Neil said, holding up the papers. He was shaking them, or maybe his hands were just shaking. Either way, he had lost his composure. Carter stared at him, terrified. His hair, usually slicked back with gel, had started to fly forward in pieces and his face was an angry purplish red.

"This is Officer Dowd," Eli said calmly, and the room turned to see the newcomer. "Unfortunately, Carter, we've made the decision to place you under arrest at this time."

"This is not happening," Neil said.

Robertson turned to him, his dark eyes blazing. "Don't push your luck, Neil," he said, lip curled. "We took your partner away in handcuffs this morning. We have witnesses, from your office, who are willing to testify to the fact that these transfers are a sham, part of a setup to make it look as though Alain Duvalier and Paul Ross were bribing David Levin. I also have a former SEC attorney, Scott Stevens—you may remember his name—who's willing to go on the record about his own experience with this case. He claims to have been forced out of the SEC for his handling of an RCM investigation a few years ago. The fact is we've got more than sufficient evidence against your client to merit an arrest. He's a flight risk. If you hadn't come in today, we would have come to you. Just be grateful the media isn't outside."

"For what possible purpose would Sol manufacture this? That's rather contrived, even for you." Neil seethed. His nostrils flared viciously as he spoke.

Robertson smiled, a cat-that-ate-the-canary smile. "My assumption—and feel free to speak up if I have it wrong here, Carter—is that setting up David Levin was a last-ditch attempt to shift the focus away from the person at the SEC who was, in fact, protecting RCM and Delphic. It's an interesting play. Also risky. Officer Dowd is going to take you down to the First Precinct now, and we'll go from there. If you'd like to discuss your relationship with Jane Hewitt with us, which I suggest you do, now is the time. Otherwise, I'm sure she'll be willing to discuss it with us when we place her under arrest."

Carter rose to his feet. He gripped the table's edge to steady himself; his whole body shook. He felt as fragile and insignificant as a leaf on a great oak tree; at any moment a gust of wind could stir the branches and he'd find himself in free fall.

He opened his mouth but couldn't speak to Robertson. To Neil he said, "Call Ines. Call Merrill. Call Merrill first. Tell her what's happened. Make sure she knows I would never hurt her."

After his rights were read and his hands were cuffed, Carter was led into a car by the state trooper; all he could think about was Merrill's wedding day. It had been perfectly clear. The sky was a light hazy blue, the color of her eyes, and of her bridesmaids' dresses, and of the cummerbunds on each of the groomsmen. There had been a tent, white and crested, its flimsy walls fluttering gallantly in the evening air. They had danced all night, almost until sunrise.

Merrill had always wanted to have a wedding at Beech House. Ines had pushed for a city wedding—easier to coordinate, fancier, a big black-tie affair—but Carter had taken a stand. He wanted to give Merrill that day, exactly how she had seen it in her mind's eye. If he could have paid for the weather, he would have. In the end, it had been perfect.

Merrill and Paul had left a day later for a honeymoon in the south of France. Carter was grateful that he had seen them off, and also that she was gone by Tuesday, when the planes hit the Trade Towers, and all was lost in New York.

# SUNDAY, 11:00 A.M.

Marion lay on the bed, squeezed her eyes shut, and waited. If she waited long enough, she figured one of the following would happen: (1) she would fall back asleep and when she woke up, everything would be fine; (2) someone would call and explain to her that there had been a horrific mix-up, but that things were on their way to being sorted out; (3) the front door would open and Sol would walk through it, calling her name and harrumphing about the idiocy of the NYAG's office. She would make him coffee while he explained away the morning's events, a web of mistakes and confusion that had culminated in his arrest and quick release. She would shake her head and pitch in the occasional affirmation ("Just awful!" and "You really handled it so well, though"), and he would apologize for giving her such a scare. Later, they would tell their friends about the arrest in gory detail, a good war story over cocktails.

Minutes ticked by. Her heart pounded out of her chest. The longer she waited, the more anxious she became. Though she knew she was fully awake, a part of her began to insist that this was all just an exceedingly real nightmare. If she just focused hard enough, perhaps she would be able to wake herself out of it.

*Open your eyes, Marion,* she thought furiously. *If you just open your eyes, you'll see that Sol is sleeping next to you, and all of this was just a very bad dream.*

The phone rang, a shrill, piercing scream.

She sat up, eyes open. The first thing she saw was Sol's pajama pants on the floor by the closet. They were splayed out in a way that made it look as though he had abandoned them midsprint. The details of the morning came rushing back, precise and horrible. Marion winced and answered the phone.

"Hello?" she said, terrified of what news might be coming. Her fingers tightened around the receiver.

"Marion?"

"Yes, this is she?"

"It's Ines Darling. What's happening, Marion? Sol's been on TV! I thought he was with my husband." Usually, Ines's coolness unnerved Marion. Everything about Ines always appeared effortless and smooth: her straight, glossy hair, her perfectly tailored clothes, the way she carried herself and moved through a room. Though Marion knew she didn't mean to, Ines sometimes made her feel the way she had in middle school: hopelessly plump and unkempt. Marion was forever losing her keys or having bad hair days or overindulging on bread at dinner. She couldn't imagine Ines, perfect, glamorous Ines, contending with such trivial imperfections.

Ines had always treated her kindly, but Marion suspected she saw her as a chore, someone she had to put up with on account of business. Ines was friends with women like CeCe Patterson and Delphine Lewis; "Page Six women," as Sol liked to call them. Marion was certainly not a Page Six woman, nor did she have any desire to be. In truth, she found them a bit dull. She was perfectly content with the friendly acquaintanceship she had cultivated with Ines; they only socialized together with their husbands and never indulged in the pretense that they might arrange to meet for lunch, just the two of them. Marion could not think of a time when Ines had called her on the phone.

"Hello, Ines," Marion replied hoarsely. "I'm sorry, I don't know where Carter is . . . Sol . . . they arrested him this morning."

"*My God, are you all right*? When did this happen?"

"It was early, around six? Sol was still sleeping. There was this banging on the door, so loud I thought they might break it down. I answered it in my bathrobe. There were five of them. Big guys, wearing NYPD vests. They flashed a warrant and just pushed past me into the apartment. I thought there must have been some sort of mistake . . ." Marion trailed off, the shaking in her voice uncontrollable. She pressed her hand to her heart as if she could slow its beating with a little pressure.

"Are you alone right now?"

A sob managed to sneak out. "I am!" Marion was trying so hard to contain herself but it *just felt so awful* . . . She fell back against the bed, clutching her torso as though she had been kicked in the ribs. In forty years of marriage, she had never been apart from Sol for more than two days at a time. If a business trip was longer than that, she went with him. If Sol was sick, she got sick; if Sol was sad, her heart felt broken. Marion knew they were different from other couples. Overly dependent, perhaps. But other couples, or at least the couples she knew, all had children. She imagined that if they had been able to, they might not have developed as they had, like Siamese twins, joined at the heart. Without him, what *was* she? Without him, well. . . Marion couldn't imagine that. She refused to imagine that.

"Can you call someone?" Ines insisted. "I think you should call someone so you're not alone. Did they say anything to you about when he would be back?"

"They said *nothing*. It was terrifying, Ines, truly. He came out to meet them, he was just in pajama pants and an old shirt, and they just started reading him his rights—you know, the way they do in the movies?—and they tried to put handcuffs on him right there in front of me—*can you imagine?*—and he had to ask them if he could put on some proper clothing. It was all so humiliating. Two of them took him back to the bedroom and he had to just throw something on, right there in front of them. They never put the handcuffs on, thank God. I just kept saying to them, my God, he's sixty-two years old."

Ines bit her lip. The image of Sol being escorted out of a police car outside 100 Centre Street was fresh in her mind; they had shown it on the news twice since 9 a.m. His hands, she was sure, had been cuffed in front of him.

"This is terrible," she said. "I'm so sorry. Listen, I'm in East Hampton now, but I'm getting a car to drive me into the city. I'd drive myself, but—well, my nerves are shot. I have no idea where Carter is. I thought he was with Sol until I saw the news—"

Marion hadn't turned on the television. She flicked it on now, muted. It was only a minute before her husband's face filled the screen.

*How on earth did the reporters know to be there? Did they have a snitch at the police department who called them with juicy tips like the time and location of the founding partner of Penzell & Rubicam's arrest? How much would a tip like that go for?*

"—I hate these fucking reporters," Ines muttered, as though she could read Marion's mind. "Excuse my language, but they're absolute vultures."

Marion wasn't listening anymore; her eyes were transfixed by the news feed. *He looks so old,* she thought, her hand still pressed to her left breast. Beneath it, her heart beat fast and hard. *My poor Sol.*

Dark circles ringed his eyes. He averted them from the camera, staring down at the cement as he walked. His hair was askew, his shirt collar half up; he still looked fresh from bed. The camera pulled out and showed a full-body shot of Sol as he entered the building, flanked by police officers. Then Marion saw it: They had cuffed his hands in front of him. Like a common criminal.

*They must have done that to him in the squad car,* Marion thought. *What else would they do? They had been rough with him this morning; not rough, but forceful, physically intimidating . . . it wasn't right, not right at all . . .*

"I'm sorry," she mumbled to Ines. "I should go."

"Yes, yes, of course. Please call me if you hear anything, anything at all. You have my cell, don't you?"

"Yes," Marion said numbly, though she wasn't sure she did.

"Everything's going to be fine. This will all get resolved."

Marion hung up the phone and slid back down into bed. She had tried to look into his eyes the whole time it was happening. But even when he was speaking to her ("*Be calm, Marion, this is just a mistake*") he was looking away, at the floor, at one of the officers. It all happened so quickly. In the moment before he left, he was allowed to hug her good-bye. He pressed his whole body flush against hers. She could hear his breathing, rapid and short, against her neck. She could smell his musty morning scent, and his morning breath, as if they were still in bed with each other, the scratch of his beard against her cheek. In her ear he whispered, "I love you, Marion. Please forgive me for this." As he pulled away from her, she caught his gaze only for a second.

Something was wrong.

Shouldn't he have been surprised? Alert? Indignant? Instead, he had looked away from her . . . as they pushed him out the door, his shoulders hung slack with resignation . . .

*He had been expecting this*, she thought. *Maybe not that morning, or that week, or even that year, but it was something he had anticipated.*

*It wasn't a mistake.*

---

Marion rolled onto her stomach, burying her face in Sol's pillow. She could smell him on it. She let herself cry now, a full, open-mouthed wailing cry, the sound muffled into the bed.

"What is 'this' Sol?" She said aloud. "How can I forgive you if I don't know what you've done?"

Hearing her own voice aloud embarrassed her. She buried her head deeper in the pillow, blocking out the room's unbearable silence.

## SUNDAY, 11:20 A.M.

The house felt still, but pleasantly so. Not at all what one would expect of a widow's home. The bedroom was a little too warm (she had told Carmen not to leave the radiator on all day, but it appeared as though she had forgotten again) but the warmth was a welcome contrast to the blistering cold outside. On the side tables, flowers bloomed. They were replaced once a week, except for the orchids, which lasted a little longer than the cut arrangements. Orchids were her favorite, but they were expensive. Morty got upset if there were too many. The lilies were cheerier, anyway. She liked it when the bedroom smelled of them; it made her feel well taken care of. As if she were at a hotel. On closer inspection, the petals were distended, in the final stages of unfurling, and some had begun to drop their stamen on the tabletop, dusting it with golden pollen. They would be dead by Monday.

She wondered if Carmen had been in the house at all that week. She never knew what Morty did with Carmen when she wasn't around, but she suspected that he let her leave early or told her not to come at all. Morty had never really gotten comfortable with the idea of live-in help.

Julianne had slept well for the first time in days. Her first thought upon opening her eyes had been that it was very nice to be back in her own bed. This filled her with a sense of sublime completeness, as though she were on her way to being whole again. Her head felt clear and her body had stopped aching, which it had been since she had gotten off the plane from Aspen. And she was wearing her own silk pajamas, the white ones with the pink piping, instead of the old sleeping shirt she kept in a drawer at the Aspen house, in case she forgot to pack one. She felt, *dare she think it*, relaxed.

Julianne had stayed in Aspen out of a sense of paralysis, as though returning would make it all real, somehow. Also, it was hard to find flights. Sol Penzell had tried to get her on someone or other's private plane and ordinarily she never would have turned that down, but at the last minute she had called his secretary, Yvonne, and declined. What would she do with herself in New York anyway? Eat Thanksgiving dinner alone in front of the television? Begin to pack up her things?

For a moment, she was seized with guilt, or at least the sense that she ought not to be, for feeling so well. But the truth of it was that it hadn't quite dawned on Julianne that Morty was actually gone. The house didn't feel any different than it did when Morty was traveling, which was often. Their bedroom was still imbued with him. His closet smelled of his cedar-scented cologne. Six dress shirts, plastic wrapped from the dry cleaners, hung on the back of the door. Morty must have picked them up himself because Carmen would have unwrapped them and placed them neatly on wooden hangers. On the bathroom counter, Julianne found Morty's razor next to her toothbrush. Its shaft was headless, as if he had shaved with it that morning and tossed away the blade. Around the basin of the sink, Julianne thought she saw traces of beard stubble. She rinsed it out with cold water after splashing some on her face, and placed his razor back on his side of the cabinet shelf.

*Why would someone pick up his dry cleaning and shave before killing himself?* She dismissed the thought after she had it, but it lingered in a back corner of her mind like a jungle cat, promising to pounce on her later.

Julianne had grown accustomed to spending Sunday mornings alone. Sunday was Morty's day to catch up on work, and he usually left the house before she was awake. When she did, she would dress in gym clothes, run on the treadmill on the third floor of their town house. Then she would get a manicure (the Koreans on the corner opened at noon on Sundays) and read the wedding announcements in the *New York Times*. She loved the wedding announcements unabashedly; it was the only part of the paper that actually caught her interest. She liked seeing pretty women, not unlike herself, with successful men. Finance guys, mostly, with impressive titles like CEO, principal, managing director. She liked to think about what they did when they were together, alone. Maybe they both loved to sail. Maybe they took shooting lessons or collected Beatles memorabilia. Maybe they both understood what it was like to lose a parent in a car accident or to go through AA or to grow up dirt poor. Maybe they weren't married for the reasons everyone assumed. The process of constructing lives for these couples could consume an hour, maybe two.

Sundays were not that distinct from the rest of the week, but they had a calmness that the work week didn't. Julianne luxuriated in the pace. There were no scheduled appointments or evening functions with Morty and his friends. Morty would be home by 5 p.m. for dinner. He liked to eat early, around the kitchen table. Angela, their cook, would leave carefully labeled Tupperware containers of pot roast or coq au vin in the refrigerator on Friday evenings before she left, so that Julianne wouldn't have to prepare anything in her absence. Though Morty had sent her to cooking school twice, Julianne was a terrible cook. Sometimes she bought bread at the bakery next to the Korean manicure place, if she remembered.

Angela had been given the whole week off because of the holiday, so Julianne was faced with the prospect of an empty refrigerator. Peering into it, her heart sank a little. There was a drawer filled with San Pellegrino, a few soft cheeses wrapped in cellophane, soy milk, a jar of cornichons (*did anyone ever eat the cornichons?* she wondered), cubed cantaloupe, beer and ketchup and assorted other sauces and condiments that Julianne didn't know what to do with. She withdrew the cantaloupe and though it was past its expiration date, fished out a square and popped it into her mouth. It was overripe and nearly fermented, and it burned a little when she swallowed it. She tossed the rest of it in the trash.

As she did, she noticed a pizza box, bent in half, at the bottom of the garbage can. The sight of it stopped her cold in her tracks. It was Morty's; she knew it. She pulled it out and inspected it, as if it were evidence of something. There was a greasy ring on the bottom, and the cardboard itself felt cold and stale. There was pizza still inside. Morty liked to save things: gift wrap, those extra buttons that came in a plastic bag in the pocket of a new coat. The Morty she knew would have saved the leftover pizza. She felt sick with sadness. She wanted to drop it back in the garbage, but was unable to let go for over a minute, too overwhelmed to move.

The weight of everything sank into her flesh like teeth. It wasn't sadness, exactly; it felt more like fear. Her skin pricked up, and her toes curled up off the kitchen tiles. She wanted to dash out into the street and hail a cab and go to the airport and get on the next flight to Texas or Provence or Cairo or Mexico. Get the hell out of there and take nothing with her, just get in the cab and go . . . but instead she stood rooted to the floor, the pizza box held with both hands, the sound of the cars amplifying outside. She could hear the earthy rumble of a motorcycle grow louder and then fade away; she wanted to jump on the back of it, allow it to take her across one of the bridges and deposit her on a deserted side street where she could quietly vanish. What had happened, here in this house? It felt foreign to her now, as if she had broken in through a window and was about to get caught inside.

She went back upstairs and fell into a dreamless sleep.

When she awoke again, the streetlamps were visible against the cobalt sky. She had made up her mind now about what to do, and she set about it with a hell-bent sense of purpose. She went to the kitchen first, and after having emptied all the shelves and cabinets of everything perishable, she took out the trash herself. Morty's cereal, his fiber bars, his Splenda and ground coffee beans. The spice rack, too, because he had given it to her. She worked her way from the bottom floor of the town house to the top, all four floors. The flowers went next, from the living room and dining room and powder room. The photographs of Morty were stripped from the shelves and placed neatly into a large suitcase that she dragged into his closet. His office was neater than expected. She knew that someone would likely come to see it, and would be angry if anything looked tampered with, so she simply shut the door and left it, still as an altar.

The process took several hours, but it was satisfying work. It wasn't altogether clear to Julianne what she was preparing the house for, but she was firm in the conviction that it was necessary. After her father had passed, Julianne's mother had preserved the house, as though he still lived there. His shoes remained lined up beneath the entryway bench, and though no one else ever drank them, bottles of A&W root beer and Bloody Mary mix lined the pantry shelves. Her father had worked on railroads all his life, and the basement was filled with his model trains, their tiny tracks running infinite loops around the wooden tables he had constructed himself out of plywood. It was a hideous way to live, for the living. No one spoke of him, but his presence was felt in every room, as if he had been there just a moment before and had run out to get the paper. Her mother grew gaunt and gray, drifting from room to room like a specter. It was as though Julianne and her sister, Caroline, lived with two ghosts. She rarely left the house except to go to church on Sunday. When she died three years later, Julianne felt more relief than she did sadness, and sensed that Caroline felt the same. They buried her next to their father, in the old cemetery on Mill Street, just past the north edge of the town.

At last, Julianne found herself back in the master bedroom suite, the edges of her hairline damp with perspiration. She had brought with her a roll of garbage bags from beneath the kitchen sink, which she carried straight to the bathroom. The razor went first, and then the shaving cream; Morty's Old Spice deodorant; his Crest toothpaste; his old contact lens case that he still kept but hadn't used since he switched to dailies. She hesitated before throwing out the contacts themselves—they were so expensive—but she did this, too, so that she didn't ever again have to look at them. When it was all gone, she sat on the edge of the bathtub and allowed herself to cry.

*Why shave?*

There would be many nights in her future when Julianne would lie awake reliving the next twenty minutes. Sitting there on the bathtub's edge, it occurred to her that she hadn't, despite her thoroughness, thrown away Morty's pills. She could name them all: Dilantin for the epilepsy, Lipitor for cholesterol, Ambien for sleep. She knew exactly what small square of real estate they occupied on the shelf. And she knew that she hadn't thrown them away with the rest of the toiletries, though she searched through the garbage, twice, just to be sure.

She didn't need to, because she knew where the pills were. Or not where they were, exactly, but whom they were with. Morty would never have left without his pills. Especially the Dilantin. He was terrified of having a seizure. Lack of control, he once told her, was worse than anything in the world.

She could see him now, standing in front of the cabinet, assessing the pills. His decision to take them with him was a calculated risk. What if someone noticed they were gone? It could be his undoing. No one needed Dilantin at the bottom of a river . . . He would have known this, but his fear of the seizures would have gotten the better of him. What if he had a seizure at the airport? What if he had one once he disappeared? Who would care for him then? He couldn't just check into a hospital; for the rest of his life, he would have to lie low. This was how he would have justified taking his pills.

He would have realized that she would have figured it out. Julianne had always been vigilant about his medication. She would have noticed the pills were gone and she would have wondered. It didn't take a genius, once you knew what to look for.

Julianne was seized with a strange mix of tenderness and anger. There in the bathroom, sitting alone on the tub's edge, was their final shared moment. Morty had let her in on his secret. He knew she would be flattered enough to keep it. She was always flattered when he paid attention to her, flattered and loyal as a dog.

His confidence in her fidelity angered her a little. It angered her enough for her to go to the phone, lugging the garbage behind her like a child with a sled. She picked it up before she thought about whom she was about to dial: Carter Darling? His lawyer, Sol? Her own lawyer, whom she had consulted once, when she had wanted Morty to marry her? She should tell someone, she thought, it seemed only appropriate. But she couldn't think of whom to tell.

Eventually, she set the receiver down and went to throw out the trash. Her anger had subsided, washed away on a wave of fatigue. When she picked up the phone again, later that evening, she made only one call, to her sister Caroline, in Texas.

"I'm coming home," she said. "If that's okay with you."

And so she did; back to where she came from. A place she never thought she'd go, and had all but forgotten about when she had arrived in New York. It was the right thing to do, or as right a thing to do as she could think of at the time.

For everything that had passed between them, and for all that he had given her, Julianne finally could give Morty something in return. It felt good to her, good enough so that she never questioned it. It somehow evened the score. Whenever it was that they found Morty—and she was almost certain that they would, eventually—she wanted to be able to sleep that night, knowing that it hadn't been she who had turned him in. In the meantime, she would wonder how long he had been planning it.

Had he flown to France to see Sophie? His true love, the woman who would, at the end of the day, always be his wife? Had they planned it all together? Or had he simply disappeared, shedding the skin of his former life like a molting snake?

Julianne wanted to hate him but as was often the case, she couldn't stay mad at Morty for very long. Even Morty's selfish acts had a strange way of charming her. There was something about the way he executed things that was so brilliantly precise and so beguilingly adept that she couldn't help but admire him. She had never known anyone so clever. Morty did everything, she thought, better than anyone. Before long, she would smile quietly when his name was mentioned on the news. *He chose me,* she would think. *At least, for a time he did. And he's smarter than all of you.*

When they found him, she would still be proud of him, for trying it at all. It had been, she thought, his best performance.

# MONDAY, 7:06 A.M.

"The arraignment's been moved up to 10 a.m.," Neil said when Merrill arrived. He gave her a swift hug, which had become their default greeting over the past forty-eight hours. "It's the first thing on the judge's docket."

"Well, that's something."

"Did you reach your mother?"

"No. I tried her cell on the way over here. I left a message with the room number for the arraignment in case she wants to join us, but I doubt she will."

"What about Lily and Adrian?"

Merrill shrugged and shook her head. She went to fix herself some coffee. There was no milk, just Coffee-mate and sweeteners. The coffee itself came out cold from the dispenser; it probably hadn't been changed since the night before. It tasted bitter. Still, Merrill drank it in a few long draughts, and once it was gone, she poured herself a second cup. She couldn't remember the last time she had eaten, though she felt strangely devoid of hunger.

"I think it's just us," she said. She tossed the Styrofoam cup in the trash.

Neil nodded. "It would look better if your mother was there."

"There's nothing I can do about that."

"I understand." Neil turned to the associate who had been quietly arranging paperwork on the conference room table. "Is everything ready for her to sign?"

"Yes," the associate said. Merrill realized he was probably close to her age, a year or two behind her out of law school, but he looked young to her, just a kid in a suit. "And the cars are downstairs to take you over whenever you're ready."

"You'll have to sign these," Neil said gently. Merrill couldn't tell whether he was genuinely empathetic or just knew how to get what he wanted in this type of situation. She had never really trusted Neil, but then, there was no one she trusted now. No one except for Paul.

"Are these for the bank check?" She asked the associate. He nodded and offered her a pen.

"They won't let us walk out of the building with a check for four million dollars without a few signatures." Neil offered a small, almost apologetic smile. "We had the money moved to your account so that you can sign for it."

"Can I speak to Dad when we get there? Alone?"

"After the arraignment. Once we post bail, he can go."

"All right," she said. "Then let's get this over with."

For days, all Merrill had wanted was a few minutes alone with her father. There were so many questions she wanted to ask, so many answers that she would never believe but that she wanted to hear from him anyway. She wanted to look him in the eye and make him answer her questions. He owed her that.

During the arraignment, Merrill perched quietly on a bench on the far side of the room. She did her best to appear attentive, but the judge's words were drowned out by the frantic chatter in her head. She could sense people were watching her, so she kept her eyes forward, trained on the judge. *What did they expect from her?* She thought bitterly. *Tears? Anger? Haughtiness?*

She wasn't sure how she was supposed to act, or even how she was supposed to feel. The truth was that she was having trouble connecting any of this to her family. Instead, it only brought to mind those role-playing exercises they used to do in law school, in classrooms that had been made to look like courtrooms. These exercises always felt so terribly contrived and unnatural, and nothing, Merrill had imagined at the time, like an actual proceeding. She half expected the judge and court officers to eventually break character, and she would see they were just law students. Instead, the judge droned on. It was just another Monday morning for him; he wanted that much to be clear. The court reporter typed away audibly. The neck of one of the court officers kept drooping like a wilted stem, as though he had been out late the night before. He looked as though he might fall asleep at any moment. Merrill scanned the room for a clock but couldn't find one. The minutes ticked by with unbearable slowness.

After bail had been set (at the staggering but previously agreed upon $4 million), the judge rose and Neil turned and nodded to her, signaling that it was over. Merrill got up and walked quickly out of the courthouse, her heart racing, eyes down, avoiding the gauntlet of judgmental stares. Ahead of her, she could see the crowd of reporters buzzing around her father and Neil like flies on meat. She waited until her father was in his town car and then she made a sprint for it.

When she opened the door, she brought with her a sudden flash of cameras and voices, and then *thunk*, the door was shut and then she was sitting beside her father in the cool stillness of the car. Outside the tinted window, she could hear muffled voices, calling her father's name. When Carter looked up at her, her mind went blank. The silence, but a second long, was suffocating. Her lips opened and closed a few times, but nothing came out; she was drowning faster than a caught fish.

"It meant the world to me to have you there." Carter reached out and tried to hug her, but Merrill couldn't move. He let his hand settle on top of hers then, pressing her palm against the smooth leather seat.

Her hand lay flat, still beneath his. She looked straight ahead, past the driver's head and into oncoming traffic. A taxi honked and darted into their lane, narrowly avoiding a cyclist.

It was too hard to look at him. Everything about him appeared diminished. When Carter had entered the courtroom, her first thought was that he probably hadn't eaten. She wondered if they fed you in jail if you were there only for the night. And he had slept in his clothes, or spent the night in them, anyway. Up close, he was wrinkled, tired, in need of a shower. She hadn't expected it, his looking so terrible.

"Someone had to be," she said lamely. She was hanging on to her composure by a single, slender thread.

"I know this hasn't been easy on anyone."

"No, it hasn't."

"How's Lily holding up?"

"I haven't spoken to her. Not since yesterday." Every word felt painful. *This was all they would talk about from now on*, she thought. They could be talking about anything—a movie they had seen or how work was going—and underlying everything would be the subtext:

*You betrayed us, Dad.*

*I know, I'm so sorry, will you ever forgive me?*

*Maybe, but I haven't yet . . .*

Merrill began to swell with resentment, tears pricking at the corners of her eyes. Carter was squeezing her hand so hard that the bones of her fingers ached. "I imagine you're all very angry with me," he said.

Merrill withdrew her hand. "I don't know, Dad. I'm a lot of things right now. Mostly, I'm incredibly tired."

"I know. I'm so sorry."

She stared out the window as the tears began to slip down her cheeks. A light snow had begun to collect on the windshield and the driver flicked on the wipers. "Weren't you thinking of us at all? How this kind of thing would affect us?" she said, her lip trembling.

"Merrill, please look at me. I never stop thinking about you. Maybe you will understand this more when you have your own children. I've made mistakes, but I've only wanted to give you everything. I think I have. Haven't I?"

"I don't know, Dad."

"I tried."

"Was it Sol, Dad? Was it Sol who put Paul in the middle of the mess with David Levin? Just tell me it was and I'll believe you." She looked him in the eye, but looked away as soon as she saw that he was crying. It always startled her to see him cry.

There was a long pause, so long that it was an answer unto itself. Then the light changed and the car stopped short, and Carter was jolted into answering. "I told him not to. I should've tried harder."

"Did you know he was going to?"

"Paul's your husband, sweetheart. I swear to you, I wouldn't have let that happen to you. If I had known."

"He's your family, too, Dad." Her voice ran cold now, free of sympathy.

"Of course he is. Please, sweetheart, I swear to you; I would never allow anyone to harm Paul. Please, please trust me."

There was something in his voice, something slippery and pathetic that she had never heard before and never, ever wanted to hear again.

"Just stop," she said, disgusted.

"I know how it feels," he said after a considered pause. "That moment when your father isn't a superhero anymore and you realize he's just a person. I remember that moment."

"I don't expect you to be perfect."

He shrugged. "You're perfect. To me you are. You always will be. When you're small, you think that about your parents. When you're old, you think that about your kids. You'll see."

"I just expect you to be *honest*." She enunciated the word as though he might be unfamiliar with it.

She reached for a handful of tissues from the box that the driver had placed for them in the back pocket of his seat and blew her nose. Her hands shook as she balled up the tissues tight in her fist. "Isn't that what you always told me to be? '*Just be honest, Merrill.* Be honest and work hard. Then everything will turn out for the best.'" Her voice had a mocking, venomous lilt. Anger had never come so easily to her before. It felt invigorating and empowering to speak this way; a good feeling, almost. "*Why* do you think I ended up in law school, for God's sake? Because I was stupid enough to believe you when you told me that's how you got ahead in life. And I so *desperately* wanted to please you. It makes me sick to think about it."

The driver cleared his throat. "We're here, sir," he said. Merrill realized they had been idling on the street in front of the Darlings' apartment building. She checked her watch.

She took a long, deep breath. "I have to get going," she said, trying to sound calm.

"Please come up," Carter said quietly. "Please. Your mother's home. I know she'd love to see you."

Merrill swallowed. The idea of the apartment, of the living room, claustrophobically thick with royal blue silks and chintz and patterned china bowls and dogs and tiny boxes clustered on the side tables, the striped walls hung with gilded mirrors, the barrel-vaulted ceiling and overstuffed couches, filled her with dread. The living room was a silent, hollow space, mostly unused except for formal occasions. The family gathered there to toast engagements and birthdays, school acceptances, job promotions. And of course, there were the parties. Merrill remembered the dresses (smocked Liberty prints in the spring; tartans at Christmastime) and patent-leather shoes that Ines would put them in when guests came over. They would get to stay up past their bedtime and Ines would shepherd them around to her friends, sometimes letting them hold trays of canapés; the guests would swoon over them, *behold the Little Darlings*! Lily always loved her parents' parties. Even then, she knew how to be a hostess. But Merrill would linger by the windows, looking out at the distant and glassed-in views of the trees in Central Park, wondering when it would all be over.

"All right," she said reluctantly. "But only to see Mom. And only for a few minutes."

As Merrill entered the building's lobby, the smell of pine marble polish, the click of her heels on the black-and-white patterned floors, the console table with its arrangement of freshly cut flowers brought on a wave of nostalgia. She inhaled sharply, forcing back her tears.

Tom, the doorman, was helping another man load suitcases into the elevator. When she saw Tom, she forced a smile. He had worked in the building for as long as Merrill could remember. She loved him the way she loved John and Carmela: not quite part of the family, but close. Throughout their childhood, Tom presided over the girls like a friendly uncle, putting them safely in cabs, casting stern glances at the boys who brought them home from dates and lingered beneath the building's brass-poled awning, hoping for a kiss. Even now, he would let Merrill up without calling first, as if the apartment would always be hers, too.

"Hi, Tom," she called when he looked up at them. She tried her best to seem calm, as though it was any other day.

Tom paused. "Hello, Merrill." He didn't come to greet her, but instead, finished with the suitcases. He offered Carter a quick nod. "Mr. Darling," he said.

There was a stiffness to Tom's voice that made Merrill's stomach sink. Usually, he seemed happy to see her; sometimes he even gave her a hug. Now he held open the elevator door for them, glancing away as they passed. Merrill and Carter both whispered thank-you's. Carter offered the man with the suitcases a polite smile that was not returned.

The elevator ride felt interminably slow. Merrill and Carter stood directly in front of the other man, and she could feel his eyes on the back of her head. She stared in silence at the panel of numbers that lit up with each passing floor.

The other man got out on the sixth floor without a word. When the elevator doors shut, she thought, *Was this the way it was going to be from now on? Would they always be greeted with such coldness?* She looked over at her father, but his face was blank, and she wondered if he had even noticed.

The door to the apartment was ajar. They marched silently through the foyer to the living room, following the sound of voices. When Merrill opened the door, Lily and Adrian smiled up at her from the sofa. They both looked tired and grateful she was there.

"Angel," Ines said after a beat, springing up from her chair. Ignoring Carter, she strode toward Merrill with arms extended.

"Mom." Merrill's eyes closed as she pressed her cheek against Ines's neck. As her mother clung to her, Merrill looked over her shoulder, taking in the familiar sight of the living room. Framed photographs jumped out at her from every surface. There were the Christmas cards, professionally taken and mildly contrived. There were black-and-white portraits of the girls at their debutante balls, and a few press photos of Carter. And there were candids: snapshots on ski lifts and blowing out birthday candles and standing in the surf with plastic pails and shovels. The girls, in kneesocks and backpacks, holding hands in front of Spence's red front doors, their perfect unlined faces basking in the ignorant perfection of their youth. Ines liked the frames to be at the same angle from the table's edge and spaced equally from one another, like soldiers in a cavalry. If a visitor picked one up, Ines would dart over to them and politely confiscate it before they were able to leave fingerprints.

*I hate being here,* Merrill thought. The thought surprised her, but the truth of it felt like an immense relief. She wanted to turn and walk out the door without a word, and just keep walking and walking until she reached the safety of her own apartment.

"Neil called," Ines announced to no one in particular. "He's on his way over to talk to us."

"About what?" Merrill said. She glanced at Lily and Adrian, but they had returned to reading a newspaper that was open between them. Merrill tried to read the headline upside down but couldn't, then decided that she didn't want to know what it said, anyway. She wondered how long they had been there.

"About everything!" Ines exclaimed, impatient. "We all have to be *prepared*. There's going to be a lot of attention on us now. There needs to be a *plan*, not just for your father but for *the family*. All right? It's not something we want to do, I understand, but it's something we *have* to do." She blinked expectantly, her eyebrows raised in a business-as-usual fashion.

"I see," Merrill said uncomfortably. "Do we have to do this now?"

Ines frowned. "You're here now."

"I know, but I'd really like to get home and see Paul. It's been a long day." Merrill turned to stare at her father, daring him to meet her gaze. Instead, he looked at Ines.

"Let her go, Ines," he said. "If she wants to go, let her go."

"Dad—" Lily started, but he held up his hand, cutting her off.

"I know this has been incredibly hard on you," he said. "I'm so, so very sorry. I can't express how sorry I am. I will try, every day, to win your trust back. All of you. But I realize that is going to take time. Right now, though, I think we might all need a little rest. So I'm going to go lie down until Neil comes. Girls, stay and talk to Neil now, if you like, or go home and we can talk tomorrow, whatever you prefer." He closed his eyes, and took a long breath. Talking seemed to tire him. His rib cage shuddered as he breathed.

Then he covered his eyes with his hand and shook his head slowly back and forth, as though he simply couldn't bear the sight of any of them. Outside, the sun shifted back and forth between the fast-moving clouds, casting long shadows across the room. It was that strange time of day, the witching hour between afternoon and evening. Soon, it would be time to turn the lights on in the apartment, but for now they remained off, the dark wood bookshelves absorbing most of the afternoon light.

Ines still hadn't said a word to him; Carter went over to her but she remained seated, her arms drawn up across her chest. He didn't try to touch her, but simply knelt at her feet like a supplicant, his arms propped on the armrest of her chair. Her head turned slowly. Finally, her eyes met his. "I just need a rest," he said quietly. She nodded mutely, and then looked away again.

Ines and her children sat together until he was gone and they heard the distant sound of a bedroom door closing.

"Are you going to stay?" Lily said meekly to Merrill, after a moment. She let her head slump against Adrian's shoulder. He cast his arm protectively around her.

"No," Merrill said firmly. "Look, I'm sorry, you guys. But I've been up since five. I need to get home to Paul."

Lily nodded. "Call me later?"

"Of course."

Ines rose to her feet.

*I'm leaving,* Merrill thought. *Even if she wants me to stay, I'm leaving.* She winced as Ines came over to her. *She's going to insist. She's going to wheedle and plead and I just can't give in . . .*

Ines reached out her hand. "Can I walk you out?" was all she said.

"Sure," Merrill said. She breathed a sigh of relief and extended her hand to meet her mother's. "I love you guys," she said to Lily and Adrian before turning to go.

"We love you!" Lily called.

When they reached the front door, Ines said, "How's Paul?"

"He's all right. Well, I think he is. I'll go home and check."

Ines nodded. "You should."

Then Ines began to cry, tears sliding down her cheeks. The tears caused her makeup to run, and her skin grew mottled, streaked with mascara and wet bronzer. A strand of hair had slipped from her bun. Merrill reached for it, intending to tuck it back behind her ear. Instead, she ended up with her mother in her arms.

"Oh, Mom," Merrill said, as she embraced Ines. "Oh, Mom."

"I don't know how I got here," Ines whispered. She clung to her daughter. Her voice was muffled against Merrill's sweater. "I spent my whole life with your father. I put *everything I had* into our life together. And now it's just gone, like nothing at all. I know this is all his fault. I know I should probably get the hell out of here, just leave him to deal with this nightmare he's created. But where will I go? I have nowhere to go. And I know it's crazy but I just can't lose him now. He's all I have. It's just too much, losing your father, on top of everything else . . ."

Merrill rocked her mother's body, as though she were lulling a baby to sleep. Her chin could almost rest on the top of Ines's head. "Shhh," she said gently. "Shhh." She closed her eyes and thought how upsetting Lily would be to Ines right now. She hoped to God Lily couldn't hear them.

"Will you ever forgive him?" Ines said after a minute. "I don't know if I can. Will you?"

Merrill's first impulse was to soothe, to reassure, to offer an *of course I will, Mom* and a kind smile, but the words got stuck in her throat. "I don't know, Mom," she said. "I think we need to take this one day at a time."

Ines held her daughter at arm's length, and examined her with an appraising eye. She smiled, then she squeezed Merrill's hands tightly before releasing them.

"All right." She sniffed back the last of her tears. " Thank you for coming over. It was so good to see you. I'm so proud of you, Merrill, I really am. You're just handling everything so well."

"I love you, Mom."

Ines stood on tiptoe and kissed Merrill on the forehead. "I love you, too," she breathed.

As Ines turned back toward the living room, she looked back over her shoulder and flashed Merrill the thousand-watt smile that she always offered the cameras. Her high cheekbones and straight Roman nose cut a fine profile against the fading light from the windows behind. Even now, haggard and pale, Ines was defiantly beautiful. She lifted her chin.

"You take care of Paul," she said slowly, "and let him take care of you." And then Ines was gone, leaving Merrill to let herself quietly out of the apartment.

---

At home, Paul had a fire going in the fireplace.

"Ooh," Merrill breathed when she entered the apartment. Her eyes stung from the cold night air. "That feels delicious."

Paul looked up from the couch where he had been reading. The gentle flicker of the flames had lulled him into a sleepy, peaceful state. On the coffee table was a glass of Merlot and a bowl of popcorn. The room felt warm and bright and welcoming.

"Hi," he said, smiling up at her. "Glad you're home."

"Thank you," she said, collapsing beside him. She didn't bother to take off her coat. Instead, she nuzzled into him, covering his chin and then his mouth with small kisses.

"Would you like some wine?" he said once she was done. He handed her his glass.

"That would be heavenly. What a day." She took a grateful sip, then paused to kick her shoes off onto the carpet.

Paul touched her cheek. His warm fingers felt good against her cold skin. "How did it go?"

She shrugged. "You know. Long. Awful. He's out on bail."

"Was there a lot of press?"

"Yeah. Neil says it will be a complete media circus by tomorrow."

"Was your mom there?"

"No, just me at the arraignment. Honestly, the courthouse was pretty overwhelming. I'm glad Lily wasn't there. I think it would have been really upsetting for her. I went over to the apartment afterward, with Dad. Mom's home. Lily and Adrian were there, too."

Paul nodded. "*You should have called,*" he started to say, "*I would've have been there for you.*" But instead he stayed silent, reflecting on the realization that he might never again be welcome in Carter Darling's house, and it was possible, too, that Carter Darling might never be welcome in his.

"I just wanted to get home to you," she offered, as though she could hear his thoughts. They sat together for a few minutes, quietly staring into the amber glow of the fire. The heat began to sink into her flesh, relaxing her muscles one by one.

"Have you spoken to David today?" she asked.

"I did. His resignation was front-page news. I saved it for you; it's in the kitchen. There'll be a press conference tomorrow. He sounded relieved. Tired, but relieved." Paul was going to tell her about Jane Hewitt's arrest, which had dominated the 5 o'clock news, but then thought better of it; Merrill looked pained whenever she heard the name Jane Hewitt.

"Did he say anything about you?"

Paul laughed. "Only that I should start looking for a new job." He put his hand reassuringly on her thigh and squeezed. "No, he said not to worry and that I should focus on taking care of you."

"That's kind." Merrill sat up on the couch and stripped off her coat. After a minute, she said, "You know who e-mailed me this morning? Eduardo. He saw the news and he wanted to make sure we were okay. He asked if there was anything he could do."

"He's a good guy."

"It'll be interesting to see who our friends are now."

"Don't think that way."

She shrugged. "Remember the job he offered you with Trion?"

"What about it?"

"Would you take it now, if he offered it to you again?"

Paul raised an eyebrow in surprise. He put his wineglass down on the table. "I honestly don't know," he said, after a moment's hesitation. He leaned forward and kissed her, his lips lingering against her cheek. "Listen, we're going to be okay, honey. You'll see. I'll find a job in New York."

"I know you will. But maybe New York's not the right place for us now." She smiled. The corners of her eyes crinkled from fatigue. Her voice shook a little, but there was a certain hopeful strength to it. "It will always be home, but . . ." She trailed off, unable to finish the thought.

"I don't know," Paul said gently. "A lot's going to change now, honey. You might want to be somewhere familiar."

"I'm not so sure New York's going to feel all that familiar from now on," she said, and sighed.

Paul paused. She was right, of course. Tomorrow, New York would feel like a different city altogether. Doors would not swing open so easily for them anymore. The stack of invitations on their hall table would thin; the hall itself might look different, a more modest entrance to a more modest home. They would take different routes now, avoiding certain places. The courthouse, the Seagram Building, the fourth floor of MoMA. Morty's town house, most of all. Perhaps it would be sold, its bright red door repainted and the stag's head knocker removed. But it would always be a haunted place for them, and if they were ever to take a turn up Seventy-seventh Street, it would come upon them like a dark wind, stopping them dead in their tracks, stirring up memories that lay dormant just below the surface.

Tomorrow, they would no longer be the Darlings of New York.

"What are you thinking?" Merrill asked nervously.

"I'm thinking I love you, and that we both need some sleep."

She nodded, her shoulders deflating slightly. "I know. I'm exhausted." The fire had burned down to a few final embers. She poured the last of the wine into Paul's glass and took a sip. "I just want today to be over."

"Okay," he said definitively. Paul rose and extended his hand, pulling her onto her feet. She smiled for the first time in what seemed like a long time. "Off we go," he said.

When he laid her down on the bed, she closed her eyes and breathed deeply. *The sheets were fresh*, she thought. *He must have changed them during the afternoon.* She felt him gently pull off her suit, her underwear, even the rubber band from her hair until she was naked. Outside, she could hear the far-off hum of the traffic on Park Avenue. Her head was swimming with fatigue. It had barely touched the pillow when she felt herself drift off into a shallow sleep.

Merrill woke in the middle of the night, heart racing. Her breath caught in her throat, jolting her eyes open. She turned onto her side: Paul was there. His lips were slightly parted and his hand, now limp, rested on the pillow just above her head.

He looked so peaceful when he slept. Just the sight of him there calmed her. After a time, his eyes flickered open and he smiled. "Those were some dreams you were having," he said.

"I'm sorry," she murmured.

He pulled her close to him. "Come here," he said gently.

She settled in against his chest. For a while, she lay awake, feeling the warm rhythm of his breath against her neck. Eventually, a trace of new light began to creep in across the windowsills. It was tomorrow. In an hour or two, the phone would begin to ring, and her e-mail in-box would fill up, and there would be reporters gathering outside her building. Neighbors would whisper in the elevator; strangers would stare; friends would ask her nervous questions when she came upon them on the street. The world would be clamoring for her. It would seep into her home through every crack, every phone line, every television screen . . . and eventually, she would have to go out and face them. But for now, she would lie in her husband's arms, her eyes closed and her body still against his, thinking that if this was all she ever had, it would be enough.

# EPILOGUE

At first, he stayed away from *Litoral Norte.* The north coast of the broader state of São Paulo was what had drawn him to Brazil twenty years ago. His memories of those hazy, sun-filled afternoons were still fresh; Sophie had taken him there. She had friends with a beach house in Barra do Una, a simple white structure with high ceilings and a large wooden deck that overlooked the sea. He liked to remember her the way she was then: napping on a chaise longue, a book open in her hand, its pages fluttering in the late afternoon air. The straps of her bikini unfastened, revealing her toasted-almond shoulders to the sun. Her hair was streaked gold, and it was long. She would stir from her nap and see him watching her; she would smile. They were happy.

Though the living would be easier for him on the coast—all fresh fish and emerald-green water—he felt more comfortable in São Paulo itself. The city was perfect: huge, gritty, too crime ridden for most tourists. Living in a dangerous city, he found, suited him. In São Paulo, everyone kept to himself, living behind guarded apartment walls, driving cars with tinted windows, departing from rooftop helipads. Even the elite wore nondescript clothing and cheap watches in public, so as not to attract the attention of thieves. Privacy was at a premium. There were no nosy small-town neighbors in São Paulo, no casual pedestrian traffic. It was a city where people slipped in and out of the shadows unnoticed.

São Paulo did, however, attract business travelers, and those were a very real threat. Business travelers read the *Wall Street Journal*. They watched CNBC. They were the ones most likely to recognize him. In the first six months, anyone could have recognized him; his picture was everywhere. He looked different, of course. Leaner nose, higher cheekbones, the distinctive jowls stripped away from his jawbone. Still, he felt a jolt through his body every time he saw himself on television or on the front page of a newspaper. More than once, it would send him into hibernation, holing up in the modest apartment he had rented for himself under the name of Pierre Lefèvre.

Some days, he would monitor his laptop for hours at a time, scouring the Internet for news about himself. He created an intricate ranking system (a front-page story that featured him and showed a photo was a 10, for example, while a small blurb about Ines Darling in a gossip rag rated only a 1 or a 2) in an attempt to gauge whether the media coverage surrounding him and the trial was rising or falling. The higher the score, the more time he would spend inside. It reminded him of New York after 9/11. Every day, the threat level had to be gauged and measured, and his behavior adjusted accordingly. If it got too high, it was time to move again, to a different apartment or to a hotel just outside town.

It was a fugitive's life: highly mobile, survival based. The point of each day was to make it to the next. But two and a half years went by without any real scares. The Darling trial was settled out of court. The news about the whole RCM debacle faded, replaced by other schemes and scandals. Morty Reis slipped out of daily consciousness, even for Morty Reis. He began to grow restless.

He started missing the deals.

He had money, lots of it, but it was stashed away in the Caymans and Switzerland. Accessing it in anything other than small bites posed an obvious security risk. Still, he couldn't help but to think about how to deploy it. The opportunities in Brazil were phenomenal. An investment in the Brazilian stock market over the last decade would have yielded him a return of 276 percent, versus a loss of 13 percent in the United States during the same period. If he had gone all in with this strategy ten years ago, not only could he have avoided the whole debacle with RCM entirely, but he would have been hailed the greatest investor of all time. He knew this was an illogical train of thought—after all, no one would invest in a fund that had a 100 percent investment in Brazil of all places—but it still dogged him. He couldn't continue to sit idly by while the Brazilian economy flew past him like a freight train.

Morty began to troll the slums, thinking, evaluating, running the numbers. He was tempting fate, he knew, like an alcoholic in a bar. But he had nothing else to do, and what difference would a few small real estate deals make anyway? All local, all in cash. If the numbers were small enough, the deals could go unrecorded. There were deals to be had in the coastal towns, too; as the economy stabilized, small beach properties were increasingly in demand.

He needed a break from the city, where booming real estate possibilities called to him like a siren's song. He decided to rent a house in Juquehy, the slightly less ritzy town just next to Barra do Una, where he would lie low and decide how to proceed. He would get a tan, at least, and keep himself away from the bigger, riskier, more tempting deals in São Paulo.

It was the end of May, the beginning of the off-season. The tourists were gone and the crowds on the beaches had begun to thin. He had been in Juquehy for three weeks or so. It was early morning, and it had rained the night before, a moist slickness coating the roads. The mountains loomed up behind his house, dark and beautiful and foreboding. The roads through them were terrifying, filled with hairpin turns that made him long for one of his race cars, preferably the Aston Martin.

He went for a stroll, his pant legs rolled so he could feel the ocean on his feet. As was often the case at the beginning or end of the day, his thoughts were of Sophie. In the distance he saw a couple walking, their hands linked. The woman's hair gleamed in the morning light. The rising sun set her figure in relief, obscuring the details of her face.

The couple stopped at the end of the beach. The man put his fingers beneath her chin and drew her in for a kiss. She stood on her toes to reach his lips.

Then the man twirled her beneath his arm like a ballroom dancer and dipped her. The edges of her hair brushed the sand.

That's when he saw her face.

She looked younger than he remembered. The morning was so bright that Morty winced and shaded his eyes with his hand; perhaps it was a trick of the light.

No. It was her. He was sure of it. Sweet Merrill Darling.

When her husband drew her back up, she stared directly at Morty. For a moment, time stood still and she froze with it, like a deer in a hunter's sight. He knew he should turn away. But for the first time since he had reached Brazil, maybe for the first time in his life, he found himself unable to act on instinct.

Then the sun slipped behind a cloud, casting a shadow on the beach. The spell was broken. The woman looked up at her husband, lifting her face to him for another kiss. She looked different now, shorter or blonder or squarer than Morty remembered Merrill to be. He shook his head; it had lasted only a second.

*Not her*, he thought. *Don't be crazy.* But his heart, pounding so hard that he could feel its pulse against his shirt, told him otherwise.

He watched them for a moment longer and then turned back to the house. His lungs pumped again; his blood flowed. His feet carried him quietly off the hard-packed sand at the water's edge to the softer sand, then up the wooden steps and into his house. Above his head, the fan's blades rotated with the same insistent whir as his heart. By afternoon he had departed, a short note of explanation left on the kitchen counter for the housekeeper: He would be gone for a while and would return, he wasn't sure when.

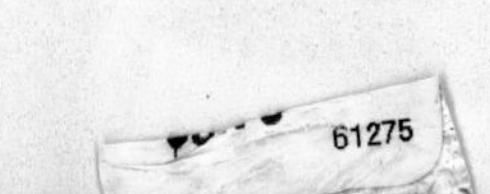

"Two parts *Too Big to Fail*, one part *The Devil Wears Prada*, Alger's debut is taut and compelling." —*Publishers Weekly*

NOW THAT HE'S MARRIED TO MERRILL DARLING, daughter of billionaire financier Carter Darling, attorney Paul Ross has grown accustomed to all the luxuries of Park Avenue. When Carter offers him a lucrative, high profile position at his hedge fund, Paul is thrilled with his good fortune. But Paul's luck is about to change: A tragic event will catapult the Darling family into the middle of a regulatory investigation and a red-hot scandal. Suddenly, Paul must decide where his loyalties really lie.

*The Darlings* is an irresistible glimpse into the highest echelons of New York society and a fast-paced thriller of epic proportions.

"One of the first novels about the 2008 financial crisis... Alger has what it takes, in the best sense." —*USA Today*

"*The Darlings* moves so fast that it feels more like a thriller than a social drama." —*Entertainment Weekly*

"Utterly compelling... as knowing about family as it is about money and social status." —Jay McInerney

A *Los Angeles Times* Bestseller

www.CristinaAlger.com

Penguin Readers Guide available online at www.penguin.com

A Penguin Book
Fiction

U.S. $16.00
CAN. $17.00

ISBN 978-0-14-312275-3

51600

EAN 9 780143 122753

Cover design: Roseanne Serra | Cover photographs: (front) David Allan Brandt / Getty Images; (back) fotog / Getty Images | Author photo: Deborah Feingold